A young boy discovers he suddenly has t
He begins by unknowingly saving his friend
saves a little girl at the Children's Cancer Center in San Diego. He even manages to bring an
elderly woman back to life after she was struck and killed by a speeding car. His name is
Thomas Grady, and he's not sure if he was given a gift or a curse because now he's being
pursued and kidnapped by several people who would force Thomas to perform his miracles for
greed, vengeance, and power. Along the way, Thomas acquires a guardian angel, Mario Reyes, ex-Navy Seal. Mario
spends a lot of his time rescuing Thomas from a host of bad actors, but Mario may have his
hands full once the government gets involved. Thomas wants to help and heal everybody, but
will Thomas Grady's power prove to be the answer to curing all the world's illnesses and in
some cases even deaths? And if so, is the world ready for the unfathomable hidden price it must
now have to pay. At Point Loma Naval Base two scientist make an alarming discovery about
Thomas and his ability to heal people; now it seems that the fate of our very existence lies in the
balance.

1

The Healing Paradox

The Second Miracle

Thomas Grady couldn't be happier now that his friend, Even Steven, was back and hanging out with him and his buddies. His real name was Steven Evans, but everyone at school called him Even Steven for no other reason than it was just fun to say. They were running around the neighborhood, riding their bikes, and getting into the kind of mischievous trouble that every 15-year-old kid gets into. Steven's parents were eternally happy and grateful to God for the miracle their son had received. Life was good in the little town of Goleta, California. But Thomas Grady was yet to put this little town, just north of Santa Barbara, California, on the proverbial map.

Thomas Grady and Steven Evans would both be ready to graduate next year and move on to high school. Being a first-year scrub was to endure a rite of passage every hormone filled kid had to go through. The fear, the hazing, the confusion and having to deal with the fact that girls actually don't have cooties. Thomas Grady was one of those kids that learned this early, in fact, he was still infatuated with Brenda Dayton and even got close to kissing her at his previous birthday party, but the moment was so onerous that his developing little brain couldn't handle it. It would go down as one of his first regrets in life.

The mid-summer days were mild, but fickle. Temperatures bounced from low seventies to the mid-eighties. It was difficult to know what to wear. But if you're a 15-year-old boy, blue jeans and a T-shirt were all you ever needed. Thomas was hanging out with Steven Evans and Johnny Engels. They were walking to the local mini mart to do some junk food grazing. Just outside the store, the boys stopped to take stock of their assets. Johnny Engels reached into his pockets and pulled out a one-dollar bill and 41 cents in change. Steven does the same and produces a $1.60, all of it in change. Thomas looks at Steven and says, "Dude, what did you, like, break into your piggy bank, ha, ha." Steven lightly slaps Thomas on the side of the head and replies, "Shut-up butthead, how much money you got?"

Both kids watched as Thomas Grady slowly reached into his pocket and began swirling his hand around, taking his time and just as he was about to take his hand out, he reached back in and kept digging around. Thomas could see the annoyed expressions on both of his buddy's

2

faces and was loving every moment. Finally, Johnny yells out, "What the fuck, stop playing with yourself and show us how much money you got, dipshit." Thomas couldn't help laughing at his own humor, "ha, ha, ha, alright, alright." Thomas pulls his hand out of his pocket to reveal his money. As he does, Johnny and Stevens' eyes pop and their jaws drop at the sight of Thomas' bounty. Thomas calmly says, "Let see, I got twenty-three dollars and 85 cents." "What the hell!" Stevens says in a fake scream. Johnny repeats the same thing, "Yeah, dude, what the hell." And just as Johnny was about to yell some other string of profanities, it happened, all three of them felt the thin hairs on the back of their necks rise as they experienced that primitive atavistic sensation of fight or flight. Like the cringing sound of nails on a chalkboard. It was the unmistakable and apprehensive high pitched sound of tires screeching on asphalt from a car just a few yards away from where they stood. They all turned just in time to see the horrific scene that would leave an indelible mark on their little young minds forever.

They watched in disbelief as they saw and heard the solid sickening thump of a white Nissan Altima slamming into an older woman that was crossing the street. They witnessed the small frail body sailing through the air and heard another, softer thump as the 98-pound body struck the rough black asphalt then rolled for another ten yards before coming to a bloody, mangled stop. Screaming came from every direction as people ran to check on the old woman. But everyone knew that it was impossible to survive such a devastating blow. The kids remained frozen in time, staring in the general direction but not seeing, not wanting to see the drama as it slowly caught up to their reality. Their minds were roiling with confused thoughts and finally came to the conclusion that they didn't know what to think or how to feel, so they remained purposely confused. It was the perfect coping mechanism needed for just this kind of experience.

By now, there were dozens of people around the victim, some screaming, some remaining calm trying to give instructions. There were dozens of 911 calls and the ambulance was on its way. Anybody standing there looking down at this poor woman knew she had to be dead. Her body lay with an exaggerated flatness as if every bone had been broken. Small streams of blood slowly oozed out from every orifice on her head. It was obvious she was not breathing. The screaming turned to sobs and sighs and then to silence.

Thomas Grady could not fight the irresistible impulse to go and see. It wasn't anything morbid, he just felt a compelling force to go and see this woman, this broken body that was on

3

the ground void of life. As he walked closer and closer to the crowd, he could catch glimpses of her among the crowded bodies surrounding her. Thomas could not explain why he was doing this, he could now hear his friends, Steven and Johnny yelling from behind him telling him to come back. Thomas Grady could hear them, he could hear the soft cries in the crowd, muffled sounds of sympathy and in the distance, the low siren of the ambulance getting closer, and closer.

As Thomas reached the outer edge of the crowd the people seemed to part and create an opening for him to walk through. Maybe because they thought he was a relative, maybe a grandchild. Why else would they move out of the way? Thomas approached the inner circle of the crowd. Now people were staring at Thomas just as much as they were staring at the old woman, but nobody stopped him or said anything. Thomas Grady continued towards the broken bloody body. The sirens were getting louder and higher pitched. People were moving to make room for the approaching ambulance. The crowd grew more intense as they watched Thomas moving closer and closer to the body lying on the hot asphalt. One lady moved towards Thomas, but her companion pulled her back.

Thomas could hear the commotion around him, the screaming started again as the ambulance pulled up and the paramedics jumped out. Thomas was now standing directly over the body, he slowly bent down and at the exact time that he *touched* one of her fingers, he felt himself being lifted off the ground by two strong arms. A paramedic had grabbed Thomas and set him down away from the body so they could start work on her, though it was apparent to the paramedic that it wasn't going to take much more work other than to simply pronounce her D.O.A., Dead on Arrival.

Thomas Grady stood there, watching the men work. They moved quickly, checking pulses, blood pressure, elevating her head, listening for heartbeats, but nothing, she refused to yield any sign of life. They looked at each other and nodded their heads as one of them covered the body's face with a blanket they had brought. Thomas never took his eyes off the body. As the two paramedics stood up and began to gather their equipment, they practically jumped with shock when they heard the old woman's voice from underneath the blanket, "Oh my lord, why is it so dark?"

Quickly, one of the stunned paramedics removed the blanket to reveal a bright-eyed woman staring back at them. "What's going on?" she asked. The paramedic helped her sit up and

explained to her that she was just in an accident and that they were there to help. The old
looked at him and said, "Help me with what, young man, by the look on your face it look
you may need a little help yourself." the paramedic laughed and replied, "Well, you may
right about that, mam, it would appear that you are not in any need of help, but just for ou
please come with us to the hospital so you could be checked out properly, it's policy, you
mind, do you?" He helped her stand and as soon as she got to her feet the crowd cheered

The old woman passed by Thomas, looked and him but could not discern the expressic
his face, so she simply patted him on the head and said, "Are you okay, son?" Thomas di
reply, he turned and ran away as fast as he could back to his buddies in front of the candy

The First Miracle

1-1/2 yrs. Ago

Thomas Grady's father, George Grady, owned a small family restaurant in Goleta, CA.
George and his wife, Helen, had a son, Thomas Grady and a daughter, Paige, she was three
older and was now in her last year at Harding High School. The Grady's were, by most ac/
a typical and happy family. Normalcy was one of George's favorite mantras. It would not
however, apply to his son, Thomas.
It was in the summer of 98' in the small town of Goleta, CA. School was about to be let o
every kid in Jefferson Middle School was ready to burst with excitement as they waited fo
sound of the last school bell to ring. It would be another 3 whole months before they wo
that bell again.

Oblivious to the stares of dozens of eyes in each room, the synchronized clocks on the
stared back with their lifeless expression, effortlessly, unblinking, a testament to their ina
nature. The more they stared at the clocks, the slower the sweeping second hand moved
and slower to a painful, agonizing crawl. Even the collective will of 940 middle school
could not make time move one nanosecond faster. It was one minute before the bell, mo
importantly, it was one minute to summer break. Twenty seconds to go and not one dro
oxygen was being used in the entire school. Even the staff were holding their breath.

At 3:00pm, the pealing of the school bells was no match for the screaming and scree

5

undreds of stampeding kids as they raced down the hallways and out into freedom. The
umultuous moment was palatable as the kids ran out of every available door. Thomas Grady was
ne of the first kids to reach his bike. He quickly unlocked his chain, backed out of the bike
ack, and pushed himself upstream through the current of kids coming his way. He couldn't wait
o get to his friend's house and tell him all about the last day of school.

Thomas Grady's friend was Steven Evans, he was 13 1/2 years old. Less than 3 years ago,
Steven Evans had been diagnosed with Ewing's Sarcoma, a rare cancer that accounts for only
bout 3 percent of all childhood cancers. A five-year survival rate is less than 30%. Steven was
n his fourth year and was not doing well. He had been bed ridden for the last 14 months.
Steven Evans could remember when he dreaded waking up to go to school. Now, he would give
anything to feel that familiar misery again. At least he knew it would mean meeting up with his
friends at the playground.

Steven had good and bad days, though the bad days seem to outnumber the good ones lately.
Today, however, seemed to be a new level of bad. He was feeling exceptionally weak and felt
like something was...imminent. Strangely enough, it also made him feel a little more at peace,
ke this feeling was an answer to his suffering. After all, he believed that if you die, there is no
more suffering, for everyone, himself, and his parents, even his stupid sister, which he secretly
oved and looked up to.

As Steven lay there contemplating this newfound peace, he was startled back into his aching
eality by a light knock on the door. His head felt like it weighed a hundred pounds as he tried to
ean it forward to see if his friend was coming to see him. Steven didn't have the strength to
peak loudly enough to say, come in, but Thomas knew this, so after a few soft knocks on the
oor, Thomas would just walk in. Seeing Thomas always raised Steven' spirits.

There was no reason in the world that today was going to be any different than any other day.
here were no sightings, mysterious winds, eclipses, or distant sounds of singing angles. But on
is day, at exactly 3:24pm, something in the universe twitched, and the ripple emanating in the
her of space passed through Thomas Grady and shifted him into a dimensional flux that
owed him to exist with all of us and at the same time, somewhere else, where, it appears,
racles reside. In other words, nothing perceptible happened.

As Thomas walked in through the door, Steven summoned all his strength to force a barely
ticeable smile, Thomas sensed it more than saw it. Steven could hear the excitement in

Thomas' voice as he started speaking to him about the last day at school. "Hey, man, dude, you should have been there!" Thomas exclaimed with eyes as wide as he could make them, "Everybody in school was running, I mean everybody. Even Tommy, you know Tommy never runs, even when we play kickball he walks around the bases. Ha, ha." Steven was transfixed on Thomas' story. Thomas continued, "Dude, I saw Brenda, she's stupid, but I think I like her. She was all like, see you during the summer Thomas, and I was all like, whatever, but you know what, I think I'm gonna invite her to my party. Oh, yeah! Hey, I know you're comin, right? I know you didn't forget my birthday. It's like the first party of summer break."

Steven could keep up with what Thomas was saying, but he could not physically respond as quickly as he wanted to. But Thomas was used to the slow reaction, so he waited for a response. This time, however, he noticed that Steven was reacting even more slowly than before. Nevertheless, he waited with the mature patience of a priest.

Steven raised his hand a few inches into the air, which was the equivalent of a 'high five' and said in a very low and barely audible voice, "Yes." was the only word he could manage without total exhaustion." Great!" Thomas exclaimed, "I know you're gonna bring me an awesome present, ha, ha" Thomas always laughed at his own little jokes. He went on, "So, listen, I talked to my mom, and I asked her if she'll rent us the new movie that just came out on DVD, I think it's called 'The House of Zombies," or something like that. Anyway, you want to see it?"

Steven acknowledged with a slight movement of his head. "Great! Okay, I'll be back after supper, and we'll watch the movie here in your room." Thomas leaned in, touched Steven's arm, and looked into his eyes and said, "I'll see you around 6 o'clock, alright?" With that, Thomas quickly turned and ran out the door. Many years later, when asked about this day, Steven Evans would describe it as follows:

" I remember thinking about dying that day and how it made me feel at peace. I also remember my best friend, Thomas Grady, coming to visit me. It was the last day of school, and he couldn't wait to come and talk to me about it. Although I think he just wanted to tell someone that he liked Brenda Dayton from his 8th grade science class. Anyway, that day I had resigned myself to dying. The doctors, there were always doctors around, they told me to hang in there and fight. But I didn't see the use, I knew what I had and what my chances were. The way I felt that day, I knew I probably wasn't going to make it another week, maybe not even another day.

But on that day, when Thomas Grady leaned in and touched my arm to tell me he'll see me later, I remember feeling a warm sensation starting at the tip of my toes. I didn't know what it was or how to interpret it. As Thomas left and closed the door behind him, the warmth continued slowly to move up my body. At first it scared me because I was wondering if this is how death begins. But I noticed that after the warmth reached my mid-section, I was starting to feel better. As it progressed up my spine through my chest and all the way to the top of my head, I remember feeling.... well,...great! I jumped, yes, jumped out of bed, went running down the hall and screaming, mom, dad, over and over again. I will never forget the confusion, the screaming, the crying and the joyful laughter that occurred on that day."

The Third Miracle?

Summer came and went, as did the next two years, mostly uneventful, with the exception of Thomas Grady falling deeply in love with Brenda Dayton. Unfortunately, it was not to be. Brenda's father got a job offer in another state and Thomas would be left alone to figure out how a broken heart is mended. The first six months was a miserable existence, but the greatest physician, time, was able to heal him almost completely by the end of the next six months. Thomas Grady still hung out with his same best friends, Steven Evans and Johnny Engels.

They were in high school now, and their days were filled with video games, hanging out with other friends and thoughts about girls. They thought a lot about girls. Steven and Johnny both had girlfriends, but not Thomas. Not that he wasn't looking, in fact, he had his eyes on a particular little blonde in his science class, her name was Daniella Rios, she was also in Thomas' history class. Thomas was mesmerized by this exotic looking little girl with perfect olive skin, green eyes and golden hair. Thomas himself had a slight golden tan on his skin. Most likely due to his mother's side of the family. Thomas' grandmother was a first generation Armenian. The rest of his looks he got from his father, light brown hair and eyes, a little thin and two big dimples on each cheek.

When he first met Daniella Rios outside of the classroom, she introduced herself as Danni. Which of course, threw Thomas off balance for just a moment. He responded to her saying, "Danni? Isn't that like, a boy's name?" Danni was used to the reaction her name got, so she answered him calmly, "Yeah, my dad wanted a boy, but he got me instead, so he called me Danni since the day I was born."

8

"It's kind of cool." Thomas said.

"Yeah, I like it." Danni replied.

"Cool." Thomas repeated.

"Cool." Danni confirmed. And they walked to their next class together while Thomas tried desperately to make small talk on the way. He just wanted her to keep talking to him, and, to Thomas' surprise, she did, and it felt good. Since then, he's been trying to work up the nerve to ask her out.

It was late Wednesday, it had been almost two weeks since his encounter with Danni and he had decided, with some help and some contemptuous coaching from his friends, that he would ask her to go out with him next Friday. *'What's so hard,'* he thought, *'just walk up and ask her if she wants to go to the show or just go eat something. If she says no, well, what are you gonna do, right? 'Damn it, what if she says no? I'm gonna look stupid. What did my dad always say? Oh yeah, nothing worth doing...no, that's not it, ah, nothing ventured, nothing....something, what, let me see, ah, was it, don't give up....damn it, oh, yeah, nothing ventured, nothing gained. That's right, right? Gotta go for it.'*

Friday came around and Thomas was feeling those butterflies in his stomach. He had that dreaded feeling of apprehension, fear and a little bit of nausea. Thomas was standing outside his science class when he spotted her. He immediately felt a little calmer just watching her. She was just wearing a simple summer dress, mid length, flat shoes, and some sort of headband thing. Thomas didn't know what to make of the headband thing, but it looked nice on her. She was carrying her backpack over her left shoulder and was talking to one of her friends. She hadn't noticed him yet.

As Danni approached the classroom, she looked up and saw Thomas, he seemed to have a silly grin on his face and she thought, *'What's up with that goofy look.'* She gave him a half grin and said, "Hey."

"Hey." Thomas replied.

"So," she said, "you gonna let me in?"

Thomas noticed that he was completely blocking the doorway, so he quickly jumped to one side. "Oh, yeah, sorry about that."

"No problem. You okay?"

"What? Yeah, fine, you okay? Cause I'm okay. You're okay, right?" Thomas wanted to slap himself, he was totally losing control. Danni could see his befuddled state and helped him out. "Yes, I am okay. So, did you do your homework?" Thomas was instantly grateful for the change in topic.

"Yes, I did. I, ah, thought it was kind of interesting. How about you?"

"Yes, I did my homework, too."

"No," Thomas said smiling normally now, "I mean, did you find it interesting also?"

"Yes, Thomas, I did." Thomas loved it when she said his name.

"Good, I mean, great. I mean, I think I'll shut up now." Danni gave him a reassuring smile and they each went to their respective seats. Thomas would just have to wait until the end of class. Hopefully by then he will have regained his composure.

Thomas had no idea what the teacher said that day, all he was thinking about was Danni. *'Would she say yes? She seems like she likes me. Hey, I'm sorta cool. Maybe she likes that. I am pretty smart, maybe she likes that, too.'* Slowly, Thomas began to build his confidence up and had come to the conclusion that he was going to ask her out as soon as this class was over.

The bell rang and startled him back to reality. He got up almost too fast, Thomas walked over to Danni and tapped her on the shoulder. She turned and stared right into his eyes and said, "Hey, Thomas, what's up?" That was all he needed, for her to say his name one more time. "Well, I was wondering, if you're not busy this Friday, if maybe you might want to go out to eat a movie, I mean, see, see a movie, or just get something to eat?" Thomas was mentally hyperventilating. "Okay," he thought, "nothing to do now but wait for her answer." Though Thomas felt like he was sitting on a thousand pins and needles.

Danni took a couple of seconds, which gave Thomas a slight sickening feeling in his stomach, like maybe this was not the best thing to do. Danni took a few more seconds while staring up at the ceiling. *"She looks very pensive."* Thomas thought. Pensive, he had just learned that word. He spelled it to himself in order to give his mind something else to do besides wait...for total rejection. Danni touched Thomas' shoulder with the tips of her fingers as if to steady him, but for what? *'Did she think he might faint, oh my God, did she think he was frail and weak? This is not good.'*

But Danni just had the habit of touching people on the shoulder when she wanted to make sure they were paying attention. She replied, "Well, actually, I'm busy....*'Damn it,' Thomas thought, 'the ole, I'm busy line. Shit, I knew I shouldn't have done this, now I'm gonna look like a total fool.'* Danni continued, "but how about Saturday? I'll be free after 5pm."

"What? Oh, yeah, Saturday would be awesome!" *'Tone it down, Thomas,'* he told himself, *'It's not that awesome.'* "I mean, that would be great. So, I'll come by around 6 and we'll do whatever."

"Sure, sounds good."

"Yeah. Okay, then, I'll see you in history class later."

"Bye."

"Bye."

That day, Thomas and Danni hung out together during lunch and Thomas even walked her home after school. They talked about a lot of different things. Mostly just idle chit-chat. But that day, Danni said something to Thomas that evoked a confluence of feelings and emotions. He couldn't tell if it was nostalgia, deja'vu or fear. Thomas could not describe it because he had never felt the grip of destiny pulling him towards his inevitable place in the history of humankind. Danni had briefly mentioned her friend, Dorothy Keller. She recounted the story of how she and Dorothy were very close while growing up. But Dorothy had contracted a rare blood disease, and she may not have long to live.

The story rang of familiarity to Thomas, as he recalled his friend Steven. Danni went on about how her friend is now being home schooled because she never knew when she's going to have a bad day, and a bad day for Dorothy was a very bad day which includes seizures and convulsions so hard that they cramp her muscles which only exasperates the problem.

For no apparent reason, Thomas chose not to tell Danni about his friend Steven. He didn't want any rumors or stories about his friend being spread at school. But still, what are the odds. They both became a bit melancholy, but quickly snapped out of it when they reached Dorothy's house. They said their good-byes and Danni reminded Thomas about their date. As if he would ever forget.

George and Helen Grady were both considered to be educated parents. They were careful to be a part of their sons' life, as well as their daughter, Paige. They attended almost every event at their schools and although they were not in the PTA, they did give what they could of their time to whatever cause the schools were sponsoring. George had a master's in business and administration and Helen finished with a communications degree. They both decided that they would first try their hand at a small business before surrendering to the drudgery of working 9 to

11

5 for the rest of their lives. As with most successful people, it always helps to have a little luck on your side. And as luck would have it, a small family restaurant went up for sale in town and it was exactly the kind of business that would allow the Grady's to test their business acumen and see if they were worthy.

They went through the usual slow and bumpy start, made a few mistakes, lost a little money, but in the end, they were able to fine tune their goals and ideas and it began to work. They went from working seven days a week, sometimes 12 hours a day, to having 5 full and 3 part-time employees, allowing them to enjoy the fruits of their labor...once in a while. They were both still very hard workers. They just didn't need to work all the time. Life was good, stable...normal. But today, Friday, something will happen that will start to pick away at George and Helen Grady's cherished normalcy and will leave something behind that will not even come close to resembling....normal.

Helen Grady walked over to the stair banister and leaned on it as she yelled, "Thomas, Paige, come on you guys, it's time to go. Your dad and I do not want to be out all day, so let's move it!" From upstairs Helen could hear them. Paige yelled back from somewhere in the hallway, "Mom, I told you, I can't go to the mall with you and dad because I'm going to a study group. I told you that earlier today, I can't believe you don't remember." Helen thought about it, and realized that Paige was right, she had mentioned the study group. It was a small group of her friends that were trying to brush up on some of the subjects for the SAT's. '*What mother would deny her child that*', she thought. "Okay, Paige, I remember, I'm not senile...yet. Tell your brother to come down, I know he's not studying for anything."

"Mom!" Helen heard Thomas yelling. Thomas was not amused, "I am not studying like my egghead brainiac sister because I don't have any test coming up."

"I know, sweetie. Let's go, dads in the car waiting." Helen knew that her kids were always aware of when she was teasing them. It was all just playful banter. Helen looked up to see Thomas walking down the stairs. "And where do you think you're going dressed like that?"

"Mom! What's wrong with what I'm wearing?"

"Nothing if you're going skiing in Alaska. It's still over 80 degrees outside, why would you want to where a hoody?"

"Mom!"

"Fine, suit yourself. Come on, your father is gonna start yelling at both of us if we don't get out

12

there now."

As Helen and Thomas walked outside and headed towards the car, Helen could see George pointing at Thomas and making a 'what the heck' gesture about the hoody. But Helen just threw her hands up in surrender and that was the end of that. George put the car in reverse to back out of the driveway while saying, "Okay, here we go, we're going to Alaska. Good thing you brought your warm clothes, Thomas."

Thomas yelled out, "Dad!" Helen only smiled and buckled up.

They were on their way to the mall. George and Helen had told the kids that they were going to have dinner there this Friday. It was a break from cooking, and they knew that it was one of Thomas' favorite places to eat. Fortunately, the food court offered a couple of healthy choices for George and Helen to pick from. It was a beautiful day, warm and sunny, with a few scattered clouds loitering above the horizon. There was a gentle breeze coming in from the ocean and the familiar scent of salty ocean water lingering in the air.

The weather was perfect if you didn't have a hoody on. However, as it turned out, when the Grady's made their way inside the mall, the air conditioner had been working over-time and there was definitely a chill in the environmentally controlled mall. When they finally sat down to eat at the food court, George leaned over to Helen and said, "To bad we didn't bring our hoody's, it's freezing in here!" "I know." Helen said, coveting Thomas' hoody which now looked very inviting and practical.

There was little conversation between Thomas and his parents. It wasn't because they didn't try to make small talk, they just noticed that Thomas was more interested in looking around to see if there were any of his friends walking around the mall. George and Helen didn't mind, they knew that sometimes Thomas would talk their ears off, and other times, not so much. They mostly spoke to each other and left Thomas to survey his domain.

The Grady's were about halfway into their meal when a young girl walked by casually near their table. The Grady's were located at a table near the edge of the food court, so Thomas was able to have a full view of what was going on in the mall. As the young girl walked past Thomas, they briefly made eye contact, but then the young girl immediately looked away. But there was something not right. Her movements appeared slightly erratic, missing the simple fluency of natural movement. A few seconds later, it was apparent that she was having a problem standing on her feet. Thomas watched her with his eyes strained wide open, he didn't know what was happening, he just knew something bad was about to go down.

The young girl looked around, she was obviously disoriented and began to cry out, "Mom, mother!"

Thomas couldn't take his eyes off of her. George and Helen were about to stand and offer the young girl help but it was too late. The young girl fell to the floor and began to convulse. Her cries became yells, and her yells became screams of shear panic. "Mom, mom, mom, mo...!" Her voice was cut off by the convulsions, her body started to twist and contort into grotesque positions that didn't make any sense. Helen didn't know what to do and began dialing 9-1-1. George looked around to see if he could spot the young girl's parents. He was about to go to the girl and try holding her arms in some sort of normal position because it looked like they might break the way the young girl's muscles were bending them.

That's when George noticed Thomas moving slowly out of his chair and move towards the girl, and slowly, almost hesitantly, his arm reached out and as Thomas was moving his hand slowly towards the young girl, he made eye contact with his father. It was only for split second. They looked into each other's eyes with a solid intensity. Neither of them had words to share. Thomas looked back in the direction of the girl and finally, lightly, gently, merely grazed the young girls shoulder, then quickly recoiled and moved back to his chair, folded his hands and stared at the ground. George remembered thinking, *'Why did Thomas touch her shoulder of all places? Why touch her at all?'*

There was a series of loud screams, George noticed a woman, running towards them, she had a couple of shopping bags in her hands, and he remembered the woman throwing them in the air as she ran towards the young girl. He noticed Helen, concentrating on her conversation with the emergency operator. He noticed Thomas sitting perfectly still in his chair after touching the girl and staring at the ground intently. But most of all, he remembered the young girl, she had almost immediately stopped convulsing, she became completely calm for just a moment, she tilted her head, as if she was trying to listen to something, or was feeling something, he couldn't tell. When the young girl's mother reached her, the young girl sat up and began speaking to her mother, "Mom, I feel something."

"What is it, darling?" Her mother asked as she stooped down to meet her.

"It's something." The young girl simply said.

"What, what is it you feel? Are you in pain, honey?"

"No."

The mother was frantically looking around the young girls body trying to see if there was anything physically wrong, but she couldn't see anything.

"Are you sure you're not hurt?"

"Yes, I'm sure. I,...I feel warm."

"Warm? Are you hot? Do you need to lie down?"

"No. Mom, I can feel it."

"Feel what? Feel what?" The mother was absolutely confused and scared. She didn't know what to do or how to respond to the strange comments her daughter was making.

"Mother." The young girl said as she slowly began to rise.

The mother was more scared than she had ever been. She was starting to think that she was losing her daughter that her little girl was losing her sanity, and hers would soon follow. Finally, after what seemed like an eternity, the mother noticed the calm smile on her daughter's face. The smooth movements of her body as she rose and stood next to her. The young girl reached out and took her mother's hand and said, "Mom, I think I'm going to be okay."

"Yes, yes, you will be okay, my dear."

"No, mother, I mean, okay." The young girl said with a reassuring smile.

George and Helen would come to find out later that the young girl, whose name was Dorothy Keller, was actually dying of a rare form of blood disease. She was not expected to live for more than a year. However, the local news stations got wind of the story and they put Dorothy Keller on every morning and late-night TV show. It was quite a story. Every professional in the health care industry swore that it was nothing less than a miracle. Dorothy had made a full recovery. George caught the tail end of an interview on a late-night news show. "She is not in remission," one doctor was quoted as saying, "she is, in fact one hundred percent cured. As a doctor, I can only say that I am completely baffled. I examined Dorothy's case, and by all practical indications, she would not have been expected to be with us much longer." The commentator asked, "Well, how do you explain something like this, Doctor?"

"I can't." The doctor replied, "This is actually what a real miracle looks like." George turned off the TV. No one in the house spoke about the incident since it happened over a month ago. George didn't want to confront Thomas about his odd behavior in the mall and he could tell that Thomas did not want to talk about it either. So, for now, he would simply let the subject rest.

15

As time went by the Grady's noticed a little blonde girl coming around more often. Her name was Danni. They liked Danni. She was a good girl and seemed to help keep Thomas on top of his schoolwork, so, there were definitely no complaints from George and Helen Grady.

The Grady's were planning a small barbecue for the upcoming weekend. They told Thomas he could invite his little friend, Danni, and extend the invitation to Danni's parents as well. Later, Danni thanked Mr. Grady for the invitation but she told him that her parents were going to be busy that weekend, and wondered if she could instead bring a friend. Mr. Grady told her that of course she could. And that was settled. The week went by quickly and Saturday rolled around. It was another great summer day in August. The Grady's had been given perfect outdoor party weather. The guests started to trickle in around 3:30pm, and all the food was prepared, with the exception of the burgers that were on the grill. By 4:30, almost everyone had shown up.

George and Helen were mingling about greeting friends and making small talk, while making sure everyone's drink was refreshed. It was a picture-perfect backyard party. George was speaking to one of his managers, Raul Mendoza, who took care of the restaurant in the evenings. He was one of George's favorites. Raul was a hard worker, honest and best of all, smart. He was a great hire. Just as George was insisting on getting Raul another beer, he turned almost bumped into Danni,

"Oops, almost knocked you over, Danni. Where's Thomas?" Danni gave George one of her disarming smiles and said, "I think he's with Mrs. Grady in the kitchen." George smiled back, padded her on the shoulder and said, "I think you better go find him and rescue him, because if I know Mrs. Grady, and I do," George said with a wink, "She is going to keep Thomas in there for hours." Danni offered a little laugh and said, "Oh, Mr. Grady, I would like you to meet my friend." George looked at the girl standing next to Danni, and he almost dropped his drink. His surprise was more than noticeable. Danni said, "Mr. Grady, are you okay?"

"Yes, Danni, I'm fine." he said, unconvincingly.

"Well," Danni continued, "this is my friend, Dorothy Keller. Dorothy, this is Mr. Grady, Thomas' dad." Dorothy extended her hand and said, "It's a pleasure to meet you, sir."

"What?" Said George.

"It's a pleasure to meet you, Mr. Grady. I know your son, Thomas. I go to the same school as he does."

"Ah, really?" George said, finally reaching out to take her hand to shake it. George went on, "Thomas hadn't mentioned you were coming?" Danni stepped in, "Dorothy is my friend, remember, Mr. Grady, I asked you if I could bring a friend. It's okay, isn't it?"

"Of course it is, it's fine, just fine. Listen, ah,.."

"Dorothy."

"Yes, Dorothy, right, of course, ah, it's a pleasure to meet you too, any friend of Thomas and Danni is welcomed here." He finally let go of her hand, which he noticed he was hanging on to all the while they were talking. "Listen," George said, "I gotta go see how Mrs. Grady is doing. I'll see you two later. Oh, and Danni, I'll send Thomas out." And before any of the two girls could say anything, George turned and quickly walked away. Dorothy looked at her friend, then they both lifted their shoulders up at the same time and started giggling.

Helen was in the kitchen making Thomas take out a tray of tuna quarter sandwiches when George almost burst in, startling both Thomas and Helen. She looked to see who the charging invader was, it turned out to be her husband. She looked at him and was about to say something admonishing when she noticed the look on his face. So, instead, she calmly said, "What's going on, George?" George froze for just a second and asked Thomas if he could speak with his mother alone. Thomas shrugged his shoulders and said, "Okay. I'm gonna go find Danni." They both watched Thomas as he walked away. As soon as Thomas was outside George put his hands on Helen's shoulder. Helen couldn't tell if he was doing this for her sake, or for his.

"Helen, you'll never guess who came to our party!"

"We have a surprise guest?" Helen was immediately intrigued.

"Yes. And you'll never guess who it is."

"Well, you're right. So why don't you just tell me."

George told Helen the story about how Danni and Dorothy Keller were friends.

"Oh, my God, you're kidding."

"No, I'm not, she's right there." George said, pointing out the kitchen window. Helen watched the three teenagers interacting in the backyard. It all seemed so normal. George noticed that Helen had a very pensive look on her face. She never took her eyes off the children as she spoke. After a few seconds of thought she said, "Well, let's not say anything, they're just kids, and besides, what is there to say?" And with that, the Grady's went out and enjoyed the party. It wasn't until later, after 7pm, when almost all the guests had left and Thomas and his friends went

17

upstairs to watch a movie, that George and Helen got into a conversation with the last few remaining friends that stayed. They sat around the kitchen island, which comfortably sat four people, but they were six.

Aaron and Sandi Taul, two longtime friends of the family, Paul Whittle, one of George's high school buddies and Joe Arroyo, a longtime friend and employee. Paul Whittle and Joe Arroyo offered to stand around the kitchen island and allow the couples to sit. The conversations took many directions, from politics, to current news and all the while trying to top each other with crazy stories. Paul Whittle was winding his up, "...and so, if we hadn't taken off at that very moment, I think we would have both been killed by that thing." Joe Arroyo stepped in and said, "You mean, by Big Foot?"

"Yeah, Big Foot, what else could it have been? This thing was huge and hairy and walking upright."

"Ah, like a bear?" Aaron said.

"No," Paul insisted, "it was not a bear, it was too....agile. It moved like a person."

"Bears kinda move like people." Helen said.

"What part of Big Foot do you guys not get." Paul said with a strong hint of frustration. But getting someone frustrated only fed into the group, so they heckled Paul for a few more minutes before they finally showed mercy on him. "Okay, Paul," George said, "We concede to your Big Foot story. But the night's not over, I still have a story to tell." All eyes shifted to George. They watched as George reached for the wine bottle and refilled the glasses of those who were drinking wine and grabbed a couple of beers for Paul and himself. Joe made himself a scotch and soda. Finally, the short-lived silence was broken by Sandi, "Looks like we're in for one doozy of a story."

"Here, here!" Aaron said, holding up his glass for a toast. "Let us toast to the biggest bull..I mean, story we are about to hear." They laughed and tapped their glasses. But Helen noticed that George didn't have his usual wry smile that he wore before he was about to say something funny or amusing. In fact, she thought he was looking a little too serious. Everyone else in the room picked up on it and the kitchen fell into a revered silence as they waited for George to speak.

"Let me ask you all something," he began, "How many miracles has anyone here witnessed or been a part of?" George saw no hands and heard no comments. The interest in what George was saying now reached a palpable moment as he went on. "Does anyone here think that being a part of a miracle, be it directly or indirectly, be pretty amazing?" No one spoke, but he got a nod of acknowledgment from everyone in the room. "What if you knew, personally, about two miracles? Would that be considered odd, coincidence, providence?"

"Depends on what you're calling a miracle, George." Aaron replied, "I mean, people now a days call a lot of things miracles. What are we talking about here, George, like finding your keys in a field of tall grass or parting the red sea?" George looked at Aaron, and without blinking said, "Parting the Red Sea." The group got a little excited and everyone started speaking at the same time, all asking the same questions, but in different forms, "What kind of miracle?" Paul blurted. "When did you experience these miracles?" Sandi said, "Wait, wait, what happened? What did you see, George?

What the hell, say something, George!" Joe shouted, not noticing that he had raised his voice. George held up his hands and said, "Hold on, I'm not through here. There's more."

"More?" Joe said, what you mean, like, more miracles?"

"Yes." George said with all seriousness.

"What, you cannot be serious." Joe exclaimed then said, "How many do you know of? This sounds like crap. Let's hear it, George, let's hear these miracles and we'll be the judge."

"Yeah." They all said, almost in unison. Helen had an idea of what George was about to say, but they had never discussed it, never verbalized their experiences to each other, or anyone else for that matter. George continued. "So, we all agree that experiencing two miracles is incredible, but I'm telling you guys, I have been somehow, and I can't say with a hundred percent certainty, that we, Helen and I, have witnessed, and or, have been somehow directly related to no less than three miracles. Three! I mean, come on, not even the Pope gets to be a part of three miracles."

"Alright, already, let's hear these so-called miracles of yours, George." Joe said.

George continued to weave his story of Steven Evens, their neighbor, and how his parents were counting down the days, almost hours before their son was about to die. They had never told their son that the doctor had told the child's parents that there was no way Steven was going to make it one more week and to prepare for the worse. The parents were racked with pain and despair. But on that day, just a few days before Thomas' birthday, Steven was miraculously healed. Not in remission, but the doctor said that he was completely cured of the cancer that was

19

about to take his life.

There was no explanation, no clues, no nothing as to how or what had happened. They said that Steven literally jumped out of bed and went running down the hallway, screaming for his mom and dad to come see. That's when Paul Whittle stepped in and said, "Well, George, there have always been unexplainable accounts of people being healed through unexplainable reasons. Happens all the time."

"All the time? Really, Paul. This happens all the time? When was the last time you heard of this happening?"

"Well, I'm not sure, I mean, I have heard of these kind of things happening."

"And you would not call them miracles?"

"I didn't say that. I think there may be some other scientific explanation."

"Call it what you want, Paul, for the moment, I'm calling it....a miracle."

George went on to tell them about the women, who, according to witnesses, was around seventy years old, maybe eighty years old. She gets hit by a car going about 40 to 50 miles per hour. Dozens of people watched in horror, including his son, Thomas and his friends as this woman's body went flying through the air, tumbling like a rag doll before hitting the ground with such force that some people say they could hear her bones breaking. The paramedics get there five to six minutes later, cover her body, and just as they're about to pronounce her dead, the little old lady gets up and starts talking to the paramedics. They inspect her and find absolutely nothing wrong with her. "How the hell do you explain that?" George announced.

"Oh my God," Sandi said, "you mean that poor Thomas saw the whole thing?"

"Yes, well, at least, he said he did, him and his friends."

"Oh, my, that's awful. For a child to see such a thing. Was he alright after wards, because he seems fine now." Sandi said, noticing she was padding George's hand. George replied, "Actually, he was a little affected at the time, but he seemed to pull out of it like a real trooper. You know what they say, kids are resilient."

There were a few seconds of silence, then Joe Arroyo said, "What about the third one. What happen there?" George was not sure where he was going with all this, he just knew that he had to tell someone all this crazy stuff. He continued.

Everyone was in shock when he mentioned the little girl who was at the party this very afternoon. How she was at the mall and the terrible scene that happened there. Sandi couldn't help herself, she mentioned Thomas again. "You mean that Thomas was there at this incident as well? Oh, my God, George, that poor child has already been through more traumatic experiences than most of us have in a lifetime."

The mood in the kitchen became very solemn, and George almost regretted bringing it all up. But at least it was out there. This was the first time that he had mentioned any of these things to anyone. Even Helen felt a little release. After some debating, they ended the night conceding that these were all, in fact, bona fide miracles. It wasn't until all the guests had left and George and Helen went to bed that George began to really contemplate the events that he described. And as he went over them in his head, he couldn't help but come to the conclusion that the one consistent thread in all of them was Thomas. He never forgot how Thomas had stared right into the eyes just before touching that young girl. But why did he touch her. He never asked Thomas why he did that. George was too concerned with Thomas' mental state. He didn't want to bring it up, and thus, never spoke about it.

But now, George felt it was time. He was now curious about how Thomas felt regarding these incredible things that had happened in his life. Maybe for all Thomas knows, this stuff happens all the time. Maybe Thomas feels that miracles happen every day, but they don't, and he needs to know that, too. George decided that night that he would speak to Thomas the next day.

The Revealing

Sunday morning, 8:32am, the Grady's lumbered around the house, a little tattered from the wear and tear of yesterdays' party. George and Helen stayed up a little too far past their bedtime, and Paige and Thomas had both stayed up watching movies until 3am. It was the little house of zombies at the Grady residence on this fine late morning. Everyone was mindlessly drawn to the kitchen, where the smell and sound of sizzling bacon easily overpowered their weak and pliable wills. Added to this, the ever-conducive aromatic smell of fresh coffee, and Helen knew that resistance was futile. Slowly, everyone converged on the kitchen island and sat and waited for breakfast to happen.

"Man, that smells good, honey." George slurred, in a low inaudible moan.
"What?" Helen said.
"Smells good." George replied with a clearer voice.

21

"Oh, yes, it does." Helen agreed.

"Mom." Thomas said.

"What?"

"Can I have pancakes?"

"No, you're having what everyone else is having, eggs, bacon, hash browns and toast."

"Ahhh,"

"Don't, ahhh me, young man, this is a good breakfast." Helen said, waving a bright green spatula at Thomas.

"If it's so good, you could have mine, except for the toast. I like toast." Paige slapped the back of her brother's head and said, "Thomas."

"Hey." Thomas said rubbing his head. "That hurts, quit it."

"I barely tapped you, you baby." Paige said, "Don't give mom a hard time, we're all tired and I need you to shut up."

"Paige." Helen said sharply, "that's no way to speak to your brother."

"Oh, mom, Thomas knows I'm kidding with him, right?" Paige said, while trying to slap Thomas again, but Thomas blocked it this time, and when she tried again, they got into a playful squabble. Helen knew these little playful fights sometimes turn into real ones, so she told them to stop.

Finally, breakfast was served, and they began to eat. There was very little conversation, but they were all enjoying they're breakfast, even Thomas, who looked like he was racing to finish first. "Thomas," Helen blurted, "why are you eating so fast, slow down."

"Mom."

"Slow down or you're..." Helen was interrupted by George's cell phone, his ring tone was the song 'Jump' by Van Halen, it was 8:43am. George was always changing his ring tone, sometimes he would pick songs that he liked, but would cause him embarrassing moments from time to time. One time, he had chosen another Van Halen song, 'Hot for Teacher,' and his cell went off while at a parent/teacher conference. After that, George was a little more careful with his choices. The cell kept ringing, Helen stared at George with a look that said, 'Well, are you going to answer that?' But George didn't answer because he had a mouth full of eggs and bacon. George swallowed and answered the call. "Hello, this is George." George didn't bother looking at the caller ID because he had just assumed it was someone from the restaurant. "Hello, is this

Mr. George Grady?" The voice on the phone said.

"Yes. Who is this?" George realized he did not know who was on the phone and became more attentive.

"This is Nurse Rice, with St Mary's hospital."

George's heart noticeably dropped a little, St. Mary's Hospital was where his mother was at. She had checked in for some minor complication, however, after being examined, the doctor advised her to stay a few days for observation. George's mom, Kathy Grady, feigned resistance, then complied because she felt she really did need to stay. The nurse continued, "Mr. Grady, we were wondering if you could come by the hospital today, at your earliest convenience."

"What's this about? Is my mother okay?" Grady's voice was thick with concern, Helen picked up on it immediately, as did the kids. Helen was mouthing the words, *'what wrong.'* George held up a finger signaling her to wait. The nurse continued, "Well, Mr. Grady, we believe that your mother may be taking a turn for the worse, and it might be a good idea to come down and see her. She mentioned your name a few times and so, well, that's why we called."

"Sure, that fine, I'm glad you called, we'll be down as soon as we can. Thank you for calling."

"It's no bother at all, Mr. Grady. We'll see you here, good-bye."

"Good-bye." George sat there for a few seconds staring into nowhere.

Everyone started in at the same time asking the usual questions, was she okay, what did they say, is she going to be alright, etc. George held up his hands and quietly said, "She's okay, for now..."

"For now?" Helen exclaimed.

"No, I mean she okay now, but they feel she may have taken a turn for the worse."

"What does that mean?" Paige asked.

"Look," George said, "let's just all get down there and see what's going on. Now, everyone, get dressed and get in the car." They all moved a little slower than George would have wanted, but this was no time to argue. They were out of the house in less than ten minutes. At 8:53am, they were pulling up to the hospital. Helen stopped to get some flowers at the gift shop and made the kids sign a card on the way up the elevator.

They got off on the 3rd floor. Paige felt uneasy with the antiseptic scent of hospitals, it smelled like...medicine. She didn't like it, nor did she like the color of the lime green walls. The clean floors and walls, and shiny tiles felt just a little too clean, too institutional. As far as Paige was concerned, the whole place was just too sterile. She began to feel just a little bit queasy. Thomas, on the other hand, was experiencing an entirely different conflux of emotions, confusion, apprehension, that familiar irrational compulsion to go, but to go where? Thomas knew he was being compelled, but by what, or why, he just simply could not understand.

The Grady family walked over to the nurse's station and inquired about the room number for his mother. "B-31," the nurse said, "just walk down this hallway to your left and follow the numbers."

"Thank you." George said. And they all headed towards the room. Paige was beginning to feel a bit more composed. Paige noticed that the more time she spent inside a hospital, the less queasy she felt. Thomas, however, was having a mini-freak-out in his head. He had to go, not to the bathroom, he just had to go. Go, go, go. But...where?

As they walked inside to meet George's mother, Helen was the first to walk over to the bed and hug Kathy Grady as she lay in her bed. Helen had always gotten along with her in-laws. Kathy was happy to see her, too. Kathy Grady gave Helen a big smile and thanked her for coming and bringing her son. "Oh, yeah," Helen said, "it's not like he wanted to come you know, I had to make him." George's mom made a fake disappointing grimace at George, but then quickly smiled and held up her hands for a hug. George walked over and hugged her. Right after that, the kids walked over and did the same.

"What's up, mom?" George asked, "You look great, what are they talking about?"

"Oh, George," his mother replied, "you know doctors, they don't know what they're talking about half the time."

"No, really, mom, what's going on?" There was a short moment of silence. Thomas shot up from his seat as if he were being eaten by ants, he startled everyone. "Thomas, what is up with you?" Helen scowled. "Ah, nothing. Can I go out to get a drink of water?"

"You could have that water on grandma's table, it hasn't been open."

"I...I really just want some water from the fountain. There's one just up the hall, I saw it." Helen wasn't sure what was up with Thomas, but she let him go. "Go on, but hurry back."

"Okay." Thomas said, and he walked out of the room. Helen looked back towards George and said, "Sorry, go on, Kathy, you were saying."

"Anyway, well, the doctors.." Kathy Grady could feel her composure sauntering away, she went on. "They, ah, well they said that they found an inoperable tumor in my head and that, well, it

24

could cause many problems."

"Problems?" George said.

"Yes, like maybe it could cause a stroke, or..." Kathy Grady allowed her emotions to surface, and her eyes began to water. "What is it, mom?" George said, "What else did the doctor say?" "They, I mean he, the doctor said that it may kill me or at best send me into a coma for the rest of my life." Kathy Grady broke down and cried, while Paige, Helen and George came in to hug and console her.

"Don't worry, mom," George said, "we'll all be right here for you. Besides, what do doctors know anyway, right?" George said, trying to cheer her up. Kathy looked into her son's eyes and stopped crying but could not stop the consuming sadness she felt growing inside her. They all just sat there for a while holding her hands and started some small talk to try to ease the stressful tension that was building in the room.

Meanwhile, Thomas had walked down the hallway, pushed the up button for the elevator. A few seconds later it arrived. Thomas got inside and pressed the number 4. Upstairs on the next floor, a small group of doctors and nurses were waiting for the elevator as well. As the doors opened, they revealed a 16-year-old boy with a slightly messy hair-doo standing in the center of the elevator. Proximity is sometimes a key factor to reactions. Because once the people entered the elevator and saw that the 4th floor button was illuminated, no one said a word. When they got to the 4th floor the group of professional medical personnel simply stepped aside and allowed Thomas Grady to walk out of the elevator.

On any other floor, someone would have probably questioned this 16-year kid wandering around the hospital, but if you're on the 4th floor, they just assume you have a family member in the I.C.U. or C.C.U area. Intensive Care and Critical Care Units are rarely visited because here, most patients are in some state of incapacitation. Most, if not all, of the patients here are mostly sleeping or are kept asleep with drugs. It's often the last step before hospice or death. Although some make it through their illness and or injuries, most of the patients are here for a reason, they require intensive and/or critical care.

The lights are lower in this area, which helps to promote calmness, for both the patient and the workers. The nurses at the station are on scheduled shifts and rounds to keep a close tab on their patients. Thomas walked over to the nursing station. He noticed that all the nurses sitting behind the counter were busy writing something or entering something on the computer.

9:35am, no one noticed Thomas as he walked past the nursing station then walked over to the first of only 6 small rooms in this section of the hospital.

Thomas stood outside the doorway of the first room, hesitated for about two seconds, then walked in, three seconds later, he was out and walking to the next room There Thomas also stopped, hesitated, then walked in and walked out. He continued the same pattern for each room. When he had walked out of the last room, a nurse finally took notice of him and asked him, "Excuse me, son," The male nurse said, "can I help you? Are you here visiting someone, or are you lost?"

Thomas stared into the eyes of the nurse and wished he was invisible. "Son?" The nurse said, trying to get Thomas' attention. Thomas finally broke out of his trance and was about to say something to the male nurse when pandemonium hit the 4th floor of St. Mary's Hospital, it was 9:37am.

Every one of the six rooms had loud noises coming from them. It sounded like people screaming...for joy? Was that joy? All the nurses ran from the stations and headed into the rooms. There was mass confusion. No one knew what to make of it. Patients were out of their beds and walking and jumping around. Smiling and singing and saying strange things, the nurses could hear them. "I feel great, call my wife!" and "Hey, doc, where's my clothes, I gotta get outta here." None of these gibberish comments made any sense. A couple of the patients were walking down the hallway without their IV bottles. They were just walking around looking at themselves in wonder.

In the meantime, Thomas had easily slipped away among the commotion and went back downstairs to get back to his family. At the same time, George had noticed that Thomas had been gone a pretty long time and was just heading out the door when he almost bumped into Thomas at the doorway. "Hey, where have you been?"

"Nowhere, just getting water....dad." George knew that look, he knew Thomas was concerned about something. But he miss-read him and said, "I know, Thomas, but don't worry, grandma's gonna be okay."

"Dad, no, it's not that."

"What is it? You okay?"

"Yeah, I'm fine. I just got to tell you something."

"Sure," George said, sensing Thomas' genuine concern. They moved from the doorway to the

26

hallway. "Go ahead, son, you can tell me anything, you know that."

"Well. I did something." Thomas said, without making eye contact.

"What?"

"Well, I actually don't know," Thomas said still looking at the floor.

"Well, what did you think you did, Thomas?"

"I touched some people."

"What? What do you mean?"

"You know, like I touched that girl at the mall."

George was thrown aback. Was this true? Did his son actually believe that he healed that girl simply by touching her? How would that even be possible? He kept his composure and said, "Thomas, how do you know it was you? Maybe it just happened?"

"No, dad, it was me. I was just afraid to tell anyone."

George's head was beginning to spin. Was this true? He had to ask, "Thomas, did you touch Steven Evans?"

"Yes."

"And that lady in the car accident, did you touch her too?"

"Yes." Thomas started to feel better every time he confessed. He was relieving a burden that would have eventually crushed him if he hadn't said something. His father went on, "Thomas, are you saying that you also healed that girl at the mall?"

"Yes." Thomas almost smiled that time. He wanted to keep saying yes, yes. For the first time he felt like he was the one being healed. It suddenly dawned on George that they were in a hospital. He turned to Thomas and calmly asked, "So, okay Thomas, what is it that you did?"

"I touched some people on the 4th floor."

"What? Why would you do that? Why the 4th floor Thomas? What made you go there, was there a reason?"

Thomas responded with just a hint of frustration, "No, dad, I don't know why, I just feel things sometimes and I felt like I had to go to the 4th floor." There was a physical weight of apprehension attached to every word they spoke. The moment was becoming incomprehensibly surreal. George struggled to hang on to a tenuous string of reality. He shook his head, as if to try to clear his mind, or wish it all away, he didn't know, he wasn't sure, in fact, maybe for the first time in George's life, he wasn't sure of anything right now. He looked back at Thomas, he

27

was confused, but calm. *'That's good.'* he thought, George mentally recouped his senses and asked Thomas, "Why, why the fourth floor, Thomas, what's up there?"

"Just more sick people."

"And you touched them?"

"Yes."

"And are they all healed now, Thomas?"

"I think so."

"Why do you say, you think so? Don't you now?"

"I think they are, I didn't stay around to see if they were, I just left while some of them were jumping around."

"Jesus." George said, not meaning to say it out loud. It was at this moment that reality came roaring back like a train. George started to play out the next 24 hours in his head. Trying to run as many scenarios as he could, none of them ended good. It was 9:51am, George realized that it was only a matter of time before all this gets out and someone puts it all together and places Thomas right in the middle of it all. George Grady began to formulate a plan, at least a partial plan that has his family leaving, right now. George takes Thomas' hand while he opens the door to his mother's room. He pokes his head in and tells Helen to meet him outside in the hallway. Helen saw the concerned look on George's face and quickly got up to see what the matter was.

As soon as she stepped outside she said, "George, what is it? You look worried." George took both of her hands in his and said, "Honey, you need to trust me and just do what I'm about to tell you." Helen did trust George and she was ready to stand by his side. She looked him in the eyes and said, "Okay, George, what is it you need me to do. You're not in trouble are you?" George gave her a half grin and said, "No, I'm not in trouble." Which was a half-truth, he wasn't, but maybe the whole family was. Helen went on. "Okay, just tell me what we're doing."

"First," George said, "we are getting out of here, like right now."

"Okay." Helen said as if she was checking off a list.

"Next," George continued, "We have to get as much cash as we can, we're going under the radar for a little while."

"What?" Helen exclaimed as she pulled back her hands from George's and said, "This sounds like trouble to me, George. What the hell is going on?"

"You said you would trust me, so, trust me, I'll explain later once we're in the car. Let's all say

28

good-bye to grandma."

They all went inside and said their good-byes. George noticed Thomas still standing by the door. He walked over to him and said in a low voice, "Thomas, say good-bye," Thomas started moving towards Kathy Grady, but George stopped him, put his right hand on Thomas' shoulder and said, "and Thomas,"

"Yeah, dad?"

"Don't forget to...touch grandma." Thomas looked at his dad, and they both smiled.

"Okay, dad."

The Grady's all met just outside the doorway, when George had a last second thought and said, "Helen, tell mom to come with us."

"What? Did you see the condition she's in? We can't ask her to just walk out of the hospital and..."

George interrupted her and said, "Helen, just go back inside and tell her to come with us." Helen just gave him a scowling look and walked back inside the room. What she saw was more puzzling than George's behavior. There was her mother-in-law standing up and already getting dressed with a huge smile on her face. Helen didn't know what to make of it all. Kathy Grady looked at Helen and said, "I heard George outside, I'm coming with you all." All Helen could do was smile back and say, "Of course, mom. Let's go." Helen walked back outside and looked at George with only more confusion than just a minute ago. At 10:01am, the Grady's headed out of St. Mary's Hospital.

Sunday morning, 9:40am, approximately 3 minutes after the C.C.U. incident at St. Mary's Hospital. Walter Harrington Porter is lying in his bed in the spacious master bedroom on the second floor of his 11,000 square foot mansion. He is lying in a modified bed that is designed to accommodate any position he desires. Surrounding his bed were numerous medical devices, monitors and special pieces of equipment that have been keeping Walter alive for the past 5 years. His doctors thought it was a miracle he was even alive.

These devices all have their own specific sound effects, and they cause the room to resonate with whirling sounds, rhythmic beeps and a steady hum. Walter Harrington Porter's long time trusted assistant, Charles Decatur is standing by him. Walter speaks in a barely inaudible voice, "Charles."

"Yes, Walter, what is it." Charles was one of very few people that used Walter's informal name.

"I don't think I'm going to be around for long."

"Let's not talk about that right now, Walter."

"No, it's alright, you know I'm a straight talker, Charles. I need you to know something."

"What's that, Walter?"

"I want you to know..." Walter was cut off by a loud beep on the so-called hot line. Walter was immediately distracted and strained as he raised his finger and pointed at the hot-line and said to Charles, "What's going on?" The hot line was a euphemism for Walter's worldwide invasive surveillance apparatus. It was massive. It was more like a smaller version of the NSA, but not by much. Walter had eyes on the entire world via a massive network. It was designed to spot anything that might help cure him and allow him to live so that he could continue his lifelong passion, or as some would say, his obsession, with building his wealth.

The system was simple, but efficient. It kept a look out for key words like, miraculous, incredible, unbelievable, magical and miracle, especially if it had the word cure mentioned anywhere. Walter wanted to know whenever anything made the news in regard to medical treatments and advances. He didn't care if it was based on science or voodoo, he wanted to know. He was interested in anything that might help keep him alive so that he may continue with his rapacious existence.

Charles looked at the monitor and the words "Got something" came up. Walter gave Charles Decatur a certain look and Charles goes into action. Charles went downstairs to the control room and picked up a phone. "Darren, what do you got?" Darren was head of this highly specialized search team and answered only to Charles.

"We got a hit, Charles. It looks and sounds crazy, but that's not for us to say, right?." Charles remains unperturbed and said, "That's right, now, show me what's up."

"Okay, I got this feed in just a few minutes ago, watch it." Darren pushes a few keystrokes, and a video comes up, but not just any video, it's a video of a miracle, a real miracle. Darren connects to one of their servers which is supposed to be a private server for use in medical facilities only.

It's part of a computer monitoring service called Critical View, one of Walters many companies that profess to be a benevolent entity, but really serves his malevolent purpose. The company, Critical View, is a specialized medical monitoring system specifically designed for patients in the intensive and critical care units in hospitals. It allows doctors to monitor patients from a remote location. The doctors are able to control the medical equipment in the rooms, thus they are able to view, in real time, what the patient's heart rate, blood pressure and other vital signs are while watching them on their iPad.

One of the selling features was that none of the videos were supposed to be permanent. This was done for the sake of the patient's privacy. However, there were a couple of exceptions, if, for instance, there was an emergency or an anomaly of some sort, the cameras defaulted into permanent recording mode. Which meant that everything being recorded would stay recorded until someone deleted the video. This was sold, of course, as a way to keep a record of any emergencies in an effort to reduce liability to the hospital, but it was really a way for Walter's people to keep an eye on anything unusual. And today, it was very unusual.

Charles watched the video. He didn't have to watch it twice. He quickly took it to Walter. Walter also looked at it only once and gave Charles a simple set of instruction that was composed of four simple words, "Bring me that boy." it was 10:11am, only 10 minute past the time that the Grady's left St Mary's hospital. Within minutes, the digital dossier of the entire Grady family was in the hands of Charles Decatur.

10:13am, The Grady family climbed into their Silver BMW SUV and started heading out of the hospital parking lot. George begins to explain to everyone in the car about Thomas. They react like anyone else would, with disbelief, confusion and a little freaked out. They can also tell that it is having a profound effect on Thomas, who appears to be the most worried for unknown reasons. Ten minutes later everyone is on board with the idea that they need to protect Thomas from what inevitably will be mobs of people seeking miracle cures for themselves and their loved ones. Not to mention that the medical community will want to examine and observe him, and there's no telling what the government will do.

The more George thought about it, the more overwhelming their situation appeared. He abruptly pulled into a 7-11 store and said, "I need a coffee, anyone else?" Thomas instinctively jumped out, he always wanted something from 7-11, candy or a chocolate drink. Paige got out to get a coffee also. Helen and her mother-in-law stayed in the car consoling each other. It was 10:20am.

It took five minutes to get out of 7-11 and another 10 to get home. George was already starting to formulate a plan on how to get and stay under the radar, at least for a while. He was wondering how much money he could withdrawal from a bank without raising suspicion.

31

Should he involve others for help, or go it alone? First things first, he thought, we need to get out of town. George didn't bother putting the car in the garage, he parked in the driveway, turned off the engine and got everyone's attention. "Okay, here's the drill. Everyone, pack one bag of clothes, one small bag for toiletries, and only two pairs of shoes. Mom, do we need to stop for any medications?" Kathy Grady looked at George with a smile and said, "Not anymore." While patting Thomas' head. George smiled back and simply said, "Let's go." And they all headed inside to get ready.

George was surprised that it only took twenty minutes for everyone to actually be ready to go. They all met at the front door in the living room. Helen had put some clothes together for Kathy, and the kids seemed to have taken care of themselves just fine. "Alright," George said, "Let's go." They all headed out the door towards the SUV, it was 10:55am. They all heard it, but weren't quite sure what the noise was, like a swishing sound followed by a couple of metallic clicks.

They all remembered seeing strangers around them, then the world went black. The next thing they all remembered were the paramedics around them. They stood up, looked around, they were all still a little dizzy, but they were all aware of the fact that one person was missing, Thomas was gone. It had taken less than two hours for Walter Harrington Porter's men to find, track and capture Thomas Grady, who was now bound, gagged, and being taken to Mr. Porter's estate.

Walter Harrington Porter

Walter Harrington Porter was a man of considerable wealth. He had made his fortune in the transportation business and in time his company became one of the world's biggest conglomerates. Walter Harrington Porter had his hand in almost everything you could think of from plastics to energy, to pharmaceuticals, along with a few high-tech firms. Mr. Porter was worth billions, however, at this moment, there was no amount of money in the world that would be able to sustain his life for more than a few more months.

Walter Harrington Porter has a number of ailments. He was suffering with severe arthritis in most of his joints, cataracts, kidney failure, prostate cancer, diabetes, lethargy, he was asthmatic along with a few other problems that come with old age and an over-taxed immune system. His doctor was impressed that he still had most of his faculties intact. Which may or may not be good news, depending on what side of Walter Harrington Porter you were standing on. If you were on his bad side, well, let's just say you wouldn't be standing there for long.

Walter Harrington Porter was born in Omaha, Nebraska on April 17th, 1932, to Henry and Alice Portman. Both parents were uneducated, unemployed, and unadulterated drunks. Walter never had a chance at a normal childhood. By the time Walter was 10 years old, Omaha was experiencing one of its biggest financial booms ever. Towards the end of WWII, Omaha was one of the largest producers of livestock, and the Union Stockyards Company was the biggest company in all of Omaha.

This only added to the demise of Walter's childhood because even unemployable people, like his drunken parents, were given jobs because they needed so much help. The stockyard didn't care if you were a drunk or any other kind of reprobate, they needed the bodies in the plant working to keep pace with the insatiable demands of the market. The Porters both worked in the evisceration process 10 to 12 hours a day. At its peak in the mid-fifties, the Union Stockyards Company was serviced by six railroads including one owned by the Stockyard itself. What this meant for Walter's parents was that they could get as drunk as much as they wanted to and still keep their jobs. It was an alcoholic's paradise.

The drinking got worse, and the beatings got harder. They both punished Walter for any shortcomings they had as people and parents. Walter grew up beaten, bruised, and teased by his peers. Even though both parents worked, they were always broke. Walter could only remember ever buying one pair of shoes during most of his childhood. His clothes were tattered and close to falling apart. He was an anomaly at school because it was very common for all working families to be doing fairly well. Almost all the kids in his school had decent clothing. Walter was teased about his parents being drunk all the time and about the silly holes on the bottom of his shoes.

Although Walter was teased a lot about many things, for some reason the one thing that stuck in his mind the most were the holes in his shoes. How he would place pieces of cardboard in his shoe so that he wouldn't end up with holes in his socks as well. He hated his parents, he hated the kids at school, but most of all, he hated his damn shoes. Why couldn't his parents just buy him another pair? They always seemed to have enough for their damn whiskey. By the time Walter was 14 years old, his life was worse than ever. His parents had succumbed to every

33

problem and disease associated with alcoholism. Their apartment was a mess, they hardly went to work, there was less money and more booze than ever. And Walter, he still didn't have a decent pair of fucking shoes. He swore he would leave these two idiots that call themselves parents as soon as he was able.

They never acted like parents, they were always arguing with each other and teasing Walter for not having a girlfriend and calling him a little fagot. Walter would hold his tongue and just run away while still hearing their ridiculously loud drunken laughter. It was a rare day when Walter went to bed without his rage, his hatred, his loathing, or his tears of bitterness.

One day, Walter woke up and found his dad drunk standing in front of the bed with a bottle in his hand and staring down at his mom. Alice Portman had died in her sleep. Later, the doctor told Henry that her liver gave out, and that he could expect the same thing if he doesn't stop drinking soon. But Walter knew that asking his father to stop drinking would be like asking a fish to stop swimming. A few days after Walter's mother passed away, Walters father walked out the door and never came back, and Walter didn't know what to do, but he knew how he felt, glad. He didn't seek help, he didn't want help, he hated everyone anyway. So, Walter went to the Stockyard Company and got a job. They were busier than ever and were glad to have anyone come on board with two good hands and a healthy back. And with his first paycheck, Walter went out and bought himself a pair of brand-new shoes.

Although Walter got rid of the shoes with holes, he will never be able to get rid of the permanent hole in his soul. But for the next 60 plus years, he would fill it with hate, malice, and contempt. He despised everyone around him because he knew their potential for being cruel. He knew of man's ability to cause pain for their own contorted pleasure. He knew that people only felt superior when they were able to make someone else feel inferior. He knew that people didn't care about him and anyone else, even when they could plainly see that a person was in desperate need of help. How else could Walter see people? They were all fakes, whore mongers, petty and weak.

Without the distraction of having to worry about people or relationships, Walter began to immerse himself in his work. It did not go unnoticed. By the time Walter was 17 he became foreman, then supervisor and in a few years, ran the entire shipping department. He was making great money, including bonuses. He enjoyed having money, not because he could buy things, like as many shoes as he wanted, but for some reason, it was the only thing that made him feel secure, and unbeknownst to Walter, he had an overwhelming desire to feel secure. Thus, he had an overwhelming desire to acquire money, which he equated to security.

It was shortly after Walters first promotion that he decided he would change his name. He still had plenty of hate for his parents and wanted nothing to do with them. He went down to the local courthouse and for a couple of dollars had his name changed legally to Walter Harrington Porter. It was a small change from Portman, but it felt like a world of difference to Walter. He had planned on using just two names, but he was always impressed by those who had three, and so, Walter Harrington Porter was introduced into the world.

Walter Harrington Porter had a moment of clarity one day while at work. He was helping one of his foremen with the scheduling of the next day's shipment of livestock when he realized that they were in need of at least two more railroad containers. He did some quick math and came to the conclusion that he would have to supplement their schedule with at least four or five truck loads. He didn't like to do that because it was always cheaper to ship by rail. However, on this cool November morning, Walter had an idea. He had enough money to buy a truck, and he was sure that he could get a loan for a second truck. All he would need are a couple of drivers and he could take on half of this load.

The next day he made some inquiries. Much to his surprise, it all came together quite easily. In a few short months Walter quit the Stockyard Company and opened up a small trucking business. With his connections at the Stockyard, Walters business took off from the very start. His first year he showed a profit of over twenty thousand dollars. The very thought of the money gave Walter a sense of security he had never known. Money was the only thing that seemed to mean anything to him. Walter had developed a love affair with money, and so it wasn't long before it's evil took root. To Walter Harrington Porter, all things and people took second seat to his lover. By the time Walter was 30 years old, he had become a millionaire. And although they say that luck favors the prepared, there is also just plain old luck, and Walter had more than his share of serendipity.

After the Union Stockyards Company was sold to a New York company, Walter noticed the livestock business starting to slow down. It was luck that drove his decision to sell his trucking company and decided to go into the real estate business. A couple of years later, the market went crazy, and Walter made a few more million. After that, he came to the realization that he needed real professionals to handle his money. Walter Harrington Porter hired the best MBA's from

Harvard and Yale. It wasn't long before his fortune grew to a very considerable size further feeding his rapacious appetite.

The Dying Soul

Man's soul seeks divine forgiveness, so that he may enter into eternity with a rueful spirit. But a soul roiled in greed and hate, will never see love, nor heaven's gate.

-JLC

During his most prosperous years, Walter Harrington Porter, now only 38 years young, began to notice a change in his health. He was becoming more prone to illness. Unbeknownst to anyone, except a young radiologist at Our Lady of Laredo Hospital in Van Nuys, California, Walters body was about to go into a losing battle with a myriad of systemic diseases. Less than a year ago, Walter went in for a minor checkup due to some mystery pain in his abdomen. He thought he may have eaten something bad, and everyone insisted that he have an x-ray taken. As usual, Walter hated the way everyone tried to pretend to care about him. He knew that they were all just feigning concern because he was the man with the money and the power.

Walter Harrington Porter never forgot how to hate. Even now, while genuine concern was being expressed, Walter could neither see it, nor sense it. But nevertheless, he went to have his pain checked out. Walter had a secret that he never shared with anyone. His greatest fear was that he would die while he was still young enough to enjoy his wealth. He didn't have any heirs, didn't care about anyone, and surely didn't want to give his money away to anyone or anything, unless it was to benefit him financially in some way. Walter despised the thought of having to leave his money behind. It was, after all, his only true love.

It was this perverse love for his wealth which prompted him to see a doctor. After a brief stay, the doctors examined him, checked out his x-ray and sent him home with a clean bill of health. The prognosis, tummy ache. However, there was a young and inexperienced radiologist at work that day. It would never be known that this radiologist accidentally gave Walter an excessive amount of dye. The dye that is used in radiology helps to create a contrast in the x-ray which allows the area to be seen more clearly. What was not known then was that too much of this particular dye can cause kidney damage.

A year later, Walter developed ATN, or Acute Tubular Necrosis. This disease deprives the kidney of much needed oxygen and in turn, causes severe complications. While being treated for this, Walter got a case of pneumonia. It took a long time for Walter to heal, but his body paid a heavy toll. With his immune system taxed to its limit, Walter would be dealt the final blow. Two years after that one x-ray, Walter also developed Hodgkin's Lymphoma. Although with treatment, one can expect a long survival rate, there are issues that develop from the treatment itself, like cardiovascular diseases, second malignancies, such as solid tumors and other complications. All of which eventually lead Walter Harrington Porter to where he is today, in a bed with no hope of enjoying his money...until now.

Standing before him is a small young boy with a dark hood over his head. Standing next to this young boy, were two large men in dark suits. Thomas Grady could feel the strength of these men. Their grip felt tight, almost vise-like. Thomas could hear noises, people shuffling around and that familiar antiseptic smell of a hospital. Finally, someone spoke. They knew his name. "Thomas." It was a man's voice. The voice sounded strained, old, hurting. "Yes." Thomas replied through his hood. "I understand you have a gift. That you are able to heal people by merely touching them. Is this true, son?"

"I guess." Said Thomas, not knowing which way to turn his head because it was still covered. That was not the answer Walter was hoping for. For some reason he was expecting something a little more dramatic. 'I guess,' sounds like something a kid his age would say, not some powerful all-healing sage. But, after all, he was a child. Walter continued, "Thomas," Walter said, in his kindest voice, trying not to upset the boy. For all Walter knew, maybe the boy healed only when he wanted to, and it had nothing to do with whether he touched you or not.
Walter kept trying to play his cards as well as he could. "Thomas, I want you to touch me so that I may be healed. Could you do that?"

"I suppose." Another childish remark. It was starting to irritate Walter. He wanted more assurance from this boy. Nevertheless, he went on coaxing him, "Thomas, the two men next to you are going to bring you towards me and I want you to touch me so that I may be healed. Okay?"

"Sure." Thomas was not trying to be coy, he just didn't know what to say to these people who kidnapped him and did who knows what to his family. The thought of his mom and dad and his sister helped to spark a little bit of courage, and Thomas stopped walking. The two men could easily push him forward, but they waited for instruction from Walter. "Wait." Thomas said. Walter was caught off guard by this sudden show of resistance. "What is it, Thomas?" Walter again, trying to be calm so as to not upset the boy. Once again, he did not know if Thomas' gift was intentional, or unintentional. In other words, could he simply force Thomas to touch him and be cured, or would Thomas need to touch you of his own free will in order to be cured. Walter wasn't sure and he wasn't about to jeopardize this chance, so he remained obsequies. "Is there something wrong, Thomas?" Thomas thought about that question for a second, *'wrong? Yeah, everything's wrong. Stay calm.'* Thomas told himself. *'Maybe this person just wants me to touch him, heal him, and then he'll let me go.'* Thomas spoke, "Well, sir, yes, there is something wrong. I don't know what happen to my mom and dad."

"They're fine, Thomas. I can assure you of that. They are at home, waiting for you. All you have to do is heal me, and these men will drop you off with your family." Walter lied. Thomas was young but was intuitive enough to sense that this person was not exactly honest. He began to worry, but what choice did he have. He had to touch him and hope that he would let him go home. Thomas took a step, indicating that he was ready to move forward. The two men lead him towards Walter.

Walter Harrington Porter stared at the boy walking towards him, daring himself to believe. *'Could this be possible?'* He thought. *'Could this small boy actually rid me of all these accursed maladies? Would I be able to enjoy my wealth once again?'* Thomas was only a mere five or six steps away, but the distance looked impossibly far to Walter, and Thomas seemed to be moving so slow it was actually causing Walter severe anxiety, making him feel even worse than he did a few minutes ago.

Having nothing or no one to believe in, Walter was drowning in a thick muck of baseless faith. His own desperateness and disingenuous hope threatened to exploit him, forcing him to reveal some trace of unknown goodness buried deep inside his dark heart. But years of callous and malice behavior quickly pulled on the reigns of empathy and Walter was back in his own wretched reality. *'I must be cured.'* He told himself, *'And everyone else can go to hell.'* Thomas was only two steps away.

Walter was trying to keep his hopes down but couldn't. Somehow he knew this was going to work. He felt giddy inside. His mind raced. *'What if it's true, what if I am about to be healed?'*

'This will be amazing.' he thought. The implications are mind boggling. One step away. The two men brought Thomas closer to Walter and he was now standing still at the edge of Walter's bed. Walter lay perfectly still, not knowing what to expect. The room fell void of all sound, it was as if everyone simultaneously blocked out the noise of all the medical equipment in the room, no one moved, all eyes were on Thomas' arm as he held it up, the palm of his hand facing Walter, Thomas leaned forward, then slowly, softly, through the darkness of his hood, he brought his hand down upon Walter's shoulder and touched him.

Of course, the results were not instantaneous, they never have been, there have always been a few seconds of delay. But in those few seconds, when Walter could feel nothing happening, he felt every ounce of hope emptying from his body and he wanted to scream. He wanted to kill the boy, he wanted everyone in the room dead, he wanted to thrust a knife into the heart of humankind and twist it. Walter felt he might explode with the disappointed rage that was expanding in his body. Walters eyes were darting everywhere, not knowing what to look for or what to look at. Walter knew there was a plate on the nightstand next to his bed, in his mind he could see himself throwing it as hard as he could at someone, anyone.

Walter began to reach for the plate when suddenly, he felt something, a warm sensation in his feet, almost hot, but not painful. In fact, as the warmth began to move from his feet to his ankles, then his calves, Walter was already starting to feel better. He froze and concentrated on the sensation. Everyone in the room was captivated by his reaction. As the warmth climbed into his torso and past his shoulders, Walter Harrington Porter knew that there was no doubt as to what was happening. A few more seconds later and the event was over. Walter Harrington Porter was healed.

Walters skeptical doctor was one of the persons in the room. Dr. Salinger was the best that money could buy, and although he remained incredulous, he became an instant convert when, much to his dismay, Walter Harrington Porter sat up, and almost leaped out of bed and said, in a clear, loud and strong voice, "He did it, I'm healed!" Walter began moving his arms and doing a few knee bends as if he was inspecting all his joints. Dr. Salinger spoke with amazement, "Mr. Porter, how do you feel?"

"Feel? I feel fine, no, I feel great, no, scratch that, I feel invincible. Oh, and Dr. Salinger, I not only feel fantastic, but I also don't remember the last time I thought this clearly. No, Dr., I am much more than just healed, ha, ha, I actually feel younger!" Walter continued walking and prancing around the room while everyone watched in absolute disbelief. It was a slightly repugnant spectacle watching a wrinkled dried up 87-year-old man prancing around the room. He looked like a walking talking anachronism.

They all understood that they had just witnessed something miraculous, a real honest-to-goodness miracle. Something impossible was just made possible before their very eyes and it caused much mental consternation. For some inexplicable reason they all felt their spirits being tested. This was, after all, a good thing that happened in a very perverse way. In a sense, it was a forced miracle, if there even is such a thing. Can you force God to grant you a miracle? Did this man who possessed such an ugly soul deserve to receive such a gift?

On his best day, Walter was agnostic, on his worse day, which were many, he was an awful man filled with an all-encompassing contemptuous scorn for people. Walter Harrington Porter was not the smartest man in the room, he wasn't the best looking, he had no real attributes to speak of. Walter was common in nature, in stature, and in all other ways, completely pedestrian. The one and only thing that separated Walter from everyone else in the room was his immense wealth. This incident and its implications did not go unnoticed by a certain person in the room.

On that day, there was a small contingent of people which bore witness to Walters miracle. There was Walters doctor, Dr. Salinger, two nurses, two henchmen from Walters security goon-squad. There was Charles and last but not least, there was Mario Reyes, a member of Charles' in-house security team. Mario Reyes had been standing by the entrance of Walters spacious master bedroom. Mario Reyes also had been observing the entire ordeal with absolute certainty that nothing was going to happen. In fact, Mario was sure he was going to have to help return this kid back into the streets after proving that this is all just a bunch of bullshit. But when he saw what happened to Walter, his mind raced elsewhere, to his dying child that was currently at the San Diego Cancer Center with an inoperable tumor in her tiny little brain.

After Walters' elation subsided, Walter froze and remained motionless for a few contemplative seconds then said, "Charles, clear the room, take Thomas to some comfortable, but confined accommodations." "Yes, sir." Charles replied. He made a few hand motions, and everyone left the room. The two goons took Thomas Grady and led him to some secluded section of the mansion.

Walters' mind was not only thinking clearly but was now locked back into the single purpose of making money, lots of it. With Thomas in his possession, he could extract massive amounts of wealth from rich families that he knew would gladly pay him whatever he wanted to keep death at bay. Wealthy people would pay millions, if not billions, to be cured or to have a family member cured of serious illnesses. He could very well be the next richest man in the world in a span of time that most would consider, overnight.

The very thought of it made Walter giddy again. Charles almost grimaced at the incongruous smile on Walters face, it looked unnatural, sardonic, and out of place. Walter quickly made some arrangements to have Thomas' blood drawn and checked as soon as possible. If there was anything there that could be synthesized he was going to find it...and sell it. Walter sent one of the nurses to draw Thomas' blood. The nurses knew what to do and where to send it.

Mario Reyes was in his mid-forties, ex-military with ten years in Special Forces. He joined Walters security team about four years ago. The pay was good, but it was one hell of a boring job. Mario was able to easily bear the mundane work for the sake of his wife of 14 years and his 11-year-old daughter who needed him now. Although at times, Mario felt he needed her more. Maggie was dying before his eyes, but it was she who gave him strength. If not for her smile and words of affection, Mario would have succumbed to the weight of this burden and at times it was Maggie's tiny shoulders that seemed to carry most of the crushing weight. She had been in the San Diego Cancer Center for the past 8 months and her prognosis was bleak.

They weren't expecting Maggie to make it much longer. His wife, Margaret, had become addicted to the anti-depression medication that she constantly needed, or she was sure she would go mad. Mario Reyes was living in the worst and darkest years of his life. He was losing his daughter to cancer and his wife to drugs and depression. And now, in front of him was this lanky 15-year-old kid that seemed to hold the answer to his impossible plight.

It did not take long for Mario Reyes to make a decision. He had already formulated a plan to take Thomas tonight and race him to heal his daughter. He was unclear how, or if, this miracle would work for his wife as well. But he was going to do it or die trying, and the consequences be damned. Besides, there was nothing anyone could do to Mario to hurt him any more than the pain he felt for his little girl. In fact, Mario couldn't remember the last time he felt this good about making a decision.

Walter was pacing around his room and planning, with much delight, how he was going to bleed every fatted calf he knew. Meanwhile, the security goons had placed Thomas in one of the upstairs bedrooms that had bars on the windows. There was only one way in or out, and that was through the door that was manned by the goons. Both men were big, strong and stone faced. However, neither one of them had the extensive training that Mario had received while serving with Navy Seal Team 5. Mario Reyes prepped himself mentally for any confrontation and being well practiced in the martial arts, he would make a more than worthy adversary for anybody who would try to stop him from his objective. Mario entered the hallway of the second floor, looked to his left, and saw the two men standing in front of the room where Thomas was. He went for the easy way first.

Mario calmly walked up to the two men and said, "I need to take the kid back to Mr. Walters." The two men looked at each other. They knew Mario well, in fact, they had great respect for him, for some reason, it felt like something wasn't right. Mario was more of an outside guy. Kept an eye on the outer parameter, handled exterior security. So, one of the men, the bigger one of the two, whose name was Jimmy, said, "Ah, we didn't hear anything about taking the kid back to the boss." Mario didn't flinch, and quickly replied, "Old man sent me up, what do I care. You guys can take him, I got shit to do." Jim looked at his partner, there was nothing odd about Mario taking the kid back to Walters downstairs master bedroom, so, they called the kid outside into the hallway, placed the dark sack over his head again and gave him to Mario. "You need any help, Mario?" Jim asked,

"With what?"

"With the kid,"

"What, are you kidding? Mario said with a big smile. Jim looked at his partner, they both just hunched their shoulders and said, "Okay, then, we'll be right here when you bring him back, Mario."

"No problem, Jim, thanks. See you guys in a bit." The two men simply motioned their heads in an affirmative gesture, and Mario was on his way.

'Okay, that was easy.' Mario thought to himself. Next step is to get in the car and get the hell out of here. Thomas was trying to say something, but Mario bent down and whispered in his ear in a stern voice, "Don't talk, I'm getting you out of here, did you hear me?" Thomas simply nodded his covered head.

Mario and Thomas walked to the center of the hallway where the stairs were located. Mario warned him that he was about to go down some stairs. Thomas had to walk a little slower than Mario would have liked, but, so far, so good. Once they get to the bottom, they would have to go down one more set of stairs to the six-car garage. Then, just outside of that, there was a small parking area for workers and outside guests. That's where Mario's car was parked. *'So far, it's been nothing but a cake walk. Just a couple of minutes and we're out of here.'* Mario thought. But before he reached halfway down the steps, Mario heard the crackling of the two-way radio, the whole security team could hear whoever was about to speak, it was Charles, the head of security, he was addressing Jim, and his goon partner, Leon, "Jim, this is Charles, over."

"This is Charles, go ahead, over."

"Jim, bring the kid back here to speak with Mr. Porter, over."

"Ah, he's already on his way, over."

"What?"

Experience kicked in, and both Jim and Leon moved quickly and gave chase while speaking on the radio. "This is Jim, boss, I think we got a problem, Mario already took the kid, he said he was told to bring him to you. Over."

"What the hell is going on. Get Mario and bring him to me and make sure you get that kid, your jobs depend on it. Go."

Mario heard the entire conversation and could hear Jim and Leon closing in. Thomas was moving way too slow for Mario, so he scooped him up, slung him over his shoulder and began running towards the exit and to his car. Things were getting complicated fast. There were two more men outside that Mario would have to deal with. He could hear Jim and Leon yelling now, "Mario, stop, don't make us stop you. Come on, don't do it." Mario knew that he would not have time to reach his car, get inside, start it and take off. He needed to buy some time. He made it outside, ran about halfway to the car, carefully placed Thomas on the floor and waited for the goons.

Both Jim and Leon drew their guns and yelled at Mario, "Don't move, Mario. Don't make us take you down. You're totally fucking up our jobs here, Mario, what the hell's wrong with you?" Mario didn't say anything, he simply held up his hands in surrender. Mario Reyes pretended to be more tired than he really was, faking deep breaths as if he couldn't go on any further and acted like he was about to collapse on the ground. Jim and Leon fell for it, they looked at Mario and thought he would be too tired to put up any resistance. They were wrong.

Mario moved so fast that it actually startled Leon when, sensing that Jim was at the right distance, Mario shifted his weight on one leg and swept Jim's legs right out from under him.

43

Jim's body went up parallel to the ground and fell hard on his back causing him to drop his gun. In the same instance, while Leon was temporarily startled from seeing Mario move so quickly, Mario already had one of his hands on Leon's arm and with his other hand grabbed the gun and twisted it inward towards Leon's body. Leon had to release the gun, or risk having his wrist broken. Mario pointed the gun towards the two men and told Leon and Jim to stay down.

Mario went over to help Thomas up and lead him to the car. While Mario was distracted helping Thomas up, he heard one of the men shuffling, he looked just in time to see Leon reaching for his back-up weapon in his leg. Mario's instincts dictated the next few moves. Mario fired twice at Leon, both shots hit the center of mass, Jim reached for his weapon as well, thinking he might have the upper hand while Mario was busy shooting Leon. He was wrong. Mario was too well trained. He didn't miss a beat, there was no hesitation, Mario saw what was happening in his peripheral vision and knew he would have to shoot Jim as well. The opportunity that Jim thought he had was never there. Mario shot twice at Leon, but Mario never hesitated as Jim was hoping. Mario instantly shot Jim hitting him once in the chest and once in the neck. This was not how he wanted to buy time. He was hoping only to incapacitate them while he escaped. Mario didn't think they would try to kill him, but then again, why wouldn't they, it's their job.

Mario and Thomas made it to the car. He was surprised the property alarm hadn't gone off. But that would bring the police, and Mario was sure that was the last thing the old man wanted. Mario started the car, Thomas was in the front seat, head still covered, he asked Mario if he could remove it, but Mario said no, he wanted to make sure they got out first, he didn't want the kid to see what was going on around him. Mario had just left a very bloody mess behind, the kid didn't need to see it. Once they were out and in the clear Mario would then allow Thomas to remove the cover from his head.

They started down the long driveway, Mario got about twenty feet when the back window shattered. Another security man, he knew him well, Aaron Billings, he was a good guy, he didn't want to hurt him either. Mario yelled at Thomas, "Get down and stay low!" Several more shots rang out and this time the side mirror exploded as one of the bullets smashed into it. *Damn it*, he thought, almost at the front gate. Mario thought, *'I still might make it.'*

Mario was only seconds away from breaking down the thick wrought iron gate. It would scratch his car, but so what, we're almost free. Just then, the fourth and last man of the outside security team, Jack Cohen, stepped out in front of Mario's car and got into a shooting position. Mario did not like that, Jack was cool headed, that's the worst kind of opponent. He was going to take his time aiming, and he wouldn't be aiming for the tires, this guy will be looking to take him out.

Mario had no choice, he had to turn the car radically to make themselves a more difficult target. It worked, several shots rang out, but he didn't get hit. Mario floored the accelerator and yelled at Thomas, "Okay, take the bag off your head, you may need to run. The front gate is the only way out of here. They're going to guard it. It's not going to be easy now."

Thomas was momentarily glad to have the sack off his head but looked up to see grass and plants flying by. The car was on the grassy area of the large estate, and they were going fast. Thomas was scared they were going to crash into a tree or something. Mario finally put a quick plan together in his head. He moved into the estates garden area where there was at least some cover to hide in. Mario turned off the engine and said to Thomas, "Look, son. This is not going to end well for some of us.

I need to get you out of here, but I want you to promise not to try to leave without me. You won't make it alone, you understand?" Thomas nodded, Mario continued, "If we get separated, meet me right here at the car, got it?" Thomas nodded again. "Look," he said to Thomas, "I need you to hide as best you can around here somewhere. There aren't many lights and there's a lot of places to hide. I'm going back to try to eliminate our problem. Wait for me to come back." Thomas only nodded for a third time. He didn't know what to say, what do you say to someone who pretty much told you he's going to go kill people.

This was the only answer at this point. Mario went back towards the house. He couldn't see him, but Mario knew that Jack Cohen was out there moving stealthy around the parameter, looking for an opportunity to present itself. But Aaron, who was also still out there somewhere, was a brawler, he was going to try to beat Mario to death if he could. Mario was now in full battle mode. His eyes went dark, his senses tuned in to his surroundings. Mario was entering back into the house through the French-doors on the veranda. They were locked, Mario had no pretense, he simply smashed it open with his foot, not caring how much noise he made. In fact, he wanted to raise the tension level. People made more mistakes when their tense.

Mario walked into the house, concentrating on his breathing, he heard a noise, Aaron was following him, and he could hear Aaron stepping on the broken glass from the French-doors.

There was a half-moon out, it cast just enough light for Mario to see Aaron's silhouette, Mario fired his usual two rounds into the center of mass striking Aaron and fatally wounding him. Reload. Mario kept walking into the house, headed towards the downstairs master bedroom where he knew he would encounter Charles. The rest of the house staff and guest were gone or hiding.

The door to the master bedroom was locked. *"Well,* Mario thought, *this ain't no social call,* and he shot the lock several times and kicked the door open. He quickly ducked to the side as a hail of bullets came showering through the doorway. Charles had pulled out a specially modified fully automatic AR15 and was taking no chances with Mario. He knew his background, he was the one who hired him. Charles himself was from special ops., U.S. Marine Corp. and no one to be trifled with. True he had a few more years on him than Mario, maybe a little slower, but just as deadly on any day of the week.

They were a close match-up, this skirmish will be about who will make the first mistake. It would be Charles. Charles had made a classic mistake in choosing his position. He had inadvertently decided to make his stance just behind Walter's bed. The location wasn't bad, what Charles didn't realize was that Mario had an almost perfectly unobstructed view of him through Walter's dresser mirror. Mario could see him, but Charles had not yet noticed the reflection, if he did, he would have moved immediately, but he didn't. Mario simply waited for Charles's attention to be diverted for a mere second or two and he would step in and fire.

Walter was still in the room, seething with anger at this betrayal. He couldn't help himself, he yelled out, "Mario, you son of bitch, I will see you dead before the night is over." This was exactly what Mario was hoping for, the old fart was going to provide the distraction he needed. Charles is going to try to calm him down or talk to him, and when he does, it's over.

Just as predicted, Walter started on another rant, something about skinning him alive, but Mario could now see that Charles was turning his attention towards Walter and trying to shut him up, and when Mario saw that Charles shifted his attention to Walter for just a second, Mario stepped into the doorway and emptied his gun in Charles direction. Charles fell to the floor lifeless. Reload.

Walter just got more furious, he didn't care that Charles was dead, he didn't care if everyone was dead, he just wanted his money. Walter could see that Mario was intent on killing him as well, but he felt that every man had his price, so he offered Mario money. "Mario, come on, man, name your price and get the hell out of my house. What do you want, a million dollars? Two? How about five million dollars, Mario. I'll give you five million dollars for you to get the hell out of my house and never come back. Will that suffice?" Walter said, with all the indignation he could muster. Mario thought about it for a second and said, "Mr. Porter, how much cash do you have in the house, right now?"

Walter almost laughed as he said, "I have a safe right here in my room with two-hundred thousand cash. Are you telling me that's all you want? Mr. Reyes, you are an idiot. Go ahead, take the money, here, I'll open the safe for you. It's just behind that painting." Mario allowed Walter to rant and talk nonsense while he opened the safe. Mario was not listening to a word Walter is saying, Mario was watching and listening for Jack Cohen. He knew Jack would be patient, maybe try to ambush him on the way out. Mario wanted the money to give to Thomas once he healed his daughter. He didn't know what else he could do for him.

Walter opened the safe, Mario held up his gun and said, "Mr. Porter, I sincerely hope you are not going to try to pull a weapon out of there. Please, just the cash. I have my gun pointed right at your head, you won't make it if you try." Walter turned and smiled, "Can't blame an old man for trying."

Walter pulls out the money and Mario is surprised to see that two-hundred thousand dollars doesn't look like much when it's in bundles of one-hundred-dollar bills. Mario walked over to the bed, pulled a pillow out from its case and placed the money inside it. Walter started on another rant, but Mario simply held up his gun, shot Walter once in the head, turned and walked out of the room.

Walter Harrington Porter came into the world wrapped in a crumbled convoluted ball of hate, misery and emptiness, and left it the same way. Walter Harrington Porter had no heirs, no friends, no charities and no will. His estate will be a source of contention for years to come. There would be no legacy, only a void where pity would visit from time to time.

Mario was still focused on the job. He would sort all this out with his conscious later. As he walked past the threshold, Jack stepped out from behind a wall just a couple of feet away. Both men instinctively engaged. Mario moved his firearm towards Jack, but Jack rushed in and prevented Mario from leveling his gun. Both men struggled to fire their weapons, but they each had hold of the other's arm that held the weapon. Mario tried to head butt Jack, but Jack moved his head to the side then came in and bit Mario's neck, hard. Mario wrenched with pain, if he bites through his artery, it will kill him. Mario let his weight fall to the ground, forcing Jack to let go or follow him down in an awkward position which might compromise his advantage.

Both men hit the floor, but now Mario is protecting his injured neck. Jack has a slight advantage because he's on top. Both men still have their guns and struggling to get them loose. Mario decides to release his gun, giving himself more mobility with his hand. Mario uses a simple judo move to dislodge his arm which no longer holding a weapon, but now he is able to use both hands against Jacks arm that still holding a weapon. After a few seconds of struggling, Mario finally grabs the gun with his right hand and twists it in towards Jacks body and causing Jack's wrist to sprain. Jack releases the gun and then tried to grab it back from Mario, but not before Mario is able to get off three shots, and the fight was over.

Mario goes back to the car and looks for Thomas. He calls out and at first there is no response, but after a moment, Mario heard some rustling in the bushes. It was Thomas, a little shaken, but okay. Mario grabs him and hugs him. He tells Thomas, "Kid, I am so sorry for all this. You do not deserve any of this. You're gonna need to start being more careful. Start changing things in your life." Thomas just hugged Mario back, it was the first sign of affection he had felt from anybody in a while. "What should I do?" Thomas asked. "I'll help you, kid, but first, we really have to go somewhere, okay?"

"Okay." was all Thomas could say.

Mario Reyes had decided to take Thomas to his home first. He didn't know if Thomas could heal something like addiction, or if he could only heal illnesses. He asked Thomas, but Mario soon realized that Thomas was just as befuddled as everyone else. Thomas did not know what the extent of his ability was, though he had been thinking about it lately. He began to form questions that he had never asked himself before because he had never had to. Until now, his life was pretty normal. He was just another kid in the neighborhood. Playing video games, basketball, and falling in love with a girl named Danni. He wondered how she was doing. He also wondered about his parents. Damn it, if only he could remember just one phone number. He swore he would memorize at least three numbers when he got home. If he gets home. At the moment his life felt pretty unpredictable.

It was a short drive to Mario's house, Walter Harrington Porter lived in one of the most expensive zip codes in Southern California, which was in Rancho Santa Fe. Mario lived about ten miles north/west in Encinitas. They arrived at Mario's home around twenty minutes after leaving Walter's mansion. Mario Reyes pulled into his driveway, parked, turned off the engine and asked Thomas to go with him inside the house. In spite of everything that Mario had done and risked for him, Thomas was still hesitant. While they were still in the car, Mario reached over and lightly touched Thomas' shoulder and asked him to look him in the eyes. When Thomas reluctantly made eye contact, Mario said, "Look at me, Thomas, I will never hurt you. I believe you are a special person put on this Earth for a special purpose. You're like an angel sent from God. I don't know what you're supposed to do, and I'm not going to make you do anything you don't want to. But right now, I really need you. Will you help me, Thomas?" Thomas felt a little uncomfortable with every word that Mario said. But was it true? *Why me?* Thomas thought, *I'm just a kid.* Thomas kept eye contact with Mario and replied, "Yes, I will help if I can." They both sat in silence for just a couple of seconds, then they both exited the car and walked towards the house.

Mario took out his keys and fumbled a little. Finally, he opened the door, and there in front of them, stooped on the couch, was Margaret Reyes, Mario's wife. She looked like she got run over by a truck…in hell. Her hair was dirty and mangled. Her bloodshot eyes had black drooping bags under them, she looked like a women possessed. Her thin tattered summer dress was stained, her legs were bruised, and she smelled of alcohol.

Margaret Reyes was a women with a dyeing child. Unkempt, uncaring and ill prepared for such a nomination. Margaret was exactly where she wanted to be, drenched in a sorrow so deep that she would never see the sun shining again. Addicted to her anti-depression drugs, Venlafaxine, was bad enough, but when mixed with alcohol, it was nothing less than a slow death sentence. Not to mention that an overdose could be fatal. She heard and saw Mario walk in, she also noticed some skinny little kid, too, but none of it registered, she just sat there unresponsive. Thomas was getting nervous, he had never seen a person on drugs before, not this bad, anyway. She looked like one of those people you see in a scary movie that's about to contort into some grotesque shapes. It didn't help that there were only a few lights on in the next room, it was almost dark where Margaret was sitting in the living room. Thomas began noticing other smells, tobacco, vodka, body odor and a few other aromas he couldn't make out. None of them were good.

Mario walked over to Margaret, took her hand gently in his and cupped it with his other hand. He positioned himself directly in front of her, but she barely acknowledged his presence. He looked at Margaret, tattered, worn-out, beat-up and drugged out, but she was still beautiful to him. He did not want to lose her, too. He knew they would need each other, and he had to help her, because without her, nothing would make sense. He spoke, "Mag," he always called her Mag since he could remember, "Mag, listen. I have someone here I want you to meet, his name is Thomas. He's going to help you." Margaret stared straight ahead, not making eye contact with Mario, and said, "What?"

"Honey, it's me, I want you to meet someone, his name is Thomas, he's right here." Mario motioned to Thomas to walk over and stand by him. "Mag, this is Thomas, he can help you."

"Help me? Why? I'm fine."

"Yes, I know, I know you're fine, honey, but we want to make you...ah, more fine."

"What? Where's my drink?" Margaret said looking around the room. Spotting a small dirty glass on the coffee table with something in it, Margaret pointed at it and said, "There it is. Tell your little friend he can help me by bringing me that glass." She smirked at what she thought was her sharp wit. Thomas went for the glass, but Mario waved at him to stop. "Thomas," Mario said, now motioning him towards him and Margaret. "Could you try touching her now?"

"What are you talking about? Touch me, touch me where? No touching, nooo touchy, touchy." Margaret said to no one in particular, she was just repeating the words, not really caring what anyone thought.

Thomas was still nervous, he walked over to Margaret and this time there was no dramatic pause, it was more like a 'tag, your it' kind of touch. Thomas jumped back as soon as he touched her. As usual, there was no immediate reaction. In fact, this time, even when the warming sensation came into Margaret's body, she did not react. At this point, she still didn't care if she felt something warm or not, all she wanted was that drink on the table.

Thomas and Mario both stood back and observed. Margaret leaned forward to get her glass, Mario did not stop her. The warmth in her body was now moving up her torso and Margaret had a slight reaction. She hesitated, but still picked up the glass and attempted to return back to her slouching position on the couch. But before her back reached the backrest, she froze. Margaret definitely was feeling something. The warming sensation had reached her neck, and she was becoming lucid. A couple more seconds passed, and she was mentally clear.

She stared at her hands for no apparent reason, then started looking around the room. Her mind was focused, her body felt good, like after a good run, she was mentally and physically tuned. Margaret looked at the glass in her hand and felt a tinge of disgust, the glass was filthy, sticky and filled with old vodka and God knows what. She was repulsed by it and almost tossed it on the floor. Her senses were immediately assaulted by a plethora of smells and horrible sights. The living room was in shambles, filled with dirty clothes, trash and bottles of liquor everywhere. The house was filled with rank smells from rotting food and body odor. Margaret Reyes had to stop herself from throwing up.

Mario and Thomas just kept watching her, waiting for her to comment or at least acknowledge what was happening to her. They didn't wait long. "What did you do to me?" She said, standing up and staring straight at Thomas. But Mario stepped in between them and said, "He cured you, honey."

"Cured me? What...who, me? He cured me?"

"Yes, Thomas cured you."

"From what?"

"From all this." Mario said motioning around the room with his hand. Pointing out the decrepit state of their home. He continued, "He cured you from your depression. From your grief, from you pain and your addiction to these!" Mario held up a large prescription bottle of Venlafaxine, one of the few anti-depression medication that you could easily and fatally over-dose on." Mario didn't know if he was reaching her, she still seemed to be taking it all in. He went on, "Mag, you've been feeling bad, and unhappy and I was tired of seeing you like this. I want you to be happy aga...." Margaret cut him off at mid-sentence, she held up her hand in a stopping gesture and said, "Happy? You want to see me happy?"

"Yes, I..." She cut him off again, "Are you fucking kidding me?" Her voice was getting louder as she continued, she pushed Mario back with enough force to send him tumbling a few steps backwards, he nearly lost his balance. Margaret was almost yelling now, "My little girl is dying, Mario, our little girl is dying! Are you happy? Are you okay? Cause I am not! I don't want to be okay. I want my grief, I need my grief and I need my pain. You think you can come in here and rob me of that? This, this pain and grief is all I have, Mario. Without it I will go fucking crazy!" Mario and Thomas were both startled by this unexpected response. This wasn't supposed to happen, this was supposed to be a healing. But Margaret wasn't done. She was feeling normal, in fact she felt good, and she was hating it. And although Thomas cured her of her addiction to the drug, it did not interfere with her free will. She was going to take her drug anyway, so that she could return to the comforting pain and the blissful numbness.

Margaret swooped up the bottle on Venlafaxine and walked to her bedroom with determination. She slammed the door as hard as she could. Behind the closed door, Mario and Thomas could hear screams of pure frustration along with several things being thrown and breaking against a wall. Then they heard nothing, there was a silence, a few seconds later, they watched the doorknob turning slowly, then the door being pushed open. Margaret stood at the doorway, looked at Thomas and said, "Are you telling me that you can heal people?"

"Yes, ma'am."

"Just by touching them?"

"Yes, ma'am."

Mario joined the conversation, "I've seen it, Mag, with my own eyes. And look what he did to you."

Mario and Margaret were finally on the same wavelength. Margaret quickly washed her face, grabbed a pair of clean pants and a top. She didn't bother combing her hair nor did she put any make-up on. She walked straight to the front door, opened it, and said, "Let's go." The next minute they were all in the car and headed to the San Diego Cancer Center.

Jacki Calloway

Talking to yourself is normal,
but arguing with a three-foot squirrel is nuts.- JLC

Jacki Calloway never had a real chance at true love. She was in need of occasional supervision, but because she usually appears to be so normal when she's on track with her medication, no one ever notices when she stops taking her meds until it's too late. After that, the voices come back as well as her hallucination and delusions. Jacki had met Alex Landon a few months back. When things started going well, Jacki would do what she always does. She equates happiness to believing that she's fine and doesn't need her medication, and in a very short time, her neurosis quickly takes over.

She would be able to live a long normal life, though statistics show that people with schizophrenia live on an average 10 to 15 years less than those without it. Yet, if she had someone to care for her, or at least help her keep an eye on her meds, Jacki Calloway could live a very normal life. Alex Landon was not that person. He liked Jacki, but he wasn't 'in-like' with her, especially when she started showing signs of being a little on the odd side.

Alex thought it was kind of funny at first, even cute, when Jacki would tell him that she had to buy a stick at Home Depot to keep the squirrels away in her bedroom. What Alex Landon didn't know was that the squirrels Jacki was talking about were three feet long and spoke to her at night and told her they were going to eat her as soon as she fell asleep. Alex would say, *Jacki, just buy some squirrel spray.* And then Jacki would laugh because she thought he was so simple minded. But it wouldn't be long before Alex realized that she was not kidding about the talking squirrels and the voices in her head. He asked her if she needed help, and she would just reply, for what? The voices help me....most of the time.

After that, Alex told her he was breaking up because she won't listen to him about getting help, but she knew it was because he was seeing those whores at Pete's Place, the local bar on Rancho Road. She was not going to put up with such disrespect from someone like Alex, a well-known spy who worked for Google. She was convinced that Alex was trying to steal her thoughts and put them on the internet for everyone to see. *'Imagine that,'* she thought to herself, *'everyone knowing what you're thinking, oh my God, that would be simply horrible! Oh, Alex, if only you could stop trying to destroy me. Why did you allow those whores to touch you and mock me'.* Jacki's thoughts went on. *' But now look at you. Tied up in my bedroom, powerless to destroy me. And now they want me to kill you. But I won't. Oh, no, no dying for you, my dearest Alex. You deserve so much more than that.'*

Jacki was living at her uncle's house. A modest 3-bedroom, 2 bath one-story house in a very nice little track near Encinitas Beach, not too far from where Mario and Margaret Reyes lived. The house was nestled in a quaint little neighborhood at the end of a cul-de-sac. The only part of the house that was visible from the street was the door to the two-car garage. The rest of the house had a six-foot fence, surrounded by a beautiful hedge of white flowering shrubs with pink camellias and some golden-leaved bleeding hearts. In the inner yard, the parameter was lined by a row of sweet-smelling Nellie Steven Holley trees, over 9 feet tall. It was impossible to see the inside of the house from anywhere in the street. It was a beautiful house on a beautiful quite street. It was too bad that Jacki's uncle was dead and lying on the bedroom floor next to Alex, who was gagged and tied to a chair in the middle of the room.

Mario and Margaret were brimming with hope as they pulled into the hospital parking lot.

Margaret had been talking to Thomas the whole way, asking him questions about his gift, but Thomas had very few answers. As Mario parked the car and turned the engine off, Margaret reached over to Thomas in the back seat, touched his lap with her hand and said in her most sincere voice, "Thomas, I'm sorry for my behavior back at the house. I was not myself." Thomas only nodded as Margaret went on, "I want you to know that we are very grateful for this, and if there is ever anything..." Margaret began sobbing, Mario squeezed her shoulder and said, "Honey, come on, everything's going to be just fine." But Margaret wanted to get it out, "Thomas, I don't know why you are here, in our lives right now, but I know it must be God's will. And maybe you are some kind of angel, I don't know, I just want you to know that if you ever need anything, don't hesitate to call us. If it's within our power, we will do whatever you ask." Thomas touched Margaret's hand and said, "It's okay, Mrs. Reyes, I just want to help." The truth was, Thomas was very uncomfortable, he wasn't used to this admiration or this extreme level of gratitude. What was he supposed to do or say? Thomas had no idea, he was a 16-year-old kid with minimal coping skills.

They exited the car and headed towards the hospital at a brisk pace. The automatic doors opened way too slow for Mario and Margaret as they hurried through the lobby of the San Diego Cancer Center. It was just after midnight. They didn't need any help with any direction, they knew exactly where to go, they knew exactly where little Maggie was. They went straight to the elevators, to the third floor, to room 310. On the bed, fast asleep was little Maggie. With the exception of her hairless head, she looked so peaceful, so normal, as if nothing was killing her frail little body from within.

Margaret nudged Maggie until she woke up. Maggie was surprised to see them, but was nevertheless happy to see mom and dad. But who was this boy, she thought. Mario helped Maggie to sit up. Maggie was still a little sleepy, but she was enjoying this unexpected attention. "Mom," Maggie said, "What's going on? Why are you guys here? Who's that?" Margaret said, pointing at Thomas. "This is Thomas, Thomas, this is Maggie." Thomas held up his hand and said, "Hi, nice to meet you Maggie."
"Nice to meet you, Thomas."

"What are you doing here with my mom and dad?" Thomas looked at Margaret and Mario for help. Mario replied, "Maggie, Thomas has a special gift. He's a very special boy." "Is he sick also, daddy?" Maggie was used to hearing words like special and gifted from people

54

when speaking about the children in this hospital. "No, Maggie, Thomas is not sick, in fact, he's here to help you. He's going to make you better."

"Is Thomas a doctor? He seems very young to be a doctor." Margaret takes Maggie's hands and says, "Look, young lady, we just need to let....Dr. Thomas do what he does, okay?" Margaret looked over at Thomas who was sort of beaming because she called him doctor. Maggie simply said, "Okay," Margaret said, "Dr. Thomas, would you mind coming over here and touch Maggie?" Thomas was only two short steps away, but as he took the first step, he felt a little dizzy. Everyone noticed it, and Mario said, "Thomas, are you okay?" Thomas stopped for a second, took stock of his feelings and he felt a little different. Something had changed, Thomas knew it, but he didn't know what. Thomas looked at Mario and Margaret and said, "I'm okay." He took another short step towards Maggie, stretched out his hand and touched her on the side of her head near her temple.

"Is that it? Am I cured?"

"Wait." Thomas said, looking at her, but not saying anything. That was another thing that was different this time, Thomas felt a little more disconnected, not from the person, but from his surroundings.

"Now?" Am I okay, now?"

"Wait." Thomas' voice remained unusually solemn.

"How long wil..." Maggie stopped talking. She felt something, the warmth was coming. Her little lips made a faint, oh, sound, her eyes got wide, she kept her lips puckered and she looked at her mom with silent excitement. Maggie didn't know what was going on, but she knew for sure she was being cured. Her body could tell, her feelings, her insides felt good and that perpetual pressure and pain in her head just vanished. Mario and Margaret experienced elevated levels of hope and joy that reached beyond heaven, beyond explanation. Their eyes, on the other hand, were becoming redder and tear-soaked with each passing second. They could see the color returning to Maggie's face, her eyes got brighter and sparkled like those of any child with young, healthy inquisitive eyes.

Once again, Thomas had inexplicably performed a miracle. It was incredible that such a miraculous thing was happening in this little hospital room. Maggie's body was being renewed at the cellular level. Not fixed, but renewed, which means she could expect a few more years added to her life. Meanwhile, every cancer cell was destroyed and disposed of into thin air.

They simply vanished. There was no medical or scientific explanation. All these unbelievable things were taking place, yet, if you were a casual observer standing just outside the door, you would be able to see that absolutely nothing was happening inside Maggie's room.

To Mario and Margaret Reyes, however, the world had just changed. Maggie was healed, they all knew it. The Reyes family was in the middle of a group hug, when Margaret grabbed Thomas and included him in the circle. They hugged for almost a minute before they relaxed. Mario picked Maggie up and said, "Your coming home with us sweetie-pie."

"But dad, what about Dr. Li? She said she was coming to see me in the morning."

"Don't worry, sweetie-pie, you'll see her. We're coming back tomorrow to let them examine you," Mario poked her nose while saying, "for the last time!" On the way out, they had a short argument with the staff, but eventually they let the family go. There was nothing they could do about keeping their child against their will. Besides, the nurses on duty were amazed at how well Maggie looked. They saw no harm if Mr. Reyes promised to bring her back in the morning for some testing.

Ten minutes later, they were headed out the door. Once outside, Margaret stopped and spoke to Thomas. "Thomas, we will never be able to repay or thank you enough for what you did for us today, for my little girl." Margaret started crying again, but she held it together and went on. "Thomas, I just want you to know that if you ever need anything from us, all you have to do is ask and we will be there. Do you understand?"

"Yes, mam." Margaret was just a few inches taller than Thomas, she leaned down just a bit and hugged him hard. Mario joined in and soon after, Maggie got in on the action. It was group hug time all over again. When the hugs were over, they started walking back towards the car. When they got there, Mario told Thomas to meet him behind the car, because he wanted to talk to speak to him.

Margaret and Maggie got inside the car while the boys were outside talking. Mario opened the trunk and pulled out a bag. He handed it to Thomas and said, "There's something like two-hundred thousand dollars in here. Take it, you're going to need it." Thomas was shocked at the amount. He asked Mario why he 'needed' it. Mario answered, "Thomas, I told you before, you need to start thinking differently. You need to start thinking two, maybe three steps ahead whenever you do anything. People are going to find out who you are and they're going to try to use you."

"They will?"

"I did."

Thomas thought about that for a second and knew what Mario was telling him was true.

"I'm sorry to tell you this, son, but people are going to come for you for help, for cures, for revenge, or for pure greed."

Thomas was eager to hear Mario's advice. "What should I do, Mr. Reyes?"

"Call me Mario."

"Okay, What should I do, Mario?"

"Well, for starters, kid, you can't trust anyone anymore. You just have to be careful, that's all. Try to find a place to hide, change your name, and stay below the radar. And one last thing."

"Yes, sir, I mean, Mario."

"If you want, I can take you home myself. I can give you a ride in the morning after we bring Maggie to have the doctor check her out. We'll all go and drop you off wherever you want to go."

That's when Thomas looked around and realized he didn't recognize anything, he had no idea where he was. "Where are we, Mario?"

"You're in San Diego, your house is about four hours north of here. Like I said, I can take you in the morning; you're welcome to stay with us until then. Or you got enough money to take a cab to China. Just let me know what you want to do, Thomas." Thomas thought about it, he was getting really home sick and didn't want to wait till morning to go home. Thomas was yearning for the banality of his former life. Playing with friends, talking on the phone and watching silly videos on his computer. And in spite of everything that Mario had done for him, Thomas didn't know anything about him, he wasn't sure if he could trust him. Mario protected him, it's true, but then, did he want to stay with someone who just killed about a half dozen men.

Thomas decided he would take a cab home. He was wide awake and felt he could handle the four-hour drive back home to Goleta. After they drove back to the Reyes residence, Mario waited outside with Thoams for the cab. When the cab arrived, Thomas said his good-byes to Margaret and Maggie one more time. Mario watched Thomas climb into the back seat and said, "Remember what I told you, Thomas. Be careful. You have my number now so call me if you need anything." Thomas smiled at Mario and said, "Okay. Thanks."

"No, Thomas, thank you." Mario watched the cab pull away into the night.

The Prometheus Syndrome

Heaven hath no rage, like love to hatred turned,
nor hell a fury, like a woman scorned. -William Congreve

Jacki Calloway had always fallen in and out of love very easily. Some folks who knew her say that it's because Jacki was as fickle as the wind, although others would say that Jacki may have been one sandwich short of a picnic. But those who knew Jacki Calloway well, knew that she suffered from acute Schizophrenia. Just a few weeks ago, Jacki felt like one of the luckiest girls in town. She had met Alex Landon a dashing young man, Alex was handsome, smart, and fun to be around. Alex and Jacki were in the midst of a classic whirlwind relationship, that is, until things started happening.

Alex wouldn't admit it, but Jacki knew the despicable little things that Alex was doing behind her back. Talking about her, making fun of her and worst of all, laughing at her. Laughing with those sick little whores he meets with at the bar. Just the thought of those women with their hands all over Alex made her cringe. She could picture them touching Alex, fondling him with their dirty little disgusting hands that are probably full of God knows what kind of germs and diseases.

Thinking of all the awful things that Alex had been doing made her tighten the grip on the steering wheel till her knuckles were bone white. *'That son-of-a-bitch is going to be so sorry he ever did this to me.'* Jacki thought with her teeth clenched so tight she could have bitten through a piece of rawhide. She didn't notice that the car was accelerating. Alex, of course, had not done anything but had a short conversation with a stranger at the bar for less than a minute. Alex was completely unaware of the darkness that was about to enter his life.

The thing about schizophrenia is that the person suffering from it is, at times, unaware of the fact that they are not fine. Once you stop taking the medication, the mind sinks into a rabbit hole from which there is no return. Not without help, anyway. Jacki Calloway was returning to her uncle's house. She had driven down to the beach to find just the right seashell so that she could stop the headaches that have been driving her crazy.

One of the voices inside her head had convinced her, after much debate, that if she went to the beach and got a seashell, bigger than the palm of her hand, but smaller than a bagel, brought it

58

back to the house and lit a candle on it, her headaches would stop right away, and so, she drove to the beach. It only took her about 40 minutes of hunting with a small flashlight, but she finally found a seashell that was just the right size to cure her headaches.

Jacki was now on her way back to the house, thinking about what she was going to do to Alex. She couldn't have him stealing her thoughts, and she couldn't just let him go. He would run straight back to those dirty little whores. The more she thought about Alex, the more she thought about how she wanted to hurt him. She kept gripping and rubbing the steering wheel. She was also unknowingly, going faster and faster.

An odd thing about Jacki, other than the crazy parts of her illness, was that she was a news junkie. Which only made things worse. There was always something bad happening in the news, and Jacki, on many occasions, would think that all the bad stuff was directed at her. Jacki was convinced that most people knew who she was, and most of them were watching her and constantly plotting against her. So, although she was completely wrong in regard to her paranoiac assumptions, she was, consequently, rather well informed on current events.

On the radio, a talk show host was saying something about a strange rumor involving a child that had miraculously healed a half-dozen people in a hospital and was later kidnapped. The story sounded like something out of a si-fi horror movie trailer. Mobsters, magic and miracles, the perfect combination for some convoluted Hollywood script.

The streets of Encinitas were rolled up for the night. There wasn't much nightlife on a Sunday in this quaint little town. A light fog had rolled in, and the temperature dropped into the low forties. A little brisk, but not unusual for this time of year. The streets were deserted, except for two lonely cars, a white Honda Accord, and a bright green and yellow taxi. Jacki had been accelerating for the past few minutes, unaware that she was now barreling west bound up Encinitas Blvd at over 65 miles per hour.

The taxicab driver never saw what hit him, he was driving north at about 40 miles per hour when he reached the intersection of El Camino Real and Encinitas Blvd. The impact was sudden, jarring and fatal. Thomas' world was violently tossed into a painful spin, then began rolling in some direction which he wasn't able to discern. He could make out the driver's arms and body flaying about like a lifeless doll. Then, darkness.

Jacki had not seen it coming either, watching the two vehicles collide suddenly right in front of her was shocking. She watched as the White Honda slammed into the taxi, sending it into a violent tailspin and then began to roll over and over. The Honda went airborne and flipped perfectly over, landed upside down and went sliding on its roof for about 50 feet. It took Jackie a few seconds to react, her reflexes were impaired due to her inability to concentrate because of those damn voices in her head that never seem to shut up. Finally, Jackie started pulling over to the side of the road. She wasn't sure why she did, she wasn't interested in helping, it was mostly morbid curiosity than anything else. Her soul was completely void of any empathy for those involved in this horrific accident, she was just watching to see what happens next.

The taxicab driver had instantaneously broken the car door window with his head, the impact threw him across the car, but his seat belt kept him perfectly in place while every vital organ in his body kept moving to the right causing massive trauma to almost every organ in his body. The only good thing was that he had already died on impact, and so he felt none of the pain. Thomas, on the other hand, felt all of it. His head also hit the side window, but since most of the energy was absorbed at the front of the car, Thomas did not experience the full strength of the impact. It wasn't until the taxi began rolling that at some point Thomas banged his head harder against something else, and this time, he was out cold.

Unfortunately, for the young female driving the Honda, was not wearing her seat belt and was ejected from the car on impact, sending her completely through her windshield, which, though made of so-called laminated safety glass, simply served as a solid object that her body had to go through. The young female driver of the Honda Accord went sailing through the air and landed on the sidewalk, battered, tangled, and shredded almost beyond recognition.

Jackie remained in the car for a minute, still gripping the steering wheel with all her might. She found it difficult to release her grip, it was as though her hands were locked in position. Jacki had no way of knowing that this was another symptom of schizophrenia. People with this illness often experience stiffness and locking of extremities. Jackie had to will her hands off the steering wheel. She turned her head slowly and surveyed the damage. She could see the taxicab and the Honda were upside down. She stared at the passenger side tire, which was still spinning, she noticed smoke coming out of the engine area and some liquid was spilling out, *'That's probably gasoline.'* she thought. She saw the crumbled body that was thrown from the white car sprawled on the sidewalk. The body was indiscernible and covered in blood. The more she stared, the less she cared.

In the back seat of the taxicab, Thomas regained consciousness. He was completely disoriented because he awoke upside down still strapped to his seatbelt. It took a couple of seconds to gather his thoughts. He suddenly recalled what happened and where he was. He began struggling with his seat belt. He could smell gasoline everywhere, it was making him dizzy. Finally, the seatbelt came loose, and he dropped on to the ceiling of the car. Thomas didn't try to open the door, it was too mangled to even try, he crawled out through the window which had been completely shattered. Jacki was still sitting in her car, not knowing what to do, but she was observing Thomas as he crawled out of the wreck.

Thomas crawled on his hands and knees for a few feet then attempted to stand, he almost lost his balance because the fumes from the gasoline were still making his head spin. Finally, Thomas was up, stumbling and walking away from the wreck when he realized that the driver was still in the car. Thomas instinctively turned back to see if the driver was okay. As he made his way around to the driver's side of the cab, Thomas could see that the driver was definitely not okay. He could also tell that he was not going to be able to get him out because the car was so smashed up the driver was not going to fit through the small space that was once a car door with a window.

Thomas could see the driver's head, there was a huge gash and plenty of blood. Thomas really had no idea if touching him would help, but he had to try. Thomas had to kneel down low all the way to the ground in order to reach the driver. By this time, Jacki had stepped out of her car and walked over to see if anyone was seriously hurt. It was more of an impulse reaction rather than a genuine concern. As she got closer, she could see Thomas walking towards the driver and kneeling down to try and reach him. Jacki wondered if the driver was okay. As she moved even closer, she could see him through the opening of where the windshield used to be. From where she was standing, she could tell that the driver was not okay. In fact, she was pretty sure he was dead.

'So, what was the kid doing?' she thought. She watched. She saw Thomas reach in the car, he wasn't trying to get the man out, he only reached in and merely touched him. "*Strange.*" she thought. Then the boy stood up and stared at the dead body, oblivious to Jackie, who was watching him. Jacki was about to yell out and ask Thomas if he was alright, but then Jackie's eyes caught a movement in her peripheral vision. The man in the car, had he moved? Jackie looked down at the man, she was standing about ten feet away from Thomas, who still had not noticed her. Both Jacki and Thomas were now intently watching the taxicab driver. Jacki could actually see movement around his head, she saw flesh and hair moving around on their own, the gaping wound seemed to be healing before her eyes. A few seconds later, the taxi driver was moving around.

Thomas was still feeling a little shook up, he turned his attention to the woman that was driving the white Honda. Her twisted mangled body repulsed Thomas for a second. It brought back memories of the old lady that was hit by a car when he was with his friends. Thomas wasn't sure if he would be able to help this one because she was in worse shape than the old woman that Thomas had recalled. Nevertheless, Thomas walked over to her and touched her as well. It took a few extra seconds, but the woman began to heal.

Thomas was relieved, but Jacki knew this could only mean one thing, this was the boy the radio was talking about, the one who healed all those people in that hospital. Thomas looked up and noticed the woman standing nearby. He was about to say something, but Thomas had sustained a couple of injuries himself, plus the fumes from the gasoline were not helping, Thomas got dizzy again, he fell and passed out. Jackie had formulated a plan in her head the moment she realized who Thomas was. And before leaving, she noticed one more thing, there seemed to be a lot of hundred-dollar bills laying around the back seat where Thomas was sitting. She peeked inside the back seat of the inverted taxicab and saw a bag with money in it. Jackie took it and Thomas and put them both in her car.

After Jackie left, the woman in the white Honda stood up. She was confused and in shock at the site of the accident which she felt she caused. She looked down at her clothes and noticed they were completely soaked in blood. She almost started to cry as she thought, *"How can there be so much blood?"* She looked towards the taxicab and saw the driver trying to crawl out of his vehicle. She was very young and panicked because she thought he was going to call the cops and she would go to jail. She also noticed that there was no one around. She decided to run and call the police later and tell them that her car had been stolen. The young woman ran into the night and made her way home.

It was about 2:30 am, Sunday morning when Thomas woke up only to have his senses jolted by the pungent smell of old urine and defecation. He realized he was gagged, tied and kidnapped again for the second time within the last 24 hours. He was in a small bedroom, nothing like the elaborate one he was recently imprisoned in. This one was much smaller, dirtier, smellier and a little scarier for some reason. That reason became much more evident when he noticed his surroundings. Next to him, also tied and gagged was another man, it was Alex Landon, but he didn't know him. Thomas could tell that Alex had been beaten badly. But that was not the scary part, next to Alex was some old man lying on the floor who was obviously dead.

The color of his skin looked drained of blood, some rigor mortis had already set in, but the biggest clue was the large kitchen knife plunged to the hilt deep into his back. As is typical of most dead bodies, this one had evacuated all or most of its waste. Thomas could tell that Alex had also used the restroom while sitting on that chair. The stench nearly made Thomas pass out again. Thomas could see that Alex was awake, though barely conscious. Alex had not acknowledged Thomas, because Alex was in too much pain and too tired to care.

Thomas did not know it, but he too was just as beaten up by the accident and just as tired as Alex. Thomas heard the sound of footsteps coming towards them from the next room. The door swung open and standing in front of him was his captor, Jackie Calloway, smiling and appearing to be very pleasant. She walked over to Alex Landon first, put her right index finger under his chin and pushed his face up so that they were now eye to eye, and said, "Alex, your life just got so much worse. I can't believe my luck." She leaned in and kissed him on the forehead. Then she turned to Thomas. She looked at him with much curiosity and said, "I saw what you did back there at the accident. I also heard you healed a bunch of people at a hospital. Is that right?" Thomas nodded yes. "I knew it!" she said with genuine excitement in her voice, "I knew it was you. Everybody's talking about you. Some kind of miracle boy, or demon witch, people don't know what to think. But I do. You are going to play a very special role for me. You are going to make sure that our friend here, Alex the spy, doesn't die on us. Okay?"

Thomas didn't know what to do, he just nodded again. Jacki spun around on one heel and headed back to the door. She turned and said, "I'll be back in just a little while. I just gotta go get me a few things. You all just go ahead and get yourselves acquainted." She winked at Thomas and walked out the door. Thomas suddenly realized that he was very tired. He hadn't slept, hadn't eaten, bathed or had any water for hours. Not long enough to cause him any real problems, but certainly enough to overwhelm him with fatigue. He could hardly keep his eyes open, and then, Thomas fell into a hard, deep sleep, tied, and gagged for the second time in his teenage life.

Thomas Grady, Blood Sample TG-1

Monday, late morning at PMD Laboratories, Darren Bolster and Sandra Kudlow are discussing their findings regarding Thomas Grady's blood work. Nobody knew who the blood belonged to, it was marked "Specimen TG-1". The requisition that came with it had clear instructions that all results were to be kept confidential and were to be reported directly and only to the CEO of PMD Laboratories. It was not unusual for the staff of PMD Laboratories to get these type of request. Though they were common, they were nevertheless laced with a bit of intrigue.

Darren Bolster was sitting at his station peering into a microscope when he looked up at Sandra Kudlow, who was working next to him and asked, "Find anything unusual with the TG1 sample yet, Sandy?" Sandra was also looking into a microscope, but she didn't look up, she answered him while looking at the drop of blood on her slide. "Nothing here. I don't get it, what is it we're supposed to be looking for?" Darren walked over to the coffee maker and poured himself a cup. He asked Sandra if she wanted some coffee, but she said, no. Darren walked over and stood behind Sandra and said, "You know, we have gotten so many of these weird request, I don't even remember if we were ever told what it is we're supposed to be looking. It would be nice if they gave us something, anything specific would be nice."

"That would help." Sandra said, as she finally sat up and turned to face Darren. She looked at his coffee and wondered if she should have another cup, she decided against it. *'Don't want the jitters,'* she thought. Sandra went on, "If we knew what we were looking for, we might be able to construct other more specific tests to help find whatever it is they're trying to find. But this random stuff, I don't get it. It's blood, it's red, it's normal, so what?"

"Right? Every sample that ever came with these special request," Darren placed air quotation marks on 'special', "we never find anything. I would like to know what special," Darren with finger quotes again, "thing we're looking for." Darren continued, "And look at these goofy instructions. Use blood specimen TG-1 on mouse NC247. Why? We don't even know what the hell is wrong with that stupid mouse. Does it have cancer, TB, a bad case of dandruff, what?"

"I know, it does drive me a little nuts, too." Sandra replied, "But it's our job, what else could we do?"

"Nothing. Let's get that stupid mouse, at least it'll cure me of boredom." Sandra gave him an obligatory laugh, then they went to get mouse NC247.

The truth is, Darren Bolster and Sandra Kudlow have been asked to do much stranger things in the past. They have been given vials with all manner of sticky and stinky substances, including plain ordinary water said to have had certain medicinal properties. They've used these things on mice, worms, plants and in some really strange moments, were instructed to place these test items on inanimate objects. For what purpose, they would never know. What they did know was that they got paid very well and if their boss wanted to see what a gross smelling gel did to an already dead mouse, well, who cares, the mouse is dead anyway. So, from this perspective, testing human blood on a mouse would be categorized under normal.

Subject NC247 was a typical house mouse, *Mus musculus*. Unknown to Darren and Sandra, NC247 was given leukemic cancer through ionizing radiation treatments. They didn't know what NC247 had, but they could see it had traces of tumors, so they suspected cancer. Darren and Sandra got the test mouse out of the holding cage and placed it in a smaller cage then carried it over to the stainless-steel worktable. They had a syringe filled with TG-1 ready to be injected, why, they had no idea. Sandra picked up the little mouse and quickly gave it a standard subcutaneous injection. It was over in two seconds. Their instructions were to wait and see if there were any instantaneous reactions. There never were, of course, any instantaneous reactions. Afterwards, they are to check on it every 30 minutes for the next 8 hours.

Sandra placed the mouse back in its holding cage while her and Darren went to lunch. They would come back in 30 minutes to check on their patient. Meanwhile, they had half an hour to discuss the triviality of their work. At the end of the day Darren and Sandra would co-author the report regarding subject NC247. It would be noted and recorded that subject NC247 was injected with TG1 at 11:30 am and by 3:30pm, there were no changes or effects. There was nothing to report. 24 hours later, the report would have the same entry, no effects.

PMD Laboratory was a subsidiary of a larger entity owned by Walter Harrington Porter. The nurse that drew Thomas' blood had left the house prior to the commotion that Mario Reyes started. The nurse, Sara Miller, was instructed to deliver the blood sample immediately to PMD along with the usual set instructions. The results were to be reported right away, but of course, any findings will be of no consequence to the former Mr. Walter Harrington Porter.

San Diego Cancer Center

Monday, 8:00am, San Diego Cancer Center. Dr. Li is speaking with the Reyes family. They're sitting in her office, Mario was on her right, Margaret on the left and little Maggie in the middle. Dr. Li looks at Maggie and smiles then turns her attention to Mario, "Mr. Reyes, do you know what's going on here?"

"What you mean, Dr.?"

"I mean, Mr. Reyes, that you came down here last night and picked up Maggie and took her out of the hospital without even so much as calling me or seeking medical advice. How am I supposed to interpret that, Mr. Reyes?"

"I don't know?"

"That's exactly the answer I would expect from Maggie." Dr Li said with a sarcastic grin. Dr Li tried Margaret, "Mrs. Reyes, do you have any idea what's going on?"

"What do you mean, going on?"

"Well, for one thing, my staff tells me that you and your husband came rushing in last night and within a matter of minutes, you all rushed out with Maggie, whom, I am told, was already looking as if she was never sick. And, that there was someone else with you. A boy. Is this true?"

"Ah, yes, it was a friend of the family." Margaret lied.

"I see, and do you have any explanation for Maggie's remarkable recovery?" Mario and Margaret answered at the same time, "No."

"Look," Dr Li continued, "I am very happy to see Maggie doing so well. In fact, she is in complete remission. I can handle a miracle once in a while, but seven? I need some answers." Mario and Margaret looked at each other and said, "Seven?"

"Yes, six other children on this floor were healed of cancer yesterday, of inoperable cancer, and I need to know what is going on here. Did you have anything to do with this, or do you know who does?"

Mario was in deep thought, trying to recall if Thomas ever left his side during the evening. No, there was no way, he told himself. There was no explanation for the other children. Dr Li noticed Mario in his contemplative mood and asked, "Mr. Reyes, is there something you wish to tell me?"

"What? Oh, ah, no."

"Why do I feel you're not telling me the truth?"

"I don't know." Mario replied, hearing the childishness of his own answer.

Margaret too, was in deep thought. Dr. Li could tell that Margaret was genuinely confused.

Margaret said, "I wish we could help, Dr Li, but I'm afraid we do not know anything."

Then Maggie blurted out, "What about Dr. Thomas, mom?" Dr Li's ears perked up and said, "Dr Thomas? Was there another doctor here last night?" Mario stepped in and said, "No, ma'am, there were no other doctors. We had jokingly called our friend, Thomas, Dr. Thomas joking around with Maggie.

"Is this true, Maggie?" Dr. Li asked.

"Well, yes, I do remember that mommy said he wasn't a real doctor. But he fixed me anyway!" Maggie said with jubilation in her voice.

"How? Maggie, how did Dr.....how did Thomas fix you? Mario abruptly picked up Maggie in his arms and Margaret rose from her chair with the same unexpected urgency. Mario said, "Look, Dr. Li, we are so happy that these other children are cured, as I am sure their families are, too. But we had nothing to do with it, please believe me when I say that. I hope your hospital continues to receive these miracles, but we have to leave, we're sorry we can't help, I wish we could. Have a good day, Dr." Dr Li could do nothing but watch them go. She knew that they knew something, she just wasn't sure what. Well, that can wait, for now, she was going to pass on the good news about her miracle babies to their parents. A job she very much looked forward to doing. After that, she would try to find out what the hell is going on in her hospital.

Thomas was becoming a little more and more aware of the importance of his gift. He didn't know how it worked, but lately he felt himself feeling out of touch with it, he couldn't explain it. Thomas was not aware of the full extent of what happen that night at the San Diego Cancer Center. Thomas didn't know it, but his ability to heal was getting stronger, much stronger. Thomas didn't know or understand any of it, though he did wonder why he rarely felt anything when he touched someone. It always felt as if nothing was going to happen. Although the people he touched would feel something. It was all very confusing, and Thomas was always wishing his gift would just go away.

Dr. Li made sure to collect blood samples from all the children that were healed on that day.

67

She will, of course, be grossly disappointed at the lab results. Not only will they not show anything unusual but will be the perfect examples of what a normal blood test should look like, leaving Dr. Li without the slightest clue as to what healed these lucky children.

What the doctors and medical laboratories will never understand about Thomas Grady is, that for all intent and purposes, Thomas Grady is completely normal. What they didn't know, what they couldn't know, is that Thomas' power to heal doesn't come from inside his body but rather threw his body. There is an unknown energy passing through him. There are no physiological or neurological anomalies at work inside Thomas. It's all about position. His position in time, space and dimension.

Thomas Grady is caught in a perpetual state of multi-dimensional fluctuation. His ability to heal doesn't even come from our known universe, his ability to heal is being leaked into our universe using Thomas as a conduit. It's all happening beyond the quantum level. What's happening to Thomas originates at the point where string theory begins. One set of physical laws enter-mixing with another entirely different set of physical laws coagulating into something so impossibly exotic that we will never possess a method to gauge, measure or observe it directly. We will, however, be able to observe it's effects.

When Thomas touches someone, an unknown inexplicable force of unknown energy from an unknown origin passes through Thomas and enters the cells of the recipient and causes the renewal of every cell in the body. Because the cells are renewed, the telomeres are also restored to their original length which would translate to a longer mortality rate, in other words, they will live a few more years longer. How much longer is uncertain at this point but a determining factor would be the age of the recipient at the time of healing. Also, for unknown reasons, any abnormal cells are completely destroyed along with any infections, genetic disorders, abnormal brain function, not to mention any physical injuries are healed as well. However, it does not stop there.

It seems that Thomas could also bring a person or any living organism back to life. In the case of death, you may be brought back to life if Thomas can touch you within a certain time frame. Once a certain percentage of cellular degradation has occurred, the unknown energy can no longer work due to the breakdown in the cohesiveness of each cell. No one knows the full extent of Thomas Grady's power because for that to happen, scientists would have to have Thomas available for decades of testing.

The House of Pain, and Death, and Pain Again

3:40am. Thomas Grady awoke slowly, and unusually tired. He opened his eyes and allowed them to acclimate to the dim lighting in the bedroom. He could see the heavy curtains on the windows. On one of the windows, Thomas could see a small portion of the glass. It appeared to be painted black. *'Why would someone paint the glass?'* He wondered. The sense of smell is one of the last senses to wake. That's when Thomas snapped back into caution mode. A small amount of adrenaline kicked in and he was now wide awake. The smell of death loomed heavy in the air. Thomas could see the dead body on the floor, which appeared even more dead, if that were possible. Although it certainly *smelled* more dead.

Thomas looked to his left side where Alex was still sitting slumped on his chair. Thomas could see that Alex's clothes were tattered and caked in blood. It was hard to tell if Alex was alive, except for the occasional slight movement of his chest that came with his slow shallow breaths. They couldn't communicate because they both still had duct tape over their mouths.

Thomas turned his attention to the sounds in the next room. He heard voices, like someone was arguing. Thomas was half right. Down the hallway, in the living room, Jackie was having another argument with herself, or rather, the voices in her head. Her hands were clenched on the side of her hips and her head slightly tilted, staring at no one in particular, she said, "What do you mean, what am I doing with a candle lit in a seashell in the middle of the coffee table?"

Jackie began pacing back and forth, still with her hands on her sides. She stopped for a second, raised one hand over her head with her index finger extended, as if she were proclaiming this conversation to a large crowd. "You're the one who said it would help me, you said, get a seashell, so I did, light a candle on it, so I did, and guess what? My fucking headache is still killing me!" Jackie was upset and tense. Suddenly, she became relaxed, and spoke calmly, gently. It was one of her other personalities. "Jackie, sweet Jackie. I didn't say it would help you, I said it would help your pain, not you, you fucking idiot, why would I help you? I'm the one who wants to see you hurt, you're such a moron. I'm the one who wants to see everybody hurt."

Jackie now hunches over, fist clinched tighter than ever and yells, "Stop making me hurt people!" She began to cry, but only for a few seconds, then she shot up into a straight rigid posture, as if standing at attention. Her face became solemn, stern, and emotionless. The calm voice returned, "Well, maybe I will help you with your pain, my dear, that is, once we've made Alex suffer properly. We can't let him live without pain, right? Besides, now that we have that boy, we could really hurt Alex as much as we want, as hard as we want and then, start all over again. Oh my God, that sounds absolutely delicious! Don't you think?" She did not wait for a reply, she simply said, "Oh, fuck you, who cares what you think. Let's go have some fun."

Thomas could hear footsteps coming down the hallway. The floors were made of hardwood, maple, and Jackie was wearing a pair of stylish light-brown Steve Madden knee high boots which made a loud heavy clumping sound. Thomas could hear Jackie's heavy steps echoing in the hallway, which only added to the fear and anxiety that Thomas was already feeling.

Meanwhile, in the room, Alex was slowly becoming more lucid. Thomas noticed Alex was waking up and he could hear Alex moaning something, it sounded like he was just repeating the same word over and over, no...no...no....The reverberating sound of footsteps finally stopped just outside the door. The light metallic giggling sound of the doorknob turning raised the anxiety level up several notches in the room. Thomas braced for whatever was about to enter.

The door swung open, and there standing before him was Jackie Calloway. Much to his surprise, Thomas was almost calmed by her strikingly normal appearance. She was small, of medium built and she had a nice face. Thomas wondered if this is what Brenda Dayton might look like when she gets older. He liked that. Suddenly, his fears returned and once again, Thomas became acutely aware of his surroundings. The dead man on the floor, the stranger next to him who was now hopelessly squirming about in his chair, trying desperately to be somewhere else, physically, or mentally. Thomas finally noticed the reason for his panic. In Jackie's right hand she had a...tool?

It was the first time Thomas had ever seen an ice pick. It looked dangerous, foreboding, and painful. It was a tool built, forged, and constructed with one single purpose. It belonged to her dead uncle, a remnant from more simpler days, an anachronism in this quiet little house at the end of a cul-de-sac in a small middle-class neighborhood, where all refrigerators came with auto-defrost.

Without even acknowledging Thomas' presence, Jackie stepped through the door and moved towards Alex with a purposeful gait. She stopped at a well measured striking distance and said,

"Welcome to day one of your hell, Alex." And she proceeded to stab Alex continuously in every part of his body. She began with the extremities, arms, legs hands and fingers. Alex was writhing in anguish as Jackie poked, stabbed, and plunged the long rusty metal pick into Alex's body. Jackie started on the upper body, not pausing to rest, her arm was moving like a piston, in and out with maddening strength and agility. She was mindful not to hit his heart, she wanted him to live as long as possible. After minutes of non-stop stabbing, Jackie finally began to tire, that's when things went from worse to insane.

Jackie took a few seconds to catch her breath. Her face was already covered in sweat and blood, which gave her a maniacal appearance. She gave Alex a smile and said, "We're not done yet, sweetie, I saved the best for last." And she began to frantically and with more force than ever, attack Alex's groin area. Her smile got bigger with each stroke which she tried to make harder than the last. Finally, after a few minutes of that, Jackie could see that Alex was not responding. She didn't want him to pass out from the pain or worse, to die. She stopped.

It was only now that she turned her attention to Thomas, who was in complete shock at the madness of the scene he had just witnessed. Thomas was gripped with fear at the thought of being stabbed to death with that horrible instrument. He was sure she was going to kill him. Jackie grabbed Thomas' chair and dragged it closer to Alex. She brought out a knife, which only freaked out Thomas even more. Jackie reached down towards Thomas' arm, Thomas winched in anticipation of the pain, but instead, Jackie cut the bonds on his arm. She positioned Thomas a little closer to Alex, then while holding the bloody ice pick less than an inch away from Thomas' eye, and with a slight grin on her face, she snarled at Thomas, "Now, touch him."
Thomas touched Alex.

After just a couple of seconds, Jackie watched in awe as Alex's wounds began to heal right before her eyes. Within one minute, Alex was completely healed. No marks, no cuts, no pain and free to reevaluate his situation with perfect clarity. Alex had never felt better in his life. He felt great, wonderful. He felt fit and healthy, vibrant, and full of hope. But all those blissful thoughts lasted a mere few seconds. Alex watched as Jackie calmly tied Thomas' arm back to the chair, dragged him a few feet away, picked up the ice pick she had placed on the floor and walked back towards Alex. She used the inside of her Van Halen t-shirt to wipe off the blood on the handle of the ice pick. It was getting too slippery. Then, the whole thing started all over again. She repeated this scene three more times, each time trying to be more creative than the last. At one time, she tried poking his eyes first. Another time she would only strike the groin area until he passed out. Finally, after hours of repetitive torture, the only thing that stopped Jackie was pure exhaustion.

She stood directly in front Alex, breathing hard and drenched in bloody sweat. She did not acknowledge Thomas. She stared past Alex as if looking at someone else, someone not there. Her eyes were transfixed intensely on a single point in space. Then she relaxed her grip and the ice pick fell onto the hardwood floor and stuck perfectly upright a few inches away from where Alex was sitting. With a blank stare in her eyes, Jackie simply turned and walked out of the room, closing the door behind her. The room looked like a multiple murder scene, the floor was filled with blood, the walls were splattered with it, even Thomas was covered in Alex's blood. Jackie made her way to her bedroom, she walked in and almost collapsed on the bed from fatigue. She was drenched in blood, her hair was matted. Most of the blood was already caked on her skin and clothes. She fell into a short nap, smiling about how else she was going to hurt Alex again and again.

Monday, 9:15am. Mario, Margaret, and little Maggie headed to McDonalds for breakfast. They all ordered a big breakfast. Maggie had orange juice while Mario and Margaret had coffee. Maggie ate quickly so she could spend some time in the play area. The play area had matted floors, large plastic tubes that were shaped into tunnels and slides. There were netted rope ladders and bridges. Maggie couldn't wait for the last bite, "Can I go play now?" Maggie added "Please?" Margaret answered, "Yes, Maggie, but finish your juice first." Maggie picked up her small cup and drank her juice as quickly as she could, spilling a little on her powder blue T-shirt. Mom dabbed it with her napkin and said, "Okay, your good. Go play, honey." Maggie ran without saying a word.

Mario and Margaret watched with great pleasure as Maggie played like a normal child, in a normal world. They couldn't have been more grateful at that moment for any other reason in the world. They let Maggie continue playing a little longer than they would have liked, but they were getting such pleasure in watching her have fun. But it was time to go. They called Maggie over and they headed out to the car.

They pulled out of the parking lot and turned on to the streets to head home. Mario turned the radio on, mostly for background noise, because this little family was basking in the simple joy of being normal. The Reyes family arrived at their house just 15 minutes later. Maggie ran upstairs

72

to her room to play her computer games and Mario and Margaret sat on the couch to watch TV and just relax for a few moments before moving on with the day's chores. The TV came on, it was one of the local news channels. There was a woman reporter standing in the street with a NEWS 5 microphone in her hand. In the background was a scene of some sort of traffic accident. Neither Mario nor Margaret was paying attention.

The reporter's voice was barely audible. "...and as you can see, there was a horrific accident here early this morning. Now normally, the streets would be closed, and this scene would have still been an active investigation if there had been serious injuries, or a death. However, looking at these vehicles, it is a miracle that no one was killed..." Mario and Margaret both responded to the word miracle and began listening to the news a little more intently. Another reporter from the newsroom was talking to the reporter at the scene, "Jennifer, are they sure there are no serious injuries? Those cars look almost completely destroyed".

"Yes, that would seem to be the case, John, it's a bit of a mystery, but a source of relief as well. You can see by the damage caused to this taxicab that one would hardly expect to see someone walk away from this, yet, here he is, standing next to me. His name is William Cormier. William, could you tell us in your own words what happened here? How did you survive this accident without even a scratch? It seems like a miracle." The reporter pointed the microphone to William, "Well, actually, I thought I was hurt, I thought I bumped my head hard, but I guess it wasn't that hard."

"You don't even have a bruise on your body. Yet look at your car, it looks like it was, well, hit by another car quite hard. How do you explain that?" William scratched his head and noticed that he had some dry blood on his hair. In fact, both him and the reporter noticed that he had blood on his shirt, his face, hands, and clothes. They both stood there in front of the camera for a couple of seconds saying nothing, then the reporter said, "William, wait a minute, you have blood everywhere, how do you explain that? William kept scratching his head as if something was itching him, but it was only nerves. William looked down at his own clothes and looked at his hands and said, "I don't know. But I'm fine. I guess God was taking care of me."
The reporter turned and faced the camera and said, "Indeed he was, William, indeed he was." As a last-minute idea, the reporter asked one more question, "Mr. Cormier, do you know the status of the other driver?"

"No. But that other car looks worse than mine. I would definitely be surprised if that driver wasn't hurt."

"What about your fare? Did you have a passenger in the car with you when this happened?" William thought about it for a second, he didn't quite remember right away, but then, "You know what, yes, I did have a fare with me. In fact, I remember now, it was a young boy...." Mario stood up, he wasn't listening to the news any longer. He looked at Margaret and said, "That was Thomas in that car. It had to be. Look at the cab, it's totaled, and this guy is covered in blood and not even a scratch on him. And what happened to Thomas. Where did..." Margaret interrupted him, "Mario, wait, let's see what they say. Maybe they'll mention Thomas." They both turned their attention back to the bleach blond that was reporting the news. ...."that's why I think we are not getting the full story, John. You could see how this looks suspicious. William has blood all over him, his passenger is missing, and we have not seen the person in the other car. Although I do have to say that the police do not seem evasive, they appear to be just as perplexed as we are." The news station changed scenes and was now in the newsroom. The anchor person said, "That was the scene earlier this morning around 3:40am. There has been no official comment from anyone. And although as you can see for yourselves, the impact that occurred should have resulted in serious injuries, and yet, none have been reported. The other mystery is, where is the passenger of the taxicab? Where is the driver of the Honda? Where is this young boy at? We will follow up with this story as it unfolds and keep you up to date. This is......"

Mario grabbed his jacket and headed to the door. "Honey, I gotta go. I think Thomas may be in trouble again. Stay here with Maggie and I'll call you later and let you know what I find out." Margaret walked over to him and kissed him, "Just be careful. Mario?"
"I will."
"Go find Thomas."
"Right. I'll see you later. Love you."
"Love you, too, honey." Once outside, Mario walked to the back of the car, opened the trunk, and unlocked a small metal box, took out his gun, two clips and box of 9mm rounds. He was sincerely hoping not to use them, then again, he was not about to let anything happen to Thomas.

New Jackie

Jackie Collins woke up slowly from a deep sleep. As usual, Jackie awoke to confusion. It seems like the first few seconds of being awake are the most normal part of her life. Her brain hasn't quite kicked into crazy mode. For a few seconds she simply feels like it's just another day in her uncle's house and he should be making some pancakes soon. Pancakes are her favorite. Jackie loved her uncle. *'That bastard, I should have killed him sooner.'* Jackie startled herself at the thought. Then, the normal world was gone. Jackie became jubilant as she immediately contemplated how she was going to hurt Alex today. She went straight to the garage to look for a new toy.

In the rear corner of the garage, she spotted it. A sports bag with three different baseball bats. The handles of each bat were exposed. Jackie could tell that two of the bats were made of aluminum while the third was made of wood. It was a Louisville Slugger bat, made of hard maple. For some reason, it just felt more solid to Jackie than the other lightweight aluminum bats. Oh, sure, she may be able to swing it for a longer period of time but think of how much more damage a good solid hard wood bat could do. Jackie decided on the wood. She picked up the bat and pranced over to the bedroom, oblivious to her morbid appearance. Jackie's clothes were dirty and smelled of decaying blood. Her hair looked and smelled like her clothes. Her face was dirty and smeared with dry blood. Jackie looked like she was the one that was in a car accident and then tortured for hours. But she was fine. In fact, she was feeling quite invigorated. Despite the fact that she had not eaten in almost 72 hours, and was also, in fact, unknowingly suffering from dehydration.

In the bedroom, Alex and Thomas were still tied to their chairs with duct tape across their mouths. They could hear Jackie walking down the hallway. Their bodies immediately began to tense. They started suffocating on hopelessness and fear. Thomas was in the beginning stages of substituting his fears for hate, which, he found to be more useful for coping with the delirium of this woman. But Alex was the one being hurt, he could not substitute his fears for hate, all Alex had were memories of pain, and Jackie was about to give him more memories. Alex and

75

Thomas were wishing time would just stop and prevent Jackie from ever coming in through the door. Her footsteps were getting closer. There was a scream growing inside Thomas' throat. Alex was already screaming in his head, *"No, no, somebody please stop this!"* In his mind, Alex was yelling at the top of his lungs. Jackie was just outside the door, but she didn't come in right away.

She began banging on the door with the bat. First, softly, then, a little harder, until finally, you could hear the loud pounding of a heavy object against the door. It sounded like a monster trying to break in to destroy and kill everyone in the room. On the other side of the door, in the hallway, Jackie was enjoying the fear she must be causing.

Jackie was now swinging at the door as hard as she could with the bat. She actually broke parts of the door, almost made a hole right through it. She stopped for a second, put her hand to her mouth as if to say, oops. She laughed to herself then finally opened the door. Alex saw the bat and was already groaning in anticipation of the pain it was going to cause. Thomas was utterly confused by this madness. *"How could something like this even be happening? How could this be possible? She must be sick. Sick?"* Thomas was forming a thought when suddenly, Jackie raised the bat over her head and swung. Thomas heard the unmistakable sound of bone breaking, the high pitch scream. Thomas' eyes had instinctively closed before the bat made contact with Alexe's knee. Thomas opened his eyes briefly only to see Jackie as she was winding up for another blow. This time she hit Alex on the cheek bone, Thomas thought for sure it would knock Alex out, but it didn't, he just grunted in pain from the crushed orbital bones in his face. The bat had produced a deep gash just below his left eye and began to bleed profusely. Thomas wanted to scream at her and tell her to stop but didn't want this woman's rage aimed at him. All he could do was watch, as Jackie pulled the bat back for another swing.

Both of them winced and braced for impact. Both had their eyes closed as tight as they could and waited. But there was no sound, no cracking of a skull or the sound of any more bones breaking. They did, however, hear a small scream, more like a whimper. Then there was a thud, but a light one, like a small body collapsing. When they opened their eyes, they saw Jackie Collins on the floor, and standing next to her was a man with a gun in his hand. He had pistol whipped Jackie on the side of her head as he walked in, saving Alex from what surely would have been a questionable blow to the top of his head. It might have killed Alex. Not that Jackie would have cared, with Thomas in the room.

Thomas could not believe his eyes, his friend Mario had come to his rescue once again. He felt happy and proud and so glad to see him. Alex was confused but also welcomed this stranger that stopped the nightmare. Mario removed Thomas' tape from his mouth then began to untie him. Thomas jumped up and gave him a big hug and wouldn't let go. Mario hugged him back, then pushed him gently away and said, "Thomas, okay, I'm glad to see you, too. But I have to untie this man also. Wait right there." Mario pointed a few feet away. Thomas reluctantly moved out of the way.

Mario untied Alex then motioned Thomas to come back, "Thomas, come here and help this man." Thomas walked over and touched Alex on the shoulder. In seconds, Alex felt whole again, but filled with confusion.

"What's going on here? How is this happening?" Alex said, unable to phantom the possibilities. Mario looked at Thomas and said, "You want to explain?" Because Mario realized he doesn't have a clue either, he just knows what this kid can do. Thomas looked around the room, it was still covered in blood, pieces of flesh, a rotting a corpse and a deranged woman on the floor and said, "Could we talk later, I just want to get out of here." There was no argument. They all started to leave when Thomas said, "Wait." He looked down at the limb body of Jackie Calloway. Alex and Mario watched as Thomas reached down and not just touch her, as he has done with others, but Thomas took the time to softly place his hand on her and leave it there for a few seconds, as if to show her that he was sorry for her because she was truly ill.

When it came to healing the mind, Thomas was never sure what to expect. It had a profound effect on Mario's wife that he did not anticipate. That woman felt she needed her grief for her daughter. But Thomas was not sure if this woman would need her madness. After just a few seconds, Thomas got up and all three of them walked out onto the street before Jackie Calloway recovered.

Alex began thanking Mario and Thomas and asked them if there was anything he could do for them. Mario simply told him not to go to the police. Jackie will probably be charged for murdering her uncle, but they won't be able to corroborate anything else that went on in there. Mario said, "It would be great, Alex, if we could just keep this whole thing between us. I'm sure you understand what would happen if word got out that some kid can perform miracles."

"I understand,' Alex said, "and I'm grateful to be one of those who received a miracle." Alex turned to Thomas and said, "Thomas, your secret is safe with me, and thank you for saving my life. And you too, Mario." Alex walked away into the faint darkness of pre-dawn. Mario looked down at Thomas and said, "You ready to go straight home this time?" Thomas looked up at Mario and grinned, "Yes, sir."

"But this time, no cab. I'm taking you myself."

"Yes, sir." Thomas repeated.

They got in Mario's car and headed towards Santa Barbara. Just as they pulled on to one of the main streets, Thomas could not help asking, "How the heck did you find me?"

"That was easy. The hard part is figuring out how to keep you out of trouble from now on." Thomas let that thought sit for a minute, then asked again, "No, Really, how did you know where I was?"

"I told you," Mario said with a smug grin, "it was easy. I heard about the cab accident on the radio. Someone mentioned the words, miracle, and hundred-dollar bills all in the same sentence, so I knew that was your cab. By the way, I grabbed the bag on the way out. Your money's in the back seat. Next, I drove down to the area and looked at which buildings or stores might have a camera facing the streets. I found one, told them I was a cop, they believed me and let me watch their surveillance video and, there you were. I saw the license plate on the woman's car, traced it through a buddy of mine in the police force and here I am. Easy." Mario glanced over at Thomas to see if he was impressed. He could tell by the expression on his face that Thomas was indeed impressed. Mario grinned and continued driving.

Tuesday, 5:45am. Jackie Calloway opened her eyes. She was lying on the floor staring at a couple of chairs. There are pieces of rope on the floor. The room was dimly lit. *"Why are the windows painted black?"* She thought. Most of the light was coming in from the hallway. There were strange odors in the room. Nothing made sense. Jackie slowly stood up and looked around the room. She saw the bloody chairs, her dead uncle decomposing on the floor and blood absolutely everywhere, including on herself. At first, there was confusion, then, seconds later, total clarity. She realized that she was sick, but not anymore. She realized what she had done to Alex, the child, and her uncle.

She was very aware of what was going to happen to her because of what she had done. She knew that she must pay for these unspeakable crimes. Can she live a life in prison? Will a jury believe her story of a miracle child and that she was mentally ill and now she's not? Jackie almost laughed when she realized that she couldn't tell which one was worse, knowing she was mentally ill and unaware of her actions, or to be of sound mind and be completely aware of her actions.

Jackie walked over to her uncle's bedroom, went to his dresser, opened the second drawer on the right, reached in and pulled out a small revolver. She held it, it felt heavy, but nowhere near as heavy as the guilt that was building inside her like a giant wave about to break and crush her. The short cathartic release was not enough to cure her conscience. Jackie Calloway asked God for forgiveness and placed the revolver in her mouth.

Mario finally got Thomas reunited with his family. They thanked him profusely for saving Thomas and getting him home safely. Mario then explained to the family what they had to do to protect Thomas from what is sure to be a media frenzy that's coming their way. They had to pack and leave right at this moment. He would stick around until they were on the road. Mario knew that it would be a matter of days before this family would be inundated by every news station and social media platform on the planet. After a couple of hours, the Grady family was on the road with a plan. Mario watched them leave to make sure no one was following. The Grady family had Mario's number which he told them to use whenever they felt they needed him, and he would be there. They were thankful and they felt just a little more assured about the future of the Grady family.

Mario was right. Within a couple of days, the news media got hold of every video feed from both hospitals. Both linking Thomas to the unexplainable miracles that happened. The world watched as Thomas inexplicably walked into the ER department of St Mary's Hospital. Gazed in amazement as they saw Thomas purposely walk up to Maggie and heal her of her cancer at the San Diego Cancer Center. Within a week the media reached that frenzy that Mario spoke of. Calls went out from every known news entity in search of Thomas Grady. The news wanted him, reality shows wanted him, heads of states and heads of countries all wanted to speak with Thomas Grady.

For weeks that was all that the news media spoke about. Where is Thomas and why won't he come out and help people, save people and cure us all. Thomas was a mystery, a hero, a miracle worker, and at the end, a villain, for not coming forth. All the Grady family could do was hide and watch in awe and in horror. They were still thankful for Mario's advice on how to remain hidden. Mario had the names and numbers of a few wealthy individuals where he had applied for security work. Mario knew one of them to be somewhat of a good man.

Mario also knew that this good man was gravely ill. Mario gave Mr. Grady a private number to this person and told him to try to arrange a meeting and explain to this wealthy person that his family needs money to stay out of harm's way. A few days later, this wealthy individual struck a deal with Mr. Grady. They would meet, Thomas would heal him, and he would hand over eight-hundred-thousand dollars in cash. Once Thoms healed the wealthy man, he was so grateful that he wanted to give Thomas even more money, but that was the quickest amount he could come up with in cash. And the Grady's needed cash. This way they wouldn't have to worry about work, and they could focus on quietly assimilating into some small town. They just had to keep their heads low and not spend their money suspiciously. Of course, unknown to the Grady family, Mario had contacted this particular wealthy person and explained to him that if he causes any problems with this family, he will make it his life's mission to kill him right after he was healed. There was no misunderstanding, and all went according to plan.

Mario had also arranged for new identities. So, when the Grady family finally did decide to settle into a small town, they would at least have new names. The family also changed their appearance as much as they could. Hair dye and some different hair styles. It was all they could do for now. They decided that it would be easier to live somewhere where they had a rough idea of the local culture, so, they moved to a small town named Henderson, right next to Las Vegas, Nevada. It was close enough to Las Vegas so that the city and its reputation would create just enough distraction for the Grady family and allow them to blend into the community with little to no attention. For almost a year, life was as close to normal as they could expect.

Thomas and his sister, Paige, developed a closer relationship and it seemed like the entire family was a little more bonded. There were just a couple of small incidents where Thomas was able to help a few people, but only from minor injuries and illnesses. Thomas was also maturing and dealing with the fact that he had this great power and responsibility. His father would help as much as he could with opinions, thoughts, and suggestions. But in the end, he told Thomas it would be up to him to decide what he was going to do. For now, his dad simply said, "Come on, let's go get some ice cream."

Thomas never told anyone that ever since that day at the San Diego Cancer Center, his powers, or whatever they were, were changing. He didn't understand how or what, he just knew that there was something different, like he was becoming more and more disconnected from this….energy, was the only word he could think of.

The Man Who Would be God

The life of Santiago Mateo Montez Monteverde, or as his friends knew him, Mathew Montez, was simple, non-descript, pedestrian in every sense of the word. Mathew was born in the Mexican barrios of Southwest Los Angeles. The only son of loving and doting Mexican immigrant parents. Mathew's life could be described as normal by all accounts, until he reached the age of reason, or at least, the kind of reason that only a 12-year-old middle schooler can come to. You see, Mathews parents were staunch Catholics. They were heavily involved with the church. They went 3 times a week, plus bible study. All this religion was eating into Mathew's play time with his school buddies.

Mathew was beginning to resent religion all together. The parents were perhaps too involved to the point where the practices, traditions, culture, and duties of religion were blurring the lines of being good Catholics or good parents. The borders of moderation are not always easily discerned, and one can pass into obsession with such subtly, that you are unaware of the fact that you are now suddenly standing right on top of a huge pile of dogma. As the parents immersed themselves further into the church, the child immersed himself deeper into the world and soon found themselves at odds with each other. As Mathew became more vocal about his objections to spending so much time at church and less time with his friends, so too did the parents seem to staunchly dig their heels in even further and insist that not only would he continue joining them in church, but perhaps he needed to go one more day to learn the ways of repentance, humility, and forgiveness for being such a disobedient child.

But the more they both pushed each other, the more both sides resisted. A few years later, at the age of 16, Mathew decided he would run away from home. One warm summer evening, Mathew formulated a plan, one with all the knowledge and wisdom that a 16-year-old could come up with. He had a small savings from his "allowance" that he had been stashing away for just such an occasion. He had secretly sold all his electronic toys that his unreasonable parents had bought him and came to the conclusion that $347.52 was enough to go out into the world and seek his own path and make his own fortune and live life on his own terms and not anyone else's stupid ideas. So, on this warm summer evening, Mathew decided he would implement his plan. He filled his backpack with all the essentials and left everything else behind. What Mathew didn't know was that he was running away and moving directly into a head on collision with fate. A fate that would change his life, and those around him, forever.

Day one was uneventful. Mathew woke up early Saturday morning, strapped his backpack on and jumped on a bus and headed to the heart of Los Angeles, a city that would sooner see you consumed than cared for. Mathew had no idea what or where anything was outside of a five-mile radius from his home. Now, Mathew exited the bus on Broadway and Olympic Blvd, the city was bustling with early weekend shoppers. Mathew was immediately surprised and amused by the number of people that were out and about. This is what he wanted, they all looked so free, so happy and independent. Although he had contemplated much while on the bus, Mathew really had no plan. He figured he would just roam around and figure it out as he went. *"How hard could it be?"*

It was still early, around 9am. Why not start the day with a good breakfast. Mathew wandered around until he found a small restaurant that looked decent. He walked in, had a seat and with his best big boy voice, ordered scrambled eggs, hash browns, bacon, toast and pancakes. When the waitress asked if he was going to drink anything, Mathew replied, "Milk, no, wait, I think I'll try some coffee." The waitress looked at Mathew just slightly incredulously and said, "Coffee? Are you sure you don't want to try our delicious fresh squeezed orange juice?" Mathew knew that she probably thought he was a little young for drinking coffee, and, the fresh juice thing did sound really good, but he held his ground, it was grown-up time. "No," Mathew said, "I'll stick with the coffee, thanks."

"Okay, suit yourself." The waitress replied, as she walked away scratching away on her order pad.

An hour and a half later, Mathew was back out in the streets. He felt like he had conquered his first challenge, survival. But it was still early, very early. Now what? He wandered around looking at all the stores and people walking and shopping. *"Where were they all going after this?"* He thought. *'Home? Back to their families, their friends.'* Mathew had been away from home for just over three hours, and he was starting to feel home sick. Not a good sign. Mathew kept wandering around not knowing what to do next. He had no idea what he was supposed to be doing. Looking for work? He would have to wait until Monday for that. Find a place to stay? That should be easy, just find a place to hide and sleep, why pay for a hotel or motel where they would require him to show some sort of identification. Not that he had any official identification, other than his high school I.D.

The day progressed and the longer Mathew stayed out in the streets the more confident he became. *'This ain't so hard,'* he thought, *'just take it one day at a time.'* Mathew managed to make it into the night. He had no idea where he was, or what part of town he was in. But as it got later, the darkness of night gnawed away at his confidence. Mathew was getting a little worried about where he was going to sleep and had seriously considered trying to rent a room for the night, but he knew that entailed too many potential problems. Not the least of which was having some night clerk call the cops on him and having to deal with his parents picking him up from jail. The thought was enough to give Mathew a renewed hope, vigor, and vim.

That night, Mathew found a place under a bridge, it was dark and hidden and he felt that was to his advantage. There was an embankment that stopped just a few feet below the bridge. It offered protection from the elements and also provided some cover. The nights were still a little warm, so Mathew didn't have to worry about a blanket. He found a suitable spot to lay down and Mathew proceeded to go to sleep. The ground was hard, the noises unfamiliar and the smells were not very pleasant, but it was all bearable. Mathew woke up the next morning only a little confused for just a few seconds. He had awoken to very different surroundings than he was used to, such as, no walls, no windows and a concrete ceiling. After suffering a brief moment of disorientation, Mathew was up and ready to meet his new life.

The daylight brought a renewed sense of confidence. He had survived one night on his own. *'Not bad,'* he thought, *'I could totally do this.'* The rest of the day was filled with exploring. Mathew decided he would look around and see what kind of resources are available. He found a library, coffee shop and grocery store. He didn't know why these places seemed important to him, he just remembers seeing everybody hanging out at coffee shops and the library usually has clean bathrooms. So far, so good.

Day two went quite well. Mathew still had plenty of money to eat with, so food was no problem. He was contemplating where he was going to take his next shower. He told himself he would worry about that a little later. For now, Mathew was enjoying his newfound and invigorating freedom.

Nighttime came and it was time to head back to his bridge and get some rest. *'Tomorrow would be the real test,'* he thought. He wondered if he would be able to find work. Mathew was set on not begging for food or money, he was determined to find work, any kind of work. He made his way up underneath the bridge and, much to his dismay and disappointment, there were several homeless men there. They were older, dirty, and appeared to be drunk. The pungent smell of dirty clothes, body odor and wine repulsed Mathew. One of the homeless men said, "Hey, buddy, you want to join us?" The other two were staring at him with no expression. For one insane moment, Mathew thought about it, then quickly answered, "No, thanks. I can find another place. You guys take care and have a nice day." The words sounded ridiculous, take care? Have a nice day. These words just didn't make any sense here. But he was young and didn't know what else to say, and so Mathew walked away in search of another place where he might find safety and sleep.

Tonight seemed just a little colder than the last and Mathew wondered if he should go to a secondhand store and buy a blanket. But he knew money was going to be tight soon, so he decided against it. Mathew finally found a suitable spot. This one was in the stairwell of a 3-story parking lot. The stairwell was out of sight, plenty of protection from the elements and one of the lights in the center landing was out, so he could see below and above him, but he was hidden in the dark. Whether this sense of confidence was false or not, he still felt a little safer under the broken light bulb. It wasn't long before Mathew fell asleep.

The morning greeted Mathew with a few reality checks. The first one was his backpack had been stolen. Mathew had not spent enough time in the streets to know how to safeguard his possessions. The second and more disturbing surprise was that all the money in his pockets was missing, in fact, all his pockets were empty. How is that even possible? Mathew thought. After a few disbelieving moments had past, Mathew was able to gather his thoughts and went absolutely crazy. Mathew started pounding the walls, the floor, screaming at the top of his lungs and yelling every profanity he could come up with. His eyes began to tear from rage and embarrassment. He was angry and felt stupid and violated and victimized. "How could this happen?" He said to himself, and then yelled out, "People are fucked up!" Mathew had never felt so many emotions roiling around in his mind before. This felt like the ultimate screw you moment. But he saved the best for last.

Mathew looked up, and although all he could see was the concrete walls and ceilings in the stairwell, Mathew was looking directly up and yelled at God. "This was all your fault, your doing, you're just getting back at me. For what, for trying to be independent? For trying to make a life for myself? Why are you punishing me for this?" Mathew pointed his finger towards the top of the stairwell, but he was aiming it directly into the face of God and said, "You think you can run my life, you think you can control me, you think this is funny. Well, you know what? I don't give a shit, bring your worst, see if I care. Cause I don't, I don't give a shit. Out here I don't have to do what anybody says! So now you made it harder for me, well, thanks, thanks a freakin lot." Mathew calmed down a little after his rant. He had to admit, he did feel a little better, getting that out of his system. He looked around one more time in the crazy unlikely chance that his backpack might be around somewhere, but it was definitely gone. Hope can be such a cruel mistress.

Although the lack of money now added urgency to his predicament, it failed to add what he needed most, desperateness. Mathew was now just an angry young man, broke, hungry, and starting to get afraid. Afraid that he would fail at his attempt at freedom. Afraid that he might have to go back, crawling, begging his parents to take him back and forgive him. The very thought of that gave Mathew strength to keep moving forward. But today presented a whole new set of challenges. Today, Mathew had no money, he couldn't just simply walk into a restaurant to sit at a nice comfortable table and order a nice hot breakfast. The very thought of it was causing Mathew's rage to build.

As a young boy growing up, his appetite is bigger than average. Young boys are used to eating a lot. And at this moment, the only thing in Mathew's head was eating. Having all of his worldly possessions stolen was not enough for Mathew to be taken to the point of desperation, but lack of food, he got desperate real fast. It took a little longer than most, but after a few hours of perceived starvation, Mathew found himself on a corner begging for change. He had to get something to eat, soon. It was beyond humiliating for Mathew. He felt this was the one thing that would be below him, but here he was, on the streets, begging for change. And when he finally had enough for some food, he ran over to a nearby McDonald's. Heck, he only needed about four dollars for a mini meal.

Mathew ate that food so fast, he didn't even remember eating it. He just looked down at his empty tray and said to himself, "Damn it, I gotta go back out there and keep begging for money." Mathew looked up and said, "Thanks, God, thanks for letting those bastards steal my shit. Now I

85

gotta go back out there and beg for money. Is this what you wanted? Well, congratulations, mission accomplished." Mathew walked out of McDonald's and went straight back out into the streets to beg for money, like any other homeless bum, and that was the one thing he didn't want to be. Mathew could feel a hate growing inside him.

The one thing that bothered Mathew the most about begging for money from strangers was the different emotions and expressions that people had. Some were friendly, even nice. Others, most, however, were rude, disgusted, apathetic, and disrespectful. But he had to eat, and all Mathew could think about was his next meal. He lost track of time, Mathew hadn't noticed that he had been on the streets for hours, he didn't even notice that he had close to forty dollars in his pocket. He was just simply on auto pilot, asking everybody that walked by him for money.

Mathew was exhausted from standing for so long. When he did finally realize that he had enough money to eat pretty much whatever he wanted to, he was both happy and completely disgusted with himself. In fact, as Mathew stood there on the street with his money in his hand, he broke down and just started crying. Crying at his pathetic situation. His face was dirty, his clothes were dirty and when he looked down at his hands, he saw that they were almost black with dirt and grim. He didn't know where to go to clean up. Did he need to make enough money for a motel? Did he have to go to the park to clean up? For the first time in his little escapade, Mathew had no idea what he was going to do next.

He hadn't thought about laundry, soap, deodorant, shampoo, toothbrush, clean socks a hairbrush or a mirror. He realized he had no idea of what he was doing or how he was going to do it. Mathew was young and inexperienced in life all he'd ever known was living at home in his bedroom playing video games and hanging out with his friends. He had no legitimate reason for running away other than he was mad at his parents for being strict with him. For the first time in the last 48 hours, Mathew was beginning to question what he was doing. But he wasn't convinced that he should go back. And so, he wandered the streets for the next few hours contemplating his situation and trying to cope with all of these new emotions he was now feeling. Even his appetite had been temporarily suppressed.

Mathew wandered aimlessly towards an undefined destination for an indeterminate amount of time. Mathew was beginning to realize that he was quickly running out of options. Stay on the streets and beg for money every day or go back home and live under the austere rules and conditions of his impossible parents. But with each step he took towards his uncertain future, the closer he came to making a decision. It was Monday, almost 6 o'clock, but the Sun was still out. It was another hot summer day when Mathew walked into some shade, he instinctively stopped for a small reprieve from the heat. It was then that Mathew noticed he was standing in the shadow of a large Christian church.

Mathew looked up and stared at the doors, they were open. Mathew didn't give it a second thought that the church was open on a Monday, it seemed to Mathew that churches were always open. He could tell that services hadn't started yet. Mathew had never been inside a Christian church before, but he had always found solace when he needed it at the church his parents forced him to go to. Mathew was never aware of the fact that churches were different, he saw them all the same, and so he slowly walked into the church hoping to find that consoling moment that would allow his mind and heart to be at peace.

Mathew looked around and noticed this was not like any vestibule he had ever seen. There was no font with holy water for blessings. *'Strange'*, he thought. He smiled for a second, remembering the day he first saw his mom putting some holy water in a small bottle to take home. Mathew was appalled because he thought his mother was stealing from the church. It wasn't till later that day that he learned it was common practice to take holy water home for blessings.

He heard someone saying that they were in the foyer. Foyer? That must be what they call their vestibule, was all Mathew could figure. Mathew made his way into the nave, or the main area where everybody's sitting. He found a place near the back and tried to stay hidden. He looked around for the Missal and was shocked to see that there wasn't a single one to be found. How do you know what's going on? Why aren't there any confessional booths? Mathew finally surrendered to the fact that they just did things very differently here. How bad could it be? It's a church. So, he stayed crouched down and tried to stay invisible.

He did thank God that no one was bugging him. He didn't want to talk to anyone. He just wanted to be left alone and not have to think about what he was going to do today. He was already dreading the fact of having to go back out into the streets and beg for money. Mathew was unaware of how much time had passed. When he looked up, Mathew realized that the church was almost full, and there was movement on the stage. It's so odd to see a stage. He felt like he was about to see a play, or some kind of show or concert. Mathew had just noticed the two big jumbo screens on both sides of the stage as they came to life with close up pictures of the

87

people on stage. A small group gathered at center stage, a singer, a guitarist, a bassist, and a drummer along with several singers. The music started and it was like no church music Mathew had heard before. They sounded cool. Mathew was intrigued by the Hollywood-like atmosphere. The lighting, the sound, and the way the whole church came to life. People were clapping and singing along, not at all what Mathew was used to. The whole experience had piqued his interest.

Then, when the music stopped, a man walked on stage. He looked like someone who worked backstage. He was wearing jeans, a T-shirt with an open plaided shirt and tennis shoes. He introduced himself as Pastor David Berman. What? Mathew couldn't believe what he was seeing. This was the leader of their church in tennis shoes? Where's the priest? Mathew didn't know whether to laugh or be appalled. But it was entertaining. Pastor David Berman walked up to the microphone and spoke, "Hello, everyone." The audience responded, "Hello Pastor." "Today, we are in for a treat. Today we have with us a special guest speaker, the Reverend Kevin Taylor.

Reverend Taylor has been speaking all over the world on the power of spiritual healing and he's here today to talk to us about his amazing experiences and miraculous works that God has done in his presence. I'm sure you will all be captivated by his stories of adventure but mostly by the amazing faith that people have around the world. Please give a warm welcome to, Reverend Kevin Taylor." The church erupted in applause as Mathew noticed a somewhat normal, average man calmly walking onto the stage and towards the microphone.

Mathew didn't know why he was expecting to see some guy that looked like a big burly safari hunter, it only seemed like it should be someone bigger than life, or least, bigger than this guy. Reverend Taylor was a man of very average qualities in the way of appearances. Mathew also noticed that he looked young. Almost a little too young for someone with so much life experience. Nevertheless, here he was, introduced by the leader of this church as someone to listen and pay attention to. You don't get that kind of intro without something to back it up.

Mathew found himself completely engaged in this unfolding scenario. This new and different church seemed to have less rules. It exuded a sense of casualness which made Mathew feel a little more relaxed than he thought he would be in a strange church filled with strange people. And now this, this was like a show, on a stage, with giant jumbo screen monitors on the walls. Mathew was pleasantly entertained and amused. And so, he listened intently to every word that came out of this young man's mouth. And for the first time in a long time, Mathew forgot all about his problems and felt like a kid about to see one of his favorite shows on television.

Reverend Taylor was standing in front of the microphone with both hands at his side, his posture was that of a meek man, a humble man. But his circumspect appearance was misleading. As Reverend Taylor spun his tales of his adventures abroad, his voice and whole demeanor changed from mild mannered to strong, forceful, even at times a bit angry. Angry at those who would deny God and God's gifts. Reverend Taylor had taken the microphone off the stand and was now pacing the stage, waving and pointing at everyone and anyone who was listening. And they were all listening. They were all riveted to their seats and hanging on every word, for Reverend Taylor, as it turns out, was quite the dynamic orator.

Halfway into his spiel, Reverend Taylor was no longer just speaking at church, he was starting a revival. The crowd was cheering, laughing, crying and back to cheering. Every soul was moved by his stories of God's strength, His eternal hope and above all the ability to move mountains through the immeasurable faith of all true believers. Mathew himself was on the edge of being converted right then and there. Then, it happened, an event that would transform and change Mathew's life forever.

Reverend Taylor proclaimed that there were going to be healings today. He began to call out physical and mental infirmities. He pointed towards the audience and said, "I know someone here is suffering from stomach problems, I know someone here is suffering from gallstones. I know you are fighting with addiction, I know because God is telling me this right now. I know because he wants you to be healed, right now, today, right here. Do you want to be healed today?" The Reverend repeated himself, "I said, do you want to be healed today? Right here, right now, today?" The audience roared with unintelligible noises. Mathew was transfixed on this man. Was he really going to do this? Was he really going to heal these people? Mathew watched in awe as men and women walked towards the stage with their hands drawn up and praising God as they approached the stage. Reverend Taylor walked down among them and met them at the front of the center aisle. Mathews eyes were stained wide open as he watched in disbelief.

The Reverend was placing his hands on these people and as soon as he touched them they fell towards the ground. If it hadn't been for the ushers and volunteers, they would have fallen all the way down to the floor. People were hopping and dancing and smiling and praising God for the miracle of healing. That's when it happened, Mathew watched an older woman in a wheelchair that was being pushed towards the front of the church. Mathew could see the woman, she had her eyes closed tight and her hands stretched out, she was muttering some prayers. Reverend Taylor saw her coming down the aisle and many eyes were set upon him to see what his reaction would be. But Reverend Taylor stood directly in front of her, and he held out both hands as she approached.

Reverend Taylor spoke into the microphone that he was holding in his hand, "Lord, we thank you for this woman coming down this aisle. We thank you for her faith. But most of all, we are thankful for what You are about to do, Lord. Madam, come to me. Come and accept what the Lord has for you. Bring her to me so that I can bear witness and rejoice in what God has in store for you today." As the woman approached Reverend Taylor, a silence began to spread throughout the church. There was less noise, but the room was more electrified than ever. Finally, the woman and the man pushing her stopped directly in front of Reverend Taylor and all eyes were upon them, including Mathews.

Reverend Taylor placed one hand on the woman's head and raised the other to the sky. He closed his eyes and turned his face up towards Heaven. There was a small hesitation before he spoke, "Lord, we thank you for this precious life. We thank you for your promise to us, for you said, Lord, that where two or more are gathered in your name and we ask it in Jesus name, it will come to past. Do you believe?" The church and the woman in the wheelchair all said, "Amen." "Do you believe that all things are possible through Him?"

"Amen." In the background, you could hear the woman repeating, "Yes, Lord, Yes Lord." "Are we not more than two people believing and asking in His name?"

"Amen."

"Do we believe that God can heal?"

"Amen."

"Yes, Lord." Continued the woman. The Reverend now placed both hands on the sides of the woman's head and almost shouted at her, "The Lord has heard your prayers, do you believe?" "Yes!"

"Then if you believe, in the name of Jesus, stand up from that chair and walk!"

The woman grabbed the handles of the chair. You could see the muscles on her arms were straining, her arms began shaking, her eyes tightened, and her teeth were clenching. It seemed like it took forever to see even a slight movement, but there it was, her legs began to show the slightest hint of movement. The church went wild, screaming, "Yes, Lord, praise God!"

A few more agonizing moments of almost imperceptible motion and then finally, the woman slowly at first began to rise. Then, just as she was almost about to stand, she shot up during the last few inches and the church went wild. There was yelling and dancing in the aisles and praising God's name. But Mathew, Mathew was beyond awe struck. It was the most indelible moment of his life, and he knew right there and then, he was going to turn his life around to God forever. He wanted what this man had. He wanted to have that kind of faith, that kind of relationship with God and to be used as a vessel for this great and wondrous power.

Mathew almost ran to the front of the church when they made an alter call to come and be saved. He had completely forgotten what he looked like, but everyone was kind, friendly and helpful. Some offered to take him to eat, others asked if he needed help. But Mathew had no hesitation in telling his story because he told them that he is going straight home after this and make up with his parents.

It would be years before his parents would accept Mathew's decision to leave the Catholic Church. They were somewhat devastated. They fought him for many months. But Mathew was steadfast and never showed any sign of being upset. He knew what he was going to do with his life, and nothing was going to stop him. He went on to seminary school and eventually became a youth pastor. But Mathew had his eyes on one thing. Missionary work. He wanted the life of Reverend Taylor. Travel the world and heal those who need healing. Mathew had experienced a few episodes personally. A few times people, those who knew him, would come to him and ask that he pray for them to be healed. Mathew didn't see why he couldn't help. He noticed that sometimes people were healed, and sometimes not. He wrote this off to either that certain persons did not have enough faith, or he needed to strengthen his own.

Mathew had always thought that the day would come when he was ready, that the Lord would work through him and there would be nothing he could not do through Him, and all the people would be healed. And so, as years went on Mathew would experience the same percentages of some people being healed while others not, he began to question his own teachings. Maybe what he learned in school and in church was wrong? Maybe it was more up to him to make this happen.

So, Mathew made the decision to move away from the church teachings and work more from a personal perspective. After all, Mathew thought, he was the one with all the faith, and maybe that should be enough. Mathew recalled the Roman soldier that asked Jesus to come to his home and heal his son. But Jesus, realizing how this Roman was so sure his son would be healed if Jesus came to see him, basically said, "Go home, your own faith has healed your son." And so, again, Mathew rationalized that it should be his faith, Mathew's faith, that needs to be so strong, that he should be able to heal others. No one else needs faith but him. So, there should be no reason why he wouldn't be able to heal everyone.

Mathew went out into the world and tried to heal everyone he could. But to his great disappointment, he was always faced with those same proportions of some being healed and some not. In fact, the majority of people were not healed. Why? Why do some people get healed not only of simple ailments, but even cancer and severe pain, while others experience no change whatsoever? This was something that Mathew was starting to come to terms with because he had come to the conclusion that these people who are not being healed are somehow not right with God. And so, this was Mathew's way of basically writing them off. If they weren't right with God, then they weren't right with Mathew, and they didn't deserve the gift of healing.

In fact, it was this exact doctrine that Mathew preached. He would tell those who did not receive their healing that they are to go and find out what is it in their lives that they need to change to get right with God. Once you have done that, come back and receive the gift that is waiting for you. Needless to say, the response was not always well received. Some people became angry, bitter, and even violent because Mathew was questioning their own faith. But Mathew stood his ground and legitimized his position with the fact that they weren't healed, but others were. Mathew's world soon became very confusing. The duality in his life was just too conflicting and the seeds of doubt were slowly taking root.

He really did believe that God was working through him, but Mathew felt bad for those who did not get healed. And in his heart, he really felt that everyone should be healed. Now he spent most of his time being frustrated by the thought of failure and the lingering possibility that he may have been wrong all this time. Maybe it was his faith that was lacking, maybe it is he who is not completely right with God.

Mathew set out with a new philosophy. One that would only add more confusion to his life. Although it would still be through his faith, and only his faith that will heal others and if they are not healed, then it is God's will that they continue to remain sick. This was a no-lose clause. This gave Mathew complete immunity from failure. It wouldn't be his fault that someone wasn't healed, it would be their fault and Gods. Mathew went on to travel the world and used his trickery of words to shine a light on his power while highlighting the shortcomings of others. The problem was, most people believed in Mathew, he would build them up into a frenzy just like Reverend Taylor did. Mathew knew how to get a crowd excited. The excitement of the crowds fed his ego, which in turn contributed to his synthetic sense of empowerment.

And so, Mathew continued his adventures as a traveling evangelist. Sometimes he would even rent a large tent to give the appearance of those old-time revivals. People loved it, they loved Mathew and most of all, those small percentages of people that did get healed, for whatever reason, were the true testaments of Mathew's power and his connection with God. But in the back of his mind, Mathew was still obsessing with the idea that he should be able to heal all people, no matter what people think, no matter what God thinks. And so, Mathew grew a little angrier and a little more bitter every day. The Reverend Mathew, as he was now referred to, had never stopped to ask the most significant question of anyone receiving a faith healing, the question that one must ask whether you did or did not receive healing. And that question is, is it truly God's will?

It cannot be Mathew's will, or his desire, but instead, it must be God's will. This would have actually been a better way for the Reverend Mathew to recuse himself from the judgement of God. But instead, he chose to point out the sinful ways of those who were not right with the Lord. Then, one day, 16 ½ years from the day he first saw Reverend Taylor, Mathew saw the answer to all his problems. And he was sure that his life would never be the same again.

Mathew was visiting the small city of Henderson, Nevada. He had located a property just beyond the outskirts of town where he could set up his tent and throw an old-style revival. He had already procured the property and offered to pay the owner half the take, which Mathew lied was typically around 5 to 10 thousand dollars. Mathew averaged closer to 15 to 20 thousand dollars per these events. It was easy to get people to give larger donations when he announces that people will be healed, and that's when he passes the offering plates around. Ever since he found out about how that woman who got healed at Reverend Taylor's performance was a plant, a fake, he never forgave Reverend Taylor for diluting his faith. But that only made Mathew more determined than ever to prove that God will heal others through him. And those that are not healed have only themselves to blame.

One day Mathew was walking back to his hotel room after a late breakfast, it was around 1:30pm when, while walking past a small park, Mathew heard what sounded like two kids having an argument. He could tell it was coming from behind the small light gray cinderblock building that housed the restrooms for the park. Mathew walked around the building to get a look at what was going on, He was feeling a little anxious, as the conversation sounded very heated. As he peeked around the corner of the building, Mathew could see two young boys arguing. They both appeared to be around 16 or 17 years old. One was clearly bigger than the other and it looked like the bigger boy was trying to take the smaller boys skateboard away from him.

"Let go of the board, or I'll break it on your face, you little shithead." The smaller boy glared at his adversary and said "No, you let go, or I'll break it over your fat head." Mathew was slightly amused at the smaller boy's unfounded confidence. Clearly the larger boy had the advantage with 40 pounds over the smaller boy and about half a foot taller. Nevertheless, the smaller boy was relentless and would not let go of his skateboard. Finally, the larger boy saw Mathew walking around the corner of the building and began approaching them. The larger boy thought better of prolonging this confrontation. But three things happened that would change the course of the day.

One, when the larger boy saw Mathew, he gave the skateboard one last hard tug and said, "Fine! Keep your dumb-ass skateboard." And he let go of it. Because of that final tug, the smaller boy instinctively pulled back even harder, but when the larger boy let go, it made the smaller boy whip the skateboard back, fast, and hard. Unbeknown to the smaller boy, a young girl was headed to the restroom, and just as she was almost directly behind the smaller boy the skateboard came whipping around, it smashed into the young girls face with devastating force, breaking her nose and possibly damaged other facial bones as well.

In an instant there was blood everywhere. The young girl barely let out a whimper when she collapsed on the floor adding a concussion to her list of injuries. Luckily, she knocked out or she would have been screaming in severe pain. Mathew was struck with fear for the little girl and was temporarily frozen by the sight of it all. He could clearly see that the bones in the young girls face were broken, and her nose was bleeding profusely. Mathew stood there in shock. But not as shocked as he was about to become.

The younger boy saw the young girl and realized what had happened and instinctively knelt in front of her. Without so much as even looking around to see if anyone was watching, the young boy, Thomas Grady, touched the little girl on the shoulder. Mathew was confused by all this. Why did he have to touch her? Was he a little pervert? Why hasn't he run for help? Mathew was about to move into action and yell at the boy and call 9-1-1 when he saw something very strange. The little girls face was moving. Her skin was moving, her nose was moving. *'What the hell is going on?'* Mathew thought.

He stared in disbelief as he watched the young girls face appear to heal itself, the bleeding from her nose stopped, and the damaged cheek bone appeared to be fine. Within a matter of seconds, the little girl stood up and he could hear her say, "What happened?" Thomas looked at her and said, "I don't know, I think you fell down and bumped your head. Are you all right?" "Yes, I'm fine, thank you." she said and continued on to the restroom as if nothing happened. The little girl hadn't even noticed the blood on her t-shirt. When she does, she will definitely scream and yell and find her mom who will not find anything wrong with her and it will be chalked up as a mystery, but not to Mathew. He knew exactly what he saw. This was a real miracle, a real healing. Who was this boy? Mathew quickly walked back behind the small building and moved out of Thomas' sight. Thomas looked around but missed Mathew. Convinced that no one saw him heal that little girl, Thomas jumped on his skateboard and headed home. Mathew followed.

Once Mathew found where Thomas Grady lived, he went back to his hotel room and began searching the internet for anything related to the words 'boy' and 'miracle'. Much to his surprise, there were numerous articles, pictures, and stories of some miracle kid. Then Mathew saw a picture of a kid. It didn't look exactly like Thomas, but Mathew could tell that it was the same child. Just different hair doo, and a few other subtle changes, but there he was. There were stories about this kid that he cured people in hospitals, in accidents and even in malls. No one directly admitted that they were cured by this child, but there was enough circumstantial evidence that would have made any lawyer happy.

If Mathew had read these articles a week ago, he would not have given it a second thought because it sounded like some cheap tabloid headline, but now, now he had personally witnessed this miracle firsthand. He just wasn't sure what to do. But there were ideas already roiling in his convoluted mind. He still had some time to come up with a plan. His revival was scheduled to take place in exactly twenty days from now. That should be enough time to come up with something, but what?

The Reverend Mathew sat in his hotel room and began thinking about what had happened today. There were several avenues to go. He could simply ask Thomas to join him. He thought, *'What greater and nobler cause is there?'* Mathew began to pace and broke into a long soliloquy. "How could he say no? But what if he did say no? Then what? He could offer Thomas large sums of money, but surely he knows he could do this on his own. And why doesn't he? Isn't he aware of the fact that he is committing one of the most heinous crimes of all time against humanity by not using his power to heal everyone?"

The more questions that Mathew asked himself, the more frustrated and angrier he started to become at Thomas. *'This child should be shared with the world. Who does he think he is?' Every moment he hides, hundreds of people go uncured and die. This is unacceptable!'* The Reverend Mathew soon worked himself into a self-righteous frenzy. Now his mind was racing trying to conceive of a plan in which to use Thomas for the greater good of all mankind. Although, the Reverend Mathew could not suppress that omnipresent voice deep in his head that was gleefully saying, *'At last, I will be great. People will see me as having God-like powers!'* Which he would humbly profess that this power was simply given to him as a gift as one that is favored by God.

There was too much to gain. Reverend Mathew began formulating his plan. He immediately turned to the dark part of his mind. In his many travels, Mathew had been presented with many gifts, but none so strange as the one the old Haitian woman gave him. He remembered how absurd it sounded at the time. But now, now it seemed like the perfect solution to his problem. The old woman had known the infamous Dr. Max Beauvoir in the Haitian city of L'Estere. She claimed that the small vial of liquid in the small jar she had given Mathew was nothing less than the same potion that Dr. Beauvoir used to create the living dead, zombies. She told Mathew that the liquid merely had to touch the skin, preferably, the lips. For some reason, that was the most effective part. According to the old woman, it should work almost instantaneously.

Mathew could think of no other way of doing this. He couldn't raise suspicion and go out and try to buy things that would help him knock out a person. He wouldn't even know where to start. He didn't want to hit the child with anything; that would just be too cruel. Mathew did not like violence. And so, not really knowing what would happen or how long this potion would last,

Mathew decided it was still the best and safest way to go...for himself.

Although this well-known Haitian voodoo witch doctor had claimed to have controlled the minds of many famous people, even the U.S. President, William Clinton, nothing had ever been substantiated. Nonetheless, here it was, a small vial of amber colored liquid. Mathew had never really paid any attention to the old woman's story and kept the vial mostly out of amusement. But now it seemed to present itself as a very viable option. *'Vial, Viable.'* Mathew thought, *'was that a pun?'* He smiled at his serendipitous humor.

Mathew had put a rough plan together within a couple of days. He went out and rented a van then stopped at a local skateboard shop and purchased a half-dozen top-of-the-line skateboards. Mathew had no idea they could be so expensive. Also, on the advice of the helpful 19-year-old clerk, who was, apparently an expert on all matters of skating, sold Mathew a few hundred dollars' worth of accessories. Mathew threw his purchase haphazardly in the back of the van and drove off. It was a hot, but dry summer day. Mathew was thankful that the air conditioner worked so well. He drove back to the park where he had been watching Thomas Grady skate for the last couple of days. It was late afternoon when Thomas finally showed up. Mathew had been waiting less than an hour. Had it been any longer, Mathew thought he might have lost his nerve to go forward with his plan.

Mathew had backed up into the parking space so that the rear of the van would not be facing the street. This would make it more difficult for any pedestrians or vehicles driving by to see the rear of the van directly. He walked to the back of the van and simply opened the double doors to reveal the brand-new skateboards and packages of accessories. Mathew knew that Thomas would have to skate near the van to get to the skate park. Sure enough, Mathew was skating right towards him. He was wearing his headset and listening to some music on his Android phone.

Thomas couldn't help but notice the van parked in the parking lot. Thomas also noticed the man standing next to the van. Thomas couldn't resist glancing over at the open doors and noticed what was inside. Thomas came to an abrupt stop when he saw what was inside the van. Mathew was holding his arms behind his back. He didn't want to show that he was wearing latex gloves with the vial in one hand and a small cotton cloth in the other. Mathew just stood there pretending he didn't see Thomas staring at the items inside his van. Mathew was wearing sunglasses, so it was difficult to tell which way he was looking. Thomas got off his skateboard and began walking towards the van. Thomas was curious as to whether this man was selling skateboards from the back of his van or what.

What Thomas did know was that that all the stuff was top-of-the-line. There were DGK, Zero and Plan-b decks. Packages of Bones bearings and all sorts of other stuff, cool stuff. Thomas could not resist walking over to ask the stranger if this stuff was for sale. "Hey," Thomas said as he approached the stranger.

"Hey." Mathew replied.

"What's with all the cool stuff? You selling?"

Mathew nodded towards the items in the van and said, "No, these are promotional items that my company wants to give away to help boost sales. See anything you like?" Mathew said with a purposeful grin. Mathew could clearly see that Thomas got excited. "What? These are free?"

"Yeah, you familiar with these brands?"

"Oh, yeah!" Thomas exclaimed. "I know all of these brands." Thomas approached the back of the van and was about to touch one of the skateboards when Mathew decided it was now or never. Mathew, who outweighed Thomas attacked him, quickly wrapping one arm around his neck and with the other, forcing the lightly soaked cloth over Thomas' mouth. Thomas was thin, but strong, he reacted quickly and threw Mathew off, and Mathew went flying backwards and landed on the floor. Thomas turned to face his aggressor and was ready to run when he realized he couldn't move. Thomas legs collapsed and he fell on the ground. Thomas could see and feel everything, but he could not move one muscle in his body. Once again, that familiar fear that he knew so well came rushing in. Thomas Grady thought, *'Not again, please.'* A few seconds later, the van drove away with Thomas lying in the back, motionless, helpless, but lurking inside his head was also one more emotion, anger.

The Reverend Mathew had no idea if his potion was going to work or not. He had tried it on a cat a few days ago and it seemed to work just fine. When Mathew placed the small damp cloth of this elixir next to the cats nose, it took only a few seconds and the cat collapsed and just laid there. Mathew did not know if the cat was dead or dying. It just lay there, and Mathew couldn't help himself from giggling at the fact that the cat was catatonic. Mathew grinned and thought to himself, *'How do I come up with this stuff.'*

Mathew had kept notes on how long the cat remained in that state. It was hours, and that was just the result of fumes. Mathew had decided that this stuff was too strong, who knows what a good whiff would do to a boy. So, he watered the potion down a little and tried it again on a different cat. This time the cat did not pass out, but when its curiosity got the best of him, the cat licked the moist cloth and immediately its little body froze. But this time Mathew noticed that the water down version didn't last as long. The cat regained movement less than an hour later. Perfect, Mathew thought. So now, here he was, with Thomas Grady tied and gagged on the floor of the van.

Thomas woke up to the all too familiar scenario, tied up on a chair, mouth covered with tape, and of course, his hands and feet were bound. He was more angry than scared. Thomas was about a year older since his last encounter and for some reason he just felt a little braver this time. Maybe because of his age or maybe because he was a bit of a daredevil on his skateboard or his maturity. Whatever the case, Thomas was not as afraid as he was the last time he was in this same predicament.

Thomas looked around the room he was in. It appeared to be a normal small sized bedroom. It was clean, no noticeable odors, in fact, it seemed like someone had just cleaned the room and sprayed some kind of air freshener, lavender or some kind of flowery scent. The room seemed almost too clean, as if someone had just dusted. Thomas could hear some noises, but nothing out of the ordinary. No one was arguing with themselves. That was a good sign. No dead bodies, that was good, too.

Thomas decided to try to keep a cool head until his captor showed him or herself. A few minutes later, he heard the soft carpeted muffled footsteps coming towards his room. They weren't heavy steps and Thomas remembered the man by the van, he was taller than him, but not by much. The door opened with little fanfare and Mathew cautiously entered and walked towards Thomas Grady. Both men appeared to be unsure as to why they were here.

Reverend Mathew spoke, "Hello, my name is Reverend Mathew, I will not hurt you, do you understand?" Thomas nodded his head. Mathew continued, "I believe that you have been sent to me to complete my mission in life. And that mission is to heal all those who are in need while I am still in this world. I believe that you are the tool which God has sent to me with which to carry out my mission. My son, you are here not because I wish it, but because providence has brought us together. Yes, we are to begin preparing for our future eventualities." Mathew touched Thomas on the crown of his head and said, "Son, it is going to be magnificent! But for now, there is much to do." With that, Mathew turned slowly and walked back out the door and into the next room.

Thomas noticed he had been holding his breath the whole time and he finally exhaled, damn it, he thought, another crazy son-of-a-bitch. Thomas realized, more than ever, that he will always be the target of those who are drunk with power, or in this case, drunk with religion. So, for the first time, Thomas noticed that he was actually more mad than scared.

In the next room The Reverend Mathew began working on his plan. He would reconstruct the Tabernacle of Moses on his stage and will offer people the chance to enter inside with him and there, no matter what they're infirmities, they will be healed. Of course, it will be Thomas who will do the healing, because inside the Tabernacle will be the Holy of Holies, which will have no lights, and no one will see Thomas tied and gagged. No one will notice when Mathew takes the hand of those who are ill, and he will place their hand on Thomas' hand. Even Thomas Grady will not be aware of what's going on in the dark. Of course, inside the Tabernacle there will be a trap door that will allow Mathew to lower Thomas out of sight so that all could see that there was nothing in there but the presence of God...and himself, the Reverend Mathew.

It took about a couple of months, but Mathew had put together a plan and a new venue. He was excited to have his next revival. He had canceled the last event because Mathew did not have enough time to put his plan into action, besides, he had just committed a federal crime. Mathew had decided to move his next revival somewhere in the bible-belt where it would be easier to work up a crowd. Although this area was mostly ruled by the socially conservative evangelicals, there were plenty of mild to moderate Christian zealots who were always looking for signs and miracles. And Mathew would be more than happy to provide both and gain their praise and stolen adulation.

Located about 50 miles north/west of Selma, Alabama is the small town of Tallapoosa. Mathew had met a man from this small town once and found him so congenial that he swore to some day visit him there. He also remembered how grateful that man was for the healing he received. Though till this day, Mathew could not recall what that man was healed of. The point is, Mathew thought of the town. It was remote and isolated enough for him to feel safe to try out his new powers, or rather, Thomas' powers. It was all the same thing to Mathew.

Everything was set. The flyers went out, the minions were sent to spread the word by mouth. Mathew knew that he always got bad media coverage if he advertised on the local radio and television stations. The most effective way to gather a crowd while staying under the radar was to send small groups of his believers out into the populace and spread the word that God was going to do incredible things at this event.

The population of Tallapoosa was roughly 80 thousand, split about in the middle between black and white. Mathew preferred to have a black audience, for some reason, they were always more…upbeat. This always put Mathew in a more comfortable and happy mood. Mathew was becoming more and more excited. *'How amazing this will be'*, he thought. *'Think of all the people that will be healed, cured, saved, and converted. It will be a glorious testament to God. Glorious.'* Mathew was already getting inquiries about the day and time of the event. He could feel it growing. Mathew knew this would be one of his greatest moments, perhaps, he thought, maybe even create a little history.

Fifty-six days ago. George and Helen Grady knew something was terribly wrong when they hadn't seen or heard from Thomas all day. They knew only too well that he was stolen from them again. They immediately got in touch with Mario Reyes who came as soon as he could. But this time, Mario didn't have any easy clues to help guide him to where Thomas could possibly be. This was going to take some time. The Grady family was understandably reluctant to go to the police and so they gave Mario some time to find him. After a couple of months, however, they would have no other choice. Thomas' safe return was now more important than their anonymity.

Mario Reyes asked the Grady's to give him a little more time. But George and Helen were getting disparate and found it difficult to wait. They would give Mario a couple of weeks to come up with some kind of lead. Mario knew only too well, that this news will not stay quiet. There's always a leak. This town will be swarming with media in a matter of days. It would be impossible to keep this kind of news contained. *'The worst part,'* Mario thought, *that it's going to bring out the crazies. One of which I'm sure is with Thomas right now.'* Mario went back to working on the case with a new fervor. He will always owe Thomas an enormous amount of gratitude for what he did for his child.

Back in Georgia. It was a few weeks into autumn and summer was sauntering away in the southern states like a stubborn child refusing to leave the playground, it just kept lingering around. The folks in Tallapoosa were still walking around gleaming with sweat from the heat and humidity in the middle of October. The sunset was showing up a little sooner with every passing day giving the Tallapoosians a false sense of reprieve from the prolonged summer heat.

Soon it will be dark by late afternoon. But for now, it was a balmy 95 degrees with 100% humidity. One for the records, to be sure. Meanwhile, in Tallapoosa, all folks could talk about was the revival being held at the Southeastern side of town.

The city of Tallapoosa looked like something straight out of an Any Griffith episode. The town was filled with quaint streets and buildings. Everything was quaint, even the old growth that lined every street to the many scattered little steepled churches. Most were white and a few were made of red bricks, but every one of them had a steeple. It seemed like every street headed out of the town eventually took you to the entrance of a pristine wilderness filled with tall trees and big skies. This was God's country, in every sense of the word.

Everyone in town noticed the huge tent being erected. Tables and chairs were being arranged inside, even a small stage. The flyers said there would be complimentary drinks and snacks. Even people who don't normally attend church were going to be there, at least for the free food. There was also excitement because the same flyer said that there will be healings. Though some were always skeptical, there were those who were in need of some serious healing. They would be there for sure for the simple reason that they had nothing to lose. And of course, the curious will flock to see the show. Last but not least, the non-believers will be there to mock everyone and yell, "I told you so."

The one thing that caught everyone's attention was the tabernacle. Those who recognized it had varied opinions. Some thought it was pretentious, some felt it was beautiful, while most thought it was probably just going to be used for some kind of a play. No matter the reason, it was a big draw. People wanted to know what was going to happen. The Reverend Mathew made few appearances around town. Some folks met him and thought he was humble and carried himself like a man of God. Still, others just didn't like the whole traveling church thing. It reminded them of a snake oil peddler. Hit one town, then on to the next. Needless to say, the opinions were wide and varied. But this was the means to the end, all this invoked curiosity, and that's what brings people in.

On Saturday evening, after going through much preparation, Mathew was exhausted and sat in his room at the local hotel. He wasn't sure if he was going to be able to sleep. As tired as he was, he was more excited about the next day. The healings that are going to happen, the things people will say. It's going to be glorious, just glorious. The day has finally arrived. The day when the Reverend Mathew is going to heal the world, one town, one city, one state, one country at a time. Mathew couldn't fight off the thought that, after tomorrow, the seeds of fame will be planted, and history will add a new chapter that will bear his name.

Reverend Mathew was up at 3:30am, the first Sunday of his new life. He had bought a custom electric wheelchair which he had Thomas Grady strapped and gaged to. Mathew had dressed Thomas in an oversized hooded t-shirt. The hood was draped over Thomas' face to hide the duct tape that covered his mouth. Mathew took Thomas inside the revival tent, rolled him under the stage and onto the platform that Mathew had made by a local carpenter. It was designed with a crank that made it easy for Mathew to turn the crank with little effort and lift up Thomas Grady into position inside the tabernacle.

Thomas was tied at the ankles, arms, waist, and wrist. But his hands were free to touch. After setting up Thomas in the desired position, Mathew let him know that he would be sitting there for a long time, maybe as late as 8 or 9pm. He told Thomas that the light breakfast that he fed him this morning would be the last meal for today, but that he would give him some snacks if he got hungry. He also let Thomas know that he could have a few small drinks of water, but he could not drink too much, because he would not be able to use the restroom for many hours. Mathew was always apologizing to Thomas for what he was putting him through, but, Mathew said, this was not his wish, but God's will that compelled him.

Now everything was set. The event was set to start at 10am, early enough to catch a little bit of the cool morning air before the sun decided to rise up and mock winters face. It was 9am, and the tent was already near capacity. By 9:30 it was standing room only. By 10am, the crowd outside the tent was as big as the one inside. There was an unmistakable fervor in the air. The Reverend Mathew was ecstatic. At 9:45 a small church group started playing music and singing hymns. At 10:01, the Reverend Mathew walked on to the stage with no introduction. He wanted to introduce himself. As he walked towards the center of the stage there was some applause that sounded a little half-hearted. Mathew used this greeting. He was well aware of the fact that if he had someone announce him, the applause is usually a lot louder and longer. But for whatever the reason, he usually preferred to introduce himself.

Mathew walked up to the microphone at center stage. He took the mic off the stand, held it in his right hand and with his left, he pointed towards the choir and spoke, "Ladies and gentlemen, the First Baptist Church Choir of Tallapoosa and their wonderful band. Can we give them a warm round of applause?" The congregation responded with a roaring round of applause.

Mathew continued, "Yes, thank you," he said, still speaking to those in the choir. "Thank you for those wonderful songs. Now, ladies and gentlemen, may I please introduce myself, my name is Reverend Mathew, and I…" The crowd interrupted him with a larger applause as well, much bigger than the one when he first came out on stage. Again, this was expected. Mathew held up an open hand towards his audience, a humble signal to stop clapping, and they did. "Thank you so much for that. You have no idea how nice it feels to feel welcomed, thank you, thank you." Another short burst of applause. "Ladies and gentlemen as promised in my flyer, which apparently some of you have seen," A short burst of laughter. "I will be giving a short sermon today. I will not take up much of your time speaking to you about how great our God is, because you already know that."

There was a scattering of amens and halleluiahs. I am not going to speak to you about our God's forgiving grace, because you already know that, too." The praises got a little louder. "Ladies and gentlemen, I am not going to speak to you about the all-encompassing power and peacefulness of God's love." Some folks stood up and shouted, amen! The Reverend Mathew went on. "Ladies and gentlemen, most of you are here because you know Gods love and you believe in Gods ways. Some of you are here searching for that very same thing. And I know some of you are here because you heard that one of your own, a Ms. Loretta Bennet, was going to be offering her fresh baked apple and cherry pies just outside this tent which, I know for a fact, there is not one piece left cause they're that good!"

Another burst of laughter. "Don't you all go thinking that I did not have one of my staff go out there and save me a piece of those pies for later." Mathew could tell that the crowd was now officially on his side. He continued. "Folks, all jokes aside, I am not here to talk to you about all the things you always hear in church. I'm here to speak to you about the amazing and powerful love that God has for you and the gift he is going to give to you today. That's right, today. Not tomorrow, not next week, not some day, but today, my friends." The applause and praises were noticeably louder. As promised, Mathew went on for only another 20 minutes or so and then he started to wrap up his sermon. "So, ladies and gentlemen, if I may quote A.B. Simpson, the founder of the Christian and Missionary Alliance, who said, "If ever there was an age where the world needed the witness of God's supernatural working, it is in this day of unbelief and Satan's power. Therefore, we may expect, as the end approaches that the Holy Ghost will work in the healing of sickness, in the casting out of demons, in the remarkable answers to prayer, in special

104

and wonderful providences and in such a form as may please His sovereign will to an unbelieving world."

Mathew was now ready to begin his show. "Ladies and gentlemen. I believe supernatural forces are always at work with the Lord. I believe He is here today for a very special reason. I believe He is here today to heal you." Half the congregation rose to its feet and yelled out praises. Mathew was ready for his big show. He held up both hands in a jester that meant he wanted silence. The crowd obliged. "Folks, I am getting a strong message here. I must ask you all a question. With a show of hands, how many people have received healing from the Lord? Hands went up all around the congregation. "Now, and more importantly, with a show of hands, how many of you went to the Lord for a healing, but did not receive it?" Again, hands went up all around the congregation. Mathew could also see that the folks listening outside the tent were also raising their hands. "Ladies and gentlemen, you are the reason I am here. You are the reason God is here. Today, you will receive that promise. That prayer will be answered. Today, you will be healed!"

The crowd stood up, some danced some jumped up and down while others raised their hands and screamed, Amen! Even outside the tent people were jumping up and down and praising God. Mathew continued. "Ladies and gentlemen, please, please, calm down, we need a little silence, we need a little prayer. I want all of you who are in need of a special healing by God today to start forming a line right here in front of me. Our ushers will help those who may have some problems walking or standing. I want a single line, right here." He pointed to the bottom of the four steps leading up to the center of the stage. The ushers had already been given instructions that only one at a time were to be led up to the stage and they were to wait until he walked through the tabernacle with each one. Once the person received their healing, then, and only then would they escort the next person up onto the stage.

The line began to form and grow. Apparently, some folks that didn't raise their hand were also in line. Probably too scared or not sure about what to make of all this. The crowd fell into a quite murmur as the Reverend Mathew walked to center stage again and addressed the congregation. "My friends, we are all so lucky to be here today. Because today you are going to see things you have never seen before. Do you believe that?" The people screamed and clapped and yelled, "Yes. Praise Jesus. Amen." The Reverend now spoke directly to those in line. He pointed at them and said, "Loved ones, oh yes, you are all loved. The folks here love you, God

105

loves you, and I love all of God's children." Everyone was nodding in agreement. "And today, today we shall all bear testament to that love. Did He not say, in John 14:12, Verily I say unto you he that believeth in Me, and the works that I do he will do also; and greater works than these shall he do because I go to the Father." Again, the crowd erupted into praise. "Did He not say that whatever you do in my name, that I will do?" More screaming and louder praising. No one caught the small omission, that right after that last verse, the rest of it was, "…so that the Father may be glorified in the Son." Reverend Mathew subconsciously wanted that glory for himself. He went on. "He didn't say some things, He didn't say most things, He said whatever you ask in My name that I will do. So, I'm going to ask one question only this one time, to everyone here. Listen, listen to me, I'm only going to ask this question once. Listen." It took about 20 seconds for the crowd to come to a complete silence. "Listen."

The Reverend Mathew was almost whispering into the microphone. "This is the one question I have for all of you. Do….you….believe?" Reverend Mathew got the response he wanted. The congregation went wild with cheers of yes, and yeah, and praise Jesus. This continued for almost a whole minute. Reverend Mathew had to calm them down again. "Okay, okay. Let's all settle down now and get to the Lord's business." He pointed at the first person in line. It was a young man that looked like he was in excellent health. Mathew was slightly perturbed. He was hoping for something a little more dramatic. The young man was escorted up onto the stage. Mathew approached him, looked him up and down and said, "Well, son, what are you doing here, you look like the captain of the local football team." The crowd laughed. "What's your name son?"

"Jeremy, Jeremy Betters."

"Well, Jeremy, what's a strong young man like you doing in a place like this?" Again, some scattered laughter. The Reverend Mathew acknowledged his small joke and nodded towards the crowd but then walked up to Jeremy and put his hand on his shoulder. "Son, I don't mean to poke any fun at you. And you wouldn't be up here on this stage unless you needed Gods help. Tell us, why are you here?" The young man was already welling with tears. Reverend Mathew held the microphone to the young man's lips. "Well, sir. You're right. I am…was, the captain of the football team at Jacksonville State University." The Reverend quickly moved the mic to his face and said, "I knew it!" The crowd gave a low laughter. "Go on, son."

"Well, I'm here because I need help. I thought I just had a simple headache. But I have them all the time. And I'm also having a difficult time remembering things." Jeremy started crying. "I can't do stuff like I used to. I, I have something called chronic traumatic encephalopathy which was the result of a severe concussion I suffered during a game about 9 months ago." The crowd was now completely silent. Jeremy was releasing every tear he ever held back. "So, I'll never play football again and, I know that may sound selfish, but it's the thing I love to do. This is my life. This is what I do. And I am here on this stage because I believe that God will help me." The crowd went back into its praising and yelling. Reverend Mathews help up one hand and the crowd quieted down. "Folks, I don't know about you, but I think that Jeremy needs to play football."

The crowd responded, "Yes, praise Jesus."

"I don't know about you, but I think Jeremy believes he will play football."

Again, the crowd answered, "Amen, praise the Lord."

"I don't know about you, but I'm ready to see God's work today."

This time the crowd was yelling out loud, "Yes, halleluiah, yes Lord."

The Reverend Mathew led Jeremy towards the tabernacle. The crowd became silent as they both entered. Once inside, even though it was quite dark, the Reverend Mathew asked Jeremy to close his eyes. "Son, I want you to pray. I want you to meditate on exactly what it is you want healed right now. You will feel my hand on your hand. Just relax and concentrate. In the darkness of the small room, Mathew took Jeremy's hand and slowly guided it to where he had Thomas' hand exposed. He placed Jeremy's hand on top of Thomas' hand and kept it there for a few seconds.

Jeremy could feel both hands and thought it was strange how one hand felt it was facing up and the other down. However, a few seconds later, Jeremey could definitely feel something happening. There was a warm sensation around his head. It seemed to be moving from the crown of his head to his neck and down his entire body. The next thing he noticed was that his headache was gone. He started crying again and Mathew knew it was done. He guided Jeremy out of the tabernacle and walked up to the microphone and said, "Jeremy, how do you feel?" Jeremy Betters could hardly speak, he hadn't gone more than a few seconds without some kind of pain in his head. Now it was gone, and his head was clear. Clearer than it ever was before. He yelled into the mic, "I'm healed! Reverend Mathew, thank you, thank you. It's amazing! I feel great! Thank you." The crowd was going wild again, and more people joined the line.

Mathew did not give thanks to God right away, he was enjoying the praise that was directed at himself. "Who's next?"

More people came up Reverend Mathew walked them into the tabernacle to receive their healing. Some had painful back problems. Some had some serious diseases and although they were healed, no one could actually see any infirmities being healed. Finally, a few went up with noticeable infirmities like Mrs. Bilks, who had a case of crippling arthritis. When she came out healed, the crowd really went wild. But there were still a few scattered sceptics in the crowd, until Gina Wade and her wheelchair were pushed up to the front of the stage. Gina Wade was Tallapoosa's local radio celebrity.

Next to Rhubard Jones, she was the next most known name in radio in the state of Georgia. She was born in the local hospital, graduated at the local high school, went to the University of Georgia but never finished for reasons she would never reveal. She got a job as a local radio talk show host and never looked back. Everybody knew who Gina Wade was. She also made the local papers 6 years ago when a drunk driver hit her car and left her paralyzed from the waist down. And had now wheeled herself up to the front of the line. 'Deja'vu' Mathew thought as he watched her rolling up slowly, hesitant, reluctant but with a sad hopefulness as if she knew she was going to be disappointed. Yet, there was no denying what she had just seen with her own two eyes and so, with determined faith, she pushed the wheels of her chair closer and closer to the stage.

People were moving forward, and it was getting crowded at the front. The tightly joined bodies raised the temperature even higher than it already was. Everyone's faces were glistening with sweat. Everyone was vying for position to see the next miracle. Reverend Mathew held his hands up and towards Gina Wade. He motioned for those around the front of the stage to make way and allow this woman onto the stage. There was a small ramp next to the stairs built for this exact reason. Reverend Mathew stood there, arms out, smiling, almost drowning in anticipation of the praise he was soon to receive. Finally, as Gina Wade landed at the front of the stage, he motioned to a couple of ushers to push her up the rest of the way. She was gently guided to the feet of Reverend Mathew. She gazed up at him, and in the back on her mind she thought, *'He seems so...normal. So plain.'* But she knew what she had witnessed, and she wanted to be the next miracle.

Reverend Mathew felt almost too comfortable staring down at Gina, as if he held some sort of power over her, which at the moment, he did. He knew that once she stepped out of that wheelchair, he would be recognized as a true conduit for God Himself. Maybe even a new Messiah. Mathew's head was now spinning, rushing from one thought to another. What if he did claim to be the new deliverer? What if he did claim to be the second coming of the Messiah? After this moment, when this woman walks again for the first time since her accident, who would deny anything he says? Who would dare?

Reverend Mathew knelt down and took Gina's right hand and held them in both of his. He stared into her eyes. They were welled up with tears. He smiled and her tears began to pour. He placed one hand on her head, she closed her eyes, he spoke, he still had his mic on so the entire congregation could hear his words. "Gina, I know this is tough for you." She could only nod. Mathew continued, "I know you think that this is a long shot. That healing is for everyone else, but not for you. How could it be that you could just walk off this chair?" She just kept nodding in agreement. "But I'm here to tell you something. Gina, open your eyes and look at me." She opened her eyes and stared into Mathew's eyes. Gina couldn't help noticing that they were plain and empty, void of anything special, yet, she had to believe.

She held her eyes steady on his. "Gina," Mathew continued" as sure as you are looking at me right now, as sure as the next breath of air you're about to take, you are going to rise up from this chair today, and you are going to walk. Do you believe me?" She nodded and the crowd was stirring back up. There was a tamed excitement. Reverend Mathew raised his voice and said, "Then Gina, there's only one thing left to do. Let's go claim your miracle!" The crowd became a wild frenzy.

Reverend Mathew stood up and walked around Gina's wheelchair and began pushing her into the Tabernacle. A couple of ushers offered to help, but he held them back. He opened the door and pushed Gina Wade into the small dark replica. Inside, Gina could not see a thing. There were no strange odors or sounds, just darkness. She heard Reverend Mathew's voice coming out of the darkness. "Gina, stretch out your hand." She did. Mathew found it in the dark. "Gina, I'm going to ask God to heal you now. Close your eyes and simply believe." She did. Mathew slowly guided her hand towards Thomas' hand, and he placed it on top. Gina thought it felt odd, because one hand felt different than the other, but she quickly dismissed it and just meditated on her prayers. Suddenly, there it was, she was wondering if she was going to feel anything. Sure enough, there was definitely some tingling in her feet. Her excitement level rose through the roof. Her anticipation was ripping out of her skin. *'Could it be? Is this happening?'* Gina Wade could feel the warm tingling sensation moving, traveling up her legs, through her calves, her knees, her thighs. She had never felt anything in her legs since the accident, but now she could actually feel something, but what was this?

The tingling moved all the way up through her torso, even up to the top of her head. She could definitely feel her legs. Feel them, as if nothing was wrong. She was so excited she didn't realize that Mathew was speaking to her until he finally had to raise his voice, "Gina!" She was startled, "What?"

"Are you okay?"

"Yes, more than okay."

"I understand, please, remain in your chair until we get outside of the Tabernacle, okay?"

Reverend Mathew pushed her outside of the Tabernacle for all to see. While standing behind her, he placed his right hand on her right shoulder and addressed her. "Gina. You are here as a testament to God. You are here so that there may be witnesses to His power and love. Gina, in Jesus name," Mathew shouted, "stand up and walk!" The entire congregation held its breath and watched as Gina placed both hands on the arm rest of her wheelchair and effortlessly raised herself up and took a few steps with such ease, that it would have been impossible to think that she was ever crippled at all.

The crowd went mad. Praising the Lord and praising the Reverend Mathew, who was basking in the unbridled adulation that was being poured upon him. This was going to be a great day indeed. People were healed, Gina Wade was walking around as if nothing ever happened. No signs of clumsiness nor were there any hints of muscular atrophy, which would puzzle her doctors for years to come. The stage was set for the Reverend Mathew to place his mark in church history. But something happened. The line for receiving healing got longer, because it was now filled with even the most skeptical nay sayers. But there was stirring in the crowd. It started with someone saying, "Hey, my migraine is gone!" Someone else said, "My arm was hurting for weeks, the doctors didn't know what it was, and it just now healed. It feels great!" Suddenly everyone was making similar comments. In fact, unknown to everyone there, they in fact *were* all healed. Everyone, even those standing outside the huge tent.

They started asking the Reverend what was going on. Mathew didn't know what the heck was going on, but he had to play it off as if he knew. Mathew walked up to center stage and addressed everyone. He had to play this right. "Ladies and gentlemen, I have decided that the Lords work cannot be confined to the walls of this small replica." He said pointing to the Tabernacle. "No. This cannot be the way God intended to help the fine people of Tallapoosa. No! There is no time to wait for such long lines and melodramatics." He held his hand towards the congregation and yelled. "In Jesus name, you are all healed. And they all said.." "Amen!" There was much joy that evening. Everyone wanted to have the Reverend Mathew over for dinner or to give a speech somewhere or visit one of the churches in the area. It was at first, a little overwhelming, but Mathew managed to accept a few dinner engagements for the next few days. For now, he had to find out what had happened with all the healings that occurred. It was almost a disaster. Luckily he was able to think on his feet and make up a quick excuse. He was going to have a few words with Thomas, for sure.

Getting back to the hotel room was no easy task. Mathew had to hide from the crowd that was seeking him out to either thank him or to ask him to heal a friend or a relative. But Mathew had given strict instructions to his ushers that everyone was to leave and that he would not be seeing anyone after the sermon. They were to tell the people that he was always exhausted after every healing, and everyone seemed to understand and so they left him alone. This gave Mathew the opportunity to transfer Thomas secretly back to the hotel room.

The nights offered no reprieve from the weather. The air was still thick and damp. Mathew was thankful for the cool air back at the hotel, though it seemed that even the air that was blowing out from the air conditioner felt thick, and heavy. Thomas Grady was in his customary position, tied and gaged to a chair. Mathew dragged the other chair that was in the room, next to Thomas. Mathew leaned in close to Thomas and calmly said, "Thomas, if I take this tape off your mouth, do you promise not to yell? If you do, I'll just leave it on. You understand?" Thomas nodded, yes. Mathew removed the tape as mercifully as possible, but the sting didn't bother Thomas. "Okay," Mathew began, "what the hell just happened back there? Why did you heal everyone?"

"What?" Thomas replied with just a hint of confusion because he knew something happened, he just wasn't quite sure what or how. "Look Thomas, there is no reason to be coy with me. I know and you know what you did. I just want to know why? And do you plan on disrupting my services every time?"

Thomas was genuinely not sure, but still answered, "Look, I don't know what happened. I didn't do anything, you're the one controlling it all."

"Oh, I wish I was, Thomas, but this is not me healing an entire congregation of people with magic powers. Only you can do that. So, what I'm asking you right now is this, are you going to let me do my work, or are you intent on continuing to sabotage God's will?" Thomas remained calm, he felt he could maintain a little control if he didn't let the other person think he was scared. Thomas sat up a little taller and said, "Look, Reverend, or Father or Pastor, or whatever you are."

"I'm a Reverend." Mathew corrected him.

"Okay, fine, Reverend Mathew, I don't know what's going on. I don't really have control of what I do. It, this power or whatever you want to call it, kind of does whatever it wants when it wants." Thomas said. Thomas had noticed that he really couldn't feel anything during these events. In fact, he used to feel something, but now, it's like he's not even aware that anything is happening at all. However, not controlling what he did gave Thomas a feeling of being disconnected from this abnormality. But the truth is, he wished sometimes he could control it, then for sure he would have more control over his life. This way he wouldn't have to deal with the Reverend Mathews' and Walter Porters' of this world. In Thomas' mind he could feel that all of this healing stuff was incongruent with reality, with life, with everything.

Mathew thought about Thomas' response for a minute and said, "Fine. I'll just play it by ear. If I see that you somehow decided to heal everyone, I'll just throw out the same old spiel. It will only make everyone happy. What's the worst that could happen?" They both stared at each other for a few seconds and realized that neither one of them had a response to that question. Mathew slapped both of his knees as he stood and proclaimed, "Okay, then. It's settled. We'll start with a few personal healings, and then, if I noticed that everyone in the whole dang place is healed, I'll just use the same ole line." Again, they both just stared at each other. They stared into each other's eyes for another few awkward silent seconds, then Mathew said, "I'm starving." "Me too." Thomas replied. Mathew ordered food and they both enjoyed a temporary truce while they ate.

Mathew had awakened to a cool morning, and he was thankful for it. His bedroom had a small balcony and he stepped outside to feel a slight breeze which was saturated with the scent of the local indigenous flowers. He closed his eyes in an effort to enjoy the moment when he was startled by a knock on the door. Mathew was very cautious, so he slowly walked up to the door

112

as quietly as possible and looked through the peephole. It was only a hotel bus boy. Mathew spoke through the door, "Yes?"

"I have a message from the front desk." It was a young voice, a thin lad, not more than 23 years old.

"What is the message?" Mathew asked.

"Well, the message is that you have a lot of messages at the desk, sir."

"Why didn't they just call me?" Mathew winched at his comment because he remembered that he had told the front desk that he would not be taking any phone calls from anybody. The boy responded, "Well, sir, ah, you said.."

"Yes, sorry, you are right, I just remembered I left instructions that I was not to be called. Thank you."

"Your welcomed, sir." Mathew noticed that the boy remained at the door for a few extra seconds then left. Mathew then realized the boy was probably waiting to see if he would tip him. Mathew felt a little bad and made a mental note to give that kid a tip later.

Mathew looked to see how Thomas was doing. He had tied him to the extra bed next to him. Thomas appeared to be in a deep restful sleep. '*Strange*,' Mathew thought, that this young man could rest so peacefully in light of his situation. Mathew attributed Thomas' peace to God's good will and if there is peace in it, then he himself must also be doing God's will. It had always been easy for Mathew to convince himself that what he was doing was the right thing. It was in this mental manipulation of himself that Mathew found and claimed his own impunity. Mathew woke up Thomas and told him that he was going downstairs to pick up some messages and that he would bring back some breakfast. Thomas looked up with squinted eyes and simply said, "Pancakes." And went back to sleep.

About 30 min later, Mathew came back to the room with pancakes and a huge stack of messages. He must have had at least 100 messages. The hotel didn't have anywhere to put them and that's why they sent the bus boy, whom Mathew had found and gave him a five-dollar bill. The boy was thankful, and Mathew's soul was cleansed. Five bucks worth of cheap absolution. It was a bargain. Mathew opened the door to his room and found Thomas wide awake.

"Good morning, Thomas."

"Good morning. Pancakes?"

"Is that all you can think of?" Mathew said with feigned displeasure.

113

"I'm hungry."

They went through their ritual of untying and tying Thomas up from the bed to the chair. Truth be told, Thomas could have given Mathew a run for his money if they were to have a physical altercation, but why? Thomas knew that it would be a matter of a day or two and Mario was going to pop up out of nowhere, beat this guy up and take him home. It's what Mario does. It been over a year since he got rid of those images of carnage at Walter Porter's house, but Thomas had been able to live with those repressed images and managed to continue living a normal life...sort of.

Among the many messages that Mathew had at the front desk, was a letter from Gina Wade, the paraplegic woman that was healed. Mathew was just now learning that she is one of the local celebrities with her own radio talk show. In the letter, Gina was expressing her eternal gratefulness and was determined to give Mathew the fame he deserves. She asked Mathew to do her show with such deep adulation that he was simply overwhelmed.

This was always Mathews weakness, his longing for praise, wither earned or stolen, it was his secret insatiable addiction. Mathew had experienced this ineffable praise in large dosages the night before when everyone was healed, and they all thanked him. Even though he knew Thomas was the one who did it, he didn't care, he *felt* like he did it, like he was responsible and without him, Gina Wade would not be walking today and in some strange and perverted way, it was true. He was, after all, the person who brought all this to the quaint town of Tallapoosa.

It was Monday and the interview with Gina Wade was scheduled for the following Wednesday starting at 6pm and ending at 7:30. It was only two days away. Mathew had called Gina and agreed to the date and time. For some unknown reason, Wednesday's was when The Gina Wade Show got its biggest audience. Mathew realized that after this little show, he would be asked to do bigger ones and his popularity would grow exponentially. He had to start planning his next move soon. He was thinking about going to South Carolina. He was partial to the charm and seduction of Southern hospitality. Besides, nothing wrong with hanging out in the bible belt for a little while longer.

Gina Wade had asked Mathew if he wanted to come in early and go over some of the prepared questions, but to her surprise, Mathew declined and said he would rather just show up and start the show. Gina thought it was the Rev. Mathew's way of 'keeping it real.' But in truth, Mathew didn't want to go over any probing questions that would just lead to suspicion.

114

Wednesday evening arrived. "Hello and welcome to the Gina Wade Show, my name is Gina Wade and today I have an amazing guest for you all. I have sitting right here in front of me the man we all saw this past Sunday who may have possibly performed more miracles in one day than Jesus Himself. He likes to be referred to as simply, The Rev. Mathew. Hello Rev. and thank you so much for coming on my show."

"Hello Gina, thank you for having me, and the pleasure is all mine."

"Well, let's cut straight to it shall we?"

"Of course." They both had headphones on and looked at each other as they spoke into their mics. Gina continued. "Rev. Mathew, I have to tell you, after last Sunday, I have so many questions I don't know where to begin."

"Well, Gina, I hope I can help answer some of those questions. But as you know, God deals in mysteries, and I may not have an answer to all your questions. And so, I fear you may end up with even more questions than you started with. But I'll do my best." Mathew was actually enjoying the interview and was feeling quite relaxed. Gina went on.

"Rev, could you tell us how long you've been performing these incredible miracles and how is it that we and/or the world have not heard about your absolutely incredible powers until now?" Gina realized she misspoke, she meant to say incredible abilities, powers sounded a little cartoonish. But Mathew caught it and liked it.

Incredible powers, Mathew thought. He let that stolen praise sink deep into his veins for a moment and basked in the fake euphoria it created.

"Rev?"

"What? Oh, I'm so sorry Gina, I had very little sleep last night." Mathew lied.

"Oh, were you worried about our interview?" Gina teased. They both smiled and Mathew said, "No, not all, I was looking forward to it. But prayer and meditation can be hard at times for the dedicated souls. As you know, even Jesus wept tears of blood in the Garden of Gethsemane." Gina tilted her head at this comment and couldn't help herself and replied, "I believe the scripture says that Jesus prayed so hard that His *sweat* was *like* drops of blood, but not actual blood. Oh, forgive me Rev, I didn't mean to correct you."

"It's quite alright, and you are correct, Gina, that is what the scripture says. Even I fall victim to bouts of senility now and then. I'm afraid you'll just have to forgive my indulgence." Mathew said with a short fake laugh.

115

Gina continued with the same question, "Of course. As I was saying. How is it that the world does not know who Rev Mathew is? You are clearly a chosen messenger of God to be able to do such wonders as I witnessed last Sunday. And I will tell you this. After today, I will make it one of my missions in my life to make sure that the world knows who The Rev Mathew is."

"Oh, my. Thank you for that wonderful praise, Gina. But I would really just like to live a simple life. Besides, I suspect that after tonight, you may have started to accomplish your mission by making me famous, at least here in your beautiful little town of Tallapoosa, Georgia."

"Well, well, Rev. It appears some of our Southern charm is rubbing off on you."

The interview went on for just over an hour. Gina constantly praising Mathew and Mathew humbly taking just little more than half the credit from God. Gina Wade made a comment that would be repeated in the local papers and other shows. She confessed to The Rev Mathew that although before the healing, she did not pray to God every day, but from now on, she will be thanking Him every day. Although the station was willing to extend the show, Mathew had to decline the extended interview. He thanked Gina and left. The next day, Rev Mathew would be the talk of the town. Not only in Tallapoosa and many neighboring towns, but a few of the bigger news agencies got wind of what happened, and they reported bits and pieces. But once the news starts talking about healings and miracles, certain people start to pay close attention.

Mathew was standing outside the studio where he had just finished the interview with Gina Wade. It was almost 8pm. The streets were not well lit, but at this time of the year, there was still a hint of residual light in the sky from the late sunsets. Mathew started walking back to the hotel. He stopped to get Thomas something to eat figuring that by now that boy was probably starving. Young boys never seem to get enough food. He pondered his situation and fantasied about being famous. Everyone will know him. Mathew felt like he won the lottery. In fact, this kind of fame would probably somehow make him rich. He didn't know how, but the thought of it excited him. And the more excited he got, the more blind he became to the fact that it would be impossible for him to keep up such an enormous charade.

When Mathew got to his room he walked inside and placed the food on the small stationary desk which was standard in every room. Mathew went over to Thomas to slide his chair next to the desk so Thomas could eat when Mathew noticed something. He looked at Thomas and saw that he had forgotten to place a gag over his mouth. Thomas noticed Mathews' confusion and

116

said, "Yeah, you forgot to place that gag on me since yesterday." Mathew was perplexed by the nonchalant attitude Thomas was portraying. He had to ask, "Did you call someone?" Thomas didn't make eye contact, he merely stared at the food and said, "Nope." Again, with the unusual lack of concern in his voice which only made Mathew more nervous. Mathew was not sure what to think, but, if the cops don't come breaking down his door in the next couple of minutes, he'll just assume that Thomas is playing along with him…for now.

"Okay, Thomas. I believe you. Why don't I just untie one of your hands, then and you could eat."

"Sure. What is it?"

"Just a cheeseburger and some fries. This town closes early and there were very little options at this time of the night. Is that okay?" Mathew asked with just a little tinge of obsequiousness.

"Yeah. That's fine. Thanks."

"Great. Well, enjoy." Thomas began eating his food and Mathew sat on his bed mentally scratching his head. He watched as Thomas was eating his food as if he didn't have a care in the world. '*Strange.*' Nevertheless, Mathew now felt he had to take some sort of precaution with Thomas. He went into the restroom and prepared another dose of Dr. Max Beauvoir potion just in case. He heard Thomas saying something, he walked out of the restroom and asked, "Did you say something, Thomas?"

"Yeah, I was saying that you won't need that."

"Need what?"

"Look, Rev, I remember that smell. Whatever it was you used to knock me out, you don't need it. I ain't going anywhere." Mathew was still unsure as to what Thomas was up to. "Well, Thomas, I don't know what to think. I did after all abduct you and forced you to do things you don't want to do, so, I'm thinking, yes, I may need it. You see Thomas, I still think you do not understand the big picture here. This is bigger than both of us. We have been chosen to do God's work. We must continue to heal the people who are without hope. You have the power but not the divine guidance. You have the gift but lack the divine will. Surely you can see how God has placed you in my hands, Thomas." Mathew waited for the reply.

Thomas was slightly put off by the fact that he couldn't enjoy his food. He was actually quite hungry. But he had to respond, he could see Mathew staring at him with enough intensity to boil water. "Rev, I may not see your big picture, but I see mine and it's not the same as yours. You may have been chosen by God, but he didn't choose me. I don't know what this power is that I have but I can tell you this, it is not a divine power. I can't explain it to you, but it's not a gift, it's a…it's like…" Thomas was trying to come up with a word that he felt best described it. Finally, the word came to him, "It's more like…an intrusion. An intrusion into here." Thomas said while waving his one free hand around the whole room. "It's intruding into our space, our world. It's not a force of good or evil, it's simply a force. Not even a force of nature because it's so incongruous with our world. You have no idea what you're playing with Rev Mathew. And no good can come from what you are doing and especially *how* you are doing it." Thomas was making enough sense for Mathew to begin questioning himself about what he should do next. There was no time to think. Mathew felt a sense of panic and quickly pounced on Thomas and held the damp rag onto Thomas' face and waited for him to pass out. Mathew didn't want to keep experimenting with the voodoo concoction, but he had no choice. He needed time to think, and this was the only way he knew how to buy time. He tied Thomas back up and this time he remembered to gag him.

Mathew stood up most of the night pondering his plight. He wanted to stop and let Thomas go. But that meant *he* would have to stop. There would be no more fame no money, but more importantly, no more healings, and Mathew could not accept that. Mathew knew he was selected specifically for this very difficult ministry. He was chosen to carry out the Lords will. He had to continue no matter what the consequences may be to himself, he had to put God's work first.

The morning came and Mathew felt at peace with his decision to keep Thomas and use him to carry on with God's work. His panic had left him, and he felt like he was back in control. He went out for a cup of coffee and to show there were no hard feelings, he'll bring back a big stack of pancakes for Thomas. Mathew had his coffee in a small café located a couple of blocks from the hotel. Some of the locals noticed him and they all came eagerly to say hi and thank him. Mathew was enjoying the first taste of being a celebrity, and he loved it. He finished his coffee, got the pancakes to go and walked back to the hotel. Mathew was in a very good mood, recalling how one of the locals asked him for an actual autograph. '*Wow, an autograph!*' He Thought, '*that's amazing.*'

Mathew opened the door to his room and almost fell back from the shock and horror of what he saw. "Hello Rev Mathew," Thomas said while sitting on a chair, untied and ungagged. There was a tall rough muscular man standing next to him. "Allow me to introduce you, Rev Mathew,

118

this is Mario, Mario, this is The Rev Mathew." "Thomas!" Mathew almost yelled his name, he clasped his hands together in a sign of supplication. His eyes immediately welled with tears. "Thomas, please! You can't leave. We have an enormous task before us. I beg you, please don't go." Mathew dropped to his knees and begged, "Please, Thomas, stay with me and let's heal the world together, my son." Mario started walking towards Mathew, but Thomas quickly held up a hand to stop him. Mario stopped. Thomas got up from his chair, walked over to Mathew and held out a hand to help him up.

"Rev. I can't go with you. I have no idea where I'm going from here. But you claim to know your path. This is a very good thing. To know your path, your direction in life whether through self-realization or divine intervention, it doesn't matter. The truth is, it's never about the final destination, it's the path, the journey that defines who we are." Mathew and Mario were both fixated on Thomas as he spoke with an unnatural maturity. Thomas continued, "Rev. I cannot go with you, but I will tell you this. Should your path be truly divine, then there is nothing you or I can do about that because by definition, it is not an obsession. But if your path was a product of your own obsession, well, that means that you do not have control of it, that it is in fact a disorder of the brain which means, Rev. that if I touch you, it's possible that you will be cured of that obsession. Do you understand what I'm saying?"

Rev Mathew thought about it for a moment. Was Thomas saying that he would take away his desire to follow God's will to heal people? Was he saying that he is mentally ill? Was this even possible? No, this can't be. Mathew raised his hand and pointed at Thomas, "Thomas, perhaps you are mistaking passion for obsession? Desire instead of obsession. Eagerness or ambition? What makes you such a medical expert on such things? My intentions are pure and of God!" "Are you sure?" Thomas said calmly. "Did God tell you to commit kidnapping? To steal a young man away from his family and force him to do your bidding? To lie in front of a congregation about things you cannot do. Does all this sound like the work of your God to you, Rev?"

Mathew was beginning to hyperventilate. Mario went back to full alert. Thomas felt the tension increase. Finally, Thomas spoke to Mario and simply said, "Hold him." They tied and gagged Rev. Mathew to a chair. They told him they'd call someone to come get him in a couple of hours. Thomas and Mario walked through the lobby of the hotel and outside into a bright sunny day. Mario said, "Okay, let's head out to the airport. I told your parents I'd have you

119

home in two or three days."

"Can we drive?"

"Do you know where you are?"

"Georgia?"

"Yeah, Georgia." Mario said as if it shouldn't be a surprise. "That's just over 2000 miles away from home." Mario continued, "We can drive for a few hours. I suppose Alabama has an airport or two. You know your parents are worried about you, right?"

"No, they're not anymore." Thomas said with a calmness in his voice, "Because they know you came for me. But I'll call them. You got a phone?" Mario reached into his back pocket and gave Thomas a phone. They got into the rental car and started driving west.

They stopped for some road snacks and water and headed towards Alabama. They drove in silence for a few miles until finally Mario broke the silence.

"So, what was all that about back there?"

"What was what all about?"

"You know, all this talk about paths and journeys back there with Mr. Healer. That didn't sound like you. Something up?" Mario was pretending to be mildly interested, but Thomas could tell he was actually very curious. Thomas looked straight ahead while he spoke.

"I don't know, Mario, I feel like, well, like I'm changing?"

"Changing? Like how?" Mario asked, but this time with real concern and genuine interest.

"As usual, I'm not 100% sure. I just know that I am. I feel like I know stuff I shouldn't know. Does that make sense?"

"No." Thomas looked at Mario to see if he was kidding. He wasn't.

"What I mean," Thomas continued to explain, "is that, well, for instance, back there with the Rev guy, I didn't know how I knew that obsession can be a disorder. Why would I know that? I never read or studied anything about that stuff. Why would I know that?"

"I don't know."

"Look, Mario, if you're gonna give me responses that are three words or less this entire trip we could just head to the nearest airport right now."

"Okay, okay, I get it. I was just giving you room to express your thoughts."

"Okay, that's better."

"Okay."

"Okay. Anyway." Thomas continued, "I can feel things coming into my head."

"How do you mean?"

"It's hard to explain. It's like my head feels like a piggy bank and someone is steadily dropping coins inside it. But it's like pennies only. You know what I mean? It feels like I can understand things I didn't before.

"You gonna have enough pennies to buy lunch by the time we stop?" Mario said, trying to make light of the conversation because he could see that Thomas was concerning himself with his own words. Thomas looked at Mario and said, "Ha, very funny." Mario reached over and put a hand on Thomas' shoulder and said, "Look, I see you're concerned. You don't know what it is, no one does. We're all just going to have to go through it together, alright. I'll be right here for you no matter what happens." Thomas always felt better, safer, when Mario was around. Mario held up his hand and made a fist, Thomas gave him a strong bump and Mario repeated, "No matter what happens."

For the next few hours Thomas contemplated his life. He knew that there will always be people with nefarious intentions pursuing him. There will always be evil and rapacious people in the world that will be trying to take him and control this thing he has. During this long drive, Thomas made a decision. He decided that he will stop ignoring this power, or force, or whatever it is, and he will try to understand it. He always wished he had some control of it, he also had a fear of it as well. But one thing was certain, if he *could* somehow control it, then that means he would be responsible for the outcomes, good or bad. Perhaps Thomas would not be so eager to accept this responsibility if he knew what happened to Jackie Calloway.

Hours later, the Rev Mathew was still sitting in his hotel room contemplating his future. As it turns out, he was not cured of being obsessed. Turns out he was actually passionate about what he was doing. He really did want to help and cure people, he just didn't have the power, and at times, he didn't have the faith either. But faith can be fickle. It comes and goes in different magnitudes. At this moment, faith is modulating in Mathew's heart. Does he have the strength and the will to continue God's work as a mere mortal? Performing healings on a hit and miss bases? The one thing he did receive from Thomas was some clarity in his thinking. Not from his touch, but from his words.

Mathew concluded that he did not think he could face his own shame. Lying to people, breaking the law and not to mention breaking a few commandments. Maybe he would follow his

121

dream another time. Was it even his dream? Was he simply chasing that euphoric feeling of pure faith he had when he witnessed that fake healing so many years ago? For now, The Rev. Mathew decided he would simply leave town and suspend his untenable lofty goals and quietly move into a temporary state of obscurity.

Thomas and Mario drove for hours. They spoke of many things, some trivial, some a little deep for Thomas. Though there were moments when Thomas would surprise Mario with his spurts of deeper understanding of certain subject matters that a kid his age would normally not have a complete grasp of. *Maybe Thomas was becoming smarter? Older? Wiser?* Mario thought about it and couldn't quite figure out what was happening with Thomas. There was one thing for sure, Thomas was maturing.

Mario wasn't sure if that would make things better or worse for Thomas. How does someone come to terms with such a thing? And as if on cue, Thomas asked Mario, "Do you think that I'm committing a sin by not sharing this gift, or whatever it is, with the world? Should I just go around healing people all day long? I mean, why not? It's not like it's costing me anything. Why shouldn't I?" Thomas could tell he caught Mario off guard and said, "Sorry, I didn't mean to put this on you." Mario replied, "No, its fine, I just never really thought about it. Give me a minute to think about an answer." "Okay." Was all Thomas said, and let Mario contemplate the depth of a question that would have been considered rhetorical any other time in human history.

They both sat in silence for what seemed a long time. Mario was watching the road while glancing around at the countryside and Thomas was mostly staring at a fixed point in space, not noticing the beautiful countryside with lush green rolling hills and meadows. Blooming trees would occasionally line both sides of the road in a gentle silent explosion of color. All this went unnoticed as both men contemplated a scenario better left to the philosophers, scholars, and scientist of the world. Then again, who would really be best equipped to answer such a question? One thing for sure, Mario definitely believed he was not the erudite person to be tasked with the profundity of such an inquiry.

Mario looked over at Thomas and could see that he was deep in thought. Maybe too deep. A kid his age shouldn't have to carry this kind of burden. Mario decided to start a conversation and said, "Hey, Thomas." Thomas didn't reply. "Hey, Thomas." Still no reply. Mario reached over and tapped Thomas on the head while speaking a little louder, "Yo, dude!" Thomas reflectively swiped Mario's hand away and replied with just a hint of annoyance, "What?"

"What, what?" Mario said.

"Yeah, what?" Thomas replied.

Mario glanced over at Thomas and said, "What, that's what. Yeah, that's right."

"What? Mario, what the heck are you talking about?"

"You know what."

"No, I don't, what?

"I'm talking about what, that's what."

Thomas finally got that Mario was just teasing him and they both started laughing. Mario rubbed Thomas' head and said, "Look, we both need to relax here. I thought about what you said, you know, about why don't you just go around healing everybody and their mother."

"And?" Thomas said with added anticipation.

"Well, I came to a conclusion."

"Yes?" Came Thomas' word, drenched in curiosity, although he was about to be sorely disappointed.

"Well, I've come to the conclusion that I am definitely not the person best suited to answer this question." Thomas stared at Mario and responded with a perturbed taste in his voice. "What? Why would you think that?"

"Because I'm not the science guy. You know me, I'm more the soldier guy." Mario thought he was off the hook with his response. But Thomas pushed, "Okay *soldier guy*," Thomas said with air quotations, "What is your opinion, then? You don't need to be a *science guy*," More air quotes, "to tell me what you think."

"Alright, alright. I'll give you my opinion." Mario said using air quotes himself on the word opinion.

"Okay. That's all I want."

"Okay then, here it is. I think there's nothing wrong with you going around healing people. The problem is..."

"There's a problem with that?"

"Hold your horses, buddy, just calm your llama and let me finish. You want my opinion or not?"

"Okay, go on, sssch."

"Really? You're gonna ssch me?"

"What?"

"Never mind, look. I think it's okay, it's a good thing to go around healing people, but how are you going to choose who gets healed and who doesn't? What's going to be your criteria? And what are you basing it on? Good deeds? Morals? Ethics? Religion? You gonna drop everyone's name in a bowl and reach in and pick one? Also, I don't know what the unintended consequences will be. I don't have the answer, but as an example, what if you cured everyone? What happens to the hundreds of thousands of jobs depending on the healthcare industry? I'm sure it goes further than that, I'm just not the person to answer this question that way you deserve to know."

Thomas contemplated Mario's answer. It was good. It gave him a little bit more perspective. It helped him to make his next decision. Thomas looked straight ahead at the road in front of him. This time he noticed the rich colors of the flowers spreading out onto the horizon. The land was flat, the sky was a bright powder blue dabbed with scattered bright white puffy clouds. Now he could smell the flowers, taste the fresh air and he became invigorated by the feral scent of nature. It was clean, it was good.

Thomas continued looking straight ahead as he spoke to Mario. "I've made a decision."
Mario asked, "Really? Do tell."
"I've decided that I'm going to allow a select small group of experts explore this phenomenon that is happening with me."
"Hmm, I don't know if that's a good idea either, buddy. There's a lot of unknown factors in that scenario. The biggest one being trust. How do you know who to trust and who's going to try to exploit you? You do remember that you may hold the current record for number of times being kidnapped, right?"
"I know, but this is different. I understand that those people, whether mentally stable or not, were acting in their own best interest. But I'm hoping to put together a small group that has a more scientific and or at least a more benevolent outlook in life."
"Benevolent? Where'd you pick up that word?"
"I don't know, I just know it."
"Just saying, I've never heard you speak the way you're speaking now."
"That makes two of us."
"Well, it could just be that you're maturing."
"Maybe."

Secmet, Inc

It took almost five months to find a facility that suited Thomas and Mario's ideal design and location. Once they found it, they started putting out classified ads. All interviews were by phone only. All interviews were performed by Mario, as Thomas felt his voice was too high to be taken seriously. Once they were satisfied with their choices, they arranged a date to meet them individually all on the same day. They thought about meeting them on separate days, but why waste that kind of time. They were going to be in or out. May as well find out who's in and who's out as soon as possible.

They had all requested to meet in person, but Mario felt that their questions would be too esoteric and would jeopardize the goal they were trying to accomplish. Interviewing all these people that were all experts in their field was a lot trickier than Mario expected. But, at the end of the day, or rather, at the end of over 2 months of faking his way through dozens of interviews, the meetings were set.

The five people that were picked to join this venture were based solely on their abilities. It was not the best way to do this. But just in case, Thomas and Mario had at least several others in the same professions on stand-by in case one of them either didn't work out, or for whatever reason, decided not to be a part of their endeavor.

All five interviewees showed up on time. There was no one in the lobby of SECMET Inc. to greet them, only an intercom system with a handwritten note above it which stated, "Press when you have arrived." They only needed to press it once, since they all showed up on time. A voice came on the intercom and asked them to please have a seat, and someone will be with them in just a moment.

They looked around the unimpressive foray. Cheap furniture, dull paint, two fluorescent lamps on the ceiling and a slight odor of paint. They introduced each other and got to know each other's respective fields. No one really had a clue as to what exactly they would be doing here, but the pay was more than intriguing. After a few minutes, the voice in the intercom returned. "Good morning. Please enter when you hear the door buzz. Thank you." All five walked in unison towards the door. It was almost inaudible, but they heard the buzz and one of them opened the door and one by one, they walked in.

Inside, the facility looked much bigger than the outside. That's because it was. Part of the facility was constructed into the hillside. It was sparse for such a big place. A few scattered pieces of equipment. Some appeared to be still in plastic packaging. The lighting was good, and the temperature was noticeably ambient. Everything seemed normal enough. They all noticed a tall man, a bit menacing looking, walking towards them. It was Mario Reyes. He extended his hand as he greeted all of them and welcomed them to Secmet Inc. "Gentlemen, and ladies, if you'll please all follow me to the conference room.

Once they reached their destination and walked inside, that's when they knew something was up. The conference room was unlike any other room they've seen before. There was a standard long mahogany conference table in the middle of the room. At one end there were six chairs facing each other plus one at the end, or the head of the table depending, they assumed, on who sat where. The conference table was approximately 15 feet long, however, a few feet past the center of the table was a 2" bullet proof Plexiglas transparent wall. On the Plexiglas wall was a slot which allowed the conference table to continue on to the other side of the room. On the other end of the table were only two chairs, one on the side of the table, and one at the now obvious, head of the table.

The other side of the room seemed impenetrable. The slot that the table went through was so precise that they couldn't see any space around it. It was if the Plexiglas was molded around the table. Also, at the head of the table was a small, thin standalone microphone. Mario began the proceedings. "Ladies and gentlemen. My name is Mario." No last name was given. "Should you choose to be a part of our endeavor, we will need all of you to sign the non-disclosure agreements that are placed in front of you. Once you sign it, you may take a copy of it to your lawyers if you have any questions regarding its content. In a nutshell, they are standard NDA's stating that you will not speak, tell or share to anyone, including your family members, which includes spouses, about what you will be seeing here or doing here. This is not a government project, but rather a privately funded project, thus the unusual salary offers. This meeting will begin once all of you have signed your NDA's. Once the meeting is over, we will see you all here in 3 days" Dr. Anastasia Semenov, the chemist, interjected, "Sir, ah, Mr. Mario.." Mario interrupted, "Just Mario, please."

"Okay," she proceeded. "Three days from now is a Sunday?"

"And?" She thought twice before responding. "Ah, well, nothing. That's fine."

"Okay, moving on. Allow me to address the comment by Mrs…" She interrupted him, "That's Miss, but I prefer doctor."

"Okay, moving on. As Dr. Semenov stated, we will be meeting this Sunday. But we typically do not work on Sundays. However, to be clear, you will have access to this facility 24/7. Although you will not be expected to keep a standard schedule, we do ask that you perform your tasks in a timely manner, and we expect nothing less than your best. One last thing for now. Should you choose to be a part of this group, you will not be allowed to bring in or take out any pictures, videos or recording devices while you are inside this facility. You will be checked, you will be monitored, and we will know, so please, no silly attempts at breaking these rules. Besides, everything here is recorded and is available to you to see and play back any time you want. But only while you are here." There was no need to pause for suspense, as the room was already filled with it.

Dr. Derek Hurd, Astrophysicist commented. "Mr. Mar..ah, Mario, what is it exactly that we'll be doing here?" Mario walked towards the back of the room while answering him, "I'm afraid I'm not the one to tell you that, but he is." Mario motioned with his arm for everyone to look towards the head of the table and said, "Ladies and gentlemen, allow me to introduce Mr. Thomas Secmet. Thomas decided to use an alias for multiple reasons. All eyes turned to the front of the table and most of them made an audible noise that sounded like confusion. Most of their mouths were open as they witnessed a thin gangly teenager walking into the room. Probably the most unimpressive sight they've seen since they arrived.

Now the room was filled with fascination and curiosity, an alluring spice for any occasion. Thomas walked over to the chair at the head of the table and unceremoniously plopped himself down. He scooted his chair up so he could speak into the mic that was sitting there in front of him. "Hello." Came a booming sound that shook everyone to their core. The mic had been set too loud. People dropped their pens and Dr. Amy Mitchell, the sociologist had to reach for her glasses thinking they were going to shake off. Thomas became embarrassed and looked around

127

for the volume control. He could see Mario from the corner of his eyes. Mario was definitely smirking. '*Shit, not funny.*' Thomas thought. Where the hell is the volume control?' Finally, he found it on the side of the mic and lowered it. "Okay, sorry. Sorry about that. Didn't mean to startle everyone. Is everyone okay?"

They all nodded, some smiling, some not. Thomas continued. "As I was saying, my name is Thomas Secmet. I will try to make this as brief as possible. You have all been chosen for your expertise in your fields. You will all have an opportunity to be a part of something.... unique. What I am about to tell you will sound unbelievable and may even sound like a joke. But I assure you, it is neither. Here is my statement to you all in this room. My name is Thomas, and I can heal people by simply touching them. I can cure them of any disease, any illness and heal any injury. You will be skeptical, and you will have doubts, and this is acceptable. Therefore, I am asking all of you to return on Sunday, three days from now, with any person and/or family member that is or may be ill, and I will heal them. Your job is to find out how I do this, as I do not know how or why I am able to. You will tell them that you would like them to come in simply to look at a new alternative to whatever it is that is ailing them. Once they are here, I will walk up to them, say hi and simply touch them. That is when your observations begin.

You will be given the opportunity to purchase any equipment you feel is necessary to accomplish this goal. You will all be able to bring in at least one assistant, but no more than two. This precludes my speech. Ladies and gentlemen, I know you must have many questions, but first, I need all of you to be satisfied that the claim I just made to be true. I'll see you here next Sunday. Good day." With that, Thomas stood up and walked out of the room. The group didn't know what to think. Mario said, "People, you are free to go home. That was the end of your workday. You are welcome to sit and talk among yourselves if you so desire." Dr. Masahiro Kato, the mathematician asked, "Mario, do you know this young man? Can you tell us anything about him?"

Mario spoke clear and confidently, "Yes. I know this young man and everything he told you is true. I have witnessed it with my own eyes on several occasions. He healed someone very close to me as well as myself after a gunshot wound." They all just stared at each other again. Is this possible, they thought. It can't be a joke, no one is so cruel as to ask you to bring someone gravely ill and joke about not being able to heal them. A few were not sure, but then, who can be sure of something like this? They didn't even notice that they were there another half hour

128

before they decided to leave and think about what they were going to do. A few knew exactly what they were going to do.

Dr. Chris Huber, neurologist, had a sister diagnosed with acute Myelogenous Leukemia, a very aggressive cancer. Dr. Masahiro Kato had an elderly mother that was suffering from Vascular Dementia and Dr. Amy Mitchell had not told her family that she was recently diagnosed with breast cancer, however, she would be bringing her younger brother who had been in a terrible car accident that left him paralyzed from the waist down. She really struggled with this, not because of her condition, but because she didn't want to give him any false hope that he would ever walk again.

Dr. Anastasia Semenov had a friend, Fred Kasson, who had contracted AIDS. For the past several years now he's been steadily declining. Dr. Derek Hurd knew exactly who he would be bringing, his mother. He had just recently had to admit her into hospice just days ago. They all left with even more curiosity than they came in with, but with an addition of dread and plenty of doubt. This was a recipe that could only taste bitter. They walked outside the building. It seemed odd that the world looked the same after such a surreal moment like that. It was sunny, warm, normal. But inside their heads their minds were spinning from the possibilities of what was proposed. They all had very similar thoughts, they were either going to be very disappointed, or they would be a part of something historical and meaningful, nothing less than groundbreaking, noble prize winning, and would most likely change the world as they knew it. Of course, they were all in.

Thomas Grady met with Mario Reyes a few minutes later after the meeting. Thomas dreadfully asked, "What do you think about the first meeting? And don't mention the mic thing." Mario raised one eyebrow and said, "Really? Don't mention the one thing that stood out the most?" He let out an exaggerated chuckle and said, "Look, Thomas, don't worry about any of that stuff. Everyone makes mistakes. Believe me, if anyone knows that it's this bunch. Besides, the rest of it went quite well, I thought." Thomas looked down at the ground as if to find a reply. He spoke while still looking downward. "Well…" Thomas started to laugh, "That was pretty stupid and funny. Man, did you hear how load that was? I mean, who would have known that little mic could be so damn loud?" They both laughed for a few more minutes.

"Seriously," Thomas said, "What do you think?"

"I think it all went quite well. The next step is in motion. We need to make sure they're all convinced and after that, let's hope they get the science right." Mario placed his arm around Thomas and said, "Let's go get a burger. My treat."

"Yeah. I'm starvin."

SECMET Inc. was located north of Pasadena California at the foothills of Altadena. The facility was once a remote location for JPL and was almost a perfect square which measured approximately 30,000 square feet. The new main JPL building was located a few miles west of SECMET, Inc. Part of the facility was built partially inside the hillside, so anyone walking in would be surprised by its size, as it was almost twice the square footage as it appeared from the outside. The location was just secluded enough to avoid any kind of heavy walking or driving traffic but visible enough to not raise suspicions. The building was a basic design with concrete blocks, high windows, and a few loading docks. It was the perfect innocuous secret laboratory. The name Secmet came from Thomas putting together the words secret and meeting. Mario and Thomas laughed about it but decided to keep the name.

Besides performing the initial interviews, Mario Reyes had also put together a small security team. They would be monitoring the dozens of cameras that Mario had installed. The main focus of security was making sure no documentation of any kind leaked out without Thomas or Mario's approval. The men were people he trusted from his military days. It was not quite mercenary work, but it paid the same. That was all they needed to know. Mario had taken a few other safety precautions that only he knew about. When you are a part of something like this, you can't take chances. Mario remembered how he got involved with Thomas, so he took a few extra steps to protect Thomas and himself.

Unbeknownst to the other 5 members of the security team, they were all mandated to wear only the gear provided by SECMET Inc. which included a built-in tracking device, a small explosive positioned just above the L5 lower lumbar that Mario could detonate remotely. A small gas pellet located near the shoulder straps of all their body armor which Mario could also detonate. This gas was a fast-acting sedative, once it went off, you'll be knocked out within a matter of seconds. Mario trusted his people, but precaution was still the name of the game.

Amy Mitchell was a slender 33-year-old woman. She had slender shoulders, a long neck and lips that seemed a little too wide for her face. Considered a little tall, five feet, eight inches, she carried herself with just enough poise that gave her an air of sophistication. Amy had her mother's deep tanned complexion and with a little effort, could look quite attractive, but she rarely tried. Amy had too much natural depth about her. In fact, one might say that because of that depth and her genuine interest in people, Amy was practically destined to be a sociologist. Now here she was, contemplating what to do next. She wished she could call her dad. He was always so logical about things.

Her father, Ron Mitchell was born and raised in Boise, Idaho but was currently serving as emeritus professor at Michigan State University in the MSU Center for Statistical Training and Consulting Services. She could just as easily get help from her mother, Dr. Ananya Kumar Mitchell, who was also a PhD-trained sociologist and professor of Epidemiology and Biostatistics also at MSU. But Amy wanted to make her own decisions. Besides, she signed that non-disclosure agreement, so how would she be able to explain her situation. Just a few days ago she was offered a position with the federal government working on God knows what for the Pentagon. Amy was a patriot for sure, but she always held on to a healthy dose of skepticism when it came to government work, policy, and intentions.

The work sounded interesting, she wasn't quite sure exactly what it was that the government wanted her to do, but, then again, it wasn't any clearer with SECMET Inc. The government work paid very well, but paled in comparison to the crazy salary offered by SECMET Inc. Amy felt a little sense of duty to her country, but it wasn't like they wouldn't be able to find someone else. Not to mention that kid at SECMET Inc. had piqued the hell out of her interest. The problem was, is this crazy kid telling the truth? If he isn't, this is a big waste of time, and she may lose out on an opportunity that was not too shabby. Then again, there was that kid. Damn, she just had to know.

It was still early Friday evening. Amy had to think of a simple ruse to get her brother to go with her to see Thomas Secmet. She would play it off as a simple curiosity. Who knows, maybe this kid can help, hell, he couldn't hurt her brother any more than he is. She called her brother, Steven and told him she was going to pick him up on Sunday morning and they were going to go visit a friend that had some news about some possible future treatments that show some promise for people in similar situations such has his own. Steven agreed out of pity for his sister because he knows that she is always trying to find ways to help. He loved her for it, but she could sometimes grade on him when she was being too obsequious. He did not like to feel pitied. Nevertheless, he was in.

Dr. Derek Hurd was a young 43-year-old astrophysicist. Born in Brooklyn, NY, and raised by a single mother who had him late in life. By the time he was born, his mother was already in her late forties. She was strict, but fair. Chores always had to be done and schoolwork was always the priority. Derek was raised with plenty of discipline and had little time for nonsense. For Derek, it was always about getting done what had to get done. It wasn't like he didn't like fun, but there was a time and place for everything. A little fun was good, but then, it was right back to work. Derek was kingly aware of the sacrifices his mother had made to put him through school and he was determined not to waste all that effort, care, and love.

Dr. Derek Hurd was visiting Los Angeles in a collaboration project with an old colleague from school. He brought his mother along. She had not been well the past few weeks. He thought the warm climate might help. It was devastating when things took a turn for the worse and Dr. Derek Hurd had to admit her into the local hospice facility. Dr. Edward Hunt recruited Derek because of his impressive work ethic. When they were at NYU together, Dr. Edward Hunt recalled how diligent Derek always was about everything he did. But now, he got the strangest phone call. In what seemed like a highly unusual change of character, Dr. Hurd had informed him that he would not be able to continue on with their project. When Dr. Hunt asked why, he got a very curious reply. "Something has come up, but I can't talk about it. I'm sorry, Edward, I have to go. Good-bye."

That would be the last time they ever spoke for many years to come. Derek's mother wanted to go back to New York, but it didn't make any sense to travel that far. She didn't have any family left on the east coast and Dr. Derek Hurd didn't have any real friends anywhere. He didn't want to move her and taking her to see Thomas was your basic nothing-to-lose scenario. Why not? If this kid thinks he can heal her, then well, let's see what happens. His mother had been suffering from multiple problems, mostly stemming from age. Her kidneys were starting to fail, her heart was weak, eyesight was almost gone, and the list went on. There really wasn't any treatment other than trying to make her life as comfortable as possible for the little time she had left.

Dr. Masahiro Kato was a second generation 39-year-old mathematician. His mother, Hana Kato, had come from Japan to the U.S. on a work visa. It turns out that Seattle had a shortage of science and math teachers and so they started recruiting from other countries. Masahiro's father and mother both came to the states to teach. Everything seemed to be going great. Masahiro had very few problems growing up in Seattle. School was fun and as it so happened, math was easy for him. He graduated from high school with honors and went on to get his PhD in Southern California from USC. Masahiro went to work for an R&D firm right out of college that specialized in computer animation software for the medical industry.

Dr. Kato was in his 10th year of working at Anitech Inc when he found out that his mother had contracted Vascular Dementia. It wasn't long before the symptoms started showing. It's an ironic disease for an educator, as her brain was the most effected part. She would never teach again. It seemed that their family lives were taking a turn for the worse. Masahiro's father was depressed most of the time and grieving the loss of his wife's cognitive functions. Meanwhile, Masahiro's work was not as rewarding as he thought it would be, so he answered the ad from SEMTEC Inc. Masahiro, like all the others, was filled with doubt bordering on cynicism. But he also could not escape the overwhelming and alluring curiosity that this young child had proposed. Not the least of which was the remote possibility that Thomas could do what he claimed he could do. He had to dare himself to submit further into this unrealistic endeavor. Vascular Dementia was nothing to be trifled with. It was an aggressive disease and if there was to be any hope, any at all, this was it.

Dr. Anastasia Semenov was a Russian immigrant. She came to this country about 20 years ago, alone. Her family did not want her to leave Russia, but she insisted on seeing the world. Anastasia wanted to visit all of Europe and America. She was in her twenties and full of youthful idealism. She was going to take a 2-year hiatus before beginning university. Unfortunately, Anastasia had decided to start her trip in the U.S.A. The beaches, the parties, the beach parties, socializing with such a care-free lifestyle was simply too seductive. Anastasia never made it to Europe. She fell in love with California's west coast. For a short while, she even thought about attending a liberal arts college. But that was not who she was at her core and so she went to UCLA and became a chemist, more specifically, a biochemist.

Anastasia had been feeling unfulfilled in her job. It was interesting enough, but she had just recently started looking around for something more challenging. She responded to the ad for SECMET Inc. because it sounded intriguing. In her journey through college, she was lucky enough to pick up a friend, Fred Kasson. He was going to UCLA at the same time and was focused on analytical chemistry. She remembered when he told her, "Your name is too damn long, I'm calling you Annie from now on." she hated it, Annie squinted her eyes and said, "Boring." They got into an argument about which field of chemistry was the best. They never arrived at any conclusive decision.

They had been friends for almost 3 months, when one day Fred came up to Anastasia while walking across campus and told her that he had something he needed to say. "Oh, oh," she remembered saying, "What's going on? Is everything okay?" She could see Fred was hesitant, "Hey, go ahead, you can tell me. We're friends." Anastasia put her right hand on his left shoulder and said, "Hey, how can I help?" Fred Kasson looked at her with watery eyes and said, "Annie, I want you to know that I wasn't hiding anything from you intentionally."

"What? What is it, Fred?"

"Well, I'm not sure you know this, but I'm gay."

"What?" Anastasia burst out laughing. "Are you kidding me?" she said with a surprised look on her face. Fred replied with visible indignation,

"What? What's so funny?"

"Oh my God, Fred, who *doesn't* know you're gay?"

"Oh my God, am I that obvious?"

"Have you seen the way you dress?" Fred looked down at his clothes. He was wearing light blue skinny jeans that were neatly folded up just above the ankles, red leather slip-on Pope shoes, no socks, and a tight long sleeve shiny Dolce/Gabbana T-shirt. Fred opened his mouth and put his hand up to it as if he was shocked at what he was wearing. They made eye contact again and they both started laughing uncontrollably. From that day on, they were best friends.

After college they would meet up occasionally. Eventually both of their lives got busy, and they saw each other less and less. Anastasia had not heard from Fred for a long time. It wasn't until just recently, about 6 months ago, that she found out Fred Kasson had been diagnosed with full blown AIDS. Because he had tried to hide it, and was simultaneously in denial, Fred had waited too long to seek treatment. Fred had never mentioned to Anastasia that he was guilty of poor adherence to treatment, poor nutrition and alcohol abuse and so now his condition was serious, very serious. He was also ashamed to mention to Anastasia that he had developed Wasting Syndrome, which is characterized by severe weight loss and muscle wasting. So, when he heard from Annie that she wanted him to fly down to check out a new treatment she heard of, Fred jumped on a plane the same day and met up with Anastasia. They would both be there on Sunday. Fred Kasson was worried she would not recognize him in his deteriorated state.

Chris Huber was the oldest of the group, he was 58 years old. A rare born-and-raised native of California. Chris was born in Los Angeles. He was what Angelinos called a "Kaiser Baby" because he, along with so many others, were born at Kaiser Hospital. He grew up in an ideal world. He lived with both parents at home. Growing up he never had to worry about anything except his grades. He had as much potential as he had opportunity and was lucky enough to be cognizant of it. Having advantages in life and knowing that one should utilize them to their fullest potential is sometimes simply luck. People could have these advantages and more, and still end up on the streets or even worse, on drugs or in jail. There are so many factors in our lives that could make us take so many wrong directions. Sometimes one needs more than privilege and status, sometimes one simply needs to trip over serendipity to receive that personal epiphany.

Luckily this was not the case for Chris. He was very aware of his situation and made sure he used it wisely. With hard work and determination Chris made his way to becoming one of the most recommended neurosurgeons in the nation. Chris Huber did not need a job, he had been exceptionally successful and at 58 years old, he would never have to work again. He was on a few boards at a few hospitals and spent most of his time studying current events within his profession. The other part of his days he spent on the golf course and an occasional game of pickleball. In between those times he was available by appointment only for consultations with his peers to discuss special cases.

Chris was not looking for a job when he saw the ad from SECMET Inc. Like all the others, he was simply curious. But now he was downright intrigued. In fact, one of the main reasons he even replied to the ad was because it mentioned his profession. Like most people in this world, Chris Huber had someone dear to him that was ill. His younger sister, Catheryn Huber, at 49 years old, was suffering from acute myelogenous Leukemia. She wasn't going to last long and would probably be going to hospice herself in a very short while. It broke Chris's heart to see his sister suffering so much. He wished there was something he could do. And now, well, he still wishes there was something he could do because frankly, Chris Huber was not ready to accept Thomas on his word. But the young man had such a nonchalant confidence about him that Chris just had to call him out on it. Hope is an alluring mistress. Even while not allowing himself to believe that Thomas could help her, there was that heavy dull presence of hope. And it made all the difference in the world.

The ad for SECMET Inc. read as follows:

135

What if you could change the world overnight? This is real. The work is done, we need your help to put it into motion.

SECMET Inc. is seeking individuals with the following expertise to help with the delivery of an unprecedented medical breakthrough that will change the world as we know it.

Astrophysicist

Mathematician

Neurologist

Chemist

Sociologist

Salary: Substantial

Reply to the email below and you will be contacted.

SECMETINC@SECMET.com

Sunday

It was a bright autumn morning. The sun was comfortably warm, but the shade hung on to the morning chill. The SECMET crew, as expected, showed up early. They had all been given the access code to enter the building. There was a note instructing everyone to meet at conference room number 3. This was a different room than the one they originally met in. There was no Plexiglas wall, just another door besides the one they came in from. This room had a large round table which seated approximately 12 people. There was definitely a different feeling to this meeting.

Waiting for them inside was Mario Reyes and his security team. There was one man standing at each corner of the room and one pacing slowly around the table. All the men, including Mario looked quite formidable and carried an air of earned confidence. Menacing would be the appropriate word to describe them. There was no reason to be on alert with the people seated at the table, but that was irrelevant, these men were trained to look for threats and danger wherever they are. It didn't matter if they were in a jungle or in a conference room. Their eyes darted to everyone watching for anything out of the ordinary.

As per Mario's instructions, they were also ordered to keep an eye on their own teammates.

Mario remembered what happened to his team. They all ended up dead. Granted it was because of him, but that was the point. He wasn't about to take any chances. This group was designed so that there were no loyalties in the group, the only loyalty was to Mario. They are to treat each other as possible threats as well. Making them the most dangerous people in the room. Their only objective was Thomas' safety.

The SECMET group was a little nervous and apprehensive. Their guests, those who were there to be healed, were just as apprehensive and confused. They couldn't tell if they were there to be healed or interrogated with "enhanced" techniques. Before anyone could say anything, the door in the back of the room opened. All eyes went to the person entering the room. Thomas walked in wearing a white lab coat that looked like it might have been a size too big. Thomas did his best to act like a young intern.

"Good morning, everyone." Everyone nodded, some said good morning back.
"My name is Thomas. Would anyone care for some water? I'm afraid we do not have any coffee this morning as, well, we don't have a coffee maker…yet." Everyone smiled and suddenly all their guards were let down. This kid looked friendly enough and didn't look like any kind of a threat. A couple of guests asked for water, everyone else was fine.

Thomas went on, "On behalf of SECMET Inc., welcome. Now, if you don't mind, our group needs to convene for just a moment, and we'll get started. Thank you for your patience." Thomas turned and walked through the same door he came in from. Mario Reyes spoke, "Well the SECMET team please follow me into the next room." The group stood up and followed Mario.

In the next room was a small table and one chair. On the table was another non-disclosure agreement. Thomas addressed his team. "Well, I'm very glad to see all of you here today. I have an idea of how to proceed. Your suggestions are welcomed. Here's what I was thinking. I think we should address one person at a time, as healing the whole group at once would just cause chaos. We could bring them into this room, heal them, and ask them to wait in the next room, away from the others. It would be too distracting to have them go back into the same room. What do you think?"

Dr. Huber spoke first, "Mr. Secmet, are you still seriously saying that these people will be healed here, today in this room?"
"Yes sir. I thought that's why you're all here?" Thomas said a bit confused.

"Yes, well, I hope you will forgive us for our skepticism, Mr....I mean, Thomas. If you don't mind, I would like to make a suggestion."

"Please do." Replied Thomas, anxious to hear anything other than his own ideas.

Chris Huber continued. "I suggest we proceed with Dr. Mitchell's brother."

Amy was uncertain and quickly asked, "Why?"

"Because" said Dr. Huber, "he is the obvious one. If your brother is healed, then he should be able to stand up out of his wheelchair. Is that right, Thomas? Will her brother be able to stand up? Today, I mean, do we know how long this will take?"

Thomas thought about it. This was the classic person in the wheelchair scenario. He almost smiled because it was so cliché. Thomas said, "I think that's a good idea." Amy shot back, "Wait, wait." She looked like she may have started hyperventilating. Everyone could see her trepidatious body language. She held up her hand and again said. "Wait. So, Thomas, are you saying that my brother will walk today? That he will be able to stand up and walk? Today? In this room?" Thomas understood her reluctance, though he would be incapable of grasping the magnitude of her disappointment if this didn't work. Thomas tried to ease her mind.

"Dr. Mitchell. I know this sounds absurd. I'm so used to this thing that it's sometimes hard for me to see this from anyone else's perspective. But I get it." Mario watched as he saw Thomas go into his solemn mature mode. "Dr. Mitchell, please look at me." Amy met eyes with Thomas. Her eyes were on the verge of tears. "Dr. Mitchell, please trust me when I tell you, your brother will walk out of that chair in a matter of minutes, if not less. He will not only be able to walk; he will be able to run. He will be completely healed. I don't know why I am able to do what I do, that's why you're here." Thomas glanced at everyone in the room, "That's why you're all here. This is your job."

"Thomas," Amy pleaded, "Okay, but please, how long will this take? Before he can walk?" Thomas thought about the answer, he never really timed it, but he knew it was quick. He replied, "I'm not sure, but...seconds, less than a minute for sure." The group was taken aback by this incredible claim. And again, they were all filled with an internal sense of outrage. Was this kid insulting their intelligence? Was this for real? How could this be possible? Yet, they all shared one common thread, the tenuous thread of hope. And so, they continued.

For a few seconds the room was silent, but filled with doubt, dread and even some anger. But all of it was suppressed and kept in check. These claims were just too outlandish to be a joke.

Dr. Huber broke the tension that had been building in the room. He addressed Thomas and Dr. Amy Mitchell. "Thomas, Dr. Mitchell, I hope you don't mind that I examine Mr. Mitchell once he's inside this room."

"What are you saying?" Amy said.

"I'm saying that I want to verify that Mr. Mitchell is indeed paralyzed and not putting on some show. I can't continue this, this," He waved his arms around the white sterile room, "whatever this is, without some presence of science in the room. For all I know, Mr. Mitchell is involved in some elaborate ruse with Thomas and yourself. I don't know. I'm saying, let me examine him and I will give you my diagnoses. Or maybe his condition is psychosomatic. I don't know, I'm just saying, let's all be sure" Amy was about to say something again when Thomas replied. "That's a very good idea, doctor." It took another few seconds for everyone to calm down. Thomas quietly and softly said, "Dr. Mitchell, would you mind asking your brother to please join us?"

Amy took a long breath and said, "Yes." Amy walked to the door, opened it and waved to Steven to come in. Steven had a little smile on his face. For Steven, this was just another one of his sister's whacky ideas. He couldn't help but love her optimistic enthusiasm. Steven rolled into the room. He was expecting to see someone else, but the same people were in this room. He thought there might be a specialist doctor or something. *"Maybe it was this guy."* Steven thought, looking at Dr. Huber. Steven watched as Dr. Huber walked up to him and introduced himself and said, "Steven, would you mind if I do a few quick little tests to measure the extent of your paralysis?"

"Go for it doc."

Chris Huber started by feeling Steven's leg. Steven definitely had some atrophy. He obviously had an injury below the C5 area, or he wouldn't have the motor skills in his upper body. Dr. Huber pulled out a small pocketknife. It was very sharp and very pointy. He asked Steven if he could prick his skin just below the knee and on his foot. Steven's reply was the same. "Go for it, doc."

Amy was watching, she was so glad that Steven was taking all this in with a grain of salt. It made her feel better in case this entire debacle went south. After a few more questions and poking around, Chris announced, "Well, with what limited instruments I have available to me, I would diagnose this young man as a good candidate for our next procedure." Thomas thought that was really good, the way Dr. Huber made it sound like this was all planned. Dr. Huber looked at Thomas and said, well, he's all yours." Steven was a bit confused. He thought the Dr. was going to do something, but instead, he had this kid, this intern continued with whatever this procedure was.

Thomas walked over to Steven, smiled, and said, "Hi Steven. I have to let you know a couple of things first. If you don't mind, would you please sign this non-disclosure agreement? It basically says that you won't tell anyone about what we are doing here for at least 6 months. Steven looked at the form, he didn't bother to read it, after all, if this "procedure" works, he'll do whatever they say. "Thanks." Thomas handed the form to Mario. Thomas reached into his oversized coat pocket and pulled out what looked like a simple metal tin. Steven thought Thomas was going to offer him a mint. Instead, Thomas pulled out a small round Band-Aid. As Thomas began peeling the waxy paper off the Band-Aid, he spoke to Steven. "So, what this is, is a transdermal patch that will instantly release a measured amount of a natural agent that has shown a lot of promise with folks in your condition." Thomas was fumbling a little with the band-aid. Steven smiled and looked up at Thomas and said, "So, they got you doing the dirty work, eh?" Thomas smiled. It was a very sincere smile, as he knew that this young man was about to be very happy. Thomas replied, "Yup, these guys do all the thinking and I do all the work."

"Oh, yeah, I know the type." Steven said while not so secretly pointing at his sister. Steven was wearing a short sleeve shirt and jokingly said, "Should I roll up my sleeve?" While exposing his shoulder. Again, Thomas smiled and said, "That won't be necessary, I'll be placing it on your forearm. One last thing, it's very important. This is the first of 3 treatments, you must complete all 3 for this treatment to be permanent. Failure to do so may result in this whole process being reversed. Steven affirmed with a nod. He watched as Thomas handled the little round band-aid as if it was a very special and expensive drug. Steven watched as Thomas carefully lowered it onto his arm and gently pressed it and made sure it stuck.

Steven stared at it. Thomas looked at Steven as he placed his hand firmly on his shoulder, squeezed a little and said, "That's it."
"That's it?" Steven replied.
"Yup."
"Okay then, we can all go home now?"

"Yup." Thomas replied.

Steven couldn't help but notice the faces in the room. They were all deadly serious. It looked as if nobody was breathing. Their eyes were dead locked on him. Steven was about to say something glib, when suddenly he noticed something. The group was still in a state of contemptuous disbelief and were seconds away from showing it. There was an ugly anger that was threatening to raise its head. But suddenly they all saw it. An almost imperceptible change in Steven's demeanor. They could tell he was feeling something.

It started at his toes. The fact that he felt anything on his toes was already more than Steven expected. But the sensation continued. He felt a tingling moving up his feet and to his legs. Slowly, but surely, moving up through his thighs, waist. He thought it would stop there, but it went on. For a second, he grabbed the arm rest on his chair tightly, not to brace for standing, but to brace for disappointment while simultaneously feeling mad for daring to hope. The sensation was warm and prickly. It went through his torso, to his neck and all the way to the top of his head. When it stopped, Steven was 100% convinced he could walk. He just knew it. He knew he was cured. In fact, he was so confident about it that he didn't try to test his legs, he simply shot up out of his chair. The immediate response from the group was a loud gasp.

Steven exclaimed loudly, "What the fuck!" He looked around the room. "What the fuck just happened? Is this real? Is this real? What the fuck!" Steven was in total shock. Amy ran to him and hugged him as hard as she could. "Steven, oh my God, oh my God, look at you!" But Steven was bordering on total shock. "What the fuck." Amy finally put her finger on his lips. "Steven, you're cussing. Stop cussing." But she was laughing. Steven was laughing and crying. He didn't know what to think. This was impossible. Which was what everybody else was thinking. Steven's reaction was too real to be an act. Everyone in the room was convinced of what Thomas just did.

Thomas let Steven enjoy his moment before he signaled to Mario to calm everyone down. Mario raised his voice over everyone else. "Okay, okay. Quite down. Please. Steven, sit down." Steven smiled at Mario and said, "No way." Mario smiled back and said, "Okay, stand if you have to. Okay, everyone, listen up. I could hear you all asking questions to yourself, to others around you, but today is not that day. Dr. Mitchell, please take your brother into the next room so that we can continue our work today. Mr. Mitchell, I promise we won't be long. Please remember to come back for your second treatment, it's very important. And we don't need to remind you that you have signed an NDA."

Steven had a big smile on his face, "Dude, whatever, I'll sign and keep on signing whatever you want. I'll be in the next room sis." Amy watched her brother walk into the next room.

The group started to ask Thomas more questions. But Thomas wanted them to think about it. He addressed the group. "So, I know this is all very unorthodox, but let's proceed with the rest of your friends and family members. The goal for today was to convince you all that what I have told you is true. Let's move on and we'll convene tomorrow. That's when your real work begins.

They continued with the rest of the group. It went pretty much the same. A continuous flow of incredible amazement. Dr. Kato brought his mother in next. It was a very emotional scene when she was not only healed but was also very cognizant of her previous condition. As usual, one of the unintended perks of Thomas' healing is that it also comes with clarity of mind. Hana Kato was able to remember that she was not able to recall who her own son was, how she easily lost her way around the house and how she would forget what simple things were and how they worked, like a coffee maker.

She was very happy she was cured, but also very scared that she might suffer through that whole ordeal again. In those few moments of clarity, Hana seriously contemplated suicide. It would be months before the SECMET team even considers addressing phycological ramifications to those who experienced these thoughts due to their being healed. These types of patients would have to be assured that not only would they not suffer through it again, but they were no danger of ever contracting that decease again. As for Dr. Kato's mother, death will come quietly, softly, and painlessly in her sleep. But due to the regenerated cells in her body, not for another 20 to 25 years at least.

Anastasia Semenov was grateful that her friend, Frederick Kasson was given a new lease on life. Nobody was happier than he was. Not because he had the worse disease, or greatest illness, but rather because he truly loved his existence in life. He was a lover of life. He embraced it for all it was worth. Fred saw the worst in people and still loved them because he always felt that everyone is connected. As a young adult Fred remembered reading John Donne's poem, 'For Whom the Bell Tolls.' It was this poem that inspired the thought that all people are connected at some level or another. The words were in his head even now, "..any man's death diminishes me, because I am involved in mankind."

Dr. Chris Huber, who appeared to be the most serious person in the group, broke down and cried when his sister was healed. They were both very happy and cried in each other's arms for what seemed a long time. Their eyes were red, and their faces were hurting from smiling so hard and so long. Thomas never got used to it. These types of moments always made him feel good. Finally, it was Dr. Hurd's aging mother. They were about to go bring her in when they heard a loud rapping on the door. They all looked at each other and wondered who could be knocking on the door so hard? Mario told everyone to step back as he reached his hand behind his back and made sure the safety was off on his Glock 19. Mario reached for the doorknob, but he saw it was already turning. Mario quickly grabbed the doorknob and yanked it open hard while drawing his weapon. Mario had his gun pointed directly between the eyes of Dr. Derek's mother. She let out a small sigh and said, "Oh my." Mario quickly holstered his gun and apologized. "Mrs. Hurd, I'm sorry, but we weren't expecting anyone to come in here.?

"What do you mean," Mrs. Hurd said, "Everyone else has come in here. I'm the last one standing in this room all alone and I'm starving. I thought there might be food in here. Is there?" Dr. Hurd looked at her, looked at Thomas and said, "What? What's going on? Did you heal her before we started?" Thomas looked at Mario, but he had no answer. Dr. Hurd continued, "Thomas, what's going on here? Is she healed? Mrs. Hurd walked over to her son, Dr. Derek Hurd, and said, "Did someone heal me? Because I feel really good. No, actually, I feel great! Oh, yeah, and hungry." Dr. Hurd didn't know what to say, so he said, "Okay, mom, but wait in the other room for now. You sure you're okay?"

"Yup. Are you okay?"

"Ah, yup."

"Okay then, I'll see you in the next room."

Mario stopped her and said, Mrs. Hurd, please, if you don't mind, we need you to wait back in the same room for just one more minute. We'll have some food brought in." Mario lied. "Okay," she replied, and calmly walked back into the next room. Everyone looked at Thomas for the answer to the question in everyone's mind. What the hell just happened? Thomas could see everyone's face, he couldn't tell if they were mad, perplexed or a mixture of both. He held up both his hands in front of him as if he was stopping an angry mob, but nobody was moving. Thomas took a deep breath and said, "Okay, so, this thing sometimes happens. For some reason, every once in a while, it seems like other people in the general proximity are also healed while

143

I'm doing this. Again, I don't know how or why or anything. This is why you all are here. If I knew what was going on, I wouldn't need any help. But I don't know anything, I know as much as anyone here. I don't know how Mrs. Hurd was healed, but you can be assured, Dr. Hurd, that she is healed just like everyone else was healed here today in this room."

Dr. Hurd said in an almost pleading way, "Thomas, are you sure? You never touched her. Maybe you should just in case? I mean, you know, just in case." Thomas could see his reasoning. After seeing everyone else being completely healed, he didn't want to leave his mom to chance, so Thomas said, "I understand. Don't worry, I'll, make sure to touch her before she leaves." He smiled at Dr. Hurd and finished, "Just in case." Dr. Hurd nodded. "Thank you."

Thomas concluded the meeting by saying, "Thank you all for coming and following through with this. It is important that you believe and see for yourselves that this is really happening. Now I need your help in trying to figure out how all this is happening. I hope that this incident with Mrs. Hurd will actually provide some kind of clue as to how this thing works. Dr. Hurd, I'm going to the next room and make sure your mother is healed. But I suggest you get her some food before you're the one who needs the healing." Everyone in the room smiled. The ice was, finally, truly broken. "I'll see you all here tomorrow bright and early." Thomas walked out of the room with Mario. It's funny how quickly one gets used to miracles. At the end of the session, they all went their separate ways. Amazed, shocked, and excited but ready to carry on with their lives as if nothing happened.

The next day Thomas laid out what he had in mind. They would all have to make a list of what kind of instrumentation was needed to begin with. They were all allowed to have one or two assistants, but no more than two each. They were to come together as a group and determine what the best course of action should be and also, what should SECMET Inc. do next to make this available to the world. What do they see as a practical delivery system for something like this? How will society act as a whole? This was the main reason for the sociologist. Thomas was counting on Dr. Mitchell to lend cohesiveness to the group and to the endeavor. This group will be faced with situations and ideas that have never been dealt with before and Thomas was sure that they all needed some sort of mindful leadership and coping tools to deal with the implications and the unprecedented scope of what they were introducing to the world. The inexorable unintended consequences may perhaps be more than the world can handle.

As time went on the entire complex, though still mostly empty, appeared to be packed with

144

enthusiasm, zeal, and optimism. Every person moved about with a vigor they never felt before. There was a mission to accomplish, and they were dead set on accomplishing it. Things moved quickly. It wasn't long before the entire floor began filling up with equipment. Thomas was happy to see such dedication from the entire team. They were all set to meet the first set of goals they had set for themselves. Thomas' apprehension and anxiety were slowly breaking away and finally making room for some semblance of relief.

Several weeks later, the team was finally able to start testing Thomas. It was no small feat to fill most of the 30,000 square feet of the facility. A small fortune was spent on getting the vendors to move up their dates and place Secmet's orders ahead of other existing orders. And another small fortune on shipping everything next day air. A third fortune was spent on technical set-up. One of the main features of Secmet Inc was the almost gratuitous number of cameras. Mario wanted to keep very tight reigns on everything and everyone. He felt certain that there would be another attack on Thomas. It wasn't a question of if, but when it was going to happen. Mario knew that Thomas was in the position to grant the one thing that people with money and power wanted the most of, time.

Time to exist is the only commodity that can't be bought, made, or sold. To an individual it is scarce, rare…finite. Mario knew it was worth millions to some, and billions to others. That kind of money could create challenges that even Mario wasn't sure he could handle. But he was going to give it a hell of a try.

The Devils Gate and the Surprise Attack

After a series of basic tests, like x-rays, MRI's, CAT scans and ultrasounds, all of which revealed nothing, the crew had to start getting creative. They fitted Thomas into a thin neoprene bodysuit covered with sensors that were able to measure the slightest change in electrical charges coming from Thomas' body. They were trying to figure out if any kind of energy was being emitted from any point on Thomas' body. They had Thomas standing very still for long periods of time in order to establish a consistent base line reading. Then they had Thomas touch someone that needed healing from various types of maladies. These tests would also yield inconclusive results.

It was difficult to try and derive any substantive theory without any data with which to

145

formulate one. Every test they did proved that Thomas was just as ordinary as anyone else in the building, but he wasn't. Dr. Huber tried introducing Thomas' skin cells to different viruses and observed the reaction through an electron microscope. Everything behaved as it should, the virus attacked Thomas' cells and destroyed them but then the virus would die and the cells that were destroyed would inexplicably heal themselves. However, if they treated the same cells outside of Thomas' body, they would simply die. So much for synthesizing Thomas' cells. It was a good thing though, at least they were able to knock off one thing from the list.

Thomas had to be physically part of the process. In other words, somebody would not be able to simply cut Thomas' hand off and go around healing people with it. This led them to believe that there might be something in Thomas' brain that is contributing to his condition. Again, they tried sensors that measure the slightest change to any electrical changes in his brain and again they came up empty handed.

Weeks passed and Thomas had been subjected to dozens of tests. He was placed in rooms with varying temperatures, pressures, and varying frequencies. He was suspended in every direction and spun around for no other reason than to see what would happen. He was submerged in liquids, covered in oils, and constantly poked with needles. Thomas was going along with it all, but it was getting very old very fast. Thomas would sometimes feel a sense of surrender. Dr Mitchell's talents were more helpful in fending off the sense of defeat and failure. She spent a lot of time building a workplace culture that was conducive to a strong positive team attitude and an overall friendly and cooperative work environment.

It was Dr Hurd who came up with the idea of testing for any external forces that may be entering Thomas' body. Afterall, any process that produces energy, such as the power to heal, needs to replace that energy in order to maintain that process otherwise it would be unstainable. At this point, any idea was worth a shot. They were going to alter the sensor suit to measure any energy changes entering Thomas' body. They also decided to increase the sensitivity of the electrodes on the suit. It was a Monday, tomorrow they would start the new test. They let Thomas know they would like to begin as early as possible. Thomas agreed to 9:30am. This would give them time to set up the test and alter the suit.

Daniel Steger woke up at an unknown time in the morning of an unknown day. Daniel hadn't really woken up so much as he came down from last night's high. Daniel was a troubled young man whose plight in life was to walk down the path of his fate brought about by every negative thought and bad decision he had ever made, which were many. At 28 years old, there was nowhere for Daniel to go but down. Daniel was Deprived of every possible opportunity from birth. His parents were drug addicts, his friends were drug addicts and now he was one. Daniel Steger was the proverbial statistic that slips through the cracks of every good intention. It was not out of societies meanness but rather a fact that Daniel was simply wasting the oxygen around him.

He woke up by one of the tunnels to the Devils Gate Reservoir in Altadena. The Devils Gate Dam was built in 1920 and is one of the oldest dams constructed by the Los Angeles County Flood Control District. It provided flood protection to the cities of Pasadena, and Los Angeles. In the 1940's, a group of occultists held rituals inside the dam intended to open up a gateway to hell. Jack Parsons, a co-founder of Nasa's Jet Propulsion laboratory along with L. Ron Hubbard, the founder of Scientology, were among the group. But now it's a hang-out for drug users and most of the concrete around the tunnels are covered in graffiti. The tunnels were below street level and you had to walk down the side of a dirt hill to get there. So, it provided cover from police cruising by. Not that the police didn't know what was going on down there. They would raid it occasionally and make a couple of busts.

Daniel walked up the dirt hill and looked for his car that he hid behind the trees so that it would not be visible from the street. Daniel had inherited the car from his friend that overdosed on heroine. There was no will, just a set of keys. Daniel's biggest and immediate problem was that he woke up sober and needed a fix. He checked his pockets for the keys. It was not unusual for Daniel to lose his keys. With all of his blackouts, it was a wonder he still had them. The car was an old 2001 Nissan Altima. It was dirty, dingy, banged up. It had one good headlight and one good turn signal. It was a miracle that he had not been pulled over.

Daniel drove straight to Lincoln Ave and Woodbury Rd. There was a MacDonald's restaurant on the corner. He would try panhandling for some money to buy some more drugs. He tried going inside and asking for a 'free' cup of coffee, but the manager came up to him and unceremoniously threw him out. Daniel was unperturbed. Nothing mattered except getting high. He walked over to the side of the entrance and started asking people for money. Almost everyone declined to help him, because they could tell that Daniel was most likely going to spend the money on drugs. After a few minutes, the manager came out again and told him he had to leave. Daniel got a little upset and said, "Hey man, I'm not doing nothing. Why you

147

buggin me, dude?" The manager pointed his finger right at his face and said, "Look, I don't care what you're doing or not doing. You need to stop bothering our customers and get off the property before I call the cops. Got it?" Daniel became a little indignant and said, "You know what, fuck you, man. I don't need this shit. I'm leaving."

"Good, leave."

"I am. So, shut up."

The manager just shook his head and walked back inside. By this time, Daniel was getting worried he may not get the money he needed for his next fix. He only needed $10.00. But to Daniel it seemed like an insurmountable amount of money. Also, it could take him hours to make that much by asking people for change. Daniel was already getting a little jittery. His mind was starting to cloud, and his thinking was becoming erratic. It took only a matter of seconds before Daniel talked himself into a full-blown panic attack. *'What should I do?'* He thought. *'It could be hours before I get the money from these cheap-ass people.'* For Daniel, hours would feel like days, even weeks. Getting high had nothing to do with the future, it was all about right now. Right, right now.

There was only one thing he could do. Daniel walked back and waited by the door hoping the manager didn't notice him. Daniel watched as the cashier entered an order. Daniel waited until the order was about to be rung up. As soon as he saw the cash register open, Daniel ran inside. Everyone was spooked as this crazed looking man with dirty clothes and unkempt hair ran like a broken dirty scarecrow across the lobby. The young cashier at the cash register slammed the register drawer closed as if by instinct. The manager turned to see Daniel sprinting across the lobby. Daniel watched in horror as the boy closed the cash register drawer. Daniel panicked, he stopped, then froze, as did everyone else in the lobby. Everyone was waiting to see what would happen next, even Daniel didn't know what would happen next. Finally, Daniel noticed a customer that must have been in the process of paying his bill in cash and was still holding a handful of bills in his hand. Daniel quickly grabbed them and yanked the money out of the customer's hand then ran out the front door and into his car.

Everyone was in shock at the whole ordeal. Then the manager snapped out of it and began chasing Daniel. However, the manager was filled with conflicting thoughts. *'What if I catch up to him? What am I going to? Fight him? Wrestle with him? Who knows what diseases this guy is carrying?'* So, the manager stopped, and let Daniel go. He would call the cops, apologize to the customers and nobody gets chlamydia today. Daniel was still in panic mode. He had run to his car, jumped inside, started the car and peeled rubber out the driveway and headed west on Woodbury Rd, back towards The Devils Reservoir at 65 miles per hour. It was a 35 mile per hour zone. It was 6:21am.

Mario Reyes woke up at 5:30am and started his routine. Coffee, a light breakfast, a little news, and one more coffee to take on the way to work. Quick weapons check. Laptop check. Make sure all cameras are working. Make sure all GPS monitors are online. Once he was satisfied with everything, he headed out the door. It was 6:01am. It was a little cooler than he expected, but his Kevlar vest added a little extra warmth anyway. He drove down the street, made a few turns and jumped on the 210 East freeway. It only took him about 18 minutes to get to his exit. It was nice not having to commute, then again, Thomas would have bought Mario a house wherever he wanted so that he wouldn't have to commute. Mario got off on Windsor Ave and turned right. At the next intersection, Mario looked up and saw the light, it was green.

'Nice.' Mario thought, he usually misses this traffic light. Mario proceeded to cross the intersection when suddenly he was violently jolted across his car. Mario's body was flung to the right and then thrown just as violently to the left causing him to smash the window of his driver side door with his head. Mario blacked out instantly. His car continued spinning from the impact flailing Mario's limb body around like a rag doll. The white Nissan Altima tried to keep going, but the air bags deployed, and the engine was shut down.

Daniel Steger was never more sober in his life. His face was covered in some light-colored powder, residue from the air bag. He didn't know it, but one of his wrists was badly sprained, the other one was broken. Daniel's right knee was also badly hurt. It took a few seconds for the pain to come. Then, Daniel started reeling. With a frantic struggle he slipped out of the car and started to run away, but his knee was hurting too much. Daniel fell to the floor and tried to crawl away, but by this time there were bystanders and other vehicles around him. People were calling 911 and taking pictures with their phones, some were also filming with their phones.

They watched as Daniel still tried to crawl away from the scene, but people had their phones right on top of him and walked next to him while yelling at him, "Don't try to run. We all got you on camera. You better wait for the police." All the yelling only made Daniel panic even more. He tried harder to crawl away, but a man went over to Daniel, grabbed his leg, and held on to it, stopping him from moving any further. Daniel was yelling something

149

incomprehensible, but the man simply ignored him.

Mario Reyes was out cold. His head was bleeding as was his nose. It was hard to tell if he was breathing or not. The crowd could only wait for the EMP's to arrive. By the time the ambulance showed up it was 6:45am. The police had already handcuffed Daniel and took him away. Both vehicles were towed, and Mario was on his way to emergency.

Meanwhile at SECMET, the lab crew arrived early, it was 7:30am. Some of the preparations were done the day before. The body suit containing the sensors was finally reconfigured and ready for testing any energy discrepancies entering Thomas' body. There was some excitement in the air, but you could fit all of their hopes inside of a thimble. By 8am, everyone was on their second cup of coffee. By 8:15am everything was ready for the first round of tests. Thomas had decided to come in a little early. He got to SECMET by 8am and was waiting in the conference room playing with his Nintendo Switch, a handheld portable game unit. It wasn't until a few people noticed Thomas that they realized...where's Mario?

The employees hadn't noticed Mario's absence, but security noticed right away. They had already tried calling him. They also went into high alert. Mr. Barton was lead when Mario was not around. Barton instructed the security team to go into yellow alert until Mario is contacted. It also meant that Mr. Cooper was in charge of Thomas' exit plan. This means that Mr. Cooper was always to be no more than a few feet away from Thomas at all times. They are to use the designated escape route in the event of a breach depending on which protocol is initiated. It was 8:25am, Barton walked up to Cooper and said, "I don't like this. No one has had contact with the boss all morning." Cooper replied, "Copy that. I don't got a good feeling about it either." "Copy that. Go check on Thomas. Eyes open." Barton walked away and spoke into his radio, "Unit 4, come in."

"This is unit 4. Copy."

"Unit 4, give me a constant parameter check, don't wait for the scheduled time, over."

"Copy that. Over."

Barton decided to go check on the Secmet lab crew, but everyone was working oblivious to the tension the security team felt. Cooper was standing just outside the door of the conference room. He could see Thomas sitting on a chair, feet up on the table and playing his video games. James Riley was on interior parameter check when he met up with Barton. Riley noticed that Barton looked a little tense. "Hey, Barton, what's going on?" Barton's eyes were darting around the facility, and said, "I don't know Ri, don't like it when the boss is not around. Walk with me." Barton walked over to the security room. There were a dozen lockers, a small table, six plastic chairs and a supply closet. Barton used his keycard to open the closet to reveal the heavy weapons. Barton grabbed a couple of HK MPV7 sub machine guns and handed one to Riley. Riley looked at it and said, "You expecting trouble?"

"Maybe. Yes. Here." Barton tossed him a couple of 40 round mags and said, "Stay frosty."

The HK MPV7 was the perfect compact sub machine gun for close quarter combat, one of Seal Team 6 weapons of choice. Barton grabbed a couple of mags for himself and headed back into the lab area. Barton and Riley headed towards the conference room. Then, just as Barton was thinking, '*I don't like this*,' all hell broke loose. The SECMET team was heading towards the conference room to start their meeting. It was exactly 8:30am, that's when they heard it, or rather, felt it. There was an explosion, it seemed like the entire building bounced, all power was cut off. The entire facility went into total darkness. It only took a couple of seconds for the emergency lights to kick in, but it felt like minutes to those trying to find their way through the temporary darkness. Barton could hear rustling footsteps. Another explosion. SECMET has been breached. He yelled into his radio, "Cooper, initiate Delta Protocol 1, now, now".

By now Barton could hear the sounds of cannisters bouncing around, thick white clouds of noxious gas began filling the entire open lab area. Barton did not know if the smoke was just for cover or if any chemicals were involved. His men had portable breathing apparatuses built into their uniforms. Barton pulled out his small mask and attached it over his face. More footsteps, they were rushing the interior of the facility. He could barely make out the intruders. They looked like special forces, well equipped and moving with precision. *Government? Shit!*

A small group of men were walking towards him, slowly, weapons drawn in single file as to hide their numbers. They couldn't shoot blindly into the smoke cover for fear of hitting civilians. Barton Yelled out towards the intruders, "That's far enough. I got armor piercing ammo so your vest don't mean shit to me. Stand down, now." Barton could see that his words had no effect on their movement. Barton held up his hand in front of Riley, signaling him to hold his fire. "I say again, stand down." Barton heard a voice coming from the cloud of smoke. "We're just here for the boy. Your men can leave." Barton replied, "What boy?"

"Let's not do the back-and-forth dialogue, just tell us where the boy is." Barton moved his finger onto the trigger and started to apply pressure. "Okay, then, how about fuck you. Take one more step and your dead. And tell all your girlfriends to get the fuck out of my building."

"Okay," The figure in front of him said. Barton could see him holding up both hands while slowly walking backwards and disappearing into the cloud of smoke. It was at this point that Barton realized that the smoke had a sedative agent in it. He could see some of the lab crew members slowly falling and becoming motionless. Barton could hear more footsteps coming in the building. There had to be dozens of these guys out there. A few seconds later, the smoke was pierced with what seemed to be hundreds of projectiles. Riley let out a small moan. "Shit, I'm hit." Barton looked towards Riley who had fallen on the ground and was moving towards him. By the time he reached Barton, Riley could hardly move. Riley was now lying right next to Barton.

Barton looked down at Riley but didn't see any blood. "What the fuck, what is this." Riley said while checking his neck. Barton could see a small dart embedded on the side of Riley's neck. Riley looked up at Barton with eyes wide open and said, "I can't move, shit, I can't move." Riley took in one more breath and slowly passed out. Barton pulled out the dart and thought, 'Tranquilizers? Why?" No wonder there wasn't a lot of shooting going on, these guys are just biding their time until the gas, or the darts knocks everyone out. These guys were definitely government. They didn't want to suffer any unintended collateral damage if this gets out to the press.

Barton knew this was not over. He yelled into the smoke hoping his team was nearby. "Hey, whatta you guys think? Two team members were very close by, Barton could barely make them out, but he knew who they were. Roger, whom everybody called Roger Dodger and Korbin, both ex-navy seals. Roger-Dodger yelled back, "This stinks of military black ops, bullshit." Korbin also yelled out, "I'm with Dodger, these guys are definitely military. Now what?" "Now what is we're about to get our asses handed to us. Question is, are we getting paid enough to die?"

"I don't think so." Replied Riley.

"Ditto on that." Said Kelly.

Barton yelled out one more time. "Okay, Cooper's got the kid, lets bug out."

All three men moved into the cover of the thick smoke and headed towards the roof in the hopes of making an escape from there. There was another spray of darts, but they were able to

152

avoid getting hit. They ran up the stairs to the roof exit, burst through the door and onto the roof. All three men froze when they were met by over a dozen men with weapons drawn. Barton held up his hands then slowly placed his weapon on the ground. The other two men followed. A man in a uniform with no insignias or any identifying marks walked up to Barton and said, "I'm glad you boys decided to live to fight another day." He motioned to his men, "Take them."

Escape and secure package Delta Protocol 1 was in place. Cooper was charged with securing Thomas. When Cooper heard Barton initiate the plan, Cooper and James Banks headed towards the boy. Banks was squatted just outside the conference room to ward off anybody trying to get in. Cooper had already run into the conference room, picked up Thomas by the waist and carried him out the back door of the conference room. Outside in the lab area, Banks was having a hard time seeing through the smoke. He could make out a couple of figures but didn't know if they were friend or foe.

Banks heard a voice, it sounded close to his position. "Drop your weapon. You get only one warning." Banks tried to find a target but couldn't find a clear shot. He was moving his weapon sporadically hoping to see any kind of movement to establish a target but to no avail. He heard the footsteps coming closer. Banks decided to move, he shot blindly into the smoke and ran across the wall of the conference room. He could hear and feel bullets, or what he thought were bullets flying all around him. But they sounded strange.

Suddenly his head snapped back. He was hit. He stopped and was hit several more times. Banks reached for his neck to see how bad he was bleeding. But there was very little blood. He felt something strange on his neck, he grabbed it, pulled it out and looked to see what it was. "Darts?" he said to himself, "Shit!" Banks felt his body get heavier with each second until finally he passed out. In a matter of a few minutes, everyone in SECMET was sedated.

Cooper had grabbed Thomas and ran through the interior conference room door that led to the escape route. Thomas was visibly scared, he asked, "Where's Mario?" Cooper replied, "No time to explain, don't talk, just follow me." Cooper put Thomas down on the floor and said, " Let's go, run!" The conference room door automatically locks during a power outage. Whoever the intruders were, they were going to have to use explosives on that door as well and even more to open the door they just went through. All this was designed for this exact purpose, to give the runner time to get Thomas out.

Cooper and Thomas were now running down the short hallway hidden behind the conference room. In the hallway was another door, this one lead to an underground tunnel, which forked into two other tunnels. Again, all designed to slow down their pursuers. Finally, at the end of one of these tunnels was a small room. In this room was a cache of weapons, cash, passports, and a Custom Audi A8 L V10 with 532 horsepower. Cooper grabbed some weapons and ammo, opened the laptop that was sitting on a small countertop and keyed in, Delta Protocol 1, go, enter. They jumped in the Audi, the door leading to the underground exit tunnel opened, and then Cooper punched it. The acceleration caught them both by surprise.

Cooper slowed the car down a little to gain control. Thomas stared at the small space the car had to negotiate. The tunnels weren't that wide, also intentional. Thomas asked again, "Where's Mario?" Cooper looked at Thomas and said, "Can't talk right now, Thomas, we gotta focus on getting out of here and getting you to the safe house. I'll explain everything there. Just do me a favor."

"What's that?"

"Just put on your seat belt, stay low, and hang on."

Delta Protocol 1, or DP-1, was one of many escape plans Mario had put together for extracting Thomas safely. It entails one designated person to act as transporter. However, as a precautionary measure, DP-1 also initiated TVD drone or, the Trivalance Drone. The TVD is a highly specialized drone designed specifically for this protocol. The TVD incorporated multiple drones all of which are housed and controlled by the main drone. There is a Mini drone, which is used for visual surveillance. The Mini drone has high-definition cameras with a 6000mm dynamic zoom capability. It is also programmed with over 300 of Thomas' biometric points for identification in case someone tries to disguise him.

This drone can determine things like the exact size and shape of Thomas' ears, eyebrows, lips, nose, and eyes. It can ID Thomas by his hands, fingers, or arms. It is almost impossible to fool this program. The Main drone also carries a Micro-drone. The Micro-drone is used for tracking. It is deployed whenever Thomas enters any hostile vehicle. The Micro-drone is laser-guided by the Main drone. It is designed to attach itself to the underside of the target vehicle and acts as a tracking device. The Main drone carries six Micro drones in case there are multiple vehicle changes. The Mini-drone also carries and deploys Nano-drones. These Nano-drones are the size of a few grains of rice. These Nano-drones are designed for one purpose, and that is, should Thomas encounter one of them, he is to swallow it. The reason for this is so that Mario knows that if Thomas is ever captured…again, he will be checked for any tracking devices on him. Thomas has three sub-dermal tracking devices already in him. One in his arm, one on his leg and one on his back. Mario is sure that they will be found by any typical scanner. The Nano-drones are to be deployed as soon as the signals from all three tracking devices go silent. That's how Thomas knows to keep an eye out for what may look like a fly or some other small insect flying around. Thomas knows he is to try and catch it and swallow it so that Mario can find him.

Cooper and Thomas exited from the tunnel onto a quite little cul-de sac that had just one house and a small detached one-car garage. Mario had bought the property because the small cul-de-sac had just one house on it, so it was very private. The one car garage was close enough to the foothills that Mario had the tunnel connected from Secmet, Inc to the back of the garage. The garage door automatically opened when the Audi L8 tripped the infrared sensors in the tunnel. As Cooper shot out of the tunnel, he had to turn sharply and drift to the right. There wasn't much room for maneuvering, but Cooper had been well trained in defensive driving.

They were on a small street, Stonehill Drive, it was just a few hundred yards to E. Loma Alta Drive. From there, Cooper would head south to Altadena Drive which would put him right around the middle of town. Cooper stuck to the protocols, the priority now was to get Thomas to the safe house. The TVD was following overhead. Once he got to the safe house, he would try to contact Mario, wherever he was. *"Damn it, Mario, where the hell are you?"*

The safe house was less than 8 miles away in Monrovia, California. Cooper could be there in less than 12 minutes. All he had to do was jump on the 210 Interstate East. The on ramp was just a few blocks away. Cooper kept checking his mirrors for any tails. He hadn't seen another car either following them or any suspicious vehicles. Cooper unconsciously let out a sigh of relief. Thomas looked at Cooper and said, "Are we alright?" Cooper looked over at Thomas, but before he could say anything, their car was hit from the side with enough force to send them spinning out of control.

The Audi A8 came to a stop, and before they could catch their breath and get over the shock, the car was hit again from another angle. Thomas and Cooper were flailing around the interior. Thomas was shaken, but Coopers instincts kicked in. Cooper yelled at Thomas, "Thomas, look at me, as soon as I step out of the car, count to 10 then you push this button. Do you understand?" Cooper pointed to a hidden button in the center counsel. Thomas barely understood what Cooper said, but he got the gist of it and replied, "Okay."

Cooper jumped out of the vehicle with his fully automatic SCAR-16. Cooper hid behind the Audi and tried to assess the situation. There were four vehicles, SUV's, each with four men inside heavily armed. This was not going to be pretty. Cooper stayed low behind the bullet proof Audi and opened fire, spraying the lead vehicle with a barrage of bullets forcing the passengers to jump out and take cover. Cooper had two grenades on him. He threw one at the vehicle closes to him. The assailants ran back behind another SUV to take cover. The grenade went off causing minor damage to the vehicle. A few of the men got wounded but it did not deter them. Cooper was trying to make out who they were. All the men were wearing what looked like military fatigues, but not exactly. It was the same guys from the lab for sure, but no way of knowing who they were. There were no markings of any kind on their uniforms or vehicles.

Cooper began to receive fire. The Audi was designed to take on heavy fire, so Thomas was safe. Cooper banged on the side of the Audi and signaled to Thomas to push the button. Cooper stood up and laid down some suppression fire. Thomas pushed the button and the Audi suddenly started moving, in fact, it moved very quickly. Before Thomas knew it, the Audi was shooting down the street at a high rate of speed driving itself. The vehicle was on auto-drive and was programed with the address of the safe house.

As the Audi took off, it left Cooper exposed. Cooper dropped his weapon and put his hands up in hopes that they would let him surrender. One of the men walked up a little closer to Cooper and shot him. Within a few seconds, Cooper was knocked out by the dart. The men jumped into their vehicles and went after Thomas. 12 hundred feet above, the TVD was still following Thomas overhead. The men had not noticed the large drone, though it was easy to miss at that height. It was cruising at 500 feet, well over the recommended 400 max set by the FAA.

The self-defense auto drive mode on the Audi was designed to elude, but it also had to stay within safety parameters. In other words, it could go fast, but not so fast that it would jeopardize the occupant. Needless to say, with those safeguards in place, The Audi was able to be stopped. There were four vehicles, one had gone in front of the Audi, two drove along the left and right side, while the fourth covered the rear. The lead vehicle simply kept slowing down until they came to a complete stop.

156

The men surrounded the Audi and one of the uniformed men tried to coax Thomas into opening the door. Thomas, however, was reluctant. The man knocked on the passenger window where Thomas was sitting and said, "Thomas, open the door. We're not going to hurt you." Thomas would not look at the man, he kept on dialing Mario's number, but he wasn't picking up. The man knocked harder, "Thomas, we know this car is bullet proof, but it's not big bomb proof. Get my drift? We don't want to hurt you, we just need you to come with us. So, what's it gonna be? You comin' out, or you wanna go boom?" Thomas put his cell in his pocket and opened the door. He knew they weren't going to hurt him, he knew why they wanted him. "Okay, I'm coming out."

"Good boy."

The uniformed man put his hand on Thomas' shoulder as if they were good ole buddies and lead Thomas to one of the vehicles. Thomas got in the back seat. By the time they closed the door, a tracking mini drone was already attaching itself to the bottom of the SUV. Once the vehicle started moving, Thomas was blindfolded. Thomas did not panic or freak out, after all, this wasn't the first time he's been kidnapped and blindfolded and taken to an undisclosed location. It was 9:45am.

At 9:50am, in Huntington Hospital, Mario Reyes slowly opened his eyes. Mario stared straight up at an unfamiliar ceiling. There was a moment of disorientation, then all of the day's events came back to him. Mario started to get up but his whole body felt pain. He stopped to assess. He had some kind of medical wrap around his lower chest area, *'that was sore.'* He thought. He felt his head, which also had the same gauze wrapping, that too was a little sore. He didn't see anything that might be broken, so that's good. He mostly had a general soreness on every part of his body. Other than that, he didn't see any reason to stay.

He had to find his phone and check on the lab, and Thomas. He looked around but didn't see his clothes anywhere. He got up and started walking to the small closet located on the other side of the room. Each step he took he heard himself saying, "ouch, ouch." Finally, he got to the closet, opened the door, and looked inside. It was empty. Not good. He *ouched* his way back to the bed to ring the nurse. Mario waited impatiently, but it took less than a minute for the nurse to show up. She smiled and said, "I see you're up? How are we feeling?"

"Fine, I was just wondering about my clothes. Well, actually, I need my phone, it's very important."

The nurse walked towards Mario with arms stretched, she placed her hands on his shoulders and tried to coax him to sit on the bed. Mario resisted, but she was insistent. Mario gave in and sat down. The nurse said, "I'll get your stuff. Your clothes were too bloody, mostly from you head wound. Heads bleed a lot. How is you head, by the way?" Mario reached up to touch his head, it was definitely sore. He answered, "I ain't gonna lie, it hurts. But about my phone, would you mind getting it for me. I really need to call in and check on a few things."
"Sure."
"Thanks."

The nurse headed towards the nightstand on the left side of the bed and opened the drawer. She pulled out Mario's phone and handed it to him. She smiled and said, "All your things are in this drawer. We had your clothes washed. I'll bring them right in. Meanwhile, I'll have the doctor come and check you out." Mario held up his phone and simply said, "Thanks." 15 minutes later, Riley was at the front door picking up Mario. Riley filled him in on what went down at SECMET. Mario agreed that it sounded like government work, but it was probably a black ops mission. They made a quick stop at Big 5 Sporting goods where Mario bought a workout suit. He was still in his hospital robe when Riley picked him up. Mario did not want to wait for his clothes or the doctor. Mario checked his phone.

There were about 50 missed calls from Thomas' phone plus another 50 from his crew. Mario was looking at the GPS tracker data from the TVD drone. He spoke to Riley without turning his head, Mario was fixed onto Thomas' location, "Make a left on the next street."
"Copy that."
"Where are the rest of the crew right now?"
"I'm guessing either under some kind of arrest or they're at the lab waiting for your instructions, boss."
"I can't get a hold of Cooper, I'll try Barton." Riley made a left. Mario looked up and said, "Go straight for a couple of miles."
"Copy."
Mario dialed Barton. Barton picked up after the first ring. "Where the hell you've been, boss? You totally missed the shit show over here."
"I heard. How's everyone doing? Anybody get hurt?"
"Only egos. These guys were pros and were set on mitigating collateral damage. What's next?"

Mario paused for a few seconds, "Hold on, I got a bead on Thomas' location. Looks like they stopped moving. Get the men and meet me at the location I'm about to send you. Our priority is getting Thomas back."

"Copy that. Waiting on text. We'll see you there."

Mario sent the location to Barton. According to the reading on Thomas' cellphone, they were only about 15 minutes away from Thomas' location. Something about that didn't sound right. These guys were too professional to be this slow and sloppy. But this was their only lead, so, he looked at Riley and said, "Okay, let's see if we can get a speeding ticket." Riley smiled and said, "Copy that, boss." Riley floored the gas pedal and sped to the location. They arrived in almost half the time. Riley parked the car, Mario jumped out to look around. There wasn't anything or anyone around. It was a typical housing track. A few cars parked here and there but no sign of anything nefarious.

Mario checked the bushes along the sidewalk and found it. Thomas' phone. He held it up for Riley to see. Riley nodded. It was a goose chase. Mario got back in the car. Let's wait for the guys to show up. Meanwhile, I'm gonna check on the TVD trackers.

Mario pushed a few buttons and finally got a signal. "Okay, I got something. They're on the move. Start the car and make a U-turn. Head to the 210 freeway and go east, and don't go slow. We might be able to catch up to them."

"Copy that."

Mario dialed Barton. Barton picked up. "What's up, boss?"

"We're headed to the 210 East again. Stay on that course until further notice."

"Perfect, we're already on route."

"Copy that. Stand by for further instructions. Anyone heard from Cooper yet?"

"Not yet, boss, but judging by the way these guys work, I'm gonna bet he's okay."

"Copy that."

Thomas was sitting in the back seat of the SUV between to large men. The first thing one of them did was check Thomas for a cellphone. He found it and simply threw it out the window. Thomas heard it bounce around on the sidewalk and wondered if the screen cracked. Thomas also still had his portable Nintendo game station that he was playing with in the lab earlier. The men let him keep that. Thomas heard one of the men speak to the driver, "Hey, there it is. Up ahead, get ready." The driver responded, "I got it."

159

Thomas felt the vehicle slow down almost to a complete stop. Then, a little bump, and now it felt like the vehicle was going up a steep ramp. It was short, the car straightened out and the driver turned off the engine. Thomas then heard a loud rumbling noise, like a metal garage door closing. Then Thomas could feel they were on the move again. But the vehicle they were in wasn't doing the moving.

The SUV had driven into a large truck. Indeed, this was a special truck. The entire trailer was lined with lead along with a powerful RF jammer for scrambling any signals that might be emanating from any device withing the truck trailer. It was 11:01am. At 11:02am, Mario was looking at his phone, when suddenly, "Shit. The signal just went dead. I got nothing."

Riley gave a look of confusion and said, "What? What do you mean you got nothing, you just had a bead on him?"

"I'm telling you, I got nothing. They must have either found the tracker and broken it, or they're somehow jamming our signal. Either way. We're flying blind."

"What do you want to do."

"Let's keep going in the general direction for a few more miles, but go a little faster, let's see if we see anything up ahead."

"Copy that."

"Wait a minute, damn, I'm so stupid. The TVD will still follow the vehicle with or without a tracker as long as it has a visual. Let me hook up to the TVD onboard tracker. Oh yeah, what the hell was I thinking, this is way better. I got a visual on our target. It's a semi-truck, more than likely the vehicle and/or Thomas are inside it. Man, this drone is paying off. Keep going straight as fast as you can." Riley was smiling as he replied, "Copy that, boss." but he was tense as he moved the speedometer closer to 100mph. Mario was getting his hopes up. If they can continue at this rate, they may be able to catch up to the truck in less than 20 minutes.

The two large men next to Thomas removed the hood from his head. Thomas could see that they were inside of a trailer. It was well lit. There was nothing in it except them. The men unbuckled Thomas' seatbelt and asked him to hold his hands up. Thomas thought about instinctively saying 'why' but he knew it wouldn't matter. Thomas held up both his hands. The man on his right waved a large flat wand up and down his body. It beeped three times. The men looked at each other and nodded. The man on the left reached over the back seat and pulled over a leather bag and said to Thomas, "Okay, Thomas, we got another set of clothes for you. Take

160

off your clothes and put these on."

"Right here?" Thomas asked.

"Yes. And please don't make us make you, it would be embarrassing for all of us, wouldn't you agree?" Thomas frowned and replied, "Yes. I suppose it would." Thomas complied and in a few minutes was in a completely different set of clothes. They weren't exactly what he would have chosen, but they weren't too bad either. The man on the left waved his wand again over Thomas' body. It still beeped three times. The men looked at each other again. The man on the left said, "Well, sorry to tell you this Thomas, but we're going to have to remove those subdermal trackers." Thomas did not like the sound of that. His voice was a little nervous when he asked, "So, what are you going to do, cut me up?"

"Well, kind of, but don't worry, you won't feel it."

Thomas couldn't help but put on a little smile as he said, "Really?" And just as he said that he felt the needle going into his shoulder. "Ow, what was that?" The man on the right said, "It's a sedative. It won't knock you out completely, well, it might, we didn't adjust the dose to your weight, but you should be fine. It really is best if you just relax, Thomas. You know we're not going to hurt you, but we do need to get those trackers out. Sorry."

Thomas dosed off as his voice trailed off, "Okaaaaay."

Ten minutes later and a little bit of blood loss, the trackers were out. Luckily, they were not embedded too deep, so they didn't need to stitch Thomas up. The only person who had some limited knowledge about their mission and their target was the one man who was designated to remove the trackers. He had to be told because he would have to cut Thomas in order to remove the devices. He was instructed to say nothing about what he was about to see. He was told about Thomas' ability to heal himself, he was not told about Thomas' ability to heal others. So, when this man cut Thomas, he did notice that the wound seemed to start getting smaller even before he was finished removing the tiny trackers. Once removed, the man noticed that Thomas' cut was healing before his very eyes. It was creepy, but it wasn't any of his business. He had a job to do and like a good soldier, he did it and said nothing to no one.

The truck exited the 210 freeway on Grand Ave in Covina, California. The truck headed south for about one-half mile and stopped on a side street. There they removed the SUV and parked it in the street, took Thomas out, who was still a little groggy from the sedative, and placed him in another car. It was pure bad luck that for no real apparent reason, one of the men looked up and saw something strange. It looked like a large drone hovering above them. It could only mean one thing, that drone had been following them. The man who spotted the drone pointed it out to the other men. One of them went to the trunk of his car and pulled out a high-powered rifle. The man was a former Navy Seal sniper. The drone had to drop to an altitude below 200 feet in order to fully utilize the onboard biometrics system. This, however, made it vulnerable to being spotted. The sniper took aim and fired. It only took one shot to knock it out of the sky. The men jumped into their vehicles and took off.

Mario saw the whole thing through the TVD cameras. "Shit. Shit, shit, shit."

"What happen, boss?"

"They made our drone and shot it down." Riley waited a few seconds and said, "Now what, boss?"

"Let's keep going and find that truck. Maybe they left some clues behind. I got a good visual on where they got off the freeway. From there I can still remember the streets they turned on. They only went a few blocks south, turned left and stopped a few blocks after that. Shouldn't be too difficult to spot a semitruck in a residential neighborhood."

"Copy that, boss. You think the truck will still be there?"

"I don't know, don't care. Gotta check it out. For now, that's all we got."

They arrived at the sight about 20 minutes later. The truck was still there. Mario and the others inspected the truck inside and out. Except for a few broken trackers they found on the floor on the bed of the truck, they saw nothing that would lead them any closer to Thomas. Mario told the guys to head back to the lab and secure whatever data was still there. Clean out the computers and everyone's cellphones, laptops and any other devices that have any mention of SECMET.

All employees will be laid off until further notice. They would all be given a generous severance package. Mario told Riley to go back with the crew, he would stay behind for a while and think about his next move. Mario walked over to the car and sat on the driver's side and contemplated the day's events. He wondered how their location was compromised. Someone had to have said something to someone. Most likely one of the lab workers. He thought about retribution but decided it would do nobody any good. In regard to Thomas, there was still hope. There was, after all, one last chance. Mario checked his watch, it was 10:40am.

The SUV carrying Thomas was the second vehicle of a five-vehicle caravan heading towards

Brackett Field Airport, located near the L.A. County Fairplex in Pomona. Once they were on the tarmac, they removed Thomas' blindfold. By 11:00am Thomas and eight other men boarded a Gulfstream G650 private jet. Thomas noticed that there were already a couple of men inside the jet waiting. One of the men motioned to Thomas to join them. They were sitting in the only seating configuration which accommodated four people facing each other. Thomas sat in one of the aisle seats. Thomas couldn't help noticing how comfortable the seat was. *'This is nice,'* he thought.

The man sitting to his right held up his hand awkwardly in an attempt to shake Thomas' hand. They were sitting so close together it was difficult for the man to offer his hand. Nevertheless, he leaned back a little while introducing himself. "Hello Thomas, my name is Dr. Allan Burrill, and this is my colleague, Dr. Cole Rinzler. We are very happy to meet you." Dr. Rinzler offered his hand across the small table between them. Thomas shook it but did not say anything. He figured he would let them do as much of the talking as possible while he sorted things out in his head. Thomas had come to a conclusion about life, everyone had an agenda.

Dr. Burrill continued talking, "Thomas, I have to tell you that we, Dr. Rinzler and I, already know about you and your abilities. We are, well, fascinated to say the least. Could you tell us anything about how it all works?" Thomas just looked down on the table hoping they would just keep talking. They did. Dr. Rinzler chimed in, "Thomas, I'm sure you know we are not here to cause you any harm or trouble, but we would be much appreciative if you wouldn't mind cooperating with us. If you haven't figured it out yet, we are working for the U.S. government, so, we're on your side." Thomas remained quiet. Dr. Burrill asked, "Thomas, are you okay? Are you feeling ill? Is there anything we can bring you? Something to eat, perhaps?" Dr. Burrill called over one of the men and asked if they had anything to eat in the plane. The man didn't know, he simply said, "Not sure, I'll go check."
"Thank you." The Dr. replied.

Everyone was lightly jolted as the plane began to taxi towards the runway. Thomas noticed that the plane had a very pleasant scent in the air, like vanilla and cinnamon. In fact, the scent was making him a little hungry. The man came back with a couple of bags of potato chips, a candy bar and a small bag of nuts. Dr. Burrill took them and looked at Thomas and said, "I thought this fancy plane would have had some nicer food." The Dr. handed the items to Thomas. "Take what you want, there will be some proper food where we're going." Thomas finally looked up to meet Dr. Burrill's eyes and asked, "Where are we going?"

"I'm sorry I can't tell you that right now. In the meantime, please enjoy these treats. We'll have plenty of time to talk when you're ready."

Thomas opened the Hershey's chocolate bar and said, "What if I don't want to talk later?" Both Dr.'s glanced over at the man sitting across the aisle from them. Thomas looked to his right to see who they were looking at. He was a tall lean man in a dark suit. He went by the name of Mr. Pitt. It was obviously an alias. No one knew his real name or exactly which government acronym he worked for, though most thought it was NHS, National Homeland Security. All they knew was that he was in charge of security and pretty much everything else. Thomas turned back towards his snacks and ate nervously. The plane accelerated and took off. Their destination was Naval Base Point Loma in San Diego.

Thomas was eating the Hershey's candy bar while looking around the plane. It seemed a little too luxurious for a military transport. It was more like something a movie star would fly in. Thomas kept his head down but still took notice of those around him. He was not at all intimidated by the two Dr.'s, they seemed friendly enough. Dr. Burrill's appearance was very disarming, he was medium height, a little overweight and wore a brand-new light lime-green Polo and Khaki pants. His face was roundish with a gray receding hairline. He looked like the perfect TV dad. Dr. Rinzler didn't fare as well. He had a few extra more pounds than his colleague, had a long narrow face with considerably less gray hair. He had roundish glasses that appeared to be a little too small for his face. And even though he was wearing a more formal dark blazer with a white shirt, his posture and demeanor made his clothes look a little dumpy. Both men were in their late 50's.

Mr. Pitt on the other hand, appeared stern and stiff. He had been reading something on his tablet since take-off. Although he had not lifted his head once, Thomas knew that he was totally aware of everything around him. Mr. Pitt reminded Thomas of Mario. Alert, prepared, and dangerous. The intercom came on and the captain announced, "Just a heads-up folks, we're going to be running into a little turbulence. We are recommending you fasten your seatbelts. We will reach our destination in approximately twenty-two minutes."

Thomas was relieved to hear that the flight was so short. He was expecting to be on a much longer trip to who knows where. Twenty-two minutes didn't seem so bad. Maybe Mario will be able to find him. He did, after all, have one more trick up his sleeve. There was nothing else left to do but enjoy the plane ride. Thomas asked if he could sit near a window. Again, both men looked over at Mr. Pitt, who gave them an approving nod. Thomas understood and got up to sit on the chair directly behind which was a solo seat next to the window. And again, he noticed that the seats were really comfortable. Thomas looked out the window for a few minutes and decided he'd seen enough clouds. He pulled out his game boy and began playing his video game. He was glad they let him keep it. They had checked it for trackers, but it came up clean.

Back in Altadena, Mario was having a meeting with his men. They finally got a hold of Cooper. Cooper had been knocked out for about 40 minutes. When he came to, he was able to borrow a cell phone from a stranger and called Mario who instructed him to wait there, and someone would pick him up. Later, in the afternoon, they all met at SECMET. There was nobody there, the lab crew and staff had been sent away. There were some laptops missing, a couple of desk-top computers and dozens of files. These guys knew exactly what to look for and where everything was.

Mario rounded the men up in the conference room. The men sat down, but Mario started pacing, he said, "Okay, listen up. This was obviously an inside job. Someone tipped these bastards off as to who we are, what we're doing, along with some tactical intel. Ideas?" The men looked around the room at each other. Riley spoke first, "Don't look at us, boss. We get paid too much to burn you." Kelly spoke next, "Yeah, and if we did, believe it or not, it would have been cleaner than this." Mario kept pacing and talking, he said, "I agree. I don't think it was one of us. Did anyone hear anything during the battle that anyone might have said that would give us a clue as to where they're taking Thomas?" They all responded, they all sounded off,

"No."

"Nope."

"Didn't hear anything but explosions and firing."

"Nada."

"Negative."

Mario went on. "Okay, everybody is on 24-hour stand-by. I got one last ace, but it's up to Thomas to play it. I want to be ready to respond when it happens. Keep in touch with your sources in case we need help or special equipment. I want to be ready to move lightning fast if we get a location." They all responded simultaneously, "Copy that."

Point Loma Navy Base is located in San Diego, California. Its force protection mission is to deter, detect and defend the installation's personnel and assets against hostile actions. Its port operations provide multiple services for home-ported submarines and surface ships that dock there. It's been in use since 1959. It is under the command of Captain Aaron T. Price, CO of Naval Base Point Loma. In the north-west corner of the base against the hills, there is a building, approximately 3500 square feet. It used to be a warehouse facility but had recently been repurposed for Mr. Pitt's use. It was now referred to simply as the R&D facility. The back of the building was almost butted up against a 30 feet high embankment. There were no windows and only two doors. One in the front and one roll-up door on the side. There were, however, four skylights.

The Gulfstream G650 landed on an airstrip in the naval base. There were a few SUV's waiting for them when they arrived. Thomas got in the back seat of one of them while Mr. Pitt sat in the front seat of the same vehicle. Thomas started to ask a question, but he noticed Mr. Pitt quickly raised his hand up as if to say wait or stop or something. Thomas correctly interpreted the hand signal as 'stopped talking'. Mr. Pitt's hand went down slowly. Thomas was really not liking this guy.

It only took a few minutes for them to get to the entrance of the R&D facility. The short drive still yielded a fantastic view of the ocean. Thomas could hear the waves crashing as they drove down the short narrow paved road along the water. Eventually they turned away from the ocean and into the small parking lot. Thomas could no longer hear the ocean, but he could still smell the salty air. Something about the smell made him feel calm, though he didn't really have a reason to be calm. He knew what was coming. Finally, all the vehicles parked. Mr. Pitt got out first and walked straight over to the front door. Thomas followed, as did Dr. Burrill and Dr. Rinzler.

The inside was definitely not as nice as SECMET, but Thomas could see it was designed for the same purpose. To poke, stick and prod him. Mr. Pitt spoke for the first time, his voice sounded like he looked, monotoned, severe and humorless. "Dr.'s if you will, please see to your preparations, we will be starting immediately. Thomas, you're coming with me." Thomas followed Mr. Pitt to a small office on the east side of the building. The office was as severely austere as Mr. Pitt's personality. The desk, chairs and bookshelves were old. The chair that Mr. Pitt sat on behind the desk squeaked loudly. Thomas could see that the noise annoyed Mr. Pitt, and for some reason, this gave Thomas just a little bit of joy.

Mr. Pitt motioned to the chair in front of him and Thomas sat down. "Thomas," Mr. Pitt said, while locking his fingers together in front of him, "I hope we can count on your cooperation. We have an extensive dossier on you and your abilities. We've been gathering them for a while now. We know all about the test being performed at SECMET, the results, and what new test were to be performed. As you may have already guessed, we did have someone in SECMET feeding us intel." Mr. Pitt paused for dramatic effect, then continued, "I want to be clear about something, although I will not be your best friend, I will always be honest with you. You deserve that. We will be conducting some test of our own and like I said, we would very much prefer that we have your cooperation." Thomas was almost afraid to ask, but he did, "What happens if I don't want to cooperate?"

"Let's not talk about such...shall we say, bad things. If I'm not mistaken, and please correct me if I'm wrong, but, you do not have to be conscious for your healing to work, am I right. We can simply take your hand and touch someone with it and it will yield the same results, correct?" Thomas got a little pale and answered, "Yes."

"Okay. Let's get started. I would like to begin by asking you some questions you have probably been asked a thousand times, but I need to know, do you know how it works?"

"I do not. I wish I did so I can tell others, and everyone will leave me alone."

"I see. What about control, do you have any control of it. Can you touch someone and not heal them?"

"No. I mean, I never tried to control it. It all just happens."

"Do you feel anything?"

"No." Though Thomas remembered how at first, he did use to feel something. But for whatever reason, he stopped feeling anything at all.

"Before we get started in the lab, is there anything you can tell me about what is going on with your ability?"

"No."

"Very well. Thomas I will trust you, but if you ever break that trust, it will not be pleasant for you. Do you understand me?"

"Yes."

"As a reminder, I know you can heal yourself, but I also know that you feel pain. Am I making myself clear?"

"Yes sir."

Mr. Pitt stood up and motioned towards the door. "Shall we?" Thomas got up and followed him out into the lab area. He saw Dr. Rinzler and Dr. Burrill holding up the suit fitted with electrodes. Thomas thought, '*Here we go again.*' Dr. Rinzler saw Thomas approaching and called out, "Thomas, come over here, we need to put this on you." Dr. Rinzler sounded happy, almost giddy as he held up the suit in front of Thomas. "This is really very exciting, isn't it?" Dr. Rinzler asked. Thomas grabbed the suit with very little enthusiasm and said, "Yeah, it a real blast." Dr. Rinzler completely missed the sarcasm and said, "Yes, it is, isn't it?"

Dr. Burrill was more in tune with Thomas' attitude and put his hand on Thomas' shoulder and said, "Thomas, I know this isn't easy, but the sooner we can come up with any answers about all this the sooner this can all be over." Thomas thought about that, '*Will it? Will this ever be over? Will my life always be like this?* Thomas donned the suit and three hours later there was no more information to be learned other than what they already knew. In spite of all the data they got from SECMET, they still performed many of the same tests. Blood test, x-rays, PET scan and an MRI. The results were the same. Nothing. Thomas had been with them for less than one day and he could already see that they were getting frustrated. Thomas finally asked if he could take a break and if there was any food around.

They headed back to Mr. Pitt's office. There was a small table in there where Thomas could sit down and eat. They brought him a ham sandwich, a bag of chips and Coke. They told him he would have a regular meal later in the day. Thomas ate his food without complaining, he had only one request, he asked if he could play his game. He also asked Mr. Pitt if there was any way of getting hold of a charger for his portable video game. Mr. Pitt became suspicious and asked Thomas to hand over his Nintendo Switch.

Mr. Pitt gave it a quick glance then opened the drawer in his desk and placed it inside. He noticed Thomas' disappointment and said, "Don't worry, I'm just going to have it checked out first. You'll get it back tomorrow." Thomas went from feeling disappointed to indignant, he stood up from his chair and said, "What am I going to do around here? I need something to keep me busy and I know you're not going to let me use a computer." Mr. Pitt remained motionless for a few seconds, his face showed less than concern. "Thomas," Mr. Pitt said in a low voice, "I'm not here to entertain you, my only job here is to make sure you cooperate. Trust me, having something to do is one of the least things you should be worried about. I do need to emphasize to you that if all this were up to me, you would now be in a medically induced coma. You get where I'm coming from, Thomas?" Thomas actually let out a small gulp. His eyes were wide open and unblinking. Thomas merely said, "Yes sir."

It was almost 5pm and Mr. Pitt was getting a little annoyed at the lack of progress. He stepped out of his office and made an announcement, "Alright everyone. Let's wrap it up for today. We'll meet here at 7:30am tomorrow. We will begin running phase 2 concurrently with phase 1." There was a noticeable change in the air, everyone became somber. Thomas didn't like the sound of that. Thomas approached Mr. Pitt and asked him,"

"So, what's phase 2?" "I'm afraid you'll have to find out for yourself tomorrow, Thomas. Good night." Mr. Pitt walked away.

A young man appeared from a doorway and walked towards Thomas and introduced himself. "Hello Thomas, my name is Glen Ryder." He offered his hand and Thomas shook it. "I'll be showing you where everything is. I'll take you to your room and show you where you'll be eating and sleeping. Follow me." Thomas followed Glen and said, "Hey, do you know what they're talking about? I mean, about the phase 2?" "Sorry, they don't tell me anything and I learned not to ask. Although, I believe I've only heard some talk about phase 3 as well."

Thomas was about to ask another question but decided against it because he knew what the answer would be. Glen led Thomas down a short hallway. The walls look like they had recently been constructed and he would be correct. The entire building had been recently renovated. Most of the walls had not been painted. The hallway and most of the rooms were still bare drywall. Glen stopped at a door and opened it. "This is your room." Glen said as he motioned for Thomas to enter. "There's your bed, a small table, a bathroom, a TV, and a microwave. There are some snacks in the mini fridge. You can request certain snacks later, for now there's not much in there. Anyway, if you have any questions, just ask for me."

"Ask for you?"

"Yeah, oh, there's a two-way radio on the table. Just a heads up, I don't know who else is on this frequency. I'm sure Mr. Pitt is one of them."

"Got it." Thomas said with just a slight sigh of disappointment. Thomas looked around the sparse room. Drywall walls, no windows but at least he had his own bathroom. That was something. Thomas went straight to the bed and although it was still early, he fell straight to sleep as soon as his head hit the pillow.

For Thomas, the next morning went on as usual for him. More poking and prodding, more questions with no answers. *Yes, I can heal animals, no I can't grow back limbs, no, I don't know how it works, blah, blah, blah.* Thomas was more bored than concerned. Sometimes he wasn't even aware of what was being done until he felt another prick on the finger for a few more drops of blood. After another exhausting day of testing and questions Thomas walked over to Mr. Pitt and asked, "Mr. Pitt, have you had a chance to checkout my video game unit. It's just that I'm really bored and would really appreciate it if I could at least play my video games." Mr. Pitt replied, "Yes. It has been checked out. Seems everything is fine. Ask Mr. Ryder to locate a charger for you. Follow me to my office and I'll give it to you." The truth was, Mr. Pitt forgot about the game, but he knew it had been checked out once before for any bugs or tracing devices. For no apparent reason, he just wanted to make Thomas wait for it. It was probably more of a control thing than anything else.

Thomas called Glen on his radio and told him what Pitt said about the charger. Glen Ryder told Thomas he would lend him his charger until he got his hands on another one. Thomas was grateful. Thomas walked over to Dr. Burrill and said, "Hey Dr., I heard something about phase 2, can you tell me what it is?" Dr. Burrill looked at Thomas with some measure of sympathy. "Sorry Thomas, but I'm not at liberty to discuss our processes. What I can tell you is that phase 2 has already begun. We started this morning." Thomas had a look of consternation and replied, "It has?" Dr. Burrill shrugged his shoulders and said, "Yup."

What Thomas didn't know was that phase 2 was going to be an attempt at cloning. The first attempt will be to use some of Thomas' DNA to construct a simple layer of skin in the hopes that the skin will carry the healing properties which Thomas possesses. If that doesn't work, they are going to try to clone an appendage, like a hand. And if that isn't successful, they will try to clone Thomas.

It was almost 6:30 by the time Thomas was able to get to his room to rest. He finally got his Nintendo Switch back, he was happy about that, for more than one reason. The game was not only a needed distraction, but it was also a way to get help. Unbeknown to Mr. Pitt's staff, the small device was specially designed to show no trace of suspicion. However, Thomas was instructed on how to disassemble it, make a few simple modifications, and turn it into a basic tracking device. Now when Thomas turns it on, he could play with it as he would normally, but while he is playing, the device will now be sending a tracking signal. At 7:35pm, Mario's cellphone beeped.

The next morning Thomas was hoping for a break from all the testing. As it turned out, they didn't really need Thomas to be around. They had enough data to pour through without adding more. Today, however, would prove to be interesting. Dr. Rinzler was analyzing the data from the electrode suit that had been configured to detect any kind of energy anomalies emitting from Thomas. SECMET had not been able to perform this test because of the breach. Now Dr. Rinzler was puzzled over his findings. After eliminating all other possibilities there was only one conclusion he could come to. Thomas *was* emitting energy, but the signal was vague, so vague that Dr. Rinzler was still not one hundred percent sure to even mention it. Also, it was the proximity that seemed so odd. Thomas was emitting this energy in a tiny region about 5cm above his right ankle. It made no sense.

Not only did the area of emission seem a little bizarre, but the energy detected wouldn't be enough to be useful in any shape or form. He finally confronted Dr. Burrill and shared his findings. They decided it did warrant further investigation. They started preparing the suit for another run. Within a couple of hours, they had Thomas back in the sensor suit and waited with bated breath. They stared intently at the display and waited to see if they could detect the signal again. It was pure luck that they found it, the amount of energy would not have normally been caught had it not been for the fact that Derek Hurd, the astrophysicist from SECMET, had decided to calibrate the sensors for such low measurements. Typically, it is not necessary to calibrate for one teraelectronvolt, which is about the kinetic energy that a flying mosquito would put out. But Derek didn't know what they were looking for, so he went a little extreme on the target values.

Dr. Rinzler and Dr. Burrill did not have to wait for long. Within a matter of seconds, the tiny energy spikes were clearly visible on the graph. However, these spikes were normal, they merely constituted a baseline. But now what? They decided to have Thomas touch someone to see if the energy spikes got any higher. They informed Mr. Pitt about the test they were about to perform and asked if he would like to be present. He agreed and they all met to watch the results of the test.

Nobody was hurt, so Mr. Pitt pulled out a knife and cut himself on the hand. Everyone winced as he had cut himself deep enough to draw a good amount of blood. Mr. Pitt showed no emotion, or any sign of pain. Dr. Rinzler thought, '*Is this fucking guy for real?*' Mr. Pitt walked over to Thomas and told both doctors to watch the screen. He held his hand towards Thomas and instructed Thomas to touch his hand. Thomas also thought there was something wrong with this guy, but he reached out and touched Mr. Pitt's hand.

Mr. Pitt watched as his hand began to heal. His face had more reaction to the healing than to the cut. It doesn't matter who you were, it was always an amazing thing to watch this process. The blood stopped flowing, the wound began closing by itself and finally, the complete healing of the hand. No scar, no bruise no marks, nothing. His hand was as good as new, actually it was better than new. Meanwhile, Mr. Pitt looked towards the doctors.

"Well?' he asked,

"Well, Dr. Burrill replied, "there was absolutely no change." Mr. Pitt was noticeably displeased. He was hoping he could succeed where SECMET failed. "Did anything change?" Mr. Pitt asked,

"No sir, nothing. We could check our calibrations again." Replied Dr. Rinzler.

"Don't bother." Pitt was still looking at his hand as he said, "Let's keep going with phase 2. I want to have a workable sample withing a few weeks. In the meantime, I'll be working on phase 3. I'll have a prototype of the articulating device here in a matter of months. Thomas, you can go to your room. We'll send for you if we need you." "Okay." Was all Thomas said. Thomas found himself feeling quite calm lately. He always knew that they didn't want to hurt him. They weren't treating him badly. In fact, besides being an actual prisoner, he was doing just fine. Thomas went back to his room and kept sending out his signal in hopes that Mario would be able to get him out of there.

Mario had located where Thomas' signal was coming from. He had been formulating a plan for the past few days now. It was a bold plan, in fact, he would have used the word 'crazy', but he had to do something. Although the location and terrain lent itself to an amphibious approach, the Navy would probably be too prepared for that. In particular, the exit plan. It had to be by ground, he had no chance against the Navy if he wanted to escape via the ocean. It was Wednesday, Mario planned to execute his plan on the following Sunday. Less traffic, less people, less chance of something unexpected happening. Although there are always unexpected circumstances.

Thomas was enjoying a few days of rest. The lab didn't need him for any more tests, they had plenty of samples of Thomas blood and tissue to work with. They allowed Thomas to walk around freely, but he always had Glen Ryder at his side. Thomas and Glen made friends easily as they had similar interests. Glen was only a small number of years older than Thomas and so that made it easy to relate to each other. In fact, had it not been for Glen, Thomas would have been bored to death. You could only play so much Nintendo.

Operation Point Loma Extraction

Mario had called a meeting, it was Saturday, 11:30am. They met to go over the extraction plan at Naval Base Point Loma. Mario had gathered some intel and a dozen arial shots of the facility via mini drones. The plan was actually quite simple from an operations perspective. They would go in with several teams using electric SUV's for noise reduction. Both vehicles will have an electric high-speed winch attached to the back of the vehicle.

"Okay, listen up." Mario said as he walked over to the arial photo on the wall. "This utility building is where Thomas is located. Rooms are not numbered but we know he is most likely located somewhere in this hallway." Mario walked over to the second photo on the wall, "This very auspicious area right here is Fort Rosecrans National Cemetery. As you can see, if we drive out to this point, it will put us directly above the facility. Note that this incline leading to the facility is around 70 degrees and we will not be able to climb down without the winch support." Korbin raised his hand, "Yeah?" Mario said. Korbin stood up and pointed at the photo where Mario was standing and said, "It looks like that grade ends a few feet before the building. Is that a drop?" Mario answered, "Yes, but you won't have to worry about that because you and Banks are running interference in case we need it." Banks stood up quickly and said, "That's bullshit, boss. I wanna go in, what's the fun of hanging back?"

173

"There is no fun, you are back-up in case we need it." Banks was going to argue but knew it would be pointless, so he just sat back down with a disapproving pout on his face. Mario pointed at the photo again and continued, "As I was saying, and to answer Korbin's question, yes, there is a drop at the end of that 70-degree incline. This is basically a cliff, that drops down about 30 feet to the ground. We will still be tethered to the winch, so we will be rebelling from where the vehicles are parked, all the way to the ground floor of the facility."

Barton asked, "What about security?"

"Good question, most recent recon shows that there is only one guard on patrol watching that cliff area. However, once we reach ground level there are two more guards patrolling the facility. Cooper, you're going to incapacitate the guard on the high ground. And I mean incapacitate, we are not in a kill mission. These are still our guys, and I don't want anyone dead, copy?" All seven men nodded and murmured, "Copy that."

Mario went on, "Cooper and Riley, you got the two guards on ground level. Remember, these tranquilizers take just under three seconds to knock out the targets. So, make sure you get a clean shot. Now here's the fun part. We don't have any reliable intel as far as security goes once we're inside the facility." Cooper raised his hand as he spoke, "So what's the plan, boss man?"

Mario smiled at Cooper and replied, "Well, we're going to do to them what they did to us." They all started laughing, "Hell yeah!" Riley yelled out. What this meant was that they were going to knock out everybody inside the building with gas before they entered. Cooper and Riley both will be handling the 40-pound tanks of enhanced Midazolam, which they referred to as M-gas.

Mario walked over to another photo, a blueprint of the facility and pointed at an area. "This is the North-East corner of the facility. It is the main entrance, and it also happens to be the only way in or out of the facility. There was also a delivery roll-up door, but it has recently been reinforced. The front entrance requires a key card which Dr. Burrill will be providing for us tonight. Once Cooper and Riley land on the roof they will begin dispersing the M-gas from one of the skylights." Riley asked, "What's the protocol if we run into an unfriendlies?"

"We incapacitate everyone, no exceptions. If you run into someone, use your nonlethals and try not to shoot them in the face. At close range, even these rubber bullets can be fatal. Try to cover the entire area with the M-gas and hopefully we get everyone to go to sleep without having to shoot anyone." Mario held up a snap-on vest with several straps and carabiners hanging on it. "This is Thomas' vest. I will place it on Thomas and connect him to my vest. I will then use the winch to pull us back up the vehicles.

Korbin, Kelly." They both stood up. Mario said, "You guys are going to play the very critical part of making sure our escape is complete. You guys are going to make sure that once we reach the check point at the end of the cemetery, there are no tails on us. Got it?" "Yes sir." They replied in unison. Mario added, "Okay if we made it this far, then we should be fine. Everyone here has a designated place to go to once we're on the road. Do not deviate from the plan. I don't want anyone thinking they can just go home after it's over. We are all going to lay low for a few days before we move anywhere. I have booked everyone a hotel room a few miles from the extraction point. Stay in your hotels until you hear from me. Once you're there, relax, hop in the pool, and order room service, just don't go out anywhere. Copy that?"

"Copy that, sir." They all said in unison.

"Korbin, Banks!" Mario called out.

Banks replied, "Yeah."

"You two are going to bring our friend, Dr. Burrill to us. I'm thinking we need a little more intel in regard to what's waiting for us inside once we breach the facility. Make sure he has his scan card with him when you pick him up."

Banks smiled and said, "You got it, boss." Banks turned to Korbin, and they fist bumped. They were glad for a little action. When these guys get wound up for a mission they hate to sit around. Besides, Banks knew that Mario gave them this assignment because they're going to be laying low at the target site tomorrow night.

Saturday, 5:30pm. Dr. Rinzler was going over some of the readings from the sensor suit. Dr. Burrill and the staff had left for the day. Only Thomas and a few security people were still in the building. Dr. Rinzler was about to leave also, but he had run into something that piqued his curiosity. There was a strange reading from the sensor suit that he couldn't explain. The suit was designed to register the slightest of changes in energy emitting from the suit. What Dr. Rinzler had found was not so much an energy reading but more of an anomaly in the reading itself. There should not have been such a minimal, almost negligible discernible signal inside of the coherent processing interval that was preset in the suit. It resembled background noise, but that didn't make any sense.

Dr. Rinzler inspected the sensors on the suit to make sure there wasn't any damage or loose connectors. He also had to make sure the suit wasn't picking up any background noise from the radar that was located on the base just a few hundred yards from where they had been testing the suit. It was most curious, especially when you consider the area from which the anomalous signal originated. Why this area? Why 5cm from his ankle? But it was more than that, the signal itself was not right, it was strange.

It was approximately 6pm. Dr. Rinzler grappled with the thought of calling Dr. Burrill or Mr. Pitt but decided against it. He knew his colleague would come back to the lab and go over all the data, and for sure Mr. Pitt would call everybody else to come back to work on Sunday, but Dr. Rinzler was ready to go home. Besides, it was his grand daughters' birthday tomorrow and there was no way he was going to miss Loni's birthday party. This will have to wait until Monday.

It was Saturday evening and Edna Burrill was baking her husband's favorite dessert, a cherry-almond sugar cookie cobbler. It was 8pm and they were ready to sit down and watch one of their favorite old Spencer Tracy movies, Inherit the Wind, a fictionalized parable of the Scopes Monkey Trial. It always led to a semi-serious conversation with Mrs. Burrill disclaiming Darwinism. But in the end they would both laugh about who won the debate.

The Burrill's had two children, grown, married, and living out-of-state. They were expecting a visit from their eldest son, Kyle, next weekend. They were excited to see the grandchildren. But for now, they were happy to be sitting in front of the television with the comforting scent of baked cookie dough gnawing at their appetites. It was all quite pleasant.

At 11:40pm, both Edna and Dr. Burrill found themselves drifting in and out of sleep. They knew it was bedtime. Dr. Burrill picked up the remote and turned off the TV. They both went through their evening rituals. They got into bed and in less than 15 minutes they were both fast asleep. At 1:30am, Korbin was in Dr. Burrill's backyard. He walked over to the bedroom window and peeked inside. He couldn't see anything, it was dark, and the curtains were drawn. Even though the curtains were slightly sheer, it was impossible to see inside with any clarity. It didn't matter, the plan was still the same. Break the window to enter and hopefully not trigger any alarms. Not that any of that mattered because this should be a quick and easy extraction. Korbin got on his radio to Banks. "Banks, copy?"

"Go ahead."

"I'm about to go in. meet me in the driveway in one minute."

"Copy that."

Korbin put his radio back in his side pocket of his cargo pants then pulled out a small lead window breaker. He took a one short back swing and crashed it into the window. It was loud, but not loud enough to alert the neighbors. It did, however, wake up Mrs. Burrill. She immediately woke her husband, but Korbin was already inside the room and running towards her. Edna Burrill was terrified and froze with fear as the strangers hand covered her mouth. Then she felt a sting in her left shoulder and in a few seconds she was fast asleep again.

Dr. Burrill never woke up, so Korbin woke him rudely at gunpoint. Korbin placed his hand over Dr. Burrill's mouth and signaled to him to be quite by holding up a finger to his lips. The doctor understood and remained quiet. Korbin spoke slowly, clearly, and calmly, "Dr. Burrill, we're going on a little ride. Your wife is not hurt, she is sedated. She will wake up in about 8 to 10 hours and she'll be fine. Do you understand me?" Dr. Burrill nodded. Korbin continued, "Okay, now, I need you to grab some clothes, your swipe-card to the base, don't get dressed, you'll get dressed later. Grab your things and come with me. If all goes well you will be right back here tomorrow, and nobody gets hurt. Got it?" Dr. Burrill nods again. "Good man. Now, let's move, we're in a hurry."

Dr. Burrill grabbed some clothing and before walking out of the room he glanced back at his wife. He could see she was still breathing, and this allowed him to remain calm himself. He believed this stranger because he hadn't stolen anything or asked for money. He figured as long as he cooperates the better his chances. He stopped by the bedroom door and picked up a pair of shoes, turned to Korbin and said, "Okay, I'm ready." They both headed out the front door. As soon as they opened it the alarm went off. Korbin didn't care, they would be gone in a matter of seconds, but Dr. Burrill stopped and went over to the alarm and put in his code. The noisy high pitch beeping stopped. He looked up at Korbin and said, "I don't want the neighbors finding my wife sedated." Korbin shrugged his shoulders and simply replied, "Okay."

Banks was in the driveway waiting. They jumped in the black SUV and Banks calmly pulled out and drove away. Dr. Burrill was in the back seat with Korbin. Korbin handed Dr. Burrill a small pillowcase. Dr. Burrill was about to ask what it was for when he realized and just said, "Oh." and then placed it over his head. "Thanks, doc." They drove for about 40 minutes before reaching their destination. Dr. Burrill could hear a garage door opening then closing. Once he was inside the house he was allowed to remove the pillowcase from his head, which he did calmly and slowly.

Dr. Burrill noticed that he wasn't feeling anxious or nervous. He could tell that these men were not here to hurt him, they were after information, most likely about the young man at his facility, Thomas. Once the pillowcase was removed, Dr. Burrill looked around. He was surrounded by six men. They looked like combat tested mercenary types. The house itself was sparsely furnished, with blackout curtains on every window and minimal décor. Must be some kind of safe house, he thought. He couldn't tell who was in charge until one of them walked up to him and said, "Dr. Burrill, please, sit down, we have a few questions. The sooner we get our answers, the sooner we can all go home. You okay with that?" Dr. Burrill sat down and replied, "Yes."

"Okay," Mario continued, "Here's the first thing we need to know, is Thomas still there at the base?"

"Yes."

"How many guards are outside the building at night?"

"I don't know the answer to that, but I will tell you what I do know. I usually see two men near the front entrance when I leave at the end of my shift. They patrol the facility. And I think there may be more near the rear of the facility, but I cannot confirm that." Mario watched the doctors body language and facial expressions. It looked like he was telling the truth so far. Mario asked, "Okay, what about inside. How many men do they have guarding Thomas?"

"They don't really guard him. Inside the facility he is mostly free to move about. But in the evening there are usually two or three men inside, again, I just don't pay much attention to these things. I am usually more involved in my work. This young man is quite

178

remarkable. And he's a good boy, too. I must ask you, do you plan to do any harm to this young man? You must know that he is an extraordinary person and may hold the key to humanities greatest ailments."

"No, I'm not going to hurt him. That young man happens to be my friend, and he doesn't like being a prisoner and I don't like it either, so, I don't really care about the key to anything, I'm just going to get him out." Mario smiled at Dr. Burrill and said, " You okay with that?"

"Ah, sure. That's fine. I'm glad he has friends."

"Great, then we're all on the same page. Now, regarding your swipe-card, do you simply swipe it, or is there also a code we need to know about? And just as a reminder, you don't go home until I get Thomas out of there. We clear?" Dr. Burrill let out a small gulp and said, "Yes, we're clear. There is no code, just swipe. But just so you know, I am telling you all I know." Mario said, "Don't worry, doc, if your information is good, your good."

Mario looked over at Korbin and nodded. Korbin walked over to Dr. Burrill and injected him with the same sedative as his wife. Dr. Burrill was out in a matter of seconds. Mario grabbed a duffle bag that was lying next to him and said, "Okay, grab the swipe-card and suit up." All eight men grabbed their gear and headed out to the two SUV's parked in the garage. Both vehicles had high speed wenches with plastic gears controlled by an electronic stepper motor which made them virtually silent when operating. They had all gone over the plan minutes before Dr. Burrill showed up.

The plan was pretty simple. They would approach the facility from the west. There would be a steep ravine which they would repel down using the electric winches. The ravine runs down for about 140 feet at which point it drops straight down another 30 feet. Halfway down that 30-foot drop two men will stop and use a grappling hook to maneuver their way onto the roof of the facility. Four others will continue down to the ground. There, they will split up into two teams. One team will move around to the north side while the other moves around through the south side. Both teams will meet at the main entrance.

All men were equipped with quick acting tranquilizer darts. They also had plenty of lethal ammo to be used only as a last resort. The two men on the roof will create an opening on one of the skylights. From there they will insert a thin hose that will be used to

179

insert the enhanced Midazolam vapor gas that should put everybody in the facility to sleep. The ground teams will incapacitate any guards located around the facility.

Once inside, they will locate Thomas, carry him out and take him up to the waiting vehicles and drive straight to the Dana Hotel in Mission Bay. The next day, Mario and Thomas will take a short drive over to Sea World. Mario would remember thinking that he'd never been to Sea World and wondered if Thomas had ever been. They would lay low for a few days before going anywhere.

Sunday, 2:30am, they arrived at the extraction point. Fort Rosecrans National Cemetery is a small cemetery that stretches for only a couple of hundred yards. At the West end of the cemetery was a steep bluff, that's where they will repel from. As they approached the entrance of the cemetery one of the three SUV's would wait there to run interference in the event that something goes wrong. Banks would stay behind. The other two SUV's drove to the bluff and parked.

Mario was the first to jump out but there was no need to give instructions. They all knew what they had to do. They all walked calmly but with purpose in their gait to the front of the SUV's, disconnected the cable from the winch and hooked it on to their harnesses. All the men then approached the edge of the bluff, turned their backs to it and began their descend. Halfway down the bluff, Roger and Korbin made their way onto the top of the facility, Kelly continued down and began surveying the rear of the facility.

Mario, Barton, and Cooper hit the ground and quickly made their way to the front entrance. Riley stayed several steps behind Mario to act as backup in the event of any unexpected surprises. Roger and Korbin landed quietly on the roof and checked for any guards. There were two standing at the front edge of the facility looking out towards the ocean. Roger tapped Korbin and signaled that he will take the one on the right. Korbin nodded. Both men walked slowly and silently closer to the guards. Once they were approximately twenty-five feet away, they both raised they guns and shot. Both men hit their targets in the neck, that was where the drug works the quickest. The two guards grimaced and immediately raised their hands to their necks, but by the time the shock wore out, they were both on the ground unconscious.

Roger and Korbin quickly made their way over to the nearest skylight. The cover was made of some polyurethane material which had been battered by the sun. The material had become brittle over time. They didn't want to break it and make any unnecessary noise. Korbin pulled out a small metallic bottle that was filled with an acetone mixture that when poured onto any kind of plastic material would basically disintegrate it. Much like gasoline dissolves foam. Korbin poured the liquid until he created a hole just large enough to insert the 1-1/2" tube. Once inserted Roger took off his backpack and pulled out the cannister of enhanced Midazolam gas. He looked up at Korbin and nodded. Korbin nodded back. Roger turned the knob on the cannister and began pumping the vapor into the building. Roger looked back at Korbin with a smirky look on his face and said, "Nighty night motha-fuckers." As they both donned their respirators.

In the rear of the building Kelly was walking crouched low to the ground looking for any movement. The rear of the facility did not have any kind of illumination. He flipped down his digital night vision monocular. Nothing to his left. He glanced over to his right and saw something. There was someone behind some brush, but he couldn't tell if it was friend or foe. He crept up slowly trying to make out the figure hidden in the brush.

Suddenly the figure's posture changed, Kelly could see that the guard also had night vision capabilities. Kelly could also see that the guard had the drop on him and was pointing his weapon directly at him. All Kelly could do was brace for the impact of the .223 Remington rounds that were about to come out of the AR15. But all Kelly heard was a soft whack. He saw the guard go down. Riley had shot the guard in the neck with a dart. He walked over and peeked around the corner to see Kelly still crouched down on the ground. "You okay." Riley asked. He could hear Kelly let out an audible sound of relief. "Yeah. Thanks."

"No problem. You comin?" Kelly noticed he still hadn't moved from his position. Kelly stood up and said, "Right. Okay then, let's go." Riley slapped him on the back as he walked by and whispered. "Man, I always gotta cover your dumb ass."

"You mean like Barbados?"

"Oh yeah, did I thank you for that?"

"No."

"Oh, yeah, that's right, because Barbados was your dumb-ass fault."

"Shut up. Let's go meet up with the guys in the front."

"Copy that, croucher."

Mario, Cooper, and Burton wasted no time. They moved quickly to the front of the facility. When they reached the end of the building, Mario peeked around the corner. It was just like Dr. Burrill said, there were only two guards. Mario hand-signaled that there were two targets, then signaled to follow him. All three men came around the corner and immediately started firing. The two guards didn't stand a chance, they collapsed onto the ground. All of Mario's men met up at the front entrance. Mario clicked his mic, "Riley, copy."

"Go."

"How long?"

"Give it two minutes and go in. everybody should be fast asleep, including Thomas."

"We're not waiting two minutes, I'll give you one."

"Copy that. Then just make sure you got your masks on nice and tight, or you'll get a visit from mister sandman."

"Copy that." Mario looked at his watch. He spoke without looking up, "Okay. One minute, everyone, follow my lead. Keep those masks tight, the gas will still be active." Mario walked behind Barton and reached into his backpack and pulled out the extra harness for Thomas. After one minute had passed Mario motioned for everyone to get ready. "Okay, first two, take the right, second two, take the left, Kelly, you're with me, let's go." Mario swiped the card on the door. He was thankful that they didn't have to use explosives. It was obvious the door was reinforced recently.

The small green light indicated the door was unlocked. Mario opened the door and let the first four men in. Then he and Kelly took up the rear. There was no movement. The gas had done its job. Now it was time to find Thomas. After checking several doors, they found him. It was an unusual sight. Thomas was going in and out of unconsciousness. It was very peculiar. Mario thought it was amusing but quickly turned his attention back to getting Thomas out. He hooked up the harness on Thomas and carried him out. Thomas was still wide awake one moment and out the next.

The only thing that Mario could surmised was that Thomas' unique abilities were countering the drug, but then the drug would again try to knock him out. The results were odd and a bit funny to see watching Thomas waking up only to go right back to sleep again. Finally, they made their way to the rear of the facility. They hooked themselves up and turned on the winches. They rose quickly, and when they got to the top they unhooked themselves, jumped into the SUV's and sped out. The third vehicle met them at the entrance of the cemetery and all three drove away just above the speed limit so as not to raise any suspicion. Once they were out of the building and the effects of the gas, Thomas woke up and stood awake. He glanced over at Mario to see a silly grin on his face. Mario moved his face closer to Thomas and said, "You alright?"

It took Mario only a few minutes to find the tracker that Mr. Pitt put in the same Nintendo Switch game. It was a somewhat clever attempt, but the tracker was nowhere near as sophisticated as the one Mario had placed in it. Mario disabled it and put it in his pocket. After a few more sweeps of Thomas' body, they felt safe that there were no more trackers on him.

Mr. Pitt

Mr. Pitt, aka, Jacek Kaminski was an only child of Aleksy and Celistina Kaminski. They were second generation Poles. Jacek Kaminski's grandparents had escaped Nazi occupied Poland in 1943, just a couple of years before the war was over. They fled to the UK where, after several years, found some success. They had two sons, Aleksy and Antoni. They enjoyed a happy middle-class life into the late 60's and were able to save a little money. The Kaminski's decided to move to America mostly because they had some family in New York. Once they got there, they bought a small grocery store in the Bronx. They had a normal life, if you could call it that, the one thing about the Kaminski family was that they were raised very strictly. There wasn't a lot of time for laughter and play. It was all hard work and study.

When they did play, it was always to win, always high intensity. The Kaminski's did not like to lose at anything, nor were they graceful losers. They were always tough and focused. Aleksy Junior was always driving his sons on the virtues of education and hard work. Consequently, both boys grew up to be well educated and somewhat successful in their own lives. Antoni became a scientist with Bell Laboratories and Aleksy junior became a mechanical engineer.

Unfortunately, Antoni Kaminski was killed in a car accident. The typical drunk driver scenario, the drunk driver crashed head-on into Antoni's car at approximately 65mph. Antoni died at the scene, the drunk driver lived. Aleksy met Celistina in university and married her one year later. Nine months after that, Jacek Kaminski was born. Though he was the light of their eye, Aleksy raised Jacek with the same strictness that he was raised with. Perhaps even a little more. Aleksy felt that if it was good for him, then maybe Jacek with a little more strictness and discipline would be even better.

Jacek Kaminski was raised to work hard, play hard and never lose. Failure is simply that, failure. There is no learning from it, there is only overcoming it. Jacek grew up with a do or die attitude about everything. In sports everyone hated to play against him, not because he was physically strong, but because he was so strong mentally. You could feel his determination which seemed to drain his opponents energy. When he joined the Navy, he tried out for the Navy Seals and was accepted.

Jacek had no problem fitting in, in fact he thrived on the discipline and excelled in his unit quickly becoming the E7 Team Leader in just one year. Jacek requested to join Seal Team 8, which is the maritime component of the U.S. Special Operations Command (SOCOM). The Team specializes in direct action, strategic reconnaissance, and unconventional warfare. Jacek lasted only three years, he felt his team wasn't getting enough *real* action and he was bored with the constant training. Jacek Kaminski left the service for the private sector. He worked security details for high end clients for two years but didn't like the people he worked for, too much bullshit with all these entitled elitist.

Finally, he was offered a job through an acquaintance. The timing was auspicious, and Jacek gave his notice and joined his friend. He was now working for the government, it had a sketchy job description. All they could tell him was that he would be working for a department that does not have an acronym. They promised independence, anonymity and, more interestingly, a huge budget. Everything about it intrigued Jacek. The first day on the job, they all received aliases, Jacek Kaminsky would be simply known as Mr. Pitt.

A few weeks later he found himself traveling to 3 different countries in 3 months. Each time he had missions that were interesting, some dangerous, some that would definitely be considered black ops. Jacek enjoyed the action and the discipline needed to carry out his missions. And just as they had stated, he had enormous resources at his disposal. But now he had a new mission. They had three weeks to prep. All they knew was that the target was a teenage boy that needed to be extracted from a facility near Pasadena, California. 22 days later, they secured Thomas Grady. 5 days after that, Mr. Pitt lost Thomas. He was not happy.

Mr. Pitt immediately assembled his team again. He was going to get Thomas Grady back at any cost. Mr. Pitt was not concerned with what the government wanted with Thomas, he just didn't like losing. 30 minutes later his team had assembled inside the facility where they had been holding Thomas. There they looked over the CT cameras to see if they could pick up some clues as to who took Thomas and where they were headed. Mr. Pitt knew it had to be Mario, but he had to be sure. Pitt watched as one of the men took off his gas mask. He recognized him right away, it was Mario, Thomas' protector. He had wondered why he wasn't at the facility when they extracted Thomas. He could only surmise that he was busy with some other issue. Mr. Pitt was never aware that Mario had been in a car accident and was in the hospital during the raid.

Pitt pointed at the screen and said, "That's our man. I want to know everything about this guy. Where he lives, his family, his background, everything." He pointed at one of his men, "Mr. Landon, get me what I need." Mr. Landon gave a perfunctory salute and replied, "Yes, sir." Next, Mr. Pitt looked at the last reading his tracker picked up before it was obviously found. "Okay, we had a reading up to 5 minutes after the abduction, we know they could have only been headed south since we are located in a peninsula. After that, however, we have no info. Ideas?"

One of the men raised a hand, "Yes, Mr. Wright?"

"Well, I could see two options that I would take. One, I would go somewhere nearby and lay low and wait to make sure no one caught on to me then head out of town. Second option is, if I were confident that I was not spotted or being followed, I would have jumped on the freeway right away and put some serious distance between me and this place."

"Mr. Wright, you seem to have a talent for stating the obvious."

Mr. Wright responded in a sour tone, "You asked, so I answered."

"True, Mr. Wright, that you did. Does anyone have any other ideas?" Another gentleman raised his hand. "Yes, Mr. Amber."

"Well, I don't have a clue as to where they may be going but let's get our net out there ASAP." Mr. Pitt gave a small semblance of a smile and said, "A man after my own heart. Yes, let's get pictures out to every airport, train station, bus terminals and check for any CT cameras between here and a ten-mile radius. Let's see if we can spot them somewhere. Okay, let's get on it."

It was still early Monday morning. Mr. Pitt's team hit the road to see if they could spot any cameras on any commercial property or street cameras. Mr. Amber and Mr. James drove down the main arterial street that left from the cemetery straight through town. They did see a couple of cameras at a convenience store and one at a Well Fargo ATM. Neither one yielded any information. However, Mr. James did notice that a few houses that they passed had cameras on their front doors. When they approached one of the homeowners on the 1200 block of Catalina Blvd They asked to see the footage during the designated times.

As it turned out, one of the cameras did catch Mario's team headed North. You could clearly see all three vehicles passing by the house. And although the windows were heavily tinted, there was no doubt these were the men they were looking for. It wasn't a big help, but at least they were able to pin them at a specific location at a specific time. This could be helpful later.

Mr. Amber sent the information to Mr. Pitt. Mr. Pitt viewed the film on his laptop. Mr. Pitt examined the video. There was something about this guy. Mr. Pitt started vocalizing his thoughts, "He was smart." He said, referring to Mario. Mr. Pitt noticed that the vehicles in the film were not speeding away. "That was smart, too, no need to attract attention. This guy has done this kind of work before. I don't know who you are Mr. Mario, but I'm gonna find out. Of that, you can be sure." Mr. Pitt closed his laptop and felt a sense of excitement to have such a formidable opponent before him. He almost smiled.

Monday, 9am. Thomas woke up groggy and a little nauseous from the M-Gas. He could tell he was in a hotel room and could hear Mario's voice in the next room and it immediately gave Thomas a sense of calmness. Thomas got up and walked towards the window. They were in a room somewhere on the twentieth floor, maybe even thirtieth. It was high. He noticed he was still wearing the same clothes he had on when he fell asleep. T-shirt and jeans. They were just a little more wrinkled than yesterday. He heard a knock on the door. "Come in." It was Mario. "You ready for a little breakfast?" Thomas looked at Mario and didn't say a word, he just walked over to him and gave him a hug. "Hey," Mario exclaimed, "You alright?" Thomas let go of Mario and simply said, "Thanks." Mario put his hands on Thomas' shoulders and said, "Hey, don't worry about it. Come on, let's get you something to eat. We gotta talk." They both walked into the main room of the suite.

Mr. Pitt sat at his desk. It was made of metal, like the ones they used in schools and cheap offices. Every piece of furniture was gray or tan, all of them stood on a bare concrete floor. No bookshelves only metal file cabinets, metal folding chairs against the wall and no windows except for the scattered narrow rectangular ventilation openings near the ceiling around the entire building. The air smelled like dirt and dust. Mr. Pitt sat on the most comfortable chair in the room, which was also made of metal, but at least it had some upholstery which didn't help, because the chair was most likely at least twenty years old. The squeaking plastic wheels on the bottom of it were a constant reminder that everything in this office was a piece of shit. This only contributed to Mr. Pitts sour mood. He was reluctantly coming to terms with the fact that the trail to find Thomas was getting cold. Ice cold.

Mr. Pitt had spent the better half of the following Monday debriefing Mrs. and Dr. Burrill. He was hoping to find something that would help in his search. But it was obvious that Dr. Burrill was a victim of a well-thought-out plan. They must have been following him for several days before they broke into his house and took his badge. He couldn't blame Dr. Burrill for giving up any information to the perpetrators, hell, the Doctor never received any type of training for this kind of scenario. Not to mention they had his wife here to threaten him with. Mr. Pitt was not sure if he would have to dispatch them later. He would have to wait for orders on that decision. Mr. Pitt remembered looking around Dr. Burrill's home office and couldn't help noticing the vast contrast between the interior of the Dr.'s office and his own. Although it was decorated in good taste, it just struck Mr. Pitt as, well, kind of feminine.

By 4pm, Mr. Pitt finally got an idea and started putting a plan together. If he can't find Thomas, at least he'll make it hard for him to move around. Mr. Pitt met up with his crew back at his metal and concrete cave and announced his plan. He was going to put out a massive propaganda campaign. He had everyone on the phone within a few hours calling every major media station and began posting on social media as well. The story was that Thomas, a poor 16-year-old teenager was abducted. They began posting pictures of Thomas everywhere. On billboards, television, flyers and posters all across the country. Mr. Pitt had a massive budget and he planned on using it. All transportation agencies were notified.

Thomas would not be able to board a plane, train, or bus. Even rental cars, taxis and ride-share companies were given Thomas picture and information. There was also a $200,000 reward for any information leading to the return of this poor teenager whose mother and father are worried sick. In a matter of hours, Thomas' picture was circulating across the country. Mr. Pitt knew they would get dozens, if not, hundreds of tips that would lead nowhere, but he had to try something. There was one thing that Mr. Pitt hadn't really thought about, and that is, Thomas also had an immense budget as well, perhaps as large, or larger than Mr. Pitts.

It took Mario nearly 6 weeks to procure the necessary arrangements for Thomas' transportation. It wasn't easy considering how Thomas' picture was now everywhere on the news, on the radio, in print and in social media. Normally this would have made things impossible to move Thomas anywhere, but Mario had his ways and a few connections. Not to mention a lot of money to pay off certain people in the right positions. There was one person he didn't have to pay, a famous movie star named John Travolta. Thomas had performed a favor regarding his older brother, Robert Travolta. John Travolta owns his own Boeing 737 and was willing to take Thomas anywhere he wanted. Now Thomas was on his way to Mr. Travolta's house in New Jersey via Thomas' private jet, which is owned by one of many LLC companies that a bunch of fancy lawyers put together for Thomas. From there, the movie star offered to fly Thomas to his new location. It took a few days, but eventually Thomas reached his final destination, Athens, Greece.

John Travolta only had to get Thomas on the tarmac, from there Mario's people took over and escorted Thomas into town. It was good to have almost unlimited resources available. Paying the right people, the right amount of money got you a set of new identification documents such as visas, and passports. As far as anyone can tell, Thomas Grady, now known as, Simon Rhodes, entered Greece and is now living there legitimately.

It's been 6 weeks since Mario extracted Thomas from Naval Base Point Loma and it's been about 3 days since Thomas landed in Greece. It was time to speak to Mr. Pitt. Mario had Kelly pick up a couple of burner phones at 7-11. After Mario connected a VPN server with a kill switch on both phones. As an added precaution, he had Kelly drive out 10 miles in any direction he wanted and call him from there. Once Mario picks up the call, Kelly will then place his burner phone on conference call and dial Mr. Pitt's phone number, which Mario paid a hefty sum for. It was Mr. Pitt's hubris that got him into this mess. Pitt knew he should have taken Thomas Grady to an unlisted government black site. But he didn't want to risk being somehow caught by the press.

The optics would be seriously bad. *'Government kidnaps boy,'* that would never work. Mr. Pitt thought it would have played out better if he kept Thomas in a local facility and that way they could at least mitigate the potential damage. However, in hindsight, it was an error. If he gets a hold of Thomas again, he's going straight to La Primavera, a camp located 50 south of Managua in Nicaragua. Suddenly, to his surprise, his phone buzzed in his pocket. He took it out,

188

looked at the caller ID number and didn't recognize it. He hung it up thinking it was a wrong number, because nobody had this number except for those very few people he works with, and their numbers always show up coded.

Mr. Pitt went back to contemplating his next move when he heard and felt his phone buzz again. This was too strange to ignore so he answered it. "Hello?" There was a short pause, "Hello," the voice said, "Is this Mr. Pitt?" Mr. Pitt was now very curious as to who this person was. So, he replied, "Yes, this is him. Who am I speaking to?" another pause, "This is Mario." Mr. Pitt went through a myriad of emotions internally. There was no way for this man to have my number. *'What the hell is going on here?'* He thought. Mr. Pitt continued with feigned composure, "Mario. Nice to hear from you. Did you call to let me know where I can find Thomas Grady?"

"No. Actually, I called to set up a meeting. I have a couple of proposals I would like to discuss with you, Mr. Pitt." Mr. Pitt motioned to one of his men to start tracing the call. Mr. Pitt began speaking at a slower pace to buy some time in order to triangulate Mario's position. Now it was Mr. Pitt who paused before speaking, "A meeting eh? Sounds a bit amanous to me." Mario knew what Mr. Pitt was doing but didn't care. "Look, Mr. Pitt, I don't mind you tracing this call, it won't do you any good, we're on conference call with a burner cell phone in a remote location on a VPN server. So, what do you say we talk about that meeting?"

"Okay." Mr. Pitt replied. Realizing that if what Mario is saying is true, then tracing the call would take too much time, but he had his guy try anyway. Mr. Pitt went on but in his normal cadence, "Okay, Mario, you have my attention. Where and when?"

"There's an old, abandoned plant in Bell Garden. I'll text you the address along with the date and time."

"I'm on pins and needles." Mr. Pitt heard a click but could still make out some sounds in the background. The burner phone must be in some remote location and left there to die. He decided he wasn't even going to trace it or pick it up. Mario is right, it would be a waste of time and manpower.

Within the hour, Mr. Pitt received a text with the address, date, and time for the meeting. His team immediately researched the facility. It was an abandoned factory that was used to produce non-woven material for use in batting and filters. There were pictures on an old website which showed quite a few large pieces of machinery still inside the building but most, if not all, were presently inoperable. Nevertheless, they provided a huge logistical problem. There were just too many places for men to hide.

According to Mario's text, they were to meet at this facility in two days at exactly 8pm. Mario gave no other instructions, no terms, conditions, warnings, or threats. Mr. Pitt could only surmise that Mario also had a plan and appeared to be pretty confident about it. Mr. Pitt did not like that. '*Mario cannot be underestimated. This man knows what he's doing.*' He thought. Mr. Pitt decided to add a few more men to his team. This will help him to set up a perimeter for a contingency plan. Mr. Pitt had to play his cards close to his chest. He didn't want to give Mario any advantages. In the end, it may be necessary to eliminate Mario and his crew. Mr. Pitt could see Mario's crew being a huge hinderance in his future endeavors to recapturing Thomas.

When Mario gave him the address of the meeting location, Mr. Pitt immediately went out to survey it. The area was in Los Angeles County in the city of Florence. Florence is situated just North of Watts. If you're looking for paradise, this ain't it. At one time it may have been a hub for local manufacturing, but not anymore. The 6000 block of Avalon Blvd is home to dozens of dilapidated old buildings with broken windows and graffiti on practically every wall, inside and out. Both sides of the boulevard are occupied with sad-looking homeless tents and makeshift shacks that look like they would fall apart in a strong wind. The streets were cracked, and the sidewalks were littered with trash. This is where you came when your last semblance of hope is extinguished...or if you're mentally ill.

The Meeting

The building that Mario chose was situated on a corner. There were actually two buildings used by the previous business owner. The two large warehouses shared one parking lot with one building on each side of the lot facing each other. The one Mario chose was on the South side of the parking lot. Mr. Pitt and a few of his men went to the front door. It was locked. Next to the door was a long rectangular window that measured about 12 inches wide and 60 inches tall. One of his men pulled out his gun and struck the window just hard enough to break it. The man reached in and around and was able to unlock the door. Once inside they surveyed the factory floor. It was strange to see so many large pieces of machinery frozen and rusting away. The machines were also covered with graffiti, cobwebs and plenty of trash.

Mr. Pitt didn't like the layout. He decided to station his men on the rafters in the ceiling. There were a number of catwalks along the walls and a couple of them went across the entire building. These catwalks were almost 30 feet high which would give his men an excellent view of the entire facility with the exception of a few blind spots, it was a perfect set up. Of course, he would expect Mario to have the same idea, however, Mr. Pitt was certain that if Mario's men met up with his men up in the rafters that would at least nullify the advantage for both parties. He was also sure that Mario would be thinking the same thing, but all's fair.

As an added precaution, Mr. Pitt decided to station a sniper on the roof of the building on the North side of the parking lot. From there a sniper would have a clear view of both Mario and him as long as they kept one of the receiving doors on the dock open. Mr. Pitt will make sure he gets there early and have one of his men open it. He was certain that Mario wouldn't mind, considering that the facility smelled of old liquor and urine. After an hour of looking around the facility, Mr. Pitt was convinced he had enough ducks in a row to handle most contingencies. It was Tuesday, the meeting was set up for Thursday, all they had to do now was wait.

Thursday, 7:55pm, both men arrive at the appointed location. Mr. Pitt walked over to the loading dock where one of his men had already opened the roll-up door. Mario could see Mr. Pitt standing on the edge of the loading dock. The dock is about 4 feet above the parking lot. There's a small metal ladder on the West side of the loading dock. Mario walked over to it and climbed up. Both men were now facing each other for the first time. They didn't show it, but they were measuring each other up looking for any signs of strengths or weaknesses. They both concluded that they were formidable opponents. Neither man extended a hand. Mr. Pitt began the conversation with a wry smile on his face, "Well, Mr...?"

"Just Mario is fine." Mario replied with no smile. Mr. Pitt continued,

"Okay, Mario. We're here. Let's hear your proposals." Mr. Pitt put his hands in his pants pockets. Mario's eyes darted down to Pitt's hands. Mr. Pitt pulled them out slowly and raised his hands with open palms. "No need to worry, Mario, I am unarmed." Mr. Pitt opened his coat to show Mario he was not carrying a weapon then placed his hands back in his pockets. Mario stood with crossed arms on his chest and said, "First things first". He motioned to someone hidden behind a large machine. Kelly came out carrying two boxes, one larger than the other, and placed them on a small counter that was next to where Mario was standing.

"What's this?" Mr. Pitt asked.

"We'll get to that in a minute. I just have one question before we start."

"Yes?" Mr. Pitt said with little interest.

"I want to know what the governments intentions are for Thomas."

"Who?"

"The boy, Mr. Pitt. The one you kidnapped for your bosses within our government."

"I assure you, I don't have the slightest idea of what you're talking about, Mario."

"The boy, Thomas, the one you kidnapped, but I was able to free him. That boy."

"I'm afraid you have me at quite the quandary, Mario. If you're missing a boy, I would be happy to ask the local authorities to help you find him in any way they can."

"Okay, Mr. Pitt. Can't blame a man for trying." Mario was hoping to record Mr. Pitt stating that he worked for the government and use that information to take the heat off of Thomas. But Mr. Pitt was no fool.

Mr. Pitt said, "So, what kind of proposal are you offering for the safety of your merchandise, Mario?"

"Right. Look, I'm going to radio my guy to stop the recording so we can speak plainly. Are we going to trust each other for the sake of having a plain conversation?"

"Sure. Just let me know when you're ready." Mario signaled Kelly back and told him to have Banks stop recording the conversation. Kelly spoke into his radio, and a couple seconds later got a reply. Kelly held up his thumb, indicating it was done.

Mario went on, "So, are we good?"

"I think I can trust you, Mario."

"Thanks. Okay, here's my first proposal." Mario reached for the smaller box on the counter and held it in his left hand. It was about the size of a normal shoe box. Mario pointed at the box with his right hand and said, "In this box are several items. There is about two ounces of Thomas' blood." Mr. Pitt's eyes went a little wide with a small look of surprise. Mario continued, "There are also some small pieces of clothing and a shoe. They are not in the best condition because I had them in a container in which I ignited a small amount of plastic explosives which will leave taggants on all of these items. Those taggants will allow your people to trace the explosives and identify them. I did this for legitimacy."

Mr. Pitt was definitely intrigued. "Legitimacy?"

"Yes, you see, my first proposal is this. That you allow Thomas to live a normal life without the

192

world, including yourself, and the government chasing him around the rest of his life. So, my proposal is this, I will stage an explosion and you and a member of your team will witness it. You will say that you saw Thomas get on a small private plane, and that you saw that plane explode over the Pacific Ocean 60 seconds after take-off. You will have all the evidence you need in this box to tell your bosses that Thomas is dead and that there is no longer any need to pursue him. This would be you doing the right thing and letting this young boy live a life that a normal young boy should."

Mr. Pitt paced in small slow steps. He seemed to be actually contemplating what Mario said. After about 20 seconds Mr. Pitt replied. "You know, Mario, as much as I like that plan. It's a good plan. I like it, but it's not going to work. The forensics alone would be a logistical nightmare. Are you aware that they would have to dive into the ocean and retrieve every single piece of that plane along with anything and anyone that was in it? They would reconstruct the whole damn thing and they would come to the conclusion that there just isn't enough of Thomas in the wreckage to confirm he was even on the plane. Sorry, I got to pass on that one. What else you got?"

Mario reached over to the counter and picked up the other box. It was just slightly larger than the previous one. Mario held up the box in front of him and waited till they made eye contact and said, "Will, Mr. Pitt, inside this box is half a million dollars in cash. This amount can be sent to you any way you choose. Cash, check, offshore account, gold, whatever. If you abandon this pursuit this amount will be paid to you every month for one year. That's six million dollars. You and your family will want for nothing. You'll be able to help your friends and family. You could start your own security company or live on a yacht and drink champaign all day."

Mr. Pitt also took a moment to contemplate this proposal. Mr. Pitt stared at the floor as if there was an answer to be found on the dirty loading dock. Mr. Pitt responded, "You know, Mario, if I quit today, they'll just have someone else replace me tomorrow, hell, maybe even by tonight."

"I don't care about that. This proposal is for you. I'll deal with the next one in whatever way I think works."

"Really? You have that kind of money, Mario?"

"You have no idea what kind of resources I have, Mr. Pitt. I know yours are formidable, but trust me when I tell you, that my resources are just as formidable, if not, bigger than yours."

"So, you say. You do understand that I have the entire might of the U.S. government behind me?"

"Yes, but I have something else, Mr. Pitt. I have power. I have information, and information is power. How do you think I got your phone number?"

That one has been troubling Mr. Pitt. There is no way any civilian should have his number. There was, of course, only one answer to that question, and that is, Mario must have someone on the inside at a very high level. Mr. Pitt countered, "Maybe you do have information, but I have information as well."

"Really? Do you know my last name? Do you have any idea where Thomas might be? Do you have any information, Mr. Pitt, because I do." Mario reached into his coat, which made Mr. Pitt flinch a little, but he saw that Mario pulled out a small stack of papers. Mario held up the papers and threw them on the floor at Mr. Pitt's feet. "Do you have a dossier on me? Because I have one on you, Mr. Pitt. I know your history, your past employment records, your health records, your address, and your family history. Do you have that, Mr. Pitt? Are you beginning to see what power looks like." The only thing Mr. Pitt was thinking as he stared down at the folded papers was, '*fuck! How did this motherfucker get all this information'?*

Mario continued in a less friendly tone. "Look, all you have to do is simply resign from this assignment and your rich. The next guy has nothing to do with you. I'll deal with whoever comes next. You, Mr. Pitt can go home tonight and think about having breakfast in Paris or New York or wherever you want to go. It's a no-brainer."

"Fuck you Mario. Where did you get this information from? I want a name now or we are going to have a big problem." Mario replied in a calm voice and said, "By problem you mean, your guys on the rafters will shoot me? Or your sniper across the parking lot will blow my brains out? I hate to tell you, Mr. Pitt, but they have all been neutralized. Feel free to check." Mr. Pitt pulled out a small ear plug and placed it in his ear and pushed in the transmitter. "This is Pitt. All station report. I repeat, all stations report." There was only silence.

Mario could see that Mr. Pitt was getting agitated. Mario said, "Look, Mr. Pitt, before you do something foolish, like reaching for your back holster where I know you have a gun. Let me assure you that there are multiple weapons pointed at you. If you would just look down at your chest." Mr. Pitt looked down to see five laser dots moving around his chest. Mario said, "Okay, so let's end this meeting. You refused my first proposal, but you have not given me an answer on the second one. Mr. Pitt, I would encourage you to take the offer, you have nothing to lose and much to gain, in the end, this is just a job. What do you say?"

What Mr. Pitt wanted was to simply shoot Mario in the head and the hell with the consequences. But he knew better than to make decisions based on emotions. Mr. Pitt composed himself again and spoke calmly. "Mario, that money sure sounds good. But it doesn't buy loyalty, dignity, or honor. I must respectfully decline your generous proposal so that the next time we meet, I will have no choice but to blow your fucking head off." Now Mario put his hands in his pockets and spoke with the same calmness. "Well said, Mr. Pitt. I hope it doesn't come to that. But if you're in my way while I'm protecting that boy, well, we will all do what we have to do. Your men will revive in about 20 to 30 minutes. By the way, Mr. Pitt, I agree with your loyalty, but there is no dignity or honor in hunting down a teenage boy for someone to experiment on." Mario turned and walked away, leaving both boxes behind. *'You never know,'* he thought.

Greece

It's been six months since Thomas Grady landed in Greece. It took a while, but Thomas was beginning to acclimate. Thomas had never been to another country and found many things unusual, besides the language. The streets, buildings, even the sky had a different feel to it. When he went down to the beach to gaze out into the Aegean Sea, it gave him a kind of calmness he couldn't describe. Thomas remembered the first few weeks when he first arrived, how he had to hide inside Mr. Travolta's plane until those men came and snuck him off like a bag of contraband. Which, technically, he was.

Thomas was always impressed with Mario's ability to do things. Like having everything in place like false identifications, and this safe house. Also, there was the security. Not only was the house amazing with its whitewash walls on the outside and manicured lawn, but there were cameras, motions detectors, heavy doors and even the glass on all the windows were tempered. Then there were the men. Thomas had four men for security. Two were always making sure that the parameter was secured. One man was always in the small guest house on the East side of the property where all the cameras and sensors were being monitored. In the house, there was always one man, Korbin, Gene Korbin, one of Mario's men. Korbin could be a menacing figure at 6foot 3inches and 210 pounds. He had the classic chiseled jaw line, squarish face and short hair. His looks screamed of military. But his most helpful feature was that he spoke Greek semi-fluently.

Thomas, who is now known as Simon Rhodes, was constantly intrigued and amused in his new home. The weather was mostly nice and the area where he lived was quaint. The streets were lined with old growth Black Acacia trees which permeated the air with scents of orange blossoms with notes of sweet balsamic. The streets were not in great shape, the cracks on the sidewalks and paved roads spread throughout the city like dark vascular veins. It wasn't the best look, but it seemed to add character to the overall feel of the city. The streets were clean and at about every other 30 or 40 feet there was a large trash bin. People in their houses and apartments place their trash in these bins and it seemed like everybody used these bins to keep the streets clean because Thomas could not find one piece of trash on the ground.

Thomas was enjoying his stay in Greece. He got around in a little Piaggio scooter. You didn't really need a license to operate the smaller engines. He recalled the first time he drove down the street to a shopping center that had various stores and places to eat. He smiled thinking about the time he walked into McDonald's and saw that the menu there they featured a "Greek Mac" which is a Big Mac variant made with pita bread with tzatziki sauce. They also had a McToast as well as a ham and cheese sandwich. Thomas tried the Greek Mac and an order of potato wedges. The other thing he thought was funny was that you could order Heineken beer at all the McDonald's. Thomas was starting to feel safe and felt happy to have this peaceful time. Free of all the crazy things that have been happening in his life, Thomas thought, it felt good to feel normal.

Well, at least as normal as could be expected. After going out to eat or walking around, Thomas still had to come back home to his "safe house". The fact that the house had a panic room with a thick metal door was a constant reminder that anything could happen at any time. Thomas had the usual briefing on the various escape plans. The panic room had a hidden exit which led to the adjacent property, which they bought. So, although the house itself was quite beautiful with its manicured lawn, trimmed bushes along with various types of palm trees, it was still a safe house and a constant reminder to Thomas that his life isn't exactly "normal."

In the seven months that Thomas has spent in Greece, he has only experienced two incidents where he had to heal someone. Fortunately, they both occurred in remote locations just outside of town. The first was a woman he saw lying on the side of the road. She had been riding her bicycle into town to do some shopping. Thomas thought she had fallen off her bike. But what happened was that this woman had collapsed due to an undiagnosed Mycotic Aneurysm. Because it was never diagnosed, this incident would simply go down as some unknown cause that made this woman double over in pain as she was riding her bike. After Thomas healed her and helped her up, she simply thanked him for his help and went on her way, oblivious to the fact that she was just about to die.

The other event happened in a quiet little neighborhood. Again, Thomas was merely scurrying about in his little scooter when he noticed a small male child playing on the balcony of a small apartment building. The child was attempting to climb up on the metal railing when he lost his footing and fell. Thomas stopped his scooter and ran to see if the child was okay. There were a few people around, but Thomas got to the child first and tried to see where the child was hurt. Thomas could see no sign of serious damage. The child wasn't even bleeding anywhere, in fact, he seemed fine, but unconscious.

Thomas picked the boy up as his parents ran down to see him. When Thomas handed the boy over to the father, the child had awoken. The child looked up at his father and said with a smile, "Geia sou bampa." Which roughly translates to "Hi Daddy." The father and mother laughed and were ecstatic to see that their child was fine. What no one knew, not even Thomas, was that the boy had actually suffered a severe concussion and would have died the next morning had Thomas not intervened. So, so far so good, Thomas thought. He was glad it wasn't something serious, at least not something serious that someone would notice, like a wound miraculously healing before their very eyes.

Thomas was definitely feeling pretty good these days. He was feeling relatively safe and for the most part, and content. Things were just going well. He was happy, having fun on his scooter while exploring a new country. Thomas was able to keep in touch with Mario and his family via burner cell phones. He had about 30 cell phones constantly available and made sure to destroy them after one use. Yes, Thomas was feeling good and was getting used to being happy. It was early December, and the weather was still pleasant. Day time temperatures fluctuate between the upper 50's and 60's. The low temperatures weren't too bad either, on average around the lower 40's at night. It was Monday, January 21st, Thomas went to bed early feeling warm, comfortable, and safe.

Back at Naval Base Point Loma, Dr. Allen Burrill was going over the sensor data with Dr. Rinzler. They were discussing the readings they recorded off the sensors on Thomas' suit. They both agreed that although the signal was weak, excessively weak, it had a very unique signature that neither one of them had ever come across before. Dr. Rinzler held up a printed graph of the strange signals and spoke to Dr. Burrill without taking his eyes off the graph. "Look at this. I don't understand. Typically, these ELF readings would come from external sources, but these are clearly coming from Thomas." Dr. Burrill walks up slowly behind Dr. Rinzler and says, "You're right, but there it is". They both just stared in silence for a few seconds analyzing the graph. Dr. Burrill pointed to a section on the graph and says, "You see this, right here?" "Yes."

"That signal makes no sense."

"I agree." Dr. Rinzler said while scratching his chin.

A few seconds later, Dr Burrill also starts scratching his chin. Both men notice what they're doing and immediately stop scratching at the same time, neither one of them acknowledging how silly they looked. Dr. Burrill decided to break the awkwardness by saying. "You know, there's been a lot of anecdotal evidence suggesting that people have significant effects, health-wise, due to ELF's, but this, this is the opposite. These reading shows that Thomas is the source. How is that possible, Cole?"

"I don't know, but what worries me even more are these spikes. It looks like Thomas emits intermittent spikes of this energy at random times." Dr. Burrill exams the spikes on the graph that Dr. Rinzler is referring to. "I see what you mean. This is very disturbing. That fact that there was never any indication that Thomas was conducting or absorbing any energy from any external source means that Thomas is somehow producing this energy. Which makes no sense. Hell, these readings don't make any sense. And how is this even possible?" Dr. Burrill pointed to the spike on the graph, "Look, our equipment isn't even design to make a vertical line at the crest of a spike."

"I know . These readings also show that, theoretically, Thomas should be losing energy, but instead, it seems like he is creating energy from nowhere out of nothing, which would really piss off Newton because it flies in the face of his very 1st law, the law of thermodynamics." They stare at each other again and go back to pondering the profundity of the implications. "Maybe we should call our friend, Bill Rakowski." Dr. Rinzler said in a soft voice. "Bill? What is he, a, eh, neural engineer, right?" "Yes. Technically a neuroscientist." Dr. Burrill said, and then added, "But that guy has so many PhD's I don't think even he knows how much he knows." Dr. Rinzler laughed and said, "That's when you know you're smart, right? When you don't know how smart you are. Where is Bill at these days?"

"I believe he is still at Caltech."

"Marvelous. They must have better testing equipment than we do. In fact, I believe they have a S.Q.U.I.D. (Super conducting quantum interfering device) Let's take the suit in case he wants to exam it for any defects we might have missed."

"Excellent. We should call him right away."

Daniella Rios

The complexity of love lies within its simplicity,
for all one simply needs to do is, love. -JLC

Thomas woke up early in the morning. It was another beautiful day in Athens and Thomas couldn't wait to go outside. Greece was really starting to grow on him. He enjoyed the varied landscapes, rugged coastlines, rolling hills and mountainous terrain. The countryside had small villages with traditional stone houses and narrow streets. There was always a strong sense of community, and a very rich culture evidenced by the local festivals and celebrations which occur throughout the year.

Thomas enjoyed going to the small local shops in his area. The food was great, and the people were very friendly. Quite a few of the local vendors knew Thomas by name. He was becoming a local himself. Today, Thomas thought he would go to one of his favorite places, Monastiraki, specifically, the famous Monastiraki Flea Market. The neighborhood of Monastiraki is an amazing area of ancient and roman ruins, hotels restaurants, cafes, bars, and small shops. Monastiraki means, "little monastery" in Greek because that's where a monastery once stood. Now it is one of the quaintest and ineffably beautiful places for both locals and tourists alike.

Monastiraki was only ten minutes away by scooter and Thomas couldn't wait to get there. He loved all the food, and the bustling crowds filled with people from all over the world. The smells were rich and thick, filled with promise of culinary delights. Today Thomas was headed to one of his favorite places, 'Oven Sesame,' which served the quintessentially Greek "koulouri" which are oven baked rings of bread. Oven Sesame fills them with various fillings from feta cheese with thyme and extra virgin olive oil to more substantial options like chicken, beef, or eggplant. Thomas loved the feta cheese and thyme. He would get the chicken on occasion, but the feta cheese was definitely his favorite.

Thomas jumped on his scooter and headed into town. Ten minutes later he was parking on a side street and ready to go get some food and who knows, maybe some dessert, as well. Thomas smiled at the idea of some sweet treat as he headed into the crowd of people. Thomas parked on the opposite side of where "Oven Sesame" was because there was never any parking on the other side of the flea market. Thomas walked up to the vendor and smiled as he said, "Geia sou, Yiorgos." Which roughly translates to "Hello, George." Yiorgos always responded in English, "Hey, Simon, how are you my friend? You are here for your favorite?" Thomas was already digging into his pockets for money. "Yup, I mean, Nai."

"Simon, you are no very good at Greek. Maybe learn first and then try to talk it."

"Speak it." Thomas corrected Yiorgos.

"Oh, look who is such a language expert now. You come here to teach me, Simon? Or you come here to eat my koulouri?" Thomas laughed and said, "Okay, today I'll just have some koulouri with feta cheese. You know what, make it two." Yiorgos smiled at Thomas and couldn't help jabbing him one more time. "Simon, you say koulouri like it's some kind of cool bird."

"What?"

"Yes, you say, cool bird. Because you cannot pronounce kou."

"What? No way, listen, koulouri. See?"

Yiorgos laughs again and says, "Look, Simon, you don't try to say koulouri and I won't use the word talk instead of speak."

"Whatever, George."

"Yeah, whatever Mr. Simon." Thomas always wondered why so many foreigners like to use the first name when using the conventional title of Mr.

Yiorgos began making Thomas' order. Thomas pulled out a few Euros to pay for his food. As he began uncrumpling the bills Thomas could have sworn he heard his name in the crowd. He looked up but didn't see anything. A couple seconds later, he heard it again. Thomas looked around the crowd. He couldn't see anyone, but he could definitely hear his name. Not only that, but they were also yelling, Thomas, not Simon. There it is again. Finally, Thomas looked towards the North end of the market, and there, waving frantically at him was Danni Rios. She had a huge smile on her face, she looked so excited to see him. Thomas didn't know what to do. So, he panicked.

Danni kept getting closer, and Thomas was quickly approaching fight or flight mode. Yiorgos looked at Thomas and could tell something was bothering him. "Simon, are you okay? Why is that girl yelling at you and calling you Thomas?" Thomas looked at Yiorgos, then looked at Danni coming closer and closer. She was about 40 yards away. Thomas looked back at Yiorgos and threw the money at him and said, "I gotta go. Sorry."

Thomas ran away and managed to quickly duck behind a crowd of people. Once he was out of Danni's sight he ran behind a row of street vendors. Once he got to the end of the block Thomas quickly turned right. He ran down another block and turned left. Halfway down that street Thomas looked back to see if he had lost her. Danni was nowhere to be seen. His heart was racing it felt like his entire body was pounding. Thomas began pacing in the street and talking to himself. "Why am I running? What's the problem? What the hell am I doing? Shit! Damn it!" Thomas sat on the curb and contemplated his next move.

Thomas had decided that it was too late to fix this. He can't just go back and tell her that he ran away like a drunken monkey because he didn't want to see her. In fact, just the opposite, he was actually very happy to see her. She looked as pretty as ever. Different hair style than he remembered, different color, too, but he liked it. Thinking about her calmed him down. Then he got upset again because of his stupid reaction. Well, no matter now, he would just look like an idiot if he ran into her now.

Thomas decided he would just go home and hide out for a while. Thomas wandered down the side streets for almost an hour before heading back to his scooter. Surely Danni wouldn't wait around that long for him after pulling that ridiculous stunt. *'She probably hates me now for acting like a fool.'* Thomas thought as he walked back into the flea market. It was almost noon, and the market was still very busy. Thomas made sure to look around very carefully as he sneaked back to where he parked his scooter.

Finally, he got to his scooter. He unlocked his helmet, pulled out his keys, and then he heard, "Hi Thomas." Thomas turned his head to see Danni standing there with her arms crossed and leaning on one hip with her head slightly tilted. Thomas knew that look. It was the 'what the hell do you think you're doing' look.

"Ah, hi Danni." Thomas said fumbling with his keys.

"Hi Danni? That's what you have to say?"

"What? Oh, you mean that whole running away thing? That was just, you know, I was, just, going…to….see.."

"Yes?"

"Ah, see….ah…nothing. Okay, I get it. I was a total moron. I don't even know why I ran, okay. I was just surprised. Like, totally surprised."

"And so, you were so happy to see me, that your first reaction was to run like a maniac down the street?"

Thomas dropped his head as low as it could possibly go and said, "Sorry."

Danni was just torturing him, she was still very happy to see Thomas. She finally let him off the hook and said, "Well, you knucklehead, are you going to give me a hug or not?" Thomas' face lit up and said, "Oh, yeah, yes, I mean, for sure." They both hugged and began talking. It would be hours before they realized just how much time had passed. Danni looked at her phone and said, "Oh my God, it's almost 2 o'clock." Thomas looked down at his watch and said, "Wow, no wonder I'm starving. You want to get something to eat?"

"For sure. I'm starving, too!" "Okay, but let's not go to the Open Sesame. I think George might be piss off at me for running also." They both laughed and took off to find some food.

The smell of freshly baked bread still permeated the air, and it only made them hungrier. They walked into a small restaurant for some Mediterranean food and continued their conversations. Thomas took a sip of his coke and said, "So, you're going to university. That sounds great. John Hopkins no less. Impressive." Thomas didn't realize how silly he looked as he moved his face down to his drink and gazed up at Danni while speaking with the straw still in his mouth. It reminded Danni of some 6-year-old kid. She thought it was cute. Thomas noticed her odd stare and lifted his head off the straw. "What?"

"Nothing."

"Why are you looking at me like that?"

"Like what?"

"Like that. Like I'm doing something weird." Danni smiled and said, "Look, it's nothing, I just thought you look kinda cute with that straw in your mouth." Thomas quickly sat up and displayed his best posture. "Better?" he said. Danni reached out and tapped his forearm, "Yes. Much better." Thomas continued, "Anyway, John Hopkins, eh?"

"Yeah. It was the only place I applied to because that was the only place I wanted to go. I did a little research, well, who am I kidding, I did a lot of research and found that JHU puts more money into research than any other university and they were the first to combine research and education into a cohesive unit and although I'm not sure I'm going to be all that crazy about Baltimore, I think that…am I boring you?"

"What? No. Sounds super interesting. Really!"

"Yeah, well, anyway. I told my parents that I was going to take a few months off before I go. You know, see the world, or at least as much as I could in a few months. Greece was on my list of places I wanted to see and so, here I am." Danni said with arms stretched out. Thomas was about to take another sip of his coke, but stopped midway and replied, "That's great!" Danni moved her drink closer to her to take a drink of her Ayran, a cold yoghurt-based drink. She took a small sip and asked, "So, what's going on with you? Why are you here in Athens of all places?"

"To tell you the truth."

"Yes?"

"I'm stalking you. Been stalking you since Goleta."

"Ha, ha. Very funny. Really, what's happening with you. Are your parents here?"

"Nope. Just hanging out in Greece. You know, checking out the area." Danni looked at Thomas with a dubious smirk and simply said, "Thomas." He felt like he had to correct his posture again. What was it about Danni that just made him so nervous. He felt like the same elementary school kid when he first met her. Nervous, jittery, hard to speak normally, like every word had to be silly. Thomas took a few seconds to compose himself and finally said, "Look,

I'm just hanging out here until I decide what I'm going to do with my life. Kind of like you."

"Are you going to a university when you leave here?"

"No."

"Working?"

"No."

"No school, no work. Must be nice. So, you're retired." She said with the same smirk on her face. Danni tilted her head downward while gazing up at him and said, "Thomas?"

"What?"

"Thomas, what the hell is going on with you? Where are you staying. Do you have a place to stay? Do you need help?"

"What? No! I'm fine. Really, everything is fine. I can't believe how fine everything is." The Waitress arrived with their food and Thomas was glad for the small distraction. Thomas pointed at the server and said, "Hey, look, our food is here. Let's eat and talk later. I'm starvin." Danni could tell Thomas was being evasive so she decided she would let him off the hook…for now. They ate their food and Danni steered the conversation to some very idle non-intrusive chatting. When they were done, they had agreed to spend the next day together.

This soon turned into a routine and Thomas and Danni were quickly becoming an item around town. They both had scooters, but Danni was renting hers. They would take turns picking each other up and sometimes Thomas would have to ride behind Danni. She noticed that Thomas would never invite her to come inside where he was staying. Danni found this odd and a little awkward because one time she needed to use the restroom and Thomas fed her the old line that the toilets were out of order and that they could stop at McDonald's a few blocks away.

By the third week, however, she had it with his mysterious crap. She came over one day and simply demanded that Thomas let her go inside to use the restroom. She could see that Thomas was still hesitant, but she held her ground. "Thomas, I'm going inside with or without you. Are you coming?"

"Yeah, sure, just don't make a big deal about it." Thomas said faking aggravation. Danni continued towards the front door. she glanced back at Thomas and said, "What are you talking about? What's the big deal, it's just a house Thomas. What? Are you hiding dead bodies in the basement that I should know about?"

"What? No. That's crazy. What are you talkin' about? Dead bodies, shish." Danni could still

204

sense his nervousness, and it only compelled her further. She stopped at the front door and allowed Thomas to walk in front of her so he could open the door. As he did, Danni looked around and it wasn't until now that she really noticed the house and the yard. "Wow, Thomas, this is a really nice place. I love all the landscaping. You got a gardener?

"Eh, yeah. We have a gardener. They come around like three times a month."

"Must be nice."

"Yeah, it's pretty cool. I mean, at least I don't have to pull weeds, right?" Thomas said, not realizing he sounded like a spoiled kid. Once inside, the first thing Danni noticed was a man standing in the kitchen next to a large window. He stared intently at Danni while also peering out the window as if he was looking for something. '*That's kind of strange*,' Danni thought. She touched Thomas' shoulder and asked, "Who's that?"

"Him? Of that's my uncle. Uncle Mike." Danni felt a little unsettled. She turned to Thomas and asked, "So, where's the bathroom?" Thomas pointed to a hallway and said, "Down the hall, second door on your right." As Danni walked down the hallway, Thomas noticed "his uncle" staring at him. Thomas shrugged his shoulders and smiled. Michael gave a half smile back and pointed his index finger at him which Thomas always knew it meant, "be careful." Thomas replied with an affirmative nod. Thomas waited patiently for Danni. She was taking a few minutes longer than anticipated but finally he heard the toilet flush. A minute later Danni appeared and said, "Hey Thomas, you have a very nice house."

"Thanks."

"Is it your parents' house or is it a rental?"

"It's a rental." Thomas answered almost too quickly.

"Well, it's very nice." Thomas tried to guide her towards the door, but then Danni noticed another man coming from a room next to the kitchen and walked up to Uncle Mike and they began speaking in a low voice. Danni asked Thomas, "And who's that?"

"Oh, he...is...my...uncle...my uncle's friend, Paul."

"Okay." Danni said, incredulously.

"No, really, that's his friend. They stay here sometimes."

"Who's they?"

"They, you know, my uncle's friends."

"Friends? There are others?"

"Sometimes."

"Okay, fine. Let's get going." As they left the house, Danni noticed another man coming around the corner of the house. She also just noticed that they are all about the same built. Tall, athletic with a very focused look, like they're paying attention to everything around them. Danni grabs Thomas' arm and stops him from moving forward. Thomas stops and meets Danni's stare. She points at the man and says, "Another one of your uncle's friend?"

"Yeah, that's Andre." Thomas waves at Andre and says, "Hi, Andre."

"Hello Simon." Andre continues to walk right past them and walks around the other side of the house. Danni is now standing with a severe posture and folded arms and says, "Did you not see that? He's just walking around your house. He didn't acknowledge me, and just walked around the side of your house. Don't you think that's kind of weird?"

"No. Andre likes to go for walks."

"Around the house?"

"Yeah, he doesn't like being out there with people. He's like a loner or something like that."

"And why did he call you Simon?"

"Oh, that, well they just started calling me that when we got to Greece. Paul started it, when we first met he said I look like Simon, so it stuck. It's like a nickname. Can we just go now?"

"Look, Thomas, I don't know what you're doing here or what you're up to. Right now, I don't care. Clearly there is something you are not telling me and I'm not going to push it. I'll wait till you're ready to let me know. So, for now, can we just go get something to eat. I'm famished." Thomas was relieved to hear Danni say that. "Okay. Now you're talkin. I got a surprise for you."

"Oh, really? I'm not sure I could handle any more surprises right now."

"Surprises?, what are you talking about?"

"Nothing. Never mind. What's the surprise." Danni watched as Thomas reached into his pocket and pulled out a single key with a small foamy toy attached to it. Danni eyes lit up and said, "Is that what I think it is?"

"Yup. I got us a boat for the day. I figure we could just cruise along the coast where it's safe because I don't know anything about boating."

"Sounds like fun. We'll pack a lunch and just hang out on the water."

"Yeah, that does sound like fun." Thomas enjoyed making Danni happy. He loved her smile, the way she laughed, her one left dimple. Thomas checked his feelings and thought, '*Oh my God. Am I in love with Danni?*'

Thomas and Danni bought some sandwiches and drinks along with a few snacks and headed down to the small marina where the boat was docked. No one gave them a second look, they were just two young kids going on a little boat ride in the Aegean Sea. They rode along the coast for hours stopping occasionally whenever they spotted some place that looked interesting. They stopped at a very small island. It wasn't really an island, more like an islet. They docked and walked around and saw the whole thing in like two minutes. It was mostly rocky ground with very little greenery. But still, they found a small patch of grass and decided to have lunch there.

It was early afternoon, and the sun was shining bright above a clear blue sky. The weather was warm with a slight breeze coming in from the south. They sat there and talked while they ate and listened to the sound of the ocean water lapping against the rocks. Thomas enjoyed talking to Danni, but it was difficult because he felt nervous around her, mostly because he knew he would have to continue telling her lies and he didn't like that.

Danni was chewing her food with a contemplated look and Thomas knew a question was coming. And sure enough, it did. "So, Thomas, or Simon, or whatever your name is. How long are you planning on staying here?" Thomas spoke with a mouth full of food. "On this island?" Danni laughed, "No, dummy, in Greece. How long are you planning on staying in Greece?" Thomas swallowed his food and replied, "Ah, I'm not sure."

"So, you're just gonna stay here? Retired at 17 years old?

"What? No. Ha, ha. That's funny. No, I'm just gonna hang out for maybe a few more months. Why?"

"Well," Danni answered, " I'm going to be here about another month. I was going to leave in a couple of weeks, but I'm enjoying Greece a little more than I thought." She gave Thomas a flirty smile.

Thomas was oblivious to her playful provocativeness and said, "Yeah, it's pretty cool here. I'm really starting to like it. Even more when you're with somebody you like. I mean, you know because I like you, I guess."

"You guess?"

"No, I mean, yes. I mean yes, I like you."

"Well, I like you too, Simon." Danni said in a sarcastic tone.

"Whatever. Hey, so what do you want to do tomorrow?"

"Really?" Another date? Mr. Grady, just what are your intentions, sir.?"

"Ha, ha. Funny. Look, how about we go and see the Parthenon. It's only like 20 euros to get in."

"Look at you all mister European."

"Whatever. You want to go?"

"It's a date."

"Great. Let's head back because I don't know if the weather is going to change on us. We should have checked it before we left."

"Okay. Sounds good. Let's go." They jumped back on the boat and headed back to the little marina. When they got back they hung out a little longer and went their separate ways. Thomas was really enjoying Danni's company very much. Thomas was also getting comfortable with the idea of maybe he is in love with Danni. And it made him feel sad that she would be leaving in about a month.

The next day Thomas picked up Danni at the apartment where she was staying. They drove to the Parthenon. They did a lot of walking. They climbed up the Acropolis and from there just did more walking. The ancient ruins were interesting, and they both pondered the perplexity of constructing such an incredible piece of architecture without modern equipment. As they stood on the steps of the Acropolis they noticed there was an area behind the Doric columns that looked like there might be some people hiding behind them. They decided to go explore thinking that maybe these people know something special about this place. But when they got there they saw three young men sneaking around and it looked like they were doing some kind of drug. The three men spotted Thomas and Danni and one of them yelled out, "Hey, you two, get the hell out of here." Another shouted in Greek, but they couldn't understand him. Though it sounded like a lot of curse words.

Thomas held up his hands and said, "Okay, okay. We're leaving." Thomas grabbed Danni's hand and guided her back towards the stairs where they came from. But one of the young men walked quickly towards Thomas and grabbed him by his t-shirt and said something in a very mean and loud voice. The young man's eye's looked a little crazed as he raised his fist to strike Thomas. Thomas braced for impact but as the young man's fist came flying towards his face, a hand came out of nowhere and caught it in midair. Thomas just stood there frozen with his eyes wide open. The young man was surprised, he turned to see who it was that stopped him. It was a menacing figure. But the young man did not want to look weak in front of his friends, so with his other hand he tried to swing at the man still holding his fist. But the man caught the other punch with his other hand, and they stared into each other's eyes for a brief second. That's when the young man heard the other man say, "My turn." With one swift blow to the young man's jaw, he sent the young man flying back causing him to fall onto the floor unconscious. It was Gene Korbin.

Korbin turned to Thomas and asked, "You okay?" Thomas said, "Ah, yeah." Korbin turned to look at the other two young men to see if any of them were going to attack. They didn't, they both held up their hands and spoke in Greek. Korbin understood them and replied back. Then he allowed the two men to pick up their friend and leave. Thomas looked at Korbin and said, "What are you doing here?"

"What do you mean, what am I doing here? I'm always here. Thomas you are never alone. Don't you know that? We all take turns keeping an eye on you. It's for your own safety."

Danni immediately picked up on the word . "Safety?" She said, "What are you talking about? Why would Thomas not be safe?" Korbin looked at Danni then glanced over at Thomas, and he realized he just made a mistake. He had to think quickly. Before Thomas could interject, Korbin answered. "Yes, mam. You see, Thomas was roughed up a little by some of the locals a few weeks ago and well, he caught a pretty good beating. So now, we keep an eye on him whenever he goes out. Make sure nothing serious happens because, you know, you never know?" Korbin turned to look at Thomas and said, "Right?"

Thomas tried his best to follow through. "Yeah, I forgot to mention that I got beat up a while back. Some local bullies, or drug users, I don't know. But they're known to cause trouble around here. And I forgot that sometimes, not all the time, my uncle and his friends will keep an eye on me." Thomas and Korbin stopped talking and stared at each other then, both their eyes darted over to Danni to see if she was buying any of it. To their surprise, Danni simply said, "Okay." She then pivoted on one foot turned and walked away. Thomas and Korbin didn't quite know how to interpret her response. Is she mad? Is she really okay with it? As Danni walked away, Thomas called out to Danni, "Hey, are you okay?" Danni simply replied, "I'm fine." Korbin put a hand on Thomas' shoulder and said, "Oh shit. She's mad."

The rest of the day did not go as planned. Danni was cold and Thomas was in over his head.

209

He never had to deal with a woman before. He wasn't sure what to do next. So, he did what any other man would do. Start apologizing for everything. But nothing was working. Danni was curt with all her comments. They had been walking for hours when finally, Thomas stopped her, and turned her shoulders so they were facing each other and said, "Okay, I know you're upset. What can I do to make it up to you?" Danni stared directly into eyes and said, "Look, Thomas. I am a very understanding person. You are obviously keeping something from me, and I can tell it seems to be bothering you just as much as it's bothering me. This tells me that you care about me, but it does not negate the fact that it hurts. It hurts to not be trusted Thomas. I'm going to give you more time to figure this out and I'm hoping you'll let me know what is really going in in the future. The near future Thomas. Even I have my limits. So, figure it out." They got on Thomas' scooter, and he dropped her off. There was nothing to say, she was right. But what could he do?

A couple of weeks went by, and Thomas and Danni kept enjoying each other's company though there was still some underlying tension. But Danni had decided she was going to give Thomas more time to figure things out. She knew Thomas was hiding something and it was also evident that Thomas needed time to sort things out. Danni could tell that this secret that Thomas is holding in is really bothering him just as much as it's bothering her.

Today they went out to the countryside. The countryside in Greece is a beautiful and varied landscape. Thomas was still taken by the quaintness of these older towns and the people that appeared to be so steeped in their old traditions. They were each driving their own scooters. It was a warm and sunny day. Blues skies with a few faint wispy clouds lingering in the air. The air was clean and the sounds of birds in the background gave the day an almost Disney feel to it. But like most Disney films, tragedy was looming.

As Thomas and Danni drove down a small two-lane road, they could see something up ahead. They couldn't quite make out exactly what it was. But as they got closer, they both felt a sense of panic. They could tell something wasn't right. As they got even closer they realized that it was a car accident. It appeared to be a head-on collision. A high-speed head-on collision as both vehicles were mangled almost beyond recognition.

Thomas and Danni quickly parked and got off their scooters to inspect the scene. Danni got off her scooter first and ran to see if anyone was still in any of the vehicles. Danni noticed some movement on her right side about fifty yards away off the road. She saw what appeared to be a man running through a large open field. He was stumbling and running as fast as he could. She could only surmise that he may have had something to do with the accident. She watched as he kept running over a small hill and then disappeared on the other side.

She turned her attention back to the accident. Both cars were still smoldering. One vehicle looked empty, the other had one passenger in the driver's seat and one in the back seat. Upon further inspection, she saw a third person about 30 to 40 feet away from the vehicle. It was a woman. She must have been ejected from one of the vehicles. Danni could see that the woman on the asphalt was moving a little which meant she was still alive. The people inside the vehicle looked like there was no way they could be alive. Their bodies were almost completely crushed and folded in impossible ways. One of the cars must have been moving at a very high speed.

Danni ran to the woman on the floor. Thomas yelled out, "Danni, wait!" Danni ignored him and ran straight to see if there was any way of helping her. Danni yelled back at Thomas, "Call 9-1-1." Thomas kept walking towards Danni as he called. Danni knelt down beside the woman. Danni could see that she was in very bad shape. Her body was battered and bruised, probably from going through the windshield. Her head was bleeding profusely, and she appeared to have a couple of ribs protruding from her left side. One of her legs was grossly twisted in several directions and her entire body was covered in small lacerations. Danni stared at Thomas with tearful eyes that were also filled with fear.

"Thomas, did you call for help?"

"Yes, but they told me it would be at least 30 min before they get here."

"What? She's not going to last that long, Thomas. What should we do?"

Thomas could hear the desperateness in Danni's voice. She was genuinely concerned for this person. But what should he do? What's the right thing and what's the smart thing to do? Thomas was frozen in thought and Danni could see it. She reached up to hold his hand and said, "Thomas, what's wrong? Are you okay?" Thomas just stood there and stared into Danni's eyes as if he wanted to say something. Danni was felling scared and confused, she asked him again, "Thomas, what's wrong?" neither one of them noticed the whining sound of an engine racing towards them at high speed.

Danni was becoming concerned about Thomas. Finally, she stood up and faced Thomas, forced him to look her in the eyes and she said, "Thomas, what is the matter? Is this accident too much for you? Do you need to sit over on the side of the road? You don't need to stand here and look at it if it bothers you too much, okay?" Thomas stared back Danni and said, "I…"

"What? You what, Thomas. Tell me."

"I…I think I can help." Danni looked at Thomas concerned and confused and said, "What? What do you mean you could help her? Thomas, what are you saying, you have some kind of medical training? Can you really help her? I mean, I don't think she's going to make it, Thomas. What is it you think you can do? Because we are all this woman has right now, so if you got some trick up your sleeve, now is the time to use it. This poor woman has nothing to lose. So, do you have like some kind of first-aid kit in your scooter?" Thomas just kept staring into her eyes. Danni grabbed Thomas' shoulders and shook him almost too hard and yelled, "Thomas! Snap out of it. You're scaring me. Listen, we have a situation, this woman is going to die, Thomas, and you are out of it. Is there anything you can tell me that would help this woman? Tell me and I'll try to do it. Now, do you have a first aid kit in your scooter?" Finally, Thomas snapped out of his confused state and decided he was going to help this woman. Thomas blinked and shook his head as if it helped clear his mind. He slowly moved Danni's hands off his shoulders and place his hands on her shoulders and simply said, "Stay right here." Thomas began walking over to the woman lying on the ground.

Danni watched as Thomas walked slowly towards the woman. He didn't have anything in his hands, 'what was he going to do?' She thought. That's when Danni noticed the sound of a vehicle racing towards them. She looked down the road. It was coming really fast. It was still about a mile away, but she could also hear that the vehicle was honking it's horn incessantly, as if to cause attention to itself. 'Was it an ambulance? No,' she thought,' it's definitely a car. Maybe it's a vehicle with medical aid of some sort.' It was strange, watching the vehicle race towards them and seeing Thomas, now kneeling next to the woman. It seemed like all of Thomas' movements were very slow as if he were apprehensive, but why? The moment struck her as surreal. She yelled out to Thomas, "Thomas, there's a vehicle coming towards us. Maybe they can help?" Thomas didn't hear her, he was too focused on what he was about to do. Still not sure, even now as he stood in front of the woman who was gazing at him as if she was glad that she would not be dying alone.

"Thomas!" Danni yelled again. "I said there's a car coming. Maybe they can help." He seemed to not hear her still, so Danni decided to walk up to him and tell him again. Then it all happened. Thomas was reaching down to touch the woman, the vehicle was just a quarter mile

212

away still blaring it's horn. Danni looked at the vehicle, then at Thomas. When she turned to look back at the vehicle, it was almost upon them. The driver of the vehicle slammed on the brakes and the tires locked and screeched as it skidded for about twenty-five feet and stopped about fifteen yards away. Danni looked down at Thomas. She could see Thomas reach down and place his hand on the woman abdomen and left it there for a few seconds.

Danni now moved her attention back to the car. As it came to a complete stop, she saw two men quickly jump out and immediately started yelling at Thomas. She could hear one of them saying, "Thomas, don't! don't do it! Stop!" Danni was getting more confused. What did they want Thomas to stop? Stop what? He isn't doing anything. Now the two men were running as fast as they could, she recognized Korbin. He was the one yelling. If Danni was confused now, she was about to be completely confounded as she looked down at the woman. Danni could suddenly see things moving around.

The healing looked just as grotesque as the injuries as she saw bones moving back inside her body. The woman's hair was also moving as the flesh on her head began to heal. Multiple lacerations were closing at the same time and her leg began to unfold as bones reconnected into their correct positions. As Danni watched, she could feel the Earth spinning, her legs felt weak, her eyes rolled back. Danni fainted and collapsed on the floor.

Danni was unconscious for less than a minute. She opened her eyes and found herself lying down in the back seat of a car. As she stood up, she recalled all the crazy things that happened and she almost fainted again, but she kept her composure. Danni sat up on the seat and looked outside. She could see Thomas and the two men arguing about something. One of them had a gun in his hand. She got scared, for herself and for Thomas. She opened the door and ran towards Thomas. Thomas saw her and said, "Danni, stay in the car, please." But she just kept on running until she was able to wrap her arms around him. "No. I'm staying right here." She looked at Korbin and said, "What the hell is going on? And what are you doing with that gun?"

It wasn't until now that Danni noticed the woman that Thomas helped standing next to the other man that came with Korbin. He also had a gun in his hand. The woman's hands were tied behind her back, and she appeared confused and agitated. She wanted to say something, but she was also gagged. Danni let go of Thomas, stepped back and looked at all of them and said, "What the hell is going on? Thomas, I just saw that woman's injuries heal, as if by magic. And now she's being held by a man with a gun in his hand. Tell me what the hell is going on, right

213

now! Right fucking now." It was the first time Thomas ever heard Danni curse. Thomas sighed and said, "Look, it's a very long story. But right now, I just need you to give me a minute. Could you wait in the car, please?"

"Hell no. I want to know what's going on. I just happen to have time for a long story right now."

"Okay, okay. Let me just wrap this up with Korbin. Please."

Danni folded her arms and said, "Wrap away. I'll be right here."

Korbin signaled his partner to turn the woman around, so she isn't facing them. Korbin spoke first, "Look, Thomas, we need to minimize your exposure here. You know you can't go around doing this stuff. Now we have a witness." Korbin glanced over towards Danni and said, "Two witnesses. That's not good." Thomas looked at the woman he just healed and said, "So, what are you going to do? Kill everybody? That's not going to happen. If you can't figure it out, call Mario and see what he says."

"I already called, he's not picking up right now. And I need an answer right now because there's an ambulance on its way and who knows who else is going to be coming down this road. We gotta move now and we gotta move fast. So, what do you propose, Thomas?"

"I'm not proposing anything, we are going to let this woman go and you guys are going back home or back to following me around or whatever it is you do, but we are not going to kill anybody. That's not happening."

Korbin thought about it for a second and said, "Okay. We'll play this your way, Thomas. I don't have a problem with it. We'll see what Mario wants to do when I get a hold of him. For now, you want me to drop off this woman at the nearest hospital?"

"Ah, no. I think we'll wait here with her until we see the ambulance arriving then we'll take off just before they stop."

"And what do you think she's going to say?" Korbin said, pointing to the woman Thomas healed.

"What do you think they'll believe, is the question. Let her say as much crazy stuff as she wants. They'll write off her story caused by some kind of brain injury."

"Okay, but look, Thomas, we can't have you doing these things anymore. Mr. Pitt is no joke. I'm pretty sure that guy has people everywhere keeping an eye out for you. He'll find you eventually and we'll move you again. But for now, let's not make his job any easier than we have to, okay?"

"Got it. No more healing stuff."

"What about your girlfriend?"

"What? She's not my girlfriend."

"Really. That's how you wanna play this. Okay, Fine."

"Fine."

"Fine. See you at the house." Korbin signaled his partner to get back in the car. They left just as quickly as they got there, racing down the road and some crazy high speed. They didn't want to be seen anywhere near this accident. Thomas walked over to Danni and said, "Come on, let's go untie her."

Thomas held up his right index finger to halt the barrage of questions that Danni was about to start throwing at him and said, "Wait. Before you ask all your questions, let's take care of this woman first. And Danni, please let me do all the talking, okay?" "Okay." She replied. Thomas untied the woman's hands and removed her gag. The woman was wide-eyed and astounded at what she witnessed, and she suddenly dropped to her knees and began thanking Thomas. "Thank you, thank you. You are like an angel. You gave me a miracle. I know God has sent you to me."

Thomas felt very uncomfortable as he grabbed the woman's arms and helped her up. "No, please. Don't worry about it. But I would like to ask you for a very special favor."

"Yes, anything. Anything you want."

"The thing is, miss."

"Please, you can call me, Ella."

"Yes, okay, well, Ella, the thing is, I would very much appreciate it if you would please not tell anybody about what happened to you here today. Can you help me with that?"

"No. I cannot do that. You are a miracle worker. Everyone should know about your great powers."

"Well, listen. It will make my life very difficult. And I could get into a lot of trouble. I really need your help. Will you help me, please?"

The woman thought about it for a moment and realized that maybe it *would* make his life very problematic and he's only a boy. So, she said, "Okay. I will never tell anyone what happen here today." Thomas sighed in relief. "But" Ella continued, "You must first help my husband and my sister. They are still in the car." Thomas looked at Ella with a sad expression on his face and said, "I'm sorry, but I cannot bring people back once they are…gone." Thomas lied, "Do you understand? You were not gone, you were just hurt. I'm afraid your husband and sister are beyond my help. I'm sorry."

"No. You must try. Please. Please try." Thomas lowered his head and said, "I'm sorry. I have tried before, and it has never worked. I would also have to wait for them to be removed from the car and I can't stay here when other people arrive. We have to go. I'm sorry. Please keep your word and don't tell anyone about what happen to you." The woman started sobbing uncontrollably as she fell to her knees in anguish, but with understanding. Thomas and Danni could see the ambulance coming, it was about a kilometer away. It was difficult to walk away from this grieving woman, but they had to leave. They walked towards their scooters and headed back into town. They didn't speak or even look at each other until they got to the Monastiraki Flea Market. There they found a table in a quite spot and ordered some food and a drink. Thomas told Danni everything.

The Death of the Atom

Bill Rakowski told Dr. Burrill and Rinzler to meet him in front of the Athenaeum Club, located inside the Caltech Campus. It was a little awe inspiring knowing that the likes of Albert Einstein once actually lived inside this building which is currently used more as a private club for dining now. Dr.'s Burrill and Rinzler were sitting at one of the patio tables just outside the club. Bill emerged from inside the building and greeted his two friends. "Allan, Cole, so good to see you two again." Allan Burril and Cole Rinzler stood up to meet their friend. They shook hands and padded each other's shoulders. Dr. Burrill spoke first, "Good to see you also, my friend. You look good. Did you lose some weight?"

Bill slapped his belly lightly and replied, "No, not really, I think maybe only my posture improved." He said while exaggerating his posture and tucking his stomach in. They all laughed, then Dr. Rinzler said, "It's great to see you, Bill. What's got you busy these days?"

Bill answered, "Oh, you know, the usual, attempting to pry into the human brain and try to figure out how the internal impression of the world gets translated into the experience of our daily lives. Searching for the answer of what is consciousness." Dr. Rinzler said, "Hell, you could have just called us, and we would have told you what consciousness is." Dr. Rakowski took the bait, "Oh, really, do tell." Dr. Rakowski asked with as much amusement as he could mustard up.

"Well, it's quite simple," Dr. Rinzler said, "consciousness is the ability of the brain to be able to determine whether to have a healthy breakfast or have a couple of chocolate donuts instead."

"I think you're confusing consciousness with healthy eating habits."

"No, I'm comparing it to eating donuts."

"Same thing, Dr. Rinzler." They both laughed.

Dr. Burrill stepped into their conversation, "So, Bill, about that thing we talked about. Are you sure you have a little time on your hands? I know you must be busy, but we are really at a quandary here." Dr. Kaminski could sense the tension in Allan's voice. "Sure, Allan, I always have time for old friends." He said putting his hand on Dr. Burrill's shoulder. "Come, let me show you guys my new digs. You're gonna love it. The CNRB building was somewhat recently dedicated to neuroscience. It's a 3-story facility with floor-to-ceiling windows. We have labs for research, labs for teaching and a 150-seat lecture hall. It's really very nice!"

Dr. Burrill and Rinzler could tell that Dr. Rakowski was very excited about his work. Hopefully it will help answer some questions regarding Thomas. When they arrived at the facility, they could see why Dr. Rakowski was so excited. The building was quite impressive and very modern looking. They walked inside and headed to Dr. Rakowski's office. Once inside, Dr. Rakowski sat behind his desk while the other two sat in front of the desk. Dr. Rakowski started the conversation, "Okay, boys. What have we got here? I noticed Cole has been dragging that case around. Let's take a look." Dr. Rinzler opened the case and pulled out the sensor suit while Dr. Burrill pulled out a file from his leather satchel and placed it on top of the desk.

Dr. Rakowski first reached for the file and opened it. He glanced over the readings and said, "What am I looking at here, because it doesn't make any sense to me. You said these were taken via the sensors embedded in the suit."

"That's right." Said Dr. Burrill. Dr. Rakowski leaned back on his chair and said, "I don't think so, unless you have some kind of new equipment I never heard of. Do you?"

"What?" Said Dr. Burrill.

" Have a new piece of equipment I never heard of?"

"No."

"So how do you explain a horizonal mark on this graph?"

"We can't."

"Then I can only conclude that your equipment is faulty."

"It isn't. we checked and recalibrated dozens of times."

"Well, then, maybe you have a bad sensor."

"Nope. Sensors are all good."

"Then you must have an anomalous reading."

"No sir. As you can see, these readings are consistent over several attempts."

"What's the sensitivity maximum on your equipment?"

"Nowhere near the sensitivity that you can get in the equipment you have laying around this facility."

"That won't do you any good. We would need the test subject here in order to run these test again. Is this person available?"

"No."

"Okay, so how is it you want me to help, Allan?" Cole stepped into the conversation, "Well, we were hoping you could do a few things for us here. One is, we would like you to check out our suit and make sure it is in good working order. Maybe we missed something, though I doubt it. Also, we wanted to know if you could inspect the suit itself. You see, here, near the area where the test subject's ankle would be, is where the original signal came from. We noticed that there is some kind of change in the material as well and we were wondering if we could take look at it through a more powerful imaging system since all we have are a few microscopes laying around."

Dr. Rakowski reached into one of his drawers and pulled out a pipe. He placed it between his lips, but never lit it. He noticed the stares of his two friends. "It's a mental crutch. I'm afraid I had led myself to believe that I can think better with this thing." Both men smiled, and Dr. Rinzler said, "I think I may give that a try." Dr. Rakowski stood up somewhat abruptly and proclaimed, "Gentlemen, the game's afoot, lets head off to the lab." The other two men smiled again, stood up and followed him out the door.

The very first thing they were able to conclude was that the sensors were working fine. The next step was to take a look at the material. Dr. Rakowski did notice that the area where the original signal was taken did have some kind of abnormality around it. It was very subtle, but more noticeable on the inside of the suit. Dr. Rakowski thought nothing of it, could have simply been a blemish during the manufacturing of the suit. Someone could have rubbed it against a rough surface, or even scraped it with a fingernail. It could have been a dozen different things that could have caused it to look the way it did.

Nevertheless, he promised his friends he would exhaust every means at his disposal to help solve their mystery. Dr. Rakowski help up the suspect area of the suit close to his face and said, "What do you say we take a look at this guy with our TEM."

"What's that?" asked Dr. Rinzler.

"That's a Transmission Electron Microscope."

"Oh, I knew that." Dr. Burrill said with a guilty smile.

Dr. Rinzler said, "Ah-huh. Yeah, sure you did." Dr. Burrill just kept smiling.

They made their way to the lab that had the equipment they needed. After a small waiting time they were allowed to go in and begin inspecting the material. It took a while to set up. Sample preparation is vital to ensuring a good high-quality image. Dr. Rakowski asked Dr. Burrill, "Hey, Allan, you mind if I do a little damage here? I need to do a little ultramicotomy on this thing. I need a slice of this material thin enough to place on a TEM grid." Dr. Burrill shrugged his shoulders and said, "Do what you need to do, you're the expert here."

"I'm usually the expert wherever I am."

"There's the Bill I remember, overconfident, cocky, but right most of the time."

"Most of the time?" Dr. Rakowski said with a feigned surprised look on his face. Dr. Burrill replied, "Alright, Bill, just do your ultra-what-ever."

45 minutes later, Dr. Rakowski was through with taking all the images he needed. Once they were downloaded, he pulled them up on his laptop and began sharing them with Dr.'s Burrill and Rinzler. Rinzler and Burrill were not exactly sure what they were looking at, but Dr. Rakowski did. Dr. Rakowski kept shifting from one image to the next, then back again. His bewilderment was noticeable. At first, he just started talking to himself. "What the hell is this? This makes no sense. But if I'm seeing this correctly, we have a very strange situation on our hands. We may have to take this sample to our S.Q.U.I.D."

219

Dr. Rinzler leaned closer to the screen of the laptop and said, "What are we looking at here, Bill?" Dr. Rakowski pulled his pipe out of his blazer pocket to use as a pointer, he clicked it at the screen and said, "Something that should not exist. Something very scary." Dr. Rinzler and Burrill looked at each other and both noticed that they each had that mixed expression of concern and fear. Dr. Rakowski started walking at a very brisk pace anxious to get to the bottom of this unusual situation. Dr. Rinzler reached out and held on to Dr. Rakowski's shoulder and said, "Hey, Bill, slow down buddy, you're going to lose us. And what do mean, shouldn't exist? What shouldn't exist. You mind sharing a little information with us."

"What? Oh, yes, of course, I beg your pardon. It seems you two are not the only ones with a piece of equipment that shouldn't be producing these odd readings. However, I know that this TEM unit is working fine. And if it is, well, I don't know how to explain this, but, well, I can't, it makes no sense. We need to get more data off this material before I can even begin to contemplate my hypothesis." Dr. Rinzler replied, "Okay, Bill. Let's get more data. I have to tell you, I'm excited, but I just can't shake this eerie feeling."

"You and I both, Cole. This thing, this suit, or I should say this neoprene material should not be producing the anomaly that I just saw. And if these reading are true, it's not only concerning me, but it is also scaring the hell out of me. I can only hope that whatever is happening to your suit is a localized event. If not, well, I don't even want to think about it." They made their way to the research facility that housed the S.Q.U.I.D. Once inside, Dr. Rakowski was able to set it up and take another look at the suit. When he was done running some test, he was even more concerned once he reviewed the reading.

"Damn it. This just does not make any sense at all. Where did you say you got this suit from?" Dr. Burrill answered, "We simply had it made at a tailor shop. We gave him the neoprene and he made us a suit with the sensors sewn on in the designated areas that we specified."

"And tell me once again, who wore this suit, and why?"

"That is a long story. And one that may be hard to shallow."

"Try me."

Dr. Burrill explained the whole story about Thomas Grady and his unique abilities. Dr. Rakowski would have normally asked Dr. Burrill if he'd been smoking his lunch, but when he considered the readings on the suit, he quickly capitulated to the outrageous story. Dr. Rinzler chimed in, "So, Bill, what can you tell us about your findings?"

"Well, that also is a story that will be hard to swallow."

"Try me."

"Well, there's no easy way to explain it but, what I'm seeing shouldn't be possible in the realm of physics. These readings are telling me that there are fundamental changes going on at the molecular level of this material. It's as if the atoms in this material are losing their spin."

"What?" Dr. Rinzler said.

"You see, spin is a fundamental property of all atoms, all matter. This cannot be altered or stopped by any external means. It is an intrinsic property of all the components in an atom, the electron, proton and the neutron. The most immediate consequence would be the loss of the magnetic moment of the nucleus. The magnetic moment of a nucleus arises from the spin of its protons and neutrons, and the loss of spin can result in the loss of the magnetic moment this will have significant implications for the way the nucleus interacts with magnetic fields and will likely lead to changes in the behavior of the atom."

"But what does all that mean, Bill?" Dr. Rinzler asked.

"That part is still puzzling me. You see, stopping the spin of a nucleus would likely have energetic consequences, as it would require the absorption or release of energy to alter the intrinsic properties of the nucleus. This could then lead to the emission of particles or radiation, or changes in the stability or chemical properties of the atom. I wouldn't be surprised if we get gamma radiation readings from this suit."

"Okay, Bill, but I ask you again, what does it all mean?" Dr. Rakowski pulled out his pipe from his coat pocket and placed it on his lower lip and said, "It means that your kid, this Thomas fellow you mentioned may be the one source of an unknown energy that has the potential to end our world and possibly the known universe. We must find this boy and find out if there is a way to stop it, or…" Dr. Rakowski placed the pipe between his teeth and said, "…stop him."

"Come on Bill. Are you serious? The end of the universe. Aren't we being a little melodramatic?"

"I wish I was being glib about this whole thing, Allan, but what is happening here is plain and simple molecular decay of matter. There must be an energy force that we have never seen or heard of. In the simplest terms, the atoms on that suit seem to be losing their charge and just falling apart. It's as if this unknown energy is actually destroying the quarks inside the nucleus

221

which makes no sense. There should at the very least be a rearrangement of elements and isotopes occurring first. This would result in unknown isotopic alterations. But this, this energy is taking a short cut and simply disintegrating the very fabric of matter itself and it appears to be occurring one atom at a time at an unusually slow rate. It may take years to completely destroy the suit, it may take millions of years, there is just no way of knowing. And there is no way of knowing if it will pick up speed. And if it does, we'll have an unimaginable crises on our hands. And I can tell you this, as of this moment, there is no way for us to stop it. We must find this boy. He may be our only hope of understanding what we are dealing with. Meanwhile, we need to confirm my observations. I have a few colleagues here that can help with that. "

Flea Market Confession

Back in Greece, Thomas Grady had just finished telling Danni his whole story. Danni was sitting across from Thomas at a small table inside a small restaurant. The lighting was dim, and it was a little noisy. Danni could hear the constant tingling of silverware coming from all around the room as the people around her ate their food oblivious to the absurdity of her conversation with Thomas. Danni realized that she hadn't said a word in almost half a minute since Thomas finished telling her his plight. She was conscious of the fact that she was still processing the information. Finally, she spoke. "Thomas, if I hadn't of seen it with my own eyes, I would have written off your crazy story as just that, crazy. But I saw it." She furrowed her brows and said, "I…did…see it, right?"

"Yes." Thomas said as he instinctively reached for her hand and held it.

Danni looked into Thomas' eyes and said, "Thomas, what are you going to do? How can I help? Oh my God, I have so many questions that I'm sure you've heard a million times. Thomas, you are a once in a lifetime historical event. The more I think about this the more excited my brain gets. I have a hundred thoughts running through my head. Thomas, I, I can't imagine what you must be going through."

"Believe it or not, I'm actually kinda getting used to it."

"Used to it? How could you…okay, I get it. This has been your life for a long while. I guess you could get used to it. But Thomas, what's your next move going forward?"

"Next move is not getting caught and placed in a locked room and getting prodded and poked again."

"Oh my God. I can't imagine. But Thomas, you can't go on ignoring this gift. You can literally change the world."

"Okay, look Danni, here is just one scenario. I heal everyone and cripple the entire medical industry, ruin the insurance industry, bankrupt some pharmaceutical companies, send hundreds of doctors to the unemployment line, and create one of the biggest overall job loss events in the history of mankind. Millions of people all around the world will be unemployed and who knows what the unintended consequences of that will be. I don't know, but I can tell you this, it will not be pretty."

"Wow, I never even thought about how much harm it could cause. So, what are you going to do? Nothing? Thomas, that would be a sin and a crime against humanity. How could you think that doing nothing is the right thing to do? No, Thomas, you must find a way to help people with this unique ability of yours. Let me help you figure it out."

"That's very tempting, you know, us working together. I think I would like that. But I'm not sure exactly what I want to do, Danni. Could we just think about it for a few days, or weeks, or decades." Danni gave Thomas a mercy grin at his attempt at being glib.

"Okay, Thomas. I get it. This is a big decision. I'll give you two weeks to figure it out. If you're willing to move forward, I'll help you come up with a plan. If not, well, I'm not really going to accept no for answer, so, basically you have a two-week vacation from me insisting that you do something."

"Sounds good to me. Why don't we get together tomorrow for breakfast and just hang out. Try to forget everything that happened today. Okay?"

"Thomas, that would be impossible. I will never forget what happen today."

"Right. So then let's just hang out."

"Okay." Danni said, sensing how Thomas was getting edgy about the whole conversation. So, she simply said, "See you tomorrow, Thomas."

Thomas and Danni hopped on their respective scooters and headed home. Thomas was only thinking about meeting up with Danni again the next day. Danni, however, her mind was racing with possibilities. Imagine the things that Thomas could accomplish, the difference that he could make in the world. The people that he could help. It was all so overwhelming and exciting. Danni would find it very difficult to sleep that night.

When Thomas got home Korbin asked for a meeting. They sat at the kitchen island on tall adjustable stools. Korbin offered Thomas a bottle of water. "Here, drink this. I know you haven't drunk water all day. You should stay hydrated." Thomas took the bottle and began drinking. Korbin continued, "So, I've been thinking about the accident earlier today. I'm sure that lady you helped will sound like she's crazy, but then I realized that when the EMT's check out her bloody body they're going to find it strange that she doesn't even have a bruise on her."

Thomas stared at his water bottle while contemplating his response. "Maybe they'll think it's someone's else's blood." Korbin replied, "I don't think so. There was too much blood on her body, clothing, and on her hair. Not to mention the car was basically FUBAR'ed. They're going to have questions and something like this will get out. And when it does, we'll be expecting a visit from Mr. Pitt. So, I think we should start thinking about getting out of Greece, soon." Thomas kept staring at his water bottle as he said, "What does Mario think?"

"It's Mario's idea."

"When did Mario say we have to leave?"

"Soon. Like a couple days at the most. We're just now formulating a plan. If I were you I would let your girl…" Thomas glanced up at Korbin, then he continued. "…your friend, know as soon as possible.

It was 6:35pm. Thomas called Danni and asked if she could meet him somewhere. She said, yes. 30 minutes later they met at McDonald's near Syntagma Square. They parked their scooters next to a dozen other scooters that were there. Thomas and Danni walked in and ordered a small meal and a drink. Thomas explained what happened and about the plan to leave Greece. Danni was not sure about how she felt about that. On the one hand, she wanted Thomas to be as safe as possible, but on the other hand, she wanted to spend more time with him. She decided to throw out the question, "So, what do you think about me going with you to wherever you're going? Or I could meet you wherever you're going. Just let me know and I'll meet you there." Thomas reached out and took Danni's hand in his and said, "I'm not sure about what to do about us. I mean, I want to keep seeing you, but I don't want to place you in any potential danger. This Mr. Pitt guy is a whack job." Danni responded, "I don't care about who or what Mr. Pitt is. I just know that I want to be with you, Thomas. Let me be with you."

Thomas was overwhelmed by Danni's show of affection. He realized at that moment that he was in love with Danni. Best of all, he felt like Danni loved him, too. Thomas looked into her eyes and said, "Okay, look. Let me speak with Korbin and Mario and see what they say. I would love for you to be with me, and Danni…"

"Yes?"

"Danni, I think I'm in love with you."

"Oh, you *think* you are?" she said in a sarcastic tone.

"No, I mean, yes, I love you." Thomas said while completely blushing.

"Okay, that's better, cause I love you too, Thomas." They smiled at each other and finished their food.

At Caltech, Dr. Rinzler, Burrill and Rakowski were still contemplating the incredible ramifications of their findings. Dr. Rakowski called another colleague, Dr. Cullen Mitchell, head of research in Wavefront Shaping Technology. Dr. Rakowski was hoping that Dr. Mitchell could use his equipment to get a different look at what was going on with the suit. Dr. Mitchell uses refractive light with mirrors and lasers to produce sharper images of biological tissue, but Rakowski was hoping he could use it on the suit to see if he could see anything that would help him solve this mystery. He also called Dr. Nasir Ashraf, a notable atomic physicist in order to get better clarity on exactly what is happening with the neoprene material.

Dr. Rakowski was able to gather everyone within a few hours. It would take the rest of the day and part of the evening to come to a conclusion, albeit an enigmatic one at best. After several attempts at producing better images and more precise readings on various pieces of equipment, the results were pretty much the same. Although each person had a slightly different description of what they observed, the interpretations were similar. Dr. Ashraf defined the problem as most dire. To Dr. Ashraf, it appeared to him that the nucleus of the atoms in the neoprene were losing their charge, which would be very similar to Dr. Rakowski's interpretation. Nevertheless, the consequences are the same, a complete destruction of the atom.

The one question that was the most troubling was, how long will the process take and will it speed up. There's no way of knowing because they were dealing with an unknown form of energy. The only thing they were able to agree on was the deleterious effects it will have on all matter. There was no way of knowing if the effects would end when the neoprene material was completely destroyed or if it would continue onto other matter near it. If it does continue, it would cause havoc on all existing matter in the world. And if it speeds up, there is no telling how fast it will continue to destroy matter.

225

Dr. Mitchell stared at his images that were created using his equipment. "You see this, gentlemen," he said pointing to a rough edge of what looked like a group of spikes, "This area is completely missing on the next image. This means that the material we are looking at is, well, for lack of better words, disintegrating. There are no remnants or debris, it's just simply gone. What we are looking at here should be impossible." Dr. Ashraf interjected, "Yes. The only way that could happen is if the atoms themselves were destroyed. Which is exactly what will happen should the protons in the nucleus lose their charge. The atom simply falls apart. The words sound simple but what we're talking about here is the removal of the strong nuclear force, one of the most powerful and fundamental forces in the universe."

Dr. Rinzler scratched his head and said, "I thought Dr. Rakowski said it was the loss of the magnetic moment due to the loss of spin?"

"Yes, that is exactly what would happen should the nucleus lose its charge. It would appear to lose its spin." Dr. Ashraf answered. Rinzler added, "So, which is it? Are the atoms losing their spin or their charge?"

"Both, they are each the consequence of the other. The important thing now is, we need to figure out if there is a way to stop this process from continuing. Perhaps the answer could be as simple as destroying this suit, maybe that will put an end to this unknown...event. By destroying the suit, we destroy the source." Dr. Rakowski looked at Allan and Cole. Dr. Mitchell noticed the eye contact and said, "Is there something you're not telling us, Bill?" Dr. Burrill stepped up and went on to explain that the source of the energy is not the suit, but a young boy whose whereabouts are presently unknown.

Dr. Ashraf crossed his arms and said, "Well, gentlemen, the situation appears to be a little more dire than expected. I'm afraid that the key to our potential dilemma is this young man. Any clue as to where we might start looking for this fella? Dr. Ashraf said looking at Dr. Rinzler. Dr. Rinzler answered, "Not a clue. However, there is one little fact you may want to know." Everyone in the room stared at Dr. Rinzler, waiting and hoping to hear one small piece of good news. Dr. Rinzler continued, "We do have a huge portion of resources allocated by the U.S. government to finding this young man."

"I'm not sure if that's good news or bad." Dr. Mitchell said, then continued, "What does our fine government want with the boy, as if we didn't know." Dr. Burrill said, "For now, that's not important. Cole and I will try to persuade Mr. Pitt that there is a new urgency that must take priority over their existing agenda. Either way, the goal for now is the same, we must find that boy. If he is the source of this unknown energy we need to find a way to stop it." Dr. Ashraf said, "Very true. Most people cannot even imagine the consequences of atoms being destroyed, but I most certainly can. The very thought of something existing that can completely disintegrate matter is quite horrifying. And I do not need to mention that this is all beyond the scope of current science. We must find this boy at all costs!" It was a solemn good-bye when they all went their respective ways. Dr. Rinzler and Dr. Burrill were not looking forward to explaining all this to Mr. Pitt.

Dr. Rinzler and Dr. Burrill sat on metal chairs facing a gray metal desk. The room was cold, poorly lit and there was a lingering scent of ammonia in the air. Dr. Rinzler and Dr. Burrill could not achieve any level of comfort as they sat there facing a blank beige empty wall. Mr. Pitt hovered around them as he spoke. "Allow me to summarize. And stop me if you think I got any details wrong. You two removed classified documents along with classified materials, both of which were clearly known to you to be top secret and sensitive due to their potential to cause serious damage to our national security. Then you took these items to an unsecured location and shared said information with unvetted civilians that had zero clearance of any kind whatsoever. Do I have that right so far, gentlemen?"

Dr. Burrill answered, "Yes sir, but…" Mr. Pitt held up one finger while interrupting, "Wait. I'm not done." Dr. Burrill stopped speaking and sat quietly as Mr. Pitt continued. "Now you two are telling me that when we find this young man, and we will find him, that you want me to simply hand him over to these gentlemen you spoke with at the unsecured location. So, my only question to both of you is, are you two out of your fucking minds? Let me just throw out a few words here and you let me know if you understand what any of them mean. How about, top secret, national security, black fucking ops! You're both lucky I don't put a bullet in each one of your heads. And guess what," Mr. Pitt pulled out his side arm and pointed it at Dr. Rinzler, then pointed it at Dr. Burrill and said, " I actually have permission to do so. What do you think about that?" Both doctors winced as the gun was pointed at them. Mr. Pitt slammed the gun hard on the desk which made a very loud metallic noise causing both doctors to jump in their chairs. Mr. Pitt said, " Now, gentlemen, with all this in mind, let's talk about damage control."

Dr. Burrill was afraid to ask but asked anyway. "What do you mean by damage control?" Mr. Pitt walked over to Dr. Burrill and leaned in close to his face and said, "You know, damage control, as in mitigating the damage you two idiots have already caused. You're lucky I don't send a squad over to Caltech and kill everyone you spoke to. Instead, here's what we're going to do. You two are going to call your little friends over there and tell them that we will no longer need their assistance and that we have everything completely under control. Also, you will inform them that you two jackass's made a mistake by showing them the data and material and that some of our people will be by later today to pick up anything and everything that you left with them. Got it?" They both replied, "Yes, sir."

"Great." Mr. Pitt said with an exaggerated sense of glee, "Then everything will work out just fine." Dr. Rinzler spoke nervously, "But, Mr. Pitt, what about the findings. The problems with the unknown energy? That is still a very serious matter. In fact, it could be described as a national security issue. One with enormous consequences" Mr. Pitt walked over to the door and held it open while gesturing for both men to leave. Mr. Pitt responded, "Dr. Rinzler, should there ever be an opening in the NSA or HLS, I'll let you know. Then you can play with national security issues all day. In the meantime, get the hell out of this office. Also, call your wives and let them know that you will be confined to this facility for several days. I need to access the damage you two have caused before I can let you out of here."

Both doctors left the room with their heads hung low feeling a sense of shame, but at the same time they felt justified in their actions. They knew that this unknown energy was a real problem with the potential to cause catastrophic consequences if given the opportunity to propagate. So, they both felt slightly reassured when Mr. Pitt mentioned to them as they walked out of the office, "I'll have some of our people come down and speak with both of you regarding your concerns about this unknown energy you're speaking of." Mr. Pitt was no fool, he could see the very real concern on both the doctors, and although Mr. Pitt was not a man of science, he was a man of logic and common sense.

Evangelismos General Hospital

Thomas woke up a little earlier than usual. He had made plans to meet Danni for a picnic at Polis Park. Thomas didn't want Korbin following him today, so he snuck out of the house with a backpack and a small flashlight that also worked as a taser. Korbin had bought it for him as a precautionary measure in case he ran into some minor trouble. Thomas was sure they were not going to hang around Greece for too much longer, so he wanted to spend as much time alone with Danni as possible. The morning air was cool, and it felt good on Thomas' face as he drove his scooter to Polis Park. When he arrived, Danni was already there waiting for him.

Thomas and Danni spent a couple of hours walking around the park. They stopped to buy some provisions for the picnic they had planned. Nothing fancy, some cold drinks, a small baguette, cheese, and some grapes. Thomas carried everything in his backpack as they headed into the park to find a good spot to sit and enjoy the day. The cool air had passed and gave way to rising temperatures. They both knew it would be warm today, high 80's was what the weatherman said. The sky was bright and powder blue. It was turning into a beautiful day. Thomas and Danni were holding hands as they walked into the park.

They found a shady tree to sit under. "This looks perfect!" Danni exclaimed. Then she began unfolding the small flannel blanket she'd been carrying. She spread it out onto the short Bermuda grass. Thomas reached into his backpack and pulled out their provisions. Danni asked Thomas if he brought a knife to cut the bread, Thomas said, "Knife? Why would I think of bringing a knife?" Danni held up the baguette and said, "Bread. To cut bread. Did you bring any utensils?" Thomas tried to hide his mortification, "What? You didn't tell me to bring stuff like knives and forks." Danni decided to spare his misplaced chagrin and said, "Hey, don't worry. We got this." Danni proceeded to pull the bread apart with her hands then she got the cheese, which thankfully, was pre-sliced. She placed one slice each on the pieces of bread. She then placed her roughly constructed cheese sandwich in Thomas' hands and said "There. Enjoy."

Thomas looked at the sandwich and said, "Wow, that is the saddest looking sandwich I have ever seen."

"Stop complaining and eat." Danni said as she pushed the sandwich towards Thomas' face. Thomas winced and said, "Okay, okay. I'm eating." They laughed as they ate their food. Thomas felt they were having a perfect day and could not remember the last time he actually felt this happy. Thomas found himself peacefully slipping into a state of relaxation as his whole body seemed to exhale a sigh of pure contentment. Thomas remembered thinking that this was the best dry cheese sandwich he'd ever had.

Thomas was about to take another bite of his desiccated cheese sandwich when he noticed some sort of commotion. He saw some strange movements from the corner of his eye. Just to the right of him, a few yards away, he saw what looked like a person or two persons struggling, or wrestling, he couldn't tell. There were also strange noises that seemed incongruent with what he was looking at. Finally, the picture came together, Thomas was watching a small young teenage girl being mauled by a large dog. The young girl began screaming and the noise seemed to further agitate the dog and attacked her with even more ferocity.

Danni was the first to jump up and yell, "Thomas, we have to help her." Thomas jumped up and they both ran towards the young girl. They both started yelling at the dog and waving their arms to try to frighten it to stop. But the dog was relentless and continued with its vicious attack. By now the young girl's screams easily drowned out the dog's angry growling. Fortunately, another man came running to help. The man was holding a fairly large stick. As he got closer to the dog, the man took a huge swing and made contact with the dogs hind legs. The dog yelped, jumped up and thought about attacking the man with the stick but as the man held up the stick as if to strike the dog again, the dog decided to run away instead. Danni grabbed Thomas' arm and said, "Thomas, pick her up, we have to take her inside the hospital. Polis Park was located directly across the street from Evangelismos General Hospital. Thomas looked at Danni and said, "Can you pick her up?"

"What?"

"Can you pick her up. She doesn't look that heavy. If you can't do it I will, but I rather you pick her up." Danni realized what Thomas was asking. She looked down at the young girl and figured she could do it. Danni bent down and scooped up the girl in her arms and they began to walk towards the hospital. Thomas said, "Danni, let me know if she gets to heavy, I'll carry her in, but you know what's going to happen and there are too many people around here." Danni kept walking and said, "I got it. Don't worry. She's actually much lighter than I thought." Danni was even able to pick up the pace and they all rushed towards the entrance.

Once inside the hospital, they realized it was not going to be easy getting this young girl some attention. Like most general hospitals, it was busy, very busy. They noticed people on gurneys in the hallways, people sitting on the floor with their backs to the wall, most of them with visible blood on their clothes and body. Danni finally made it to the front desk and presented the young girl while insisting they see her right away. The admissions lady took a calm look at the young girls injuries and placed a request for an immediate nurse. Of course, immediate meant another five to fifteen minutes.

Danni and Thomas walked over to a small clear area of the lobby and sat on the floor with the girl. Danni held her in her bosom while gently cradling her head. The little girl had never stopped crying and appeared very frightened. Seeing so much blood all over her little body only added to her horror. Finally, Danni said, "Look, Thomas, we don't know how long this is going to take and she is very hurt and very scared. I have an idea." Thomas knew what she was going to say and started feeling anxious. Thomas said, "What's your idea?"

"Look, Thomas, just take off your coat, place it over her leg. No one will see or notice what's going on. Just touch her and cover up the leg as it heals. She'll be fine and out of pain and we could just go." Thomas thought about it for just a few seconds and decided to go with it. He removed his coat and placed it over the girls leg. He reached down and barely touched her ankle. The young girl felt something immediately. Within a few seconds you could see that the pain was gone. The torn flesh on her leg began mending and a few seconds later, she actually smiled and said, "It doesn't hurt any more. I feel fine. I need to call my mama." Thomas and Danni only caught the word mama because she was speaking Greek.

They all smiled and watched as the girl reached into her little backpack and pulled out a cellphone. As soon as Thomas and Danni were sure she was going to be fine, they left her in the front entrance of the hospital and walked back to their picnic area to pick up their stuff. They sat there relaxing for a minute when they heard another commotion. This time, it was bordering on pandemonium. They both stood up to see what was happening. The loud noises were coming from the hospital. Thomas suspected what it was and felt a chill on the back of his neck.

Danni said, "What the heck is going on. You think maybe there's a fire?"
"Nope." Danni did not like the way Thomas answered her, as if he knew something. "Thomas, do you know what the heck is going on over there?" Thomas quickly picked up all their picnic items and told Danni to follow him. "Where are we going, Thomas?"
"Nowhere, we just gotta get out of here. I'll explain as we go."

"What's going on, Thomas?" Danni was trying to keep up with Thomas' pace. He was walking so fast that Danni almost had to jog to keep up with him. She grabbed his shoulder and forced him to slow down and said, "Hey. You want to race? Slow down and talk to me." Thomas slowed his pace to a normal walk but wouldn't stop until they got to their scooters. Thomas placed all of their stuff on top of the seat of her scooter and began to explain to Danni. "Okay, so there's one more thing I haven't mentioned yet. But I didn't mention it because I have no idea what the hell is going on. Apparently, sometimes when I heal someone, others around the general proximity also get healed. Don't ask me how or what or anything. It just happens."

Danni stared down at the ground contemplating what Thomas had just said. Finally, Danni said, "Thomas, you really need to consider getting help. This thing you have, you are not in control of it and maybe there is a way of controlling it. But this, this is too much. This is too random. You'll never be able to hide forever with this thing. You need to do something, and I want to help you deal with it. It's time to get help, Thomas."

Meanwhile, at the hospital, everyone was going crazy. Some people were screaming, laughing, crying, and dancing with joy. Broken bones were healing, cuts and wounds were miraculously being healed. Hearts were made whole, kidneys were working again. Exactly 136 people were healed that day. Nobody knew what to make of it. But everyone was claiming miracles and thanking God. Dozens of people in the hospital and outside in the streets men and women were on their knees praying and giving thanks. It did not take long for this event to travel to San Diego where Mr. Pitt was planning his trip to Greece.

Mr. Pitt had a few assets in Athens. He made a few phone calls on his way to the private jet. Within a matter of hours of the hospital event, there were several teams on the ground already out searching for Thomas. Mario didn't know it, but he had about an hour and a half head start on Mr. Pitt. Mario also made a few phone calls and also got a hold of Korbin to talk over an extraction plan. However, this one was not going to be that easy because Mario knew that all public transportation would have pictures of Thomas. Train stations, buses and airports are out of the question. Within a couple of more hours, the Greek government will be assisting Mr. Pitt on his search for Thomas. However, no one calculated the impact the hospital event would have on the general public in Greece.

Every news network was at the hospital covering the extraordinary event. Everyone wanted to know how it was all possible that so many people received these miraculous healings while others in the same hospital remained sick and hurt. People wanted to know if those who were healed were special in some way. Were they Christians, Catholic, Muslim or not religious at all. Who was responsible and why hasn't anybody claimed credit for such an amazing event. Soon other states, even other countries, were sending their emissaries and religious diplomates to investigate the miracle of Evangelismos General Hospital. In less than 24 hours, the hospital had become the biggest news story in the world.

Thomas and Danni had hurried back to Thomas' house. They explained what happened to Korbin and of course he went a little ballistic. They called Mario right away. Mario knew it was going to be close to impossible to get Thomas out of the country, so he opted to hide. There were a few contingency plans, but they needed altering now that Thomas was traveling with a companion. Korbin asked, "Okay, we can make these plans work, just let me know what we need to do boss." Mario thought for a minute and answered, "Look, we have to assume that Mr. Pitt is already on his way, so don't try to take Thomas out of the country just yet. I'm sure they're circulating photos of Thomas as we speak to every public transit stations including all airports. It'll take me anywhere from 15 to 20 hours before we can meet up and that's if I jump on a plane withing the next 30 minutes. Pitt might already be on a plane. I don't know if he's ahead of me or not, so watch your six out there."

"Got it, so what do we do?"

"Hang tight. There's no way anybody knows where you are. But not for long. I estimate we have approximately 36 to 48 hours. It may be safer to stay put for right now."

"Copy that."

"Okay, I'm on my way. Oh, and by the way, I want you to initiate, but do not execute, plan Alpha Charlie 3, no, wait, make that Alpha Charlie 4."

"Copy that."

Mr. Pitt had assembled a crew of 16 agents and a support team of 5. They were all in a plane headed to Greece. Mr. Pitt, like Mario, had no idea who was going to reach Greece first, him or Mairo. But Mr. Pitt was sure of one thing, he would catch Thomas this time. Afterall, he had the full support of the Prime Minster in Greece which means every law agency in the country would be at his disposal in what will be known as the greatest manhunt in Greece's history.

Meanwhile, at Caltech, Dr. Rakowski, and Dr. Mitchell had assembled a team to continue studying the anomalous energy lingering in the material. When Mr. Pitt sent over several agents to confiscate all of their materials and data, Dr. Rakowski was determined to hold back a small piece of the material and of course they had all the data backed up. There was no way they were about to let the government have total control of this important finding.

After 17 hours of nonstop testing, experimenting, and observations of what they termed as the ADF – Anomalous Destructive Force – they came to several more conclusions, all of them bad. This was going to be the most important finding since the discovery of gravity. A couple of the team members saw a potential Nobel Prize while others simply saw it as the potential end of our reality. All of the testing was telling them that the ADF consisted of one or more energetic particles that does not comply with our existing laws of physics.

In their report they noted the following:

The ADF is propagating. It is self-sustaining since it seems to draw energy from its own existence. Any matter that comes in contact with the ADF becomes completely inert. Somehow, the ADF literally removes the charge of the neutron in every atom, thereby eliminating the strong force that binds the nucleus. Once this is achieved, the atom simply falls apart creating useless innocuous particles with a net zero charge. Some scientists speculated that the ADF may somehow be destroying one or all of the quarks inside the nucleus which would explain the absence of the strong nuclear force.

There is also speculation that once the ADF achieves a particular density, which at this time is unknown, it increases in size. This is referred to as a 'spike'. But perhaps one of the most damning things is that the particles that make up the ADF appear to be semi-quantumly entangled. Meaning, that when a spike does occur, wherever this ADF exists on our planet or even anywhere in our universe, some of it, but not all of it, doubles in size simultaneously. So, there is no telling how much of this ADF is out there. The ADF continues to show signs that it operates under its own set of physical laws.

Dr. Mitchell had a contact at the NHS, National Homeland Security, a Mrs. Krystn Bennet had the ear of the person in charge. After Dr. Mitchell spoke with her, she mentioned that their people had received some materials from Mr. Pitt's people and had come to the same conclusion regarding the anomalous energy, with the exception of the entanglement issue, which she thanked him for. Mrs. Bennet assured Dr. Mitchell that they had already swung into action and are currently in the midst of the biggest global manhunt ever. She requested all their most recent data on the ADF be sent as soon as possible. Dr. Mitchell complied and sent everything over. This was all they could do for now. Dr. Mitchell told Mrs. Bennet that his team would continue studying the anomaly in the hopes of finding anything that might help mitigate the destructive power of the ADF. She thanked him and hung up.

Mario was getting intel that he had a head start on Mr. Pitt. How much of a head start was anybody's guess. 17 hours later after the phone call with Korbin, Mario was landing in Greece. It didn't help that there was only one major airport in Athens, AIA, which is also the largest international airport in Greece, serving both, Athens and the region of Attica. Mario arrived incognito, with hair dyed a light shade of brown and fake prescription eyeglasses. He wore frumpy clothing and a baseball cap in an effort to look less threatening. Mario was on the same flight with Cooper and Rogers. Cooper and Rogers didn't need to be incognito as they had not been seen with Mario. Kelly and Banks would be coming in on another flight. Although they too had not been seen with Mario, it was a precautionary measure. Mario wanted to draw as little attention as possible.

Mario made it through customs uneventfully. He was thankful for all the long moving walkways in the airport, Mario was a little tired from the flight and those moving walkways saved a hell of a lot of steps. Mario stepped outside the airport and spotted Korbin next to the car. They got in and as they drove away Mario noticed dozens of uniformed personnel rushing into the airport. No doubt to look for him. Once they got near the safehouse, Mario noticed that the streets were also bustling with police as well as some military people. Extraction was going to be difficult. Mario turned to Korbin and said, "How far to the house?" Korbin answered Mario while constantly shifting his eyes to the rear and sideview mirrors. "We're 15 minutes out."

"Tell me about this girl that Thomas is with." Korbin still checking the mirrors said, "She seems fine. I mean, it looks like they really like each other so I don't think she'll be a problem." Mario let that set in for a minute and said, "Okay, she can stay but we'll need to keep an eye on her for a while. She's going to have to earn a lot of trust." "Copy that." replied Korbin. 16 minutes later they pulled into the driveway at the house. As Mario got out of the car he looked up and said, "Looks like we might get some rain." Korbin looked up at the grey sky and simply shrugged his shoulders and said, "Yeah, maybe." They walked into the house together.

Once inside, Thomas walked over to Mario and gave him a hug. "Man, it's great to see you, Mario." Mario leaned back from the hug and looked at Thomas and said, "Good to see you too, buddy." Mario turned his gaze towards Danni and asked, "And who is this?" as if he didn't already know. Danni walked up to Mario and introduced herself. "Hi. I'm Danni. And you must be Mario. I feel like I already know you. Thomas speaks so much about you."
"Well, don't believe everything he tells you."
"Oh, no, it's all good stuff." Mario glances at Thomas and says, "Oh, really?" Thomas just shrugged his shoulders and said, "Well, I very well couldn't tell her all the bad stuff, right?"

They all had a brief laugh, and the room fell silent. Everyone waited for Mario to speak.

Mario walked slowly towards the center of the room they were in. All eyes were on him. Mario looked around at everyone in the room and began to speak. "Okay. Things are a little more intense than they used to be. I don't know what happened but there is definitely something going on. Something new. I don't know what it is, but the efforts put out to find you, Thomas, have gone through the roof. No matter, we need to stick with our plan. We just have to be more cautious than ever. Cooper and Rogers will be here in about 10 min. Kelly and Banks will be here in a few hours. We can go over plan Alpha Charlie 4 and update Kelly and Banks when they get here. I need a table, a map and a coffee." Everybody moved to make it happen. Andre and Alex cleared out the dining table, Korbin knew they would be needing a map, so he had picked one up a few weeks ago. Danni volunteered to make some coffee.

Mario didn't say anything, but he was feeling foolish about his choice of locations to hide Thomas. He should have placed him somewhere closer to central Europe. There would have been more options as far as movement goes. Right now, Mario is sure that all main roads out of Greece are either blocked or being watched. Their only chance is to hide in or around the city for now, which is teeming with local and foreign agents including uniformed personnel. Mario knew that they would be safer in the house if they simply held up inside. But sooner or later, there will be a door-to-door search. Mario relaxed a little when he smelled the fresh brewed coffee.

A few hours later Kelly and Banks showed up. The team was all here. Mario gathered everyone at the table and began laying out the plan to move Thomas to a new location. One that's a little more remote. No one knew about that location because Mario didn't want anyone to know about it until it was necessary. It was another safe house on the north side of Marousi, about an hour away from where they are, a straight shot up highway 83 North. The problem was, they'll have to go by street, so add about another hour to that. That's a lot of exposure. Mario didn't like it, but if they need to move, the new location will buy them a little more time to figure out how to get Thomas out of Greece. The good news is, there are a lot of streets they can use for cover and confusion.

Some of Mr. Pitts people had questioned the vendors at Monastiraki. Turns out quite a few of the vendors recognized Thomas' face and Danni as well. They also mentioned that they both rode scooters. Mr. Pitt immediately pulled up a map on his tablet and removed the stylus. He quickly drew a circle estimating the distance that someone would use a scooter to take a casual trip to this area. Pitt figured if you're a kid on a scooter you are not going to drive more than 20 to 30 minutes. Approximate speed on the typical streets would be around 30mph. That would put Thomas no more than 10 to 15 miles at the most from this location. Assuming Thomas enjoyed riding, we could add another 5 miles to that for a total of 20 miles max. Mr. Pitt drew a 25-mile radius circle around Monastiraki. He passed on the information to everyone on the search team and ordered them to start a house-to-house search within the radius provided. Mr. Pitt also instructed that all means out of the city be blocked or watched. Mr. Pitt felt more confident than ever that they were going to be successful.

Five hours later, Mario was going over their plan one more time. Going over the plan helped to find any inconsistencies, weaknesses or possibly some improvements. The plan was simple enough. On the side of the house, parked on the driveway were 4 identical Metallic Magnetic Blue Peugeot 3008's with dark tinted windows including the windshield and the sunroof, making it impossible to see inside the car. Once they knew they had to make a run for it, all 4 vehicles would take off at the same time and head straight for the second safe house. In the event that they get spotted, all four vehicles are to split up and make a run for it on their own. Once they are sure they have lost whoever was tailing them, then and only then, are they to rendezvous at the safe house. Mario would be driving with Thomas and Danni. Mario is the only one that had a switch car ready at another undisclosed location in the city.

Once Mario arrives at the first specified location, the three of them would get into another completely different looking vehicle, a white Toyota Corolla and drive to the safe house hopefully undetected. Everyone else was on their own. All the men were well trained in tactical driving skills. Not to mention they all have a few tricks up their sleeves like large tacks that can be thrown behind them used to flatten tires.

It was still winter in Greece and the days were short. A couple more hours passed since Mario went over the plan and it was starting to get dark outside. Everyone was thinking about getting a good night's sleep when it happened. Everyone had been peeking outside the windows all day looking for anything that might look suspicious. Banks was looking outside the window facing east when he saw something. Banks called out, "Mario, I think we got a couple bogies." Mario went to the window to see. "Yup. That's them alright. Looks like they're doing a house-to-house search, and it won't be long before they get here. Everyone, put your comms on and get ready to execute the plan." This was the only time that Danni felt any kind of panic. She didn't show it, but you could hear it in her voice. She grabbed Thomas' arm, Thomas looked at her and noticed how hard she was holding on to him and said, "Hey, we got this. It's going to be alright." Danni pretended not to be afraid and said, "I know. Let's go."

They all went out to the side of the house and loaded onto the vehicles. Kelly and Banks were number 1 on the comms. Cooper and Rogers were 2, Andre and Alex were 3 and Mario, Korbin, Thomas and Danni were number 4. Once inside the vehicles they all waited for Mario's instructions. Mario spoke into the comms. "Okay, stick to the plan. We're going to all exit the driveway and turn right. Move in a straight line, stay close and keep up with my pace." All drivers responded, "Copy that."

It was already dark outside, and Mario felt it may play to their favor. Mario accelerated, he was doing 90km/h in a 40km/h zone. It was a short matter of time before they were spotted. Sure enough, a police car called it in. 4 vehicles moving at a high speed in a single file down a residential neighborhood. A few seconds later all patrols in the area got the orders to engage in the pursuit of all vehicles involved. As expected, Mario and the others were now being chased by vehicles with blinking lights and sirens. Mario got on the comms again, "Okay, let's get this show started. Follow my lead on the next intersection." "Copy that." came the response from the other three vehicles.

At the next intersection Mario turned left, the second car turned right, the third car went straight, and the fourth car made a sharp U-turn and doubled back. The pursuing vehicles had to split up in four directions, but no one knew which car Thomas was in. The chasing vehicles had to also break up into four different directions. This minimized the number of cars chasing each vehicle. Mario could see that only three vehicles were chasing them. '*That's better than 10.*' He thought. Korbin was in the back seat of the car, he reached over behind the rear seat and pulled out a plastic pressurized container with a hose and spray nozzle attached to it. Korbin began pumping the container to make sure it had good pressure on it then he set it down.

Korbin then reached back in the same area and picked up a couple of small boxes, about 10" square. Korbin spoke to Mario, "Yo, boss, which one you want to use first?" Mario looked in the rear-view mirror and saw Korbin's face smiling back. He said, "Tell you what, I'm gonna make a left two street down, I'll let you pick." Mario winked at Korbin in the mirror. Korbin smiled again and said, "Copy that, boss." Thomas was in the front seat with Mario and couldn't see what Korbin was doing but he was curious, so he turned his head to see. Danni was in the back seat with Korbin, and she was watching with the same curiosity as Korbin began opening the small boxes. Mario suddenly swerved to the left and Korbin almost fell. "What the hell?" Korbin yelled. "Mario looked in the mirror again and said, "Sorry, almost hit a dog." Korbin wasn't sure if Mario did it on purpose or not although he could swear he saw Mario smile.

Mario called back to Korbin, "Here we go!" Mario turned the car sharply to the left and everybody in the car was pushed to the right. It was a quick turn, Mario pushed the button on the dashboard and opened the hatchback. The rear door of the car flipped open. Korbin almost lost his balance during the turn but regained it in time to grab two of the boxes and began dumping the contents onto the street. Inside the boxes were large stainless-steel jacks with extremely sharp points guaranteed to puncture the best of tires.

As the pursuing vehicles turned the corner they didn't have time to react. They could see the jacks scattered throughout the street, but it was too late. The first two vehicles got three flat tires each and lost control forcing them to end the pursuit. The third vehicle was able to see what was going on and was able to avoid the steel jacks by driving onto the sidewalk until the street was clear. However, once the pursuing vehicle made the left turn he was joined by another two vehicles. Mario glanced at his mirrors and saw he still had three vehicles on him. He called out to Korbin, "Hey, how many jacks we got left?" Korbin replied, "I got one more box, but we still got this baby." Korin added while pointing at the pressure container. "Okay, we're gonna need it. Wait for my signal." "Copy that, boss."

Thomas turned to face Danni and asked, "Hey, how you doin?" Danni reached to hold Thomas' hand, Thomas reached out and held it as she said, "I'm fine. Really." The whole thing was actually so surreal to Danni that it didn't seem real, so she didn't have any genuine fear. She felt like the whole thing was being played out in a movie. Thomas was a little nervous because Mario had never been up against something like this before and quite honestly didn't know how they were going to get out of it. Mario called out to Korbin, "Another left coming up. Let's see what that last box of jacks well do." "On it."

Mario made another sharp left turn and Korbin dumped the last box of jacks on the street. The lead car expected the jacks, so he swerved and avoided the jacks. The second car didn't know what was going on and went straight and got two flat tires. The third car missed all the jacks by luck. Mario could see that he had only two vehicles behind him now. Mario called out to Korbin, "Okay, we got another left coming up. Wait for my signal." Korbin replied, "Hey, boss, why not make a right this time, I think these guys might be on to us." "Sorry pal, it's gotta be a left. I gotta slow down too much to make a right and I don't want them to slow down and see what we're doing. Besides, they don't know what's coming." Mario could see Korbin smiling in the mirror. Korbin replied, "You're the boss." Korbin picked up the 3-gallon pressurized container. The spray nozzle was connected to a two-foot-long hose. Inside the container was a hyper-slippery omniphobic liquid with a friction coefficient of .04. In other words, this stuff was extremely slippery.

"Korbin," Mario called out, "left turn coming up. Start your spray well before the turn, let's make sure they get plenty of that stuff on their tires before they go into the turn." "Copy that." Just as Mario began his turn, Korbin began spraying the liquid onto the street. It didn't matter if they saw him or not. The substance he was spraying was going to pretty much render their tires completely useless. Not only will their tires simply spin in place, but they will also have no control. Since Korbin sprayed the street well before the turn, both vehicles ran over the liquid and were unable to make the turn. As expected, both vehicles slid out of control and were now unable to pursue.

Korbin called out to Mario, "Ha. That's all of them, boss. We got clear skies up ahead. Let's hope the others did as well as we did." Mario nodded while keeping his eyes on the road and said, "Let's hope so. We're not far from the location from..." Mario's car went flying to the right as the vehicle that Mr. Pitt was driving slammed into the side of them. The Peugeot 3008 went into an uncontrolled spin and stopped on the opposite side of the street facing parallel to the curb. Everyone in the car was stunned. Mario was semi- conscious, Korbin was out cold because he didn't have a seat belt on. Danni was conscious but confused. Thomas was just roughed up a little and was aware of what was happening.

Mr. Pitt had rammed their car from the driver's side. Fortunately, Mr. Pitt aimed for the front of the car and not the middle, otherwise there would have been some serious injuries involved. It was a matter of seconds before their car was surrounded by dozens of police cars with blinking red and blue lights. Mr. Pitt stepped out of his vehicle slowly and walked calmly over to the driver's side of Mario's car and pulled the door open. Mr. Pitt leaned in to see if Mario was conscious and as he did, Mario suddenly grabbed Mr. Pitt in a headlock, pulled out his gun and pressed it against his head. Mr. Pitt was surprised, but immediately regained his composure.

"Hey, relax, Mario. We're not here to hurt anyone."

"Tell that to my friend over there that's knocked out."

"Okay, okay, I could have hit your car a little softer but it's hard to judge how much is too much, you know? By the way, it's hard to breath." Mario loosened his grip a little. Mr. Pitt kept talking. "Look Mario, look around, there's no way you're getting out of here. It's over. Just let me take the boy and you can go. We're not pressing charges. You and your men will be set free. Oh, and by the way, we got your men." Mario looked around and what Pitt was saying was true. There were way too many people out there and more showing up as he sat there with his arm around Pitt's neck.

Thomas said, "Mario, he's right. There's no getting out of this one. Just let me go with Mr. Pitt and take Danni home. It's the only way." Mr. Pitt added, "See, Thomas gets it. Come on, Mario, I'm serious, we'll let all of you simply walk away. We have no interest in you or your men." Mario pressed the gun a little harder against Mr. Pitt's head and said, "You got me, and I got you, motherfucker. Let's make a deal."

"Sorry, no deals."

"That's too bad for you, Pitt, cause I ain't just handing over the kid."

"Mario, we gotta talk."

"I'm listening."

"No, I mean, alone."

"How do you propose we do that with all your friends here?"

"Let me up. You could keep the gun to my head, just let me talk to everybody out there." Mario thought about it and reluctantly released his grip on Pitt's neck and said, "You try anything funny, I don't have to tell you that it will only make me happy to blow your brains out." Mario stood behind Mr. Pitt while holding the gun to the back of his head. Mr. Pitt stood up, brushed his coat off with his hands and spoke to the large group of police and everyone else that was there. Mr. Pitt spoke loudly, but clearly, "Everyone, listen up. I need all of you to leave this area. This is not a request. It's an order. I want everyone cleared out and out of sight." A few police officers complained and wanted to arrest all of Mario's people, but Mr. Pitt said, "Look, I have the direct number to all of your supervisors. If you want, you can call them, and they will tell you to follow my instructions. And my instructions are for everyone to clear the hell out. Now!" Everyone began clearing out, a few more reluctantly than others, but in a few minutes the streets were clear. Mr. Pitt turned to look at Mario and said, "Satisfied?"

Mario pulled the hammer back on his weapon and pressed it a little harder on Mr. Pitt's head and said, "You think I don't know you got your boys out there with a sniper rifle aimed at my head right now?" Mr. Pitt smiled and said, "Okay, you got me. Yes, Mario, there are a couple of guys out there that could have taken you out already. I just need to give them the sign and they'll drop you, and it looks like your partner is kind of out of it." Mr. Pitt said pointing down at Korbin who was still unconscious. Mario was about to say something when he suddenly became lightheaded then collapsed onto the ground. A common symptom of a concussion.

Mario was out for only a minute. When he came to he noticed he was propped up against a car. Mr. Pitt had Mario's weapon, but he wasn't pointing it at anybody. Korbin also came to and was sitting on the asphalt street with his back to another car. Thomas and Danni were inside Mr. Pitts car surrounded by Mr. Pitt's men. Mario stood up with a little difficulty. Mr. Pitt reached out as if to help Mario stay balanced, but Mario held up his left hand inferring that he was fine. Mario looked around and assessed their situation. It wasn't good. He looked at Mr. Pitt and said, "Okay, Pitt. What do you want."

"You know what I want, Mario. I'm taking Thomas and I guess his girlfriend back to the states."

"You do and I'll find you and get him back."

"Not this time, Mario. You're going to let me take him and stop coming for him."

"And why would I do that?"

Mr. Pitt began walking over to one of the vehicles next to him and said, "Mario, come on, get in, let's talk." Mario was in no position to refuse so he got in. He glanced over at Thomas and simply said, "I'll see you soon." And got in the car. Mario rubbed his head, he could feel the crusty blood matting his hair. "Where we going?"

"Just for a coffee, or tea if that's your thing."

"It ain't my thing. I'll take a coffee."

"Great."

Mr. Pitt instructed his men to take Thomas and Danni back to their headquarters. As the ambulance arrived Mr. Pitt turned to one of his agents and said, "Make sure Mario's buddy is taken care of before you leave." The agent acknowledged Mr. Pitt with a simple nod of his head. Once Korbin was in the ambulance, another agent took off with Thomas and Danni.

Mr. Pitt took Mario to a small coffee shop and explained the extenuating circumstances regarding Thomas. That the current situation is no longer about them or even Thomas. It's about the safety of a nation and maybe the world. Mr. Pitt showed Mario the emails with all the data regarding the findings and the potential danger it poses to national security. In the end, Mr. Pitt told Mario that he would look into the possibility of allowing him to visit Thomas during the investigation process of Thomas' ability. But Thomas would have to remain in custody until a solution can be reached regarding the detrimental effects of the unknow energy which he seems to be spreading.

It took almost an hour to convince Mario, but he understood. Mr. Pitt drove Mario back to speak with Thomas. Once they arrived, Mario had to break the news to Thomas who was surprisingly understanding. Thomas was standing in front of Mario and said, "Mario, you're the best friend anyone can have. But this all makes sense. We don't know what to do and maybe they don't either, but we have to try something if this strange power is going to hurt people in the end." Mario looked into Thomas' eyes and simply held his arms open, and they embraced. "I'll see you soon buddy." Mario said. Thomas had watery eyes and replied, "Okay."

Back to Goleta

34 hours later, Mr. Pitt and Thomas were back in the states. But the only condition that Thomas had was that Danni be able to accompany him if she so desired, which she did. It was ironic that Thomas ended up at the Institute for Collaborative Biotechnologies, or ICB an affiliate university of the US Army located in Santa Barbara, California, literally 10 minutes away from where Thomas used to live in Goleta. ICB is known for its premier faculty which works with graduate students and postdoctoral researchers as interdisciplinary teams of biologists, chemists, physicists, physicians, and engineers. These teams develop biologically inspired technological innovations in systems and synthetic biology, bio-enabled materials and cognitive neuroscience. Once inside, Thomas was surprised to see a couple of familiar faces, Dr.

243

Burrill, and Dr. Rinzler. They had been invited to assist in the research at the ICB. They were later to be joined by Dr. Rakowski from Caltech.

A team was assembled within a few hours, but the schedule on how to proceed would take a full day. For starters, they asked Thomas if he could provide the names of some of the people that he healed so that they can be checked for any detrimental effects. It may also provide a timeline of any negative effects between exposure and duration of exposure. They began by contacting Steven Mitchell and Catheryn Huber . They were slightly hesitant to comply, but the reasons that were given were just too compelling, so they agreed.

The ICB team did everything in their power to maintain a tranquil environment. All participants had complete freedom to come and go as they wished. The team, however, would stress to Thomas that they would prefer that he stay on the ICB grounds for the simple reason that they wished to mitigate unnecessary exposure to the general public. Thomas agreed with their wishes as long as he was able to receive guests, like his family and of course, Danni. The next few months would be some of the most grueling testing Thomas had ever experienced. None of it was painful, but it was very hectic. There was a desperateness about finding out everything they could about the ADF. The ICB team kept the name of the unknown energy which was coined by Dr. Rinzler and Dr. Burrill.

Month 3 at the ICB

The ICB team had come up with a few ideas for constructing a couple of innovative pieces of equipment that may help them to get a better reading on the ADF, specifically the rate at which it is flowing from the point of origin. Also, with the help of a new discovery by three Nobel Laureates in physics which recently were able to provide a new tool for exploring the world of electrons inside atoms and molecules using extremely short pulses of light which could be measured in attoseconds. This new tool may be able to provide further insight as to what exactly is happening to the atoms when confronted with the ADF. It took a while to learn how best to use this new tool along with the new equipment specifically designed for ADF detection.

Month 6

The new equipment proved to be more useful than they expected. The ICB team was able to acquire much more data than before. Also, as they used the new equipment, they were able to adjust and calibrate them for even more accuracy. As exciting as this was for the team, they still did not have the answer to the main question. Where is the energy coming from. They know the point of its entrance, through Thomas' lower leg area, but where is the energy originating from. They also have not been able to discern any patterns regarding the proliferation of the ADF or how to stop it.

Month 9

One of the postdoctoral researchers, Rishan Arora, was taking some notes regarding the new data from one of the new pieces of equipment when he noticed some very strange readings. He didn't know what to make of them. He looked around for Thomas and found him in the lunchroom. Rishan walked over to Thomas and asked him if he had experienced anything different in the past 30 minutes. "Nope." Thomas replied. Rishan went on, "Are you sure? Did you feel anything different at all?" Thomas was a little annoyed because he was about to bite into a pastry he just bought from the vending machine. "Look, Rishan, I'm telling you, I didn't feel anything, do anything, or see anything. What's up? Is there something wrong?"

"No. Well, yes, I mean, I don't know. I just got a strange reading on my equipment." Thomas was still unconcerned and kept looking down at his pastry. Rishan finally said, "Thomas, do you mind if we take a reading."

"Right now?"

"Yes, well, after you finish your lunch."

"This ain't my lunch, it's just a snack." Thomas said a little embarrassed.

"That's okay, when you're done, please come find me, Thomas."

"I can go now if you want."

"No, no. Please finish your lunch first."

"It's not my lunch. Look, never mind, I'll see you in a just a couple of minutes as soon as I'm done with my...lunch." Rishan smiled and said, "Okay. See you soon."

Thomas had forgotten all about the wireless sensor connected to his ankle. The research team insisted on monitoring Thomas 24 hours a day. The sensor on Thomas' leg constantly

245

transmitted data to a modified variable differential transformer and produced an audible signal whenever any change occurred. They referred to this piece of equipment as the ADF Detector. And about 20 minutes ago, something had definitely occurred. Rishan was sitting at his desk when he heard a loud beeping signal from the detector. It was alerting Rishan to an unusually large spike.

It had only been a minute when Thomas walked up to Rishan. "Hey, Rishan, so what's up?" Rishan responded slightly startled, "Oh, hey, Thomas. Yeah, so what's up?"

"You tell me. You asked me to come over."

"Yes. Right. So, I just wanted to make sure that you're okay." Thomas stared at Rishan with an incredulous look as if Rishan was hiding something. "I'm fine," remarked Thomas as he placed his right hand on Rishan left shoulder and said, "Okay, Rishan, what's really going on. Just tell me." Rishan had no reason to feel embarrassed, it just felt intrusive monitoring someone's body. Rishan said, "Sorry about the weirdness, it's just that our equipment detected a very large spike coming from you. You didn't feel anything?"

"Nope." Thomas said nonchalantly. Meanwhile, the rest of the team noticed that something was happening with the detector so came over to see what was going on. Dr. Rakowski took a quick look at the detector and said, "Wow, that's unusual. Thomas, did you feel anything?" Thomas was getting a little annoyed at the question. "No. I typically do not notice or feel anything when anything happens. I have no control of whatever this is. Is there a problem?" Dr. Rakowski spoke while pointing at the detector. "You see this signal on the graph?" "Yes." Thomas replied. "Well, it's telling us that you just had what appears to be one of the largest spikes since we started monitoring you. We're just trying to figure out what it means and what the ramifications are, if any."

After everyone got a look at the signal on the ADF Detector they all started to perform other tests and experiments on the material that was wrapped around the sensor on Thomas' leg. This material was highly susceptible to any molecular changes, and they were anxious to study it after that huge spike. It took about ten minutes to set up the other pieces of equipment which were also designed specifically for testing and observing any changes in the material. Just as they were about to begin studying it, another researcher named Yulong Li, whom everyone called Tony, burst into the lab. "Holy shit!" Everyone turned to face Tony, who looked crazed but somehow in a good way. "Holy shit." He repeated. Dr. David Conti, head of the research team, grabbed Tony by the arm and said, "Hey, Tony. Calm down. What the hell's going on with you?" Tony stared wide eyed at Dr. Conti and said, "Dude, sorry, I mean, Dr. Conti, it was crazy!"

"What was crazy?" Dr. Conti asked with controlled patience. Tony began recounting his story about how he was on his way to the lab. He knew he was going to be late, but he had informed Dr. Conti that he had to run an errand first thing in the morning and that he would be in as soon as possible. Tony was riding his bike and just as he was about to enter the ICB campus, he was struck by a pickup truck. Luckly the driver of the truck saw him in time to step on the brakes, but not quick enough to avoid him. Tony ended up with multiple breaks on his left arm, plus some minor cuts and bruises. Although Tony was in terrible pain, he was able to take himself to the Isla Vista Medical Clinic just a few blocks from where he was struck. Everyone in the lab listened with anticipation.

Tony went on to explain how just as the technician who was about to take an x-ray of his arm, he suddenly felt something strange. Like a warm feeling moving through his body. Tony explained how he could feel the bones in his arm shifting around. At first it scared the hell out of him but then he noticed that the pain was going away. After what seemed like just a few seconds, all the pain was gone, and his arm felt great. The radiologist came into the room and asked him if he was sure that he had broken his arm because the x-rays appeared to be normal. Everyone in the lab just stared at Tony in silence and disbelief. Dr. Burrill said, "Maybe we should take a look at his arm. Tony, if you don't mind, we're going to need a sample."
"Wait, what? A sample of my arm?"
"No, just a skin sample of the area where the break happened. It'll just be a tiny skin graph." Tony let out an audible sigh and said, "Oh, sure. That's fine."

Meanwhile, the rest of the team went over the events. Dr. Clarke, who is heading the investigation team said, "Okay. Let's go over what just happened. Thomas produced a very large spike and Tony, who is approximately 1 mile away from here, gets healed. Comments?" Dr. Rinzler chimed in, "We need to contact that medical center and find out if any other incidents like this one happened to anyone else. The more test subjects we have the better. It would be interesting to find out if a recent healing is different from an older previous healing." Dr. Clarke agreed, saying, "Yes. We'll be able to do those comparisons since we have samples from Steven Mitchell and Catheryn Huber." Dr. Conti said, "Good. Let's start with that.

247

Meanwhile, let's take a look at what that spike did to our material."

Four hours later the team made some new discoveries. In regard to the material, there was definitely more damage done. Most likely from an increase of density of the ADF. It was always frightening to see the damage at the molecular level because you are witnessing the complete destruction of atoms. At least they were able to come to a conclusion, even though it was obvious, it had to be noted that, whenever Thomas has a significant spike, it contributes to the density of the ADF and therefore can be concurred that there will be more damage.

The other observation was, that anyone who has been healed by Thomas will also suffer increased damage due to the quasi-entanglement of the ADF, though, again, not everyone will experience it the same way. For some reason, some people are affected while others are not. At first, Dr. Burrill and Dr. Rinzler believed that the ADF is quantumly entangled, but as it turns out, it is only semi-entangled which means it's even more paradoxical than expected. They also found that once the disintegration of any matter began, the ADF would continue to grow thus increasing its density which somehow contributed to the spikes. However, they were not able to make any accurate or measurable predictions as to when a spike might occur.

Five hours later, the investigation team informed the rest of the ICB teams that there were indeed other healings at the medical clinic. But that wasn't all. They decided to call all the clinics, urgent cares, and hospitals within a five-mile radius. They experienced some form of massive healing phenomenon also. Beyond that five-mile radius there were no reports of any unusual medical anomalies. All this simply added more confusion to their endeavors to find any clues that might help stop the ADF. And it was only now that everyone in the lab noticed that they too, were experiencing healing in one form or another. Dr. Burrill noticed that his back wasn't hurting any more. Larry Fritz had been tolerating a toothache all day but now it was gone.

One morning, while Rishan was going over some data with all the members of the ICB team, they came to a realization. While Rishan was speaking and telling everyone to refer to their notes on the data sheets, Rishan suddenly became quiet. Everyone in the room stared at Rishan and waited for him to continue. After a long awkward pause, Rishan simply smiled and said, "Has anyone else here noticed that none of us are wearing our glasses?" Tony, who was the most near sighted, felt his face because he simply assumed he was wearing his glasses. After realizing he wasn't wearing them, he looked around the room and was able to see with perfect

20/20 vision. They all smiled and laughed a little.

One Year Later

Further tests confirmed previous assumptions that the ADF is basically disintegrating all forms of matter. They know that the ADF which is coming from Thomas is constantly flowing. They know that unknown densities will trigger an increase of ADF. The largest increases occur during spikes. There were various attempts to stop or slow down the ADF by wrapping Thomas' leg in multiple materials like lead, copper, plastic but none of these materials had any effect. They even tried inducing a powerful magnetic field around it, but to no avail. One of the most daunting problems was their inability to control the ADF. It simply did not respond to any attempts or any modalities that the ICB teams came up with. Another huge problem was that they had also concluded that the ADF is a massless entity. This further exasperated the hope of ever containing it. All of this data was being shared with scientists at every major university such as Caltech, MIT as well as the Department of Defense.

By the end of the first year Thomas was allowed to see visitors more often. Danni came whenever she was allowed. Mario made a few visits as well. Mario had mentioned to Thomas that he was comfortable with the security measures at the lab. He told Thomas that it looks like a small army is stationed around the entire campus. Not to mention they still got that nutcase, Mr. Pitt out there keeping an eye on things. Thomas was glad that Mario now had his life back, after all, he still had a daughter and a wife at home. As for Danni, Thomas wasn't sure what to do about her. He had very strong feelings for her, but he wasn't sure that this should be her life as well.

Thomas did love her and that made things very complicated. Today Danni came with some take-out food. One of Thomas' favorites, In-N-Out. They sat in the break room. The small room had only a few tables and for some reason, three chairs per table. The walls were bright white with white speckled tile flooring. It had a very institutional look. The lingering odors of ethnic food cooked in the microwave didn't help with the ambience.

Thomas and Danni sat at one of the tables. Danni placed the bag in the center and reached in to pull out the food. "Hey," Thomas said, "I think that's mine. I know you got me the double-double." Danni pulled it away from him and said, "How do you know I didn't get one for myself?"

"Because you never do. Now give me that buger." Thomas reached over quickly and snatched it out of her hand. "Hey, buddy," Danni exclaimed, "you better watch it, I still control the ketchup, so you better behave. I know you don't want to eat dry French fries."

"Okay, okay." Thomas acquiesced. "Keep your double-double." Danni gave him a smug grin and said, "Ha, that'll teach you. Now, here's your double-double, I got myself the single cheeseburger."

"Duh, like I didn't know." They sat and talked for hours about everything and nothing. They spoke about her school, her part time job, and other things. Time passed too quickly when they were together. Whenever she left, they always kissed and told each other I love you. Each time Thomas said it, he felt it more.

Month 16

Springtime was just around the corner. Thomas was still living in the lab. They had fixed up a spacious room for him. His bedroom was on the second floor and had a nice large picture window which faced South-East towards the main campus, but if you look hard enough, you could just make out a small view of the ocean. Thomas got out of bed and began walking towards the bathroom to wash his face and began to brush his teeth. It was 7:46am. Thomas was rinsing his mouth when he heard a pounding on the door. He could hear Rishan, "Thomas, are you awake?" Thomas spat the water out of his mouth and said, "Yeah. I'm here. What's up?" Rishan yelled through the door, "We got another spike. This one is huge."

"How did you do that?" Thomas said and continued, "I thought your equipment isn't configured for high readings?"

"We recalibrated a couple of weeks ago. Can I come in?"

"Oh, yeah, sure. Sorry. Hold on." Thomas walked over to the door and let Rishan in. Rishan said, "Thomas, are you sure you don't feel these spikes? I mean, this is crazy. We may have to recalibrate the equipment again."

"Wow. That big, huh?"

"Yes. I'm just so surprised you don't feel anything."

"Nope. Nothing."

The area of the spike would prove to be even larger than the last one. It had a diameter that reached several states including Dallas, Texas and Durango, Mexico. Unfortunately, this made matters worse for the ICB team. The news of so many incredible healings saturated the news and every internet platform. People didn't know whether to be happy or scared. Those that were gravely ill were definitely happy. Rumors and conspiracies were everywhere. No one knew what to make of it. One thing for certain, the economy was changing. The pharmaceutical industry was already seeing a decline in their sales. Their business models were about to be put to the test. Medical insurance companies started dropping their costs as people were opting out of insurance. All the smaller subsidiary companies that support the medical and pharmaceutical industry were the first to feel the brunt of the impact. The unemployment numbers continuously grew every day, and a recession was looming on the horizon. Every day saw more and more people leaving medical offices, clinics, and hospitals. In the Westcoast, medical billing was almost at a standstill.

There was something else that happened. Something subtle. A few people at the ICB laboratory were experiencing a strange phenomenon. They noticed it in the break room first. It involved a jar of peanut butter and a jar of strawberry jam. One of the lab workers, Kindra Newcomb wanted to make a P&B sandwich but couldn't open the lids on the jars. She asked her co-worker, Larry Fritz but he couldn't open it either. After what seemed like a long time they went out for help. Rishan was clever, they thought, so they asked him if he could help open the jars. Rishan tried tapping the edges with a knife. He tried wedging it between the door hinge but almost broke the door.

Finally, Rishan remembered that the last plumber that came to fix a small leak had left behind one of his adjustable pliers, he remembered the plumber had referred to them as channel locks. He found them under the sink. Rishan adjusted the pliers so that they fit the jars diameter just right, squeezed and turned. Rishan turned with all his might and finally he was able to get the lid to move. But when it did, they could all hear that distinct sound of air rushing in. That was very unusual. The same thing happened with the second jar.

They quickly looked for other jars. The same thing happened to those as well. Tony suspected something so he looked for some of the plastic containers. They were extremely difficult to open as well, and they too let out a sound of rushing air. They didn't know what to make of it. They brought it to the attention of all the team members. They decided to break up into two groups, one group would begin looking into the spike and testing the materials while the other group went throughout the campus checking on other containers that had the same characteristics as theirs. The group checking the containers found that the majority of all containers on the campus had issues while others did not. Armed with this information they concluded that this may not be as important as their other research, so they headed back to the lab.

Dr. Conti and Dr. Rinzler were going over their findings on the material that was attached to Thomas' leg. There was extensive damage. So much so that this time it was visible with the naked eye. They didn't need special equipment to see that the material had tiny sections of it missing. But it got worse. This time they could also observe some of these tiny holes appearing before their eyes. This means that the density of the ADF is now larger than ever before. To make matters worse, they noticed that their own equipment is showing signs of deterioration. Even though this is all still happening on a very small scale, it will inevitably become a very serious problem. Dr. Conti requested to have new equipment built because he was sure that their current equipment may be inoperable in the very near future.

Meanwhile, Dr. Clark's team had finally found the boundaries of the effects of the last spike, which they all dupped 'The Super Spike.' It wasn't until they reached a diameter of approximately 1500 miles. After that, there were only a few scattered incidents of healings. Larry Fritz said, "Wow, if you do the math, that covers an area of 1.7 million square miles. How is that even possible?" Dr. Rakowski answered, "If the ADF is massless as we surmised, then it's free to travel at or close to the speed of light. So technically it could cover this area in less than a second."

Rumors had got out that the source of all the healings were coming from the ICB building in Santa Barbara. It didn't take long for throngs of people to arrive from all over the country and other parts of the world expecting to be healed. Thousands gathered around the small city of Santa Barbara and Goleta. A mile away there was a massive gathering of people in wheelchairs. They were so crowded they could barely maneuver around each other. Closer to the building were hundreds of inflated mattresses with people that were barely alive stricken with life threatening diseases.

The situation was becoming a logistical nightmare. There were no facilities to handle this kind of massive crowd. The National Guard had to be deployed. Not to get rid of the people, but to bring supplies because every single one of them refused to leave. It was after all, for many of them, a matter of life or death. The ICB team was hoping Thoams would have another spike just to get rid of the crowds.

Month 19

A secret meeting of all the Dr.'s had been arranged by Dr. Rakowski. They met at the admissions building. There was a meeting room available there for staff members. Dr. Rakowski opened the meeting. "Gentlemen, we are here to discuss a grave issue. We need to come up with some options for ending this ADF phenomenon." Dr. Burrill said, "I thought that's what we've been doing?" Rakowski said, "That's not what I'm referring to here. What I am saying is, we need to come up with a way of stopping the ADF soon. Dr. Conti and I have made a very recent discovery that demands our immediate attention." Everyone looked towards Dr. Conti. Rakowski went on, "Dr. Conti, would you like to explain." Dr. Conti stood up and addressed those in the room. "Gentlemen, as Dr. Rakowski said, we made a remarkable discovery which we feel not only requires our immediate attention but requires our immediate action as well."

No one said a word, so Dr. Conti continued. "a few weeks ago, one of our staff members mentioned that they were having a difficult time opening jars and plastic containers." There were murmurs around the table and a couple of them held up their hands in a jester that said, so what. Dr. Conti was unphased and continued. "They thought that it was strange, so they went about checking other containers around the campus and found that many of them were experiencing the same issue. What was unusual was that they heard the sound of air rushing into the jar once they finally got it to open. They dismissed it as something unrelated but just recently decided maybe it's something so, they shared it with Dr. Rakowski and I. We looked into it and what we found is quite troubling."

Dr. Conti waited for any reaction, but there was none. They were all waiting with bated breath, so he went on. "What Dr. Rakowski and I found was that although the ADF is destroying atoms, it appears that it's destroying oxygen atoms quicker than other atoms. As of right now we have no idea why, but we know that the results will be catastrophic." Dr. Rinzler said, "What are you saying, that the ADF is destroying oxygen faster than anything else?" Dr. Conti replied,

"Yes. Although it is destroying all atoms around us, it would appear that the ADF has a preference for the oxygen atom. We haven't noticed that the ADF is destroying the oxygen around us because it's being replaced just as quickly. But the oxygen in these jars is not being replaced. So, what happens is, the oxygen is being removed from these containers and creating a vacuum thus making it difficult to open. The point is, we are now aware of the fact that the ADF is destroying the oxygen around us, and we have no idea as to how quickly it's doing it. And what this means is that we need to come up with a solution to the problem we are calling 'Thomas.'" Dr. Rinzler chimed in again, "Wait. What are you saying? That we need to get rid of Thomas? How are we getting rid of Thomas, Dr. Conti, if I may be so bold to ask."

"Dr. Rinzler, we cannot allow this ADF to continue for reasons that are well known to you. We now must consider one of two options. One. We could try removing Thomas' leg and see if destroying it will stop the ADF from entering into our extant reality. If it doesn't and say, it continues to come from Thomas, then option two is, we may have to consider removing Thomas from the equation. As it is, we don't know if it's already too late because as we also know, the ADF can proliferate on its own, just not as fast." Dr. Burrill stood up and protested, "We can't sit here and plan the demise of a teenage boy." Dr. Conti replied, "We can't stand here and ignore the fact that that teenage boy may very well be the end of mankind and all that it has created."

They all sat quietly contemplating their morality. Dr. Rakowski said, "I think we should consider option one. We will remove the leg and incinerate it. If the spikes stop, we will have solved the problem. If not, well, let's cross that bridge later." They all nodded solemnly. Dr. Burrill said, "I'll inform Thomas of our plans."

"You're going to what?" Thomas jumped out of his seat waving his hands around. "What do you mean you're going to cut off my leg?"

"Thomas, we have to, it's for your own good. We need to know if we can stop this energy from continuing to enter our world. You need to see that doing nothing will place all of humanity in jeopardy. Billions of people will die Thomas. Billions." Thomas let it sink in for a few minutes. He paced around his room and thought about it. No matter how hard Thomas tried, he couldn't come up with any other option either. Finally, after more than a few agonizing minutes Thomas turned to Dr. Burrill and said, "Will I get one of those cool prosthetic legs that's like

254

interchangeable with springs and stuff?"

"I'm sure we can get whatever you want, Thomas." Thomas continued pacing, not really wanting to concede. He knew he had to. What choice was there. It was him or billions of people. Thomas stopped pacing and said, "Okay. I get it, doc. It's just not an easy thing to freely give up your leg when there's nothing wrong with it."

"I get it, Thomas, but our new findings compel us to be expedient on this matter. We know it's no small thing we are asking of you, but I also have to tell you, Thomas, we are going to have to do this very soon."

"Like how soon?"

"Like within the next few days."

"All right, doc. That gives me a little time to say good-bye to my leg."

"If it's any consolation, we will only need the lower half of the leg, not the whole leg."

"It's not…a consolation. But it is what it is, doc."

Three days later a surgical team was flown in via helicopter. Within a few hours the procedure was complete. Thomas was in his room recovering. Thomas' leg was on its way to a makeshift incinerator located on the campus. Dr. Rakowski and Dr. Conti placed Thomas' leg inside the incinerator and watched through a thick glass window. They saw Thomas' leg burn and slowly become a small heap of ashes in just a few minutes. Once the ashes were cooled down, they scooped the ashes up and took them back to the lab to see if they could get a reading and find out if they were in fact able to destroy the source of the ADF.

After several attempts at trying to get a reading they were satisfied that there wasn't any trace of the ADF coming from the burnt ashes. There was a small sigh of relief from everyone. They still, however, had to make sure that Thomas was not emitting any more ADF from anywhere else in his body. They waited until Thomas was fully recovered from the procedure. Thomas woke up groggy from the anesthesia. But after 20 minutes he was fully conscious. Thomas looked down at his legs and although they were under a white sheet, he could see that part of his right leg was missing. It wasn't easy to reconcile his emotions. Did this save lives? Was it worth it? Thomas pulled the sheet off to see that his right leg was covered in blood-stained bandages. The only thing he was thinking was how it didn't hurt. He felt fine. If fact, his leg healed perfectly on its own. The only thing he needs now is a prosthetic device.

Most of the team came to visit Thomas. They were all standing around the bed and asking him how he was feeling. Rishan said, "So, Thomas, how do you feel? Does it hurt?" Thomas replied, "Nope. But I do feel like I'm missing it. you know, my leg." Rishan walked over next to Thomas' bed and said, "I'm sure you do. But don't worry, we're getting you the best prosthetic leg we can find. A specialist is coming here today to work with you and make sure he gets all the right dimensions on your leg. It should normally take about a month, but we're going to fast track it so you should see it in a couple of weeks or less."

Thomas noticed that Dr. Conti had a wheelchair in front of him. Dr. Conti smiled and said, "Thomas, I'm glad you're feeling well. Would you mind if we took you down to check you and make sure there are no more readings?" Thomas sat up by the side of the bed and said, "Sure, no problem, doc." Dr. Conti was relieved that Thomas was in such a good state of mind. He already felt bad for Thomas, and it made him feel better that Thomas had such a positive attitude. Dr. Conti helped Thomas get on the wheelchair and they rolled him over to the lab for testing.

At first they weren't sure if they were getting a reading, as they didn't know where to place the sensors along with the test material. They were getting something, but it didn't look significant. Or they couldn't tell. They tried placing the sensors in different areas of Thomas' body and checking the detector. They weren't getting a reading, but they weren't getting a zero reading either. That was cause for a little nervousness. Finally, they placed one of the sensors just below Thomas' right lower rib. The room went quiet. They all stared at each other in silence waiting for Rishan to say something. Thomas got a sick feeling in his stomach that he may have given up his leg in vain. Dr. Conti looked at Rishan and said, "Well?" Rishan kept staring at the detector hoping to see something different, but he didn't. Rishan said, "I'm sorry Thomas, but I'm getting a reading." Thomas asked, "What kind of reading?"
"It looks like all the previous readings. Exactly the same as all previous readings."
"Are you sure?" Thomas asked. Hoping for a different response.

"Sorry, Thomas. I'm afraid the ADF simply found another way through your body. The readings look like they're coming from the sensor just below your lower rib cage, on your right." "What does this mean?" Thoams asked directing his question to Dr. Conti, who replied, "Looks like we still have the same problem, Thomas. I'm sorry about your leg." Dr. Conti held his head down and walked away noticeably saddened. Dr. Conti was sad because he knew what had to be done next. Dr. Burrill walked over to Thomas and placed one hand on Thomas' shoulder then padded it while saying, "Don't worry Thomas. We'll come up with something." Thomas didn't say anything, he simply started rolling away in his wheelchair.

24 hours later there was a loud uproar coming from outside the campus. People were screaming and yelling. The ground shook from thousands of people stomping and moving around. Everyone in the ICB lab walked over to the window facing the west side of the campus. From there they could see the huge mob that had gathered. The screaming turned into a frenzy. They didn't know what to think. Should they evacuate? Do they need protection? Finally, one of the security guards came in to let them know what was going on.

Dr. Rakowski spoke to the guard, "Jim, What the hell is going on out there? It sounds like a riot. Should we be worried?"

"I don't think so, doc." Jim Hill was head of security for the campus. Jim continued, "They're not screaming because they're mad. They're screaming because they're happy. They're ecstatic, actually. Turns out they're all healed. Maybe they'll go home now." Dr. Conti said, "Well. That's good I guess. But that means we may have other problems. Thank you for the information Jim."

"Don't mention it doc. I just thought I'd come here and let you all know so you don't get worried."

"Again, thank you Jim. I'll let the others know."

Dr. Conti walked over to Rishan and said, "Well? Did we get another spike?" Rishan just kept staring at the detector while answering, "Dr. Conti. I don't think we're going to get control of this. Thomas just spiked again, and I don't think we'll be able to determine the strength because, well, we'll have to recalibrate the detector and also, I think it's starting to break down. I could see some of the material is actually missing. Parts of the metal are simply gone. If we get any damage on the IC board this thing is toast. So, yeah, we got a spike." Rishan didn't even bother asking Thomas if he felt anything. He never does.

But this was different. Rishan could feel that this spike was going to be way bigger than anything else they had before. And he was right. The ICB investigation team confirmed events in all of the U.S. And now, for the first time, they had to check other non-contiguous states and countries. By the end of the day, the team had confirmed most countries had experienced some sort of event. That was the good news for anyone needing medical help. The bad news was how much ADF had been released into the world.

By the end of the week, the ADF detector was no longer working. Machines all around the world were having problems. Every manner of machinery was breaking down for no apparent reason. Closed containers all over the world appeared to be collapsing due to the oxygen molecules being eliminated. Grocery stores had to remove large amounts of inventory due to damage. Shipping containers on large cargo ships were stuck in the middle of the ocean because machine parts in their engines just broke down. Combine this with all areas of the medical industries including the insurance industries suffering great losses, it was plain to see that mankind is about to enter a global crisis never before seen in history. And all of these things did not compare to the potential damage to our existence.

Dr. David Conti and Dr. Bill Rakowski met in secret. They had to come to a final conclusion which, if it's not too late, had to be implemented immediately. They were both seated at a small table in one of the offices in the building. Dr. Rakowski said, "David, I don't think we have much of a choice here. We need to find a way to stop this thing. Now."

"I agree. But how?"

"That's why we're here, David. We have to come up with 'the how'."

"Well, I can only think of one way of fixing this problem, Bill."

"If you are thinking what I'm thinking, then I agree. But we have to be perfectly clear, so I'll state my position." Dr. Conti said, "Go ahead."

"Well, it is my position that we must remove Thomas from Earth altogether. There is no place where he could exist without placing the world in dire jeopardy." Dr. Rakowski continued, "We must contact the White House and find out what resources are available to accomplish this mission as soon as possible." Dr. Conti said, "Okay. I agree. I have some contacts. I'll make the calls, meanwhile, why don't you construct a plan on how we're going to move forward from here." They both stood up and solemnly shook hands. Dr. Rakowski said, "We'll meet back here in two hours to finalize everything."

"Got it."

From Dust we Came

Thursday evening, Dr. Rakowski was speaking with his contact at the Pentagon, Major General Paul Olsen. Dr. Rakowski spoke slowly and calmly. He did not want to be misconstrued in any way. "General, I need to know what resources are available to us for the removal of our problem." The voice on the other end of the phone was just as deliberate, "Dr. Rakowski, I can assure you that our resources will be adequate. Now, what are we talking about here?"

"What we're talking about here is nothing short of the destruction of our world, General."

"That sounds a little melodramatic, Dr."

"If by melodramatic you mean depriving the world of breathable oxygen, then yes. I guess I am." There was a short pause, General Olsen said, "Okay, Dr. You have my attention."

"As you know, General, our subject.."

"For God's sake, Bill, just call him by his name. He's not our enemy."

"Right. Okay, as you know, Thomas is still emitting this destructive energy which we have termed, ADF."

"Right, and what does that stand for again."

"Anomalous Destructive Force."

"Got it. Go on Dr."

"Well, this force, the ADF experiences spikes. This is an occurrence where the ADF is increased significantly. As of this moment we have determined that if it continues at this rate, there will be a catastrophic event that would jeopardize mankind's existence. We have also come to the conclusion that the only way to prevent said disaster is to remove Thomas from Earth all together."

"I see. Just so you know, Doc, I have been keeping up with your reports. I didn't know how you were going to fix this problem, but your solution, prosaic as it sounds, appears to be the only solution. I'll speak with my people over here and get back to you."

"Sir, we need to know now. Like within the next few hours at the most. These spikes are unpredictable. And if the previous spikes are any indication of what to expect, well, let's just say we may be in a situation where it will be too late to do anything about it. Sir, I would like to just mention a few points and hope it will expedite my request. Generally, the oxygen level in our atmosphere is approximately 21%. Nitrogen and other gases make up the rest. If our oxygen level drops below 19.5%, we may not be able to make any decisions as we will be severely cognitively impaired. Beyond that, we will all suffer from asphyxiation on a global scale."

"Got it. I'll get back to you within an hour. Goodbye Bill." Dr. Rakowski hung up and realized he forgot to say goodbye. He walked over to his office and began designing a plan. He felt guilty, immoral and dirty. It was no easy thing to reconcile these emotions with his own personal ideology and he knew this would be an epistemic decision on his part. He was not a religious man, but he knew this was wrong. The one thing he could reconcile is the numbers. Removing Thomas will mean saving billions of lives.   And so, he began to plan the demise of Thomas Grady.

Dr. Rakowski met with Dr. Conti and shared the conversation he had with General Olsen. They both agreed they need to act soon. Most of the equipment in the lab was starting to show signs of breaking down. Another thing which hasn't been mentioned, was that if oxygen atoms are removed while they are in the shape of water, the results would mean that a jar of water, for instance, would become mostly hydrogen which is volatile and highly reactionary and could lead to fires and or explosions if ignited. Of course, that would be the least of our problems if the oxygen levels fell below the levels needed to sustain life.

Unknown to the ICB teams, the ADF has already been significantly reducing oxygen levels in the atmosphere. All types of matter are experiencing problems. Machinery all over the world are having issues due to mechanical parts simply breaking apart due to the disintegration of atoms in the metal. Cars are getting flat tires for no apparent reason, small holes are appearing on almost everything, televisions, tables, windows, eyeglasses, etc. Some items simply break apart once they are touched. And no one knows this better than the ICB teams. Their equipment keeps breaking down, making it harder to understand exactly what is going on.

By Friday morning Dr. Rakowski received instructions from General Olsen. Thomas is to be taken to an undisclosed location via helicopter. Thomas Grady is to be deeply sedated, blindfolded, and restrained. The helicopter will arrive at 1200 hours to receive Thomas. Dr. Rakowski arranged for Thomas' room to be filled with an anesthetic gas. Once Thoams is passed out they will connect an IV to keep him sedated. By 10am Thomas was incapacitated, tied and blindfolded. Dr. Rakowski worked with Dr. Conti and two military guards. They had to keep what they were doing quiet.

Around noon, Rishan was looking for Thomas. He approached Dr. Burrill, "Excuse me, Dr. Burrill, have you seen Thomas today? He wasn't in his room, and I have a few questions for him." Dr. Burrill said, "You know, I haven't seen Thoams all day. We usually meet at the break room for a coffee and a bagel. Well, he usually has a doughnut, and I have the bagel, but no, I have not seen him this morning. Is there a problem?"   Rishan shook his head and said, "No, no problem, I was just wanted to see how he's doing."

"That's nice." Dr. Burrill said, then as he walked away he turned and said, "Well, tell him I said hi." "Okay." Rishan walked back into the lab and saw Tony working, he was peering into a microscope. Rishan walked up to him and tapped Tony on the shoulder to get his attention. Tony jumped up, noticeably startled and said, "What?" Rishan was startled as well by Tony's response.

"Whoa, sorry, I didn't mean to spook you, Tony. I'm just looking for Thomas. Have you seen him?"

"Nope. But funny thing is, he was supposed to meet me here around this time. We were going to go over some of the findings regarding the effects the ADF is having on the equipment. He seemed concerned."

"Really? I didn't think Thomas was interested in this stuff."

"Oh yeah. I told him about it, and he wanted to see for himself how this ADF thing is eating away at matter. It's scary stuff."

"I know. Anyway, if you see him, tell him to come see me when you guys are done."

"Got it."

About thirty minutes later, Rishan noticed that Thoams was still not anywhere around and started to wonder if something was wrong. By the time he spoke with Dr. Rinzler and Kindra Newcomb he realized that no one has seen Thoams all day. It was 1:45pm. Rishan was about to go speak with Dr. Conti when he noticed that Dr. Conti was also missing all day. Five minutes later, everyone could hear the sound of a helicopter approaching the landing area just outside the building. Everyone in the lab walked over to a window to watch the helicopter land. It was a Seahawk, a multi-mission Naval helicopter. That's when they noticed two guards rolling a gurney down through the open area of the lab. They were coming from Dr. Conti's office. On the gurney they could see that it was Thomas. His hands were tied in front of him, he was blindfolded, and three large straps kept him secured to the gurney. They also noticed an IV going into one of his arms.

Before anybody could say something, Thomas was rushed out the door. The helicopter was approximately 36 meters away. There wasn't any paved walkway to the helicopter, so the guards had to practically carry the gurney across the grassy area. Just before they got to the helicopter, a convertible jeep came barreling through the side chain-link gate.

The guards stopped momentarily to watch the jeep coming at them at full speed. Behind the wheel was Mario. He had Korbin and Banks with him. Banks stood up from the backseat behind Mario, secured himself to the rollbar and let out a few short bursts of fire in front of the guards. The Guards froze as the bullets spewed dirt and grass in front of them. They dropped Thomas and held up their hands. The guards were totally confused as to what was happening.

Mario was 30 meters away when suddenly they were hit by heavy fire. The rotors of the Seahawk had drowned out the sound of the 4H60 Blackhawk support chopper. The sound of heavy metal slapping the side of their jeep made Mario slam on the brakes. Mario yelled out, "Hit the dirt!" Mario and his team knew these were no ordinary rounds that hit their vehicle. It was a 50-caliber machine gun. They would have no chance against it. They were right, once they jumped off the jeep the 50-cal shredded the jeep into useless junk metal. Mario and his team had to hit the ground and had to stay low.

Meanwhile, once the guards noticed that they were being protected, they picked up the gurney with Thomas in it and ran straight to the helicopter. Mario and his men could not get up to fight. The machine gun on the side of the Blackhawk was too powerful. One round would cut them in half. Mario could only watch as they loaded Thomas into the helicopter and watch it fly away. A voice came over a loudspeaker from the Blackhawk, "Drop your weapons and lay face down on the ground." Mario instructed his men to do as they say. A few seconds later a dozen men showed up and restrained Mario and his crew.

Mario had gotten a notice from his friend at the DOD that they were going to extract Thomas today, but he got there too late and underestimated the fire power they had to face. No one knew why they were taking Thomas or where they were taking him. All Mario knew was that it didn't sound good, and he was going to get Thomas out. But he was too late, he had failed, and he feared that this may be the last time he would ever see Thomas again. A few minutes later, Mario and his men were placed in back of an unmarked van.

There was pandemonium back in the lab. Everyone wanted to know what happened to Thomas. Dr. Rakowski did not spare any words. He told them all exactly what was happening. They were all horrified at the conditions of Thomas' abduction. It took 30 to 40 minutes for Dr. Rakowski to explain that the fate of the world was still in their hands. Nothing was more important than the work they were doing right here, right now. It was hard. They felt hurt and betrayed. Thomas had become a real friend to everyone at the ICB lab. But they had a job to do still, and so, they went on.

Less than two hours later Rishan got another reading. Apparently Thomas had not removed the monitor that was still strapped to his side. This time, the ADF detector went off scale again and immediately stopped working. In fact, nearly all machinery in the building stopped working. Even the door handles were not functioning correctly. This was now officially the biggest spike. Fortunately, the cell phones were still on. There was never any way of knowing what was going to be affected by the ADF.

Dr. Conti began making phone calls. Most of the people he called already knew him and why he was calling. But this time was different. This time when Dr. Conti asked about any medical events, he got more news than he asked for. Hospitals were reporting people being healed, but on top of that, their equipment was breaking down. MRI's, X-ray machines, and all types of monitors. Almost every piece of machinery was experiencing some sort of problem. It was the same with everyone else he called.

Other strange things were happening. People were reporting that they felt dizzy and had difficulty breathing. However, this happened mostly in small, enclosed rooms. And this was because they were unknowingly suffering from oxygen deprivation. Larger rooms and areas had less issues because the oxygen levels were able to be replaced sufficiently. The world was coming to a standstill. All mechanical devices were failing due to what appeared to be missing material. Bolts were just falling off, screws disappeared, springs and gauges were useless. Even fuels and other liquids experienced chemical changes that caused them to be inert or were simply converted to different chemical compounds rendering them useless for combustion.

Dr. Rakowski realized that they would probably not survive another spike. He called General Oleson and told him his concerns. The General reassured Dr. Rakowski that Thomas would be off world in a matter of hours. The plan was to place Thomas on a rocket that was already set to launch several communication satellites into orbit. But now it was programed to go into deep space, with Thomas in it. As a precautionary measure, they actually will have Thomas euthanized and his body dismembered prior to launching. They had no idea as to what Thomas' abilities or limitations were in regard to healing himself. Humanities fate was riding on this plan. There was no way of knowing if Thomas would be able to produce another spike even in his dismembered state.

Dr. Rakowski knew that it didn't matter if Thomas produced another spike or not, because the

ADF multiplies itself anyway, just not as quickly as when Thomas spikes. Dr. Rakowski feared that there may already be too much ADF in the world already. The goal now was to figure out how to stop it or slow it down. The problem so far was that they never figured out anything about how to do that. None of the ICB teams, or anyone else involved with this project, knew how to control the ADF. So even with Thomas out of the picture, the world may still be doomed. Just as Dr. Rakowski thought about this, all the lights went out.

Two hours later, the rocket with Thomas Grady onboard took off. It would be almost the same path as Voyager 1, headed towards a multi-billion-mile journey into deep space. As decided, Thomas Grady was basically murdered and dismembered, as they did not know what the results would be if they kept him intact. They still didn't know if they were in the clear. For all they know, Thomas may still be able to spike.

Back on Earth, everything was breaking down at the molecular level. Oxygen was depleted to the extent that levels were becoming critical. Bridges were falling apart, buildings were collapsing, some animals were dying from asphyxiation. Large swaths of land were dying. The entire eco-system of Earth was changing into an unsustainable environment. The ocean was covered with dead marine life. Once the algae in the oceans started to die, mankind would not be far behind because algae are one of the largest producers of oxygen.

All of the ICB teams members along with everyone else in the area passed away. Three weeks later, more than half the population on Earth was gone. Two weeks after that, there were only a few hundred people alive on the entire planet. But they were the ones who would witness the horrific sight of watching the Earth dissolve. Mountains became large clouds of thin dust and soon the moon began to exert a stronger gravitational force than Earth and slowly started pulling the Earth apart. Five days later, all life is gone, the Earth is nothing more than a thick cloud of dark dust. The moon, no longer held captive by the Earth's gravity, hurled away into empty space to find its own solar orbit. And all that was left of Earth was a wispy dark cloud of dust revolving around the Sun.

28 million kilometers from Earth, the torso of Thomas Grady spiked. A few minutes later, the Sun became a little dimmer.

THE END

265

Made in the USA
Las Vegas, NV
28 August 2024

94533136R00148